Both of them swung out over the audience—the woman hanging from the man's fingertips, and only his toes in that ring keeping them from rocketing out into the crowd. They swung high, and on their downswing it almost seemed that the audience could touch her—and some people tried, reaching and waving as she flew by. The spotlights flashed, following their trajectory.

The audience screamed in delight, pounding their seats.

And then, in a strange twist, the *ceiling* opened up— and a darkness billowed out of that opening, a darkness that swallowed the dazzling spotlights like inky black smoke. Only it wasn't smoke. And something else was moving in that darkness. For an instant, the crowd bellowed in excitement—not knowing what to think. Claudi knew instantly what to think, but she was frozen in her seat. As the crowd abruptly fell silent in sudden fear, she felt Sheki draw a deep breath.

And then the two glittering acrobats arced high—and disappeared into the darkness.

And did not come back down.

But something else did, several things—black and winged and fast.

DOWN
THE STREAM
OF STARS

Jeffrey A. Carver

BANTAM BOOKS
NEW YORK · TORONTO · LONDON · SYDNEY · AUCKLAND

DOWN THE STREAM OF STARS
A Bantam Spectra Book / August 1990

ISBN 0-553-28302-2

Published simultaneously in the United States and Canada

*Bantam Books are published by Bantam Books, a division of Bantam Doubleday
Dell Publishing Group, Inc. Its trademark, consisting of the words "Bantam
Books" and the portrayal of a rooster, is Registered in U.S. Patent and Trademark
Office and in other countries. Marca Registrada. Bantam Books, 666 Fifth Avenue,
New York, New York 10103.*

PRINTED IN THE UNITED STATES OF AMERICA

RAD   0 9 8 7 6 5 4 3 2 1

For Alexandra,
with wonder and anticipation

*"For I dipped into the future,
     far as human eye could see,
Saw the Vision of the world,
     and all the wonder that would be;
Saw the heavens fill with commerce,
     argosies of magic sails. . ."*

—Alfred, Lord Tennyson

PROLOGUE

**Starship *Elijah*
Alpha Orionis A (Betelgeuse) Remnant
Year 181 Sp.**

Clouds of ejected star matter billowed luminously into space like the breath of a mythical god. The ghostly ball at their center was all that remained of the once-mighty sun, Betelgeuse. Three years before, the supergiant had blazed forth in a vast supernova explosion, transforming itself from a living star into a funeral pyre that had briefly out-shone the Milky Way. Its ghostly appearance now betrayed the unusual nature of its death. No ordinary supernova—even one ending, as this had, in a black hole—would have contracted and darkened in quite this way. Its smoky translucence spoke eloquently of the invisible forces that had bound it into an oddity of cosmic proportion, an object of Promethean power and mystery.

Its outer layers blazed in the viewscreen as the starship sped inward through the remnant clouds. The display changed every few seconds, highlighting various aspects of its structure. Many on the bridge found their glances drawn repeatedly to the image on the viewscreen. Starship *Elijah* was diving toward the stellar remnant through the shifting reality of K-space, and tremendous computative power was at work creating that image out of the streams of data pouring into the ship.

Most of the crew were busy at their consoles. But one person, seated at the rear of the bridge, ignored all else but that irresistible vision of the star's ghost. She faced it with her eyes half closed, focusing on its presence with her memory, her imagination, her inner vision. Tamika Jones cared not at all about the astrophysical data streaming across the consoles. She was searching for just one thing, and that was the touch of a mind—a mind that she hoped still lived out there in the remnant of a once-living star. It was a mind she had not felt in three years, not since the moment of the star's death.

In that moment, she had felt *him* die, too—had mourned his death. But in the midst of her grief she had hoped, prayed, *felt* that the man without whose genius this strange, unprecedented *thing* would not exist, had somehow passed through the shadow of death, through the heat and fury of a supernova, and lived. And that was why she was here now, to search for this man who had perhaps survived death. She was here to find Willard Ruskin.

She felt the stirring and muttering of her shipmates' minds around her, like memory-voices chattering and distracting her. That was the effect of the continuous altering of the K-space that carried the ship inward toward the unknown. Transitions through K-space boundaries produced an involuntary cross-linking of neighboring minds—which could be alarming when unexpected—but they were counting upon it now to join them with Willard, or his companions, or whatever might remain of them. She hardly knew what the mind she was seeking might feel like —reaching to her across the gulf of space that separated them from the star, and from whatever lay in the twisted continuum beyond it.

She hardly knew, really, what she was hoping to find.

What her shipmates hoped to find deep within the supernova remnant, close to the black hole inhabiting its core, was the opening to a new interstellar gateway—a structure that would whisk *Elijah* and untold ships to follow at some unimaginable speed toward the galactic center. It was for that gateway that the majestic Betelgeuse had died at the hands of Project Breakstar. It was for that gateway that a fantastically stretched loop of flawed space had been caught and anchored to the resulting black hole. It was for that gateway that a man named Willard Ruskin, and his best friend Max, had died. . . .

Elijah was flying headlong toward a singularity where known space-time ended and something else began. No one knew precisely where the passage into the gateway lay. Eight robot probes had failed to find it, or to return. At a nearby console, astrophysicist Thalia Sharaane was studying the data streams with ferocious concentration. Possibly she would find clues to the gateway's opening on those consoles, but her friend Tamika had no such hope. And yet Tamika *knew* that if she could just reach out to the mind of Willard Ruskin . . . if she could locate and touch once more the man she had loved . . . she might, just might learn from him the way to enter the gateway.

She squinted at the changing image of the sun, growing visibly larger by the second, and searched outward with her thoughts, desperately trying to ignore the jabber and clamor of human intelligence around her.

A movement by the captain made her aware of an announcement. "Sixty seconds from go-around point. Let me know, people, if you're getting anything." He queried the individual bridge officers, then Tamika. "Ms. Jones?" Not answering, Tamika strained to reach out . . . beyond the prison of her own skull and her own mind . . . to reach beyond the bounds of this ship with its clamoring crew. . . .

The captain's voice became urgent. They dared not venture too close to the black hole, not even in K-space. "Thirty seconds, Ms. Jones. If you don't have anything, we've got to get out of here."

She drew a deep breath and exhaled with exquisite slowness, listening to the meaningless jabber around her, and was about to tell him, *No, nothing, do what you have to do*—

And then she saw it.

Saw him.

Saw the face of Willard Ruskin, peering at them out of the viewscreen. She pointed, unable to draw a breath, unable to speak. The captain turned, opened his mouth. "What—" And when he checked the time again, his face tightened with indecision.

Tamika, it is you . . . ?

Was that her imagination, or had she actually heard—

Tamika . . . and Thalia! Yes!

That was not her imagination. Thalia had risen at the sound of her name. And then she seemed drawn back to her console. And Tamika heard, and *felt*, Thalia tell the captain, "Keep going! Turn the nav-control over to me. I think I can get us through!" And Tamika heard, "You *think*—" and saw the captain gazing fiercely at Thalia, with only seconds to decide.

And then she was aware only of the mind that was welling up out of space and merging with her own. . . .

So long it has been . . .
. . . how long?
Can we even know?

My children, do you sing ?
Can you know ?

Who are you? Willard, is it you? And who else?

I/we know you
Otherlife . . . entering us . . . so strange
but welcome
so new

Is it you? Willard?

Tamika
I love you
we loved you
yes
and
Thalia

I don't understand . . . what is happening?

Who are we ?
and you ?

Be with us
Come

Tamika was suddenly aware of a flood of thought and knowledge pouring into Thalia, *through* Thalia . . . was aware of Thalia's connection to the cogitative console, and the knowledge streaming through her, the mapping of the gateway entrance passing through her and into the nav-control.

And Tamika was aware of the K-space fields changing dramatically, and the ship altering course, shifting through the tricky matrices of unknown space, diving perilously toward the core of what had once been a star and was now an opening in space-time itself. . . .

She was aware of space slipping and altering its very nature around her . . . and she felt Willard Ruskin's presence, and his love, or something very much like his love, now with staggering power and clarity. But it was much more, he was not just Willard now; he was different, astonishingly different, there were others present with him, or were they *part* of him . . . ?

She heard the exclamation "N-space!" and felt the ship passing through a turbulence, and then into a smoothly flowing *something*—and she had the distinct feeling that they were speeding down a fast-moving channel, and she heard cries of amazement and fear. And when she opened her eyes she actually saw in the viewscreen an ethereal channel opening like a tunnel to receive them, its banks stretching backward past them, and all around them the blurry shapes of what looked like star clusters and clouds.

As she saw all of this, her mind was filled with greetings and joy and surprise, and she felt the presence not only of what-had-been-Willard, but also a Logothian named Ali'Maksam, and an assassin named Ganz, and the mind of a sun named *Bright*. And all of her pent-up hopes and fears and joys fell away like spilling tears, and she felt herself opening to receive memories and feelings that she could not have dreamed of. . . .

And she knew, dimly, through the choir of voices and thoughts, that they had succeeded. Their starship had passed into the gateway and was speeding inward now into the galaxy . . . inward toward what, they could scarcely imagine . . . speeding down a fabulous, glowing river of stars. . . .

PART ONE
Year 269 Sp.

CLAUDI

"All the rivers run into the sea; yet the sea is not full."

—Ecclesiastes 1:7

A word of explanation . . .

I should make one thing clear at the outset, and that is that I am not the hero of this story. It is true that I followed the story and its aftereffects with great interest, and on occasion took certain actions to steer events; so I can hardly lay claim to perfect objectivity. But much of what follows I did not fully understand myself at the time, and much has been reconstructed from long, later conversations with the principal actors. If I seem defensive about certain of my actions, it's because, I guess, I am—but please understand that I was only trying to make the best decisions that I could under difficult circumstances.

Now, I know that many have blamed me for what happened to Willard Ruskin in the matter of Project Breakstar . . . in the bewildering events that opened up the inner galaxy to all of Greater Humanity. Rightly or wrongly, I took much of the blame for the nano-agents that played havoc with his memory, and even the blame for his death. And I accept a share of that responsibility. But I ask you to remember that what happened to Willard Ruskin in the creation of the gateway wasn't altogether bad.

May we talk about the gateway itself?

Unquestionably, the starstream, as it has come to be known, has been a mixed blessing for the galaxy and for Greater Humanity (a term I will use for now, if I may, to include all members of the Habitat). It has brought both wonder and peril, and who is to say which is the greater? I confess I cannot. *War*, for example, is a terrible thing to contemplate; and yet, was it a price worth paying so that our peoples might inhabit vastly larger tracts of space? Was it worth war, and penalties even more terrible, for the knowledge and opportunities gained, for the newly discovered races? How can one weigh such gain for all of civilization against the deaths of billions, and the devastation of at least one entire planetary culture?

That is a question that I have been trying to answer for the better part of the last century.

If I may briefly review:

This story starts, really, with the creation of the gateway structure by Willard Ruskin, et al., back in the year 178 Sp. The details of the political fallout from that event have filled volumes. Following Project Breakstar, two years passed before the debris from the Betelgeuse supernova cleared enough to allow even the earliest tentative efforts to chart the gateway structure. But with the famous first passage by Tamika Jones and Thalia Sharaane (and, coincidentally, the discovery that the gateway was alive and sentient), the new diaspora of Humanity into the deep galaxy had, for all practical purposes, begun. The gateway soon became the greatest thoroughfare in the history of Humanity, or of any other known race.

Within thirty standard years, dozens of star systems previously well beyond the reach of the Habitat already sported burgeoning colonies. Six intelligent races had been discovered, two of them spacefaring. In general, the interracial contacts had been friendly, or at least not actively hostile. Most of the hostilities that existed during this period could be traced to preexisting tensions among the various old factions of the Habitat of Humanity.

Then in the thirty-second year, a planet known as Riese's World was discovered orbiting an unstable sun, near the inner edge of the Orion galactic spiral arm. Also discovered was the remains of the Riesan civilization.

Their world had lain almost directly in the path of the gateway. Before Breakstar, their sun had been as stable and trustworthy as any. Not so, after. The Riesans, who coincidentally had been on the verge of achieving spaceflight, had been unintentionally decimated by Breakstar.

Guilt and self-recrimination resulted from that discovery. But not war. War came later. Forty-one years later, when the Enemy, the Karthrogen, the Throgs, came storming up the starstream from somewhere even deeper toward the heart of the galaxy. What the Karthrogen wanted, no Human knew. Where they came from, no one was sure. All that was known was that when Karthrogen and Humans met, Humans died. Usually in large numbers. Planetary numbers.

This story is about that war. But it's also about other matters—the settlers of one of the new worlds, for starters.

Even in the face of the Enemy, Human expansion into deep space continued unabated—slowed a little by the war, maybe, but only a little. One was generally at greatest risk during passage through the starstream, because that was where the Karthrogen were most likely to appear. But despite the losses, most people never saw, or ever would see, a Throg. It was often said that one was statistically at greater risk riding a shuttle into orbit than riding the starstream. (It was untrue, to be sure; but it was often said. Sometimes what is said is more significant in human terms than what is true.)

There came a time when a particular colony-ship was making its way down the starstream, stopping off at a few systems along the way. An interstellar circ-zoo was on board, along with a full complement of colonists. Among the latter were a young Human girl traveling with her parents, and a young boy who became her friend. This story is about them, and about some of their friends at the circ-zoo. And the reason their story is important is because of what they learned about the Throgs. And because of what they learned from, and taught, the starstream.

It's also about Willard Ruskin, and about *Bright*, once known to Humanity as Betelgeuse, and about the others who died with them—or what they became. And yes, it's about me, Jeaves, a cogitative intelligence.

If you want to know more than that . . . well, I suggest you let the story unfold.

May I freshen that drink for you? As you wish. I'll be right here if you need me. Just give a call.

CHAPTER 1

The starship's deck hummed beneath Claudi Melnik's feet as she stood in the empty corridor, looking both ways. There was a certain stealth to her look, because this section of the ship was not yet officially open to passengers. But Claudi (eight years and some of age, standard) was curious, and on an exploratory mission. She wanted to see what was down here, where all kinds of signs pointed to a "circ-zoo" that would be opening soon. All of the main doors to the circ-zoo seemed to be closed; but there was a small door down the corridor from the others, and that one had winked open at her casual touch on the control plate. The room beyond beckoned silently.

Like most children her age, Claudi was driven by an insatiable curiosity, and she had very little sense of fear. As far as she was concerned, if she got caught, she got caught. It wasn't as if she was doing anything *wrong*, after all. She was just looking.

She still had a little time left before she had to get to deck-school. And that room looked extremely interesting. After a momentary hesitation, she crept through the open door. Her heart beat faster as she looked around. She saw clear-domed enclosures of the sort used to hold animals in zoos. Most of those near the door looked empty and small but she glimpsed larger ones in the next section of the room. And where there were enclosures, surely, there would be animals.

Animals!

She tiptoed forward, peering around hopefully.

Something was moving out beyond the enclosure. It was a blur, and it shifted first one way, then the other. Lopo, squinting nearsightedly, could only hope that whatever it was would come closer. Something danced in his mind, a fleeting image of a small keeper; it seemed connected somehow with the blur outside. It was a startlingly pleasing image. Then it was gone. Lopo blinked in puzzlement.

The teacher, behind him, was making *hrrrrmph*ing noises, trying to get his attention. But the lupeko was bored with his teacher. He was more interested in learning what was outside. He strained to pick up the movement and the scent. But the enclosure blocked out most scent—and now the thing was retreating, fading to a blur of nothing.

In disappointment, Lopo turned back to the rear of his enclosure. A pile of comfortably musty blankets lay heaped in one corner. In the other corner were two basins, one for food and another for water. The keepers were not feeding him much lately, which made him a touch grouchy; but the water, at least, he could control. He pressed a small pedal with his forepaw, and a stream of water swirled into the bowl. Lopo lapped at the water—then raised his head, thinking he had sensed movement again. Or was he just imagining?

There it was! The blur, coming closer. And a voice, tiny and high-pitched: "What *is* it? A dog? Or a fox?"

It was almost near enough to see. It was just a little taller than Lopo was when he sat up on his haunches. The creature stepped closer, and finally came into focus. It *was* a keeper—and a small one! How extremely odd. Lopo wrinkled his nose, sniffing. The smell of the thing wafted only faintly to his nose, but he could tell that it was different from the usual keeper's—a lighter, almost flowery smell. It moved very close to the enclosure wall now, putting its face close to Lopo's. Lopo cocked his ears and studied the face, topped with yellow hair and dotted with bright blue eyes. "Hi," it said. "Are you a dog? What are you doing in there? My name's Claudi. What's yours?"

Lopo blinked, tipping his head one way and then the other. He understood the words—some of them, anyway—but he couldn't reply to them, and so he just peered back at the keeper, hoping it would say more. *Hi*, he knew. *Dog*, he knew. *Name*, he knew. But how the words worked together, he wasn't quite sure. Nor did he understand why the little keeper was asking him about dogs. *Claudi*, he didn't know at all.

The keeper glanced furtively to one side, then the other; then it pressed a small hand to the side of the enclosure. Lopo wished that the bubble-wall would go away.

Another voice came from somewhere out of sight—the voice of the regular keeper, Joe—loud with surprise. "What are *you* doing in here?" Joe's familiar large shape appeared behind the small one.

"I was just looking at your dog," said the small keeper, turning. "I wasn't doing anything."

Joe put his hands on his hips. "You're not supposed to be in here, you know. Just circ-zoo people are supposed to be here. Anyway, that's no dog. That's a lupeko." He pronounced the word "Loo-*peek*-oh." Then he went on, "Do you know what lupekos are?"

"Nope," said the small keeper.

"You haven't seen the big one we have on display out in the zooshow?"

The little one shook its head, back and forth.

"No, of course not. We haven't opened the galleries yet. Well, we'll have to get you a look at it. They're very smart animals. And they like little girls."

Little girls! thought Lopo. *So that's it.*

"What's your name?" Joe asked.

The little girl pointed at the lupeko without answering. "What's wrong with this one?" she asked.

"Why, nothing's wrong with it. He's just very young, and hasn't learned to talk yet."

"Talk?"

Joe nodded. "That's right. Say, don't you want to tell me what your name is?"

"Uh-huh." The little girl smiled, swinging her arms. "What did you say it was called?"

"A lupeko." The keeper chuckled. "And *you* are—?"

She ducked her head shyly, and in Lopo's mind her face suddenly shone, sparkling and vivid. He'd never met a keeper like this! His heart welled up. She seemed so . . . *likable*. "Why is it called a lupeko?" she asked.

"To make little girls ask questions." That brought a giggle, and Joe added, "Fair's fair, now. Won't you tell me your name?"

There was a moment of silence. Then very softly she said, "Claudi." *Of course,* the lupeko thought. She had said that before.

"That's a nice name. Claudi what?"

"Melnik."

"Claudi Melnik. Well, hi—I'm Joe. Joe Farharto."

She swung back and forth. "Hi."

"Well," Joe said, "I sure didn't expect to find a pretty girl wandering around in my back galleries. You're not even supposed to be able to get in! I'd better check and see if the door got left open."

There was no answer from Claudi, while the lupeko mulled over the fact that *Claudi Melnik* was indeed a nice name. He rolled the name over in his thoughts, wishing that he could speak it aloud.

"Since you're already here," Joe said, "I guess I could show you around a little. Do your folks know where you are?"

Claudi shrugged. She stepped closer to the enclosure again, coming back into focus for Lopo. "Can this one talk?"

"Lopo? No, like I said, he's too young. His speech hasn't been installed yet. But he can understand you, probably. Do you want to say hi?" Joe crouched beside Claudi, peering into the enclosure with her. "Hello, Lopo. Would you like to meet Claudi?" Joe tapped on the enclosure wall. Lopo backed away cautiously, then pressed his nose forward again.

"Hi, Lopo," said Claudi.

The lupeko ducked his head self-consciously and wagged his tail.

"Can I pet it?" Claudi asked.

Joe's face frowned. "Well, I don't—"

"Please?"

He sighed. "Well . . . I guess there's no harm. Wait right here." He disappeared, then reappeared with something shiny in his hand, which he touched to the enclosure wall. Lopo couldn't see anything happen, but a soft wave of keeper-smells wafted into his face. He lifted his nose toward them.

Joe's large hand came through the enclosure wall and ruffled the back of Lopo's neck. He raised one ear. The touch felt good, but he was more interested in the little girl. Her hand seemed to hesitate, then reached out to touch his nose. He sniffed at her fingers wonderingly, then licked them with a quick movement of his tongue. He caught a taste of something salty and sweet.

Claudi squealed and pulled her hand away. "It's okay," Joe reassured her. "He won't hurt you. You can pet him if you want."

Yes, please, Lopo thought.

The girl hesitated, then reached out again. Lopo kept very still, until he felt the hand brush the top of his head. He raised his head a fraction of an inch and let out a small sigh of pleasure. She began petting his head. Lopo closed his eyes, relishing the feeling; he opened them again to look up into her eyes. They flashed bright and clear and blue, just like the image in his mind. He was smitten—by her eyes, by her light flowery smell, even by her hesitation. Something made him feel as if he had always been waiting for just this person, just her touch. His tail wagged furiously. Stay, don't go, he wished.

"I think he likes you," Joe said.

Claudi didn't answer. She just kept petting him.

"I guess we'd better close it up again."

Claudi gave Lopo one last pat. Then Joe made the wall become solid again, and Lopo pressed his nose to it. "Bye, Lopo!" Claudi said. Lopo made a throaty whine.

"You want to come back and see him again?" Joe asked, ushering the girl away. They both became blurs again.

"Sure," Lopo heard her say, and his heart raced.

"Maybe you'd like to see the bigger one, too. It's out in the zooshow area. . . ."

The voices faded, and Lopo was left alone with the ever-present hum in the deck. He watched a long time, whining mournfully once or twice, hoping that Claudi might return; but at last he turned back to his blanket and to the softly murmuring, dimly flickering glow of the teacher. That, at least, was always there—even if it didn't have the nice smell or the friendly touch of a little girl.

But Lopo knew now what he wanted. And it had just walked away, into the blurry distance.

If Claudi didn't know how the lupeko had gotten its name, the teacher did. It knew that the lupeko was a hybrid creature, part old-Earth wolf, *canis lupus,* part picobear from the planet Cardiff. It was one designer's attempt to create an improved, and highly intelligent, guard animal and companion. The design program was by most accounts a failure, partly due to a tendency to moody dispositions that rendered lupekos unsuitable as guard animals, but mainly because the design lab failed financially before the design could be refined.

The only lupekos still around were those in the circ-zoos. Lopo was one of two aboard starship *Charity,* as part of the J. J. Larkus Traveling Interstellar Circ-Zoo. The knowledge-teacher was responsible for seeing that the lupekos learned all that they were supposed to. But it was the ship's intelligence system, monitoring the teacher, that now observed Lopo's behavior and suspected that something important had just taken place.

The intelligence system wasn't sure what, if anything, it ought to do about it, but it was more determined now than ever that Lopo receive a proper lupeko education. And young Claudi Melnik was already a candidate for special attention.

The intelligence system wasn't completely sure why it

had made all of these judgments. Probably it would have said: Call it a hunch.

The intelligence system went more on hunches than most people would have guessed.

And quite often its hunches were correct.

CHAPTER 2

As Claudi hurried away from the back rooms of the Larkus circ-zoo, she noted the vibration of the deck through her feet. She was often aware of this feeling. She enjoyed it; it reminded her that the ship was alive, pulsing and breathing, and carrying her and her family far, far down the stream of stars, maybe even to the very core of the galaxy. That awareness always gave her a warm glow of excitement in her heart. And she was right, of course; the ship *was* carrying her down the starstream, and though they would not actually be venturing anywhere near the center of the galaxy, that at least was the direction in which they were headed.

Her awareness of the starstream was mostly in her mind. Claudi had never gotten to *see* the starstream in person—though her parents had promised to take her one day to the observation deck, which was very exclusive and took reservations and everything. In the meantime, the humming of the deck was really the only thing that let her know, day to day, hour to hour, *yes, we're still moving, we're still on our way down the stream*. And she paid attention to it. She noticed any little change in the hum and wondered what was happening in the engines, if they were changing speed or getting ready to put in at a starport. She felt a sense of responsibility. Who knew but what she might be the first to notice a problem and warn the crew? It could be her alertness that would save the ship. *That* would put her on the road to being a captain some day!

Just now, though, she realized she had better get a move on. She had been so interested in that dog-thing, the lupeko, that she'd forgotten the time. Now she was late again for the deck-school, and would probably get yelled at by the teaching-wall. And word usually got back to her parents when that happened, and then she caught it from them, too. It didn't seem right. She was already eight, and you'd think that they would understand by now that she could take care of herself. Anyhow, it was worth a minor yelling, to have seen the lupeko-dog. And tomorrow, if that man Joe kept his promise, she'd get to see the other lupeko, as well. Unless, of course, she got grounded for being late to school.

Claudi darted into an open lift. "Deck Defoe," she sang to the lift-controller. She hooked her arms over the railing in the back of the lift and made a whooshing sound under her breath as it shot upward. The door winked open, and she slipped out into the deck-school.

The lift had opened into a big, noisy room with bright green walls hung with all sorts of pictures and things that the kids had made. A class of little kids was letting out now, at least twenty boys and girls hollering and scrambling toward the lift. Claudi walked through the mob, letting them part around her. She noticed on the wall clock that she was now forty-three minutes late. Ducking her head, she tried to avoid the gaze of Mr. Seipledon, a human teacher, who was just coming out of the far classroom.

"You're late there, aren't you, Claudi?" Mr. Seipledon called.

Claudi sighed and nodded, without quite looking at him. "Yes—er, I have to get in there," she said, not quite pleading, as she glanced at the closed door of her classroom. "Could I—that is—may I be excused? Okay?"

Mr. Seipledon frowned, shaking his head. "All right,

Claudi. But you know the wall's going to ask you the same thing."

Claudi bobbed her head. She knew. That's why she didn't want to have to answer for it twice, if she didn't have to. Once was enough. Edging away from Mr. Seipledon, she opened her classroom door carefully and slipped into the back. There were six—no, seven—other kids sitting in various positions around the room. One of them was a stranger, a new boy, who looked at least two years younger than anyone in Claudi's class. He didn't turn, but a couple of the other kids did. One of them, Jeremy, peered up at the clock and grinned wickedly. Claudi glanced away; she didn't want to give him the satisfaction of seeing her embarrassed. She didn't even glance at her friends Suze and Jenny, either, but instead walked straight to her seat and slipped on her headset. They were doing individual instruction now, for which she was grateful. When the silence-screen went on around her, the room went from rustling quiet to dead silence.

An instant later, the voice of the teaching-wall filled her head. It was one of the nameless instructional programs. "Claudi, you're late again. Was there an emergency of some sort that I ought to know about?"

Claudi flushed. "No."

"Would you like to tell me why you're late, then?"

"Well—"

"Were you down on the lower decks again?"

She was glad none of the other kids could hear. "Yes," she murmured.

The teacher made a clearing-of-the-throat sound. "If you don't mind my asking, what were you doing down there?"

"Well, I was looking at something at the circ-zoo, and I just—" She hesitated.

"Just what, Claudi?"

"Forgot, I guess."

"Forgot that you had school?"

"No," she said with a flash of irritation. "The time, that's all." She sighed, wishing that she could just get on with her lesson, instead of being scolded. But you never knew what to expect from the wall in a situation like this; it was designed to be guess-proof, she was sure.

."Claudi—you know that it's important to remember the time, don't you? Isn't that one of the things we try to teach you?"

She nodded silently. "I'm sorry," she said finally.

The teacher let the moment stretch, then said, "All right, perhaps we don't need to bring this up with your parents—as long as you promise to do better tomorrow. May I have your word on that, Claudi?"

"Uh-huh." She nodded in relief.

"All right. Let's get started on your lesson, then. And pay attention! This is an important one!"

Claudi twirled her hair around her finger and nodded. She dutifully watched the screen in front of her seat. A picture was shimmering into focus there—a picture of a planet, golden and green, with swirling white cloud patterns encircling its waist like an apron around a fat lady. The voice of the teacher deepened, saying, "This is the colony world called Daugherty's Hope. It was the first planet to be colonized in the Great Second Push down the starstream. It's important to know about Daugherty's Hope because . . . well, can you tell me why, Claudi?"

She took a deep, shuddering breath. Daugherty's Hope? She'd heard of it—

"Think, Claudi. Remember, when we were talking about the world *we're* going to—"

"Heart of Heaven!" she blurted.

"That's the nickname, yes. But its real name is Sherrick Three—the third planet of Sherrick's Star. You knew that, didn't you?"

She nodded.

"Well, when we talk about Sherrick Three, we often compare it to Daugherty's Hope. Do you remember why?"

Claudi pinched her lip, thinking.

If there was impatience in the teaching-wall's voice, it was well concealed. "Let's go over it again. It's because the two worlds are very similar. But Daugherty's Hope was settled almost sixty years ago—and that means we can look to it to see what we might expect on Sherrick Three. For example, we can expect the climate patterns to be similar. . . .

"Claudi, are you listening?"

Claudi started. She *had* been listening. And then, somehow, she'd started thinking about the circ-zoo, and wondering how she could get in to see it tomorrow without getting anybody mad at her.

"Okay, then. Now, not only is Sherrick Three—"

"Call it Heart of Heaven," Claudi suggested. "Everyone else does."

The teacher was silent a moment, then *hrrrmph*ed. "All right. If it will make you pay attention. Now, Claudi, Daugherty's Hope is similar to Heart of Heaven in another way, too." The image of the planet was turning like a globe; after a moment, it presented a large ocean to her view.

"Its oceans!" Claudi guessed.

"That's true—and a good point! But just now I want to show you something else."

"Oh."

"If you're interested, we'll come back to the oceans. But look here! The other similarity is its *situation*." A map of the Milky Way galaxy appeared, with a tiny patch highlighted, showing the Habitat of Humanity. An arrow pointed inward toward the center of the galaxy, stretching the border of the Habitat like a piece of chewing gum. "When Daugherty's Hope was settled, not many other worlds had been explored that far down the starstream. It was a real pioneer world. Now, you know what that means."

"Um—"

"It means the colonists didn't have much to fall back on in case of trouble. They were in a part of space where very few people had been, except for the explorers who mapped it. And so it was a hard life, by comparison with ours. They had to fend for themselves, while the rest of us, on more comfortable worlds, had all kinds of help available when we needed it. . . ."

Claudi nodded. She couldn't help noticing that some of the other kids were getting up from their seats. They had finished their lessons, apparently. Only the new boy was still seated, gazing at his own screen. Jeremy rose and made another face at her, pulling his lower eyelid down in a big leer. Claudi curled her lip and looked back at her screen.

"Thank you, Claudi," the teacher said, with scarcely a break in stride.

"I was listening," she protested weakly.

"I'm sure you were. That's why I'm confident that you can tell me what I just said."

She flushed.

"I was explaining that both worlds were dangerous places to be, because they were exposed. There was the wilderness to contend with, and of course, like most places, there was a certain risk from the Throgs."

"Mm."

"Do you want to talk about the Throgs, Claudi?"

She shivered. She certainly did not.

"Well, that can wait a little while, I guess—until you're ready." The teacher paused. "But suppose we talk about some of the other difficulties that the colonists faced."

Claudi sighed.

"Claudi, it's important—because we need to be prepared. All of us, including you. We're going to a new world, where we won't have all of the things that kept us safe on your old world. We have to be ready—"

"I know," she muttered. If only she could watch some of those holos that they'd shown back on Baunhaven, holos of explorers on the new worlds! She liked watching them drop in their scout craft through the mists of strange worlds; she liked watching them step out onto alien landscapes, protected by their shimmering shield-suits. She liked watching them discover new creatures, liked seeing them fight for their lives. . . .

"Claudi, I get the feeling that you're not quite with me today."

She swallowed self-consciously.

"Suppose we made it more challenging, and set up a sim so that *you* had to make some decisions, the way real explorers would. Do you think that might interest you?"

She didn't hesitate. "Sure." The teacher had promised such a sim for later in the term. The sooner the better!

"Okay. I'll make you a promise, then. This seems to be our day for making deals. If you pay attention for the rest of this session, I'll set up the sim for tomorrow. It'll be a lot more challenging than the ones we've done before," the teacher warned. "But you have to keep up your end of the bargain. And that means listening today, to prepare for tomorrow. Agreed?"

Claudi nodded silently, rocking her whole body forward and backward. "Teacher—"

"Yes?"

"Can I see the bridge?"

She could imagine the teacher frowning. "You mean, *'May* I see the bridge?'"

"Uh-huh."

"Ask correctly, Claudi."

She sighed. *"May* I see the bridge—please?"

"Very well, but just for a moment. The bridge is off limits now. But here's a playback."

The whole teaching-wall at the front of the room shivered and darkened, then blossomed out into a surroundie, filling the room. Claudi was the only pupil left in the room. She gasped with delight as the starship's bridge took form all around her. Though it wasn't quite as good as realietime, it was exciting nonetheless. There was the captain sitting in his command chair, right beside her, and the piloting crew at their stations; she saw a dazzling array of screens and readouts—and best of all, down in the front of the bridge, the holopool showing the view of the starstream, the glorious starstream.

What it showed, of course, wasn't a real view such as one might see out the window, even if one could look out a window. She understood that the real view here in n-space was somehow different, though she by no means understood why. But she knew that the starship's intelligence systems took the real view and turned it into something that they could see. It was a vast tube of light, heavenly light, down which the starship floated. And pulsing in the wall of the tube were the glowing beacons of stars, slowly passing the ship by.

Claudi loved to watch the passage of the starstream, even in remote viewing—though she would have preferred to go to the bridge in person. She loved to wonder at those globes of light, to wonder what worlds lay out there beyond the tube. Even right there on the edge of the starstream, she knew, there were thousands of unknown worlds, stars that had never been visited, planets yet undiscovered. The teaching-wall had taught her about that, and she'd listened carefully. If it seemed that she didn't pay attention, that was only when the teacher talked about things that didn't interest her.

The image in the holopool suddenly changed. In the place of the starstream there appeared a complicated graphic, which she couldn't understand at all. She envied the bridge crew, who did understand it. But after a few seconds more, the surroundie vanished.

A teacher's face appeared in the wall—and suddenly she smiled sheepishly. It was the face of "Mr. Zizmer," the holoteacher who was the boss over all the other teacher-programs. Mr. Zizmer was a round-faced man with short dark hair and laughing eyes. Those eyes were sneaky, though, because the thing about Mr. Z was that he could be laughing with you and poking you into working harder at the very same time. And she could tell he was about to do that now.

He stepped out of the wall and came over to crouch by her. "Claudi, tell me something. Would you like to be able to understand all of those instruments you just saw on the bridge?" She blinked at him. "Would you like to know everything the crew knows about flying the ship?" he asked.

She hesitated, then nodded vigorously.

"Good! Well, Claudi, I want to teach it to you. As much as I can, anyway. But—" Mr. Zizmer's forehead wrinkled up. *But.* There was always a *but.*

"If you want to understand those things, there are other things you have to learn first. That's the trick, Claudi. There's always a price. And the price is, to know the things you want to know, you have to pay attention—and learn your basic science, and your math, and—"

Claudi nodded glumly as he talked. She didn't really mind learning all that stuff. She just wished it were more fun. They'd had better teaching systems back on Baunhaven, in her opinion. Except for Mr. Zizmer; she liked Mr. Zizmer.

"So let's go through some of your math challenges now, and then I'll give you just a little head start on tomorrow's sim, and then we'll call it a day."

With a sigh, Claudi leaned forward and peered at her screen, where a strange series of figures had just appeared. She nodded and began moving her lips silently as she concentrated on working out the equations in her mind.

Forgive me—I hope I'm not being overly insecure, breaking in again like this—but I thought I could hear some of you wondering at the wisdom of a teacher that allows an eight-year-old girl such latitude. I can hear you thinking, "That child needs direction. Love and understanding, yes; but she hardly needs pampering, etc. . . ." You're probably thinking that if real humans had been put in charge of educating her instead of robots, she would have known the meaning of discipline.

Well. To you, it might seem that way. But you weren't there, remember. I would put it to you that this teacher suspected possibilities that were not necessarily obvious to the casual observer. Therefore, I would ask you to reserve your criticism. The teacher might not have made perfect decisions; but it was doing what it thought offered the best hope of nurturing certain seeds of potential in an eight-year-old girl—seeds that it sensed might be of more than passing importance.

So the teacher wasn't ignoring the need for discipline in the girl's life; it was just going about instilling it in a different way. And that was part of its reason for scheduling a sim for the next day. This sim would test the children more than any the teacher had put them through before. It had its reasons for trying to steepen the children's learning curve, even if its reasons were based on a hunch.

In any case, the teacher was listening to me, so don't blame the teacher. I hope it doesn't spoil the suspense to say that on this occasion, events proved me right.

By God.

CHAPTER 3

"Are you coming to breakfast with me?" Claudi's mother called out.

Claudi started and rubbed her eyes. She had dozed off in front of her book, dreaming of something—shimmering beings flying in space. She remembered feeling a flutter of fear, but that was gone now. She sighed and let the book darken, then slid down from her bunk. "Coming," she called, sliding open the partition to the tiny suite that was their family living room on the ship.

Audrey Melnik was waiting at the door. "Let's hurry, then. I have to be on Master Deck Two in twenty minutes."

Claudi ducked out ahead of her mother. "Where's Fath'?"

Her mother looked exasperated. "Weren't you listening when he said good-bye to you? He had to get to his wood-working shop. You do know they're making a log cabin, don't you?"

Claudi nodded, skipping along ahead of her mother for a few seconds. Then she turned and waited for her mother to catch up. "I still don't understand why, though."

Mrs. Melnik rolled her eyes. "Don't you *ever* listen when we talk to you? They're learning how, in case we need to build something like that on Sherrick Three."

"But why won't we just make *real* buildings when we get there?"

"We will, Claudi. But suppose something goes wrong. Suppose something happens to our construction-specks, for instance. We'll be a long way from help, and we need to know that we can still build things the hard way if we have to. Anyway, log cabins *are* real buildings."

Claudi nodded. But she still had trouble believing it. Building a log cabin on a starship! Crazy!

With a shrug, she darted ahead of her mother into the lift.

When she arrived at the deck-school, just as the chime sounded, she found the classroom in an uproar. Some of the little kids were crowded around the door, trying to see what was happening. The rest of her class was already there. Mr. Zizmer was standing in the middle of the room, looking exceptionally solid. He was wearing a green-and-blue uniform with a snazzy patch on his left shoulder, and he was carrying a clipboard and acting very organizational. When he saw Claudi, he bellowed, "The entire crew has now checked in! Line up for your station assignments! This crew will be landing in just a few minutes on a newly discovered planet!"

Claudi slapped her forehead. The sim! How could she have forgotten that the teacher had promised to move it up to today? Her classmates were scurrying to line up. From the doorway, groans of protest rose from the younger children as they were called away from the door; the sound cut off as the door winked closed. Claudi peered down the line at her classmates. They all looked excited—except for Jeremy and Paul, who were purposely looking bored.

"Now, Jenny," Mr. Zizmer said after making the first few assignments, "you'll be navigation officer, because we all know you can find your way around with your eyes closed." That brought giggles from everyone. Jenny had gotten lost once in a darkened compartment, unable to find the door. She'd bumped all over the place, howling, until someone had come along and found her. It had happened just after boarding, and she hadn't known all she had to do was ask out loud for light.

"Sheki Hendu?" Everyone looked, as the teacher addressed the new boy. His name was pronounced *Sheck-ee*. He was a head shorter than the next-smallest kid in the class, and his brown skin looked as though it had been dusted with white flour. Claudi wondered where he was from. "Sheki, since you're new, let's get you right into the action. You'll be first officer. You'll take your orders directly from the captain and pass them on to the rest of the crew." There were a couple of mutters at that, but Mr. Zizmer just smiled and glanced at his clipboard again. He typed something in. "And now," he said, "we need a captain."

Jeremy stuck up a hand, grinning. He and Claudi were the only two left.

Mr. Zizmer regarded him thoughtfully. "Actually, Jeremy, I was thinking of making you the chief defense officer." Jeremy frowned. "In charge of gunnery." The boy's eyebrows went up, and his grin returned as Mr. Zizmer continued, "No, for captain, I was thinking of the person whose impatience led me to move this sim up in the lesson plan. You can all thank her, if you like. He suddenly looked straight at her. "Claudi?"

Her heart stopped. *She* was going to be captain? She wanted to, but . . . what if she made a fool of herself in front of everyone?

"Do you accept the assignment?" Mr. Zizmer asked.

Claudi swallowed, then nodded. "Okay," she squeaked.

"Good." Mr. Zizmer stepped back with a sweeping hand gesture. "Well, then—I'll be coming along as admiral, but you're the captain. Would you care to address your crew?"

"Um—" Claudi panicked for a moment. "I don't know! What do I say? I mean, what are we doing?"

"Good question!" Admiral Zizmer said approvingly. "You can't be captain if you don't know your mission!" There was some tittering at that. Claudi flinched, feeling put on the spot. Admiral Zizmer just smiled, though, and pointed to the wall screen. "All right—here's your mission!" A planet sprang into view. "Planet Zed Zed. We will be the first explorers to touch down upon it. We must decide—*you* must decide, together—whether or not a human colony could survive on this planet."

He turned around. "Are you ready to give it a try?"

The kids looked at each other with nervous excitement.

"Great!" Zizmer snapped his fingers. A full surroundie sprang up and filled the room. They were standing on the bridge of a spaceship, and on its viewscreen was the same image of the world Zed Zed, where the wall had been. "Captain Melnik? Command of the ship is yours. May I suggest that you send your crew to their stations?"

Claudi flushed and drew a deep breath, then squawked, "To your stations, everyone!" She stepped to the command seat and, touching it with her hands, realized that though the surroundie made it look different, it was actually her regular seat. "Everyone put on your headsets!" she added. She bit her lip, wondering if it was the right thing to say. But Admiral Zizmer was nodding. Heart pounding, she looked up at the screen. The ship was coming to life.

The sound of howling engines filled her ears, along with voices snapping information back and forth. She felt a tugging of G-forces. The headset was giving her realistic sensations to go with the images. Staring at the viewscreen, she saw the glow of their entry into the atmosphere, and wisps of vapor flying past. She wondered what she should be doing. Even as the thought passed through her mind, she heard the teacher's voice close to her ear. "Perhaps you should ask the crew to report. If everything's okay, tell them, 'Steady as she goes.' "

She nodded anxiously. "Crew," she squeaked. "How are we doing? Report."

And she heard her classmates answering: "Looking good." "Coming down fast!" "No enemies in sight." That last comment was made in a tone that sounded disappointed. All of the voices sounded deeper, more mature than the voices of kids. The surroundie was doing that. It was probably making her sound like an adult, too. She assumed the teacher was whispering into the other kids' ears, as well, helping them to understand their assignments.

"Good," she said. "Steady on—I mean, um—"

"Steady as she goes."

"Right. Um, steady as she goes!" Her heart pounded harder. In front of her, all manner of information crossed the screens. She understood none of it. But there was a whispering voice now, telling her that this was speed and that fuel, and that wind. . . .

A sudden hooting alarm made her jump. The shuddering grew harder. "What's that?"

"Something's happening—" someone cried.

"It's not me! I don't—"

"Captain! What—"

Claudi froze, watching lights flash red over the consoles. What was happening? Were they under attack? Admiral Zizmer leaned toward her, but she was already shouting, "Jeremy—Defense Officer—report! Engineer, what's happening?"

Over the hubbub, she heard Jeremy shout, "Nothing on the screens!" But from the engineer, there was no answer.

"Better ask your first officer. I think the engineer isn't sure," Admiral Zizmer murmured.

"First Officer!" she cried. "Find out what's wrong."

A small voice called, "Aye, Captain." A dark figure darted across the bridge.

Claudi glanced and saw Admiral Zizmer frowning over the scene, his eyes darting to and fro. The first officer's voice caught her attention again. "The en-engines aren't w-working! I think we're going to c-crash." She looked over to her left and saw her first officer, Sheki, stretched on his tiptoes looking over the shoulder of Rob, the engineer. Rob looked hopelessly confused. But Sheki gazed at her with steady eyes.

"Can't you do anything?" she asked.

The little boy looked puzzled, then frowned, as though listening to a voice. He shook his head. "Im-impossible. We're g-going in, Captain."

Claudi's breath quickened. Going in! Losing her ship!

"We still have some control," the admiral murmured. "Tell the autopilot to ride the controls hard." Claudi nodded and called to the autopilot to do that. "Hang on!" she yelled to everyone else.

A moment later, she felt a tremendous shaking, and the ground came into focus in the viewscreen, coming up fast. She felt the nose of the ship turning up, then heard metal tearing. "Hang *on!*" It might not have been real, but it *felt* real, and she used her hands to clutch at her seat. She felt the ship bucking, and heard shouting. Then there was a loud smashing sound, and everything went black.

When she came to—she actually felt as if she had blacked out, but there was a strange, ghostly memory in her mind, as if she'd been somehow *walking,* or calling out in a dream—she found herself sitting in a smoking ruins. Tongues of flame darted up from the consoles. She blinked in fear. "Put out the fires!" she shouted. She heard Sheki yell, "F-fire control!" and there was a whooshing sound, and the flames vanished. Claudi looked around in relief. "Is everyone okay?"

A chorus of affirmative yells came back to her. "Wow—" she heard someone say—it was Jenny—"Claudi, what were you *doing* just then?"

"Huh?"

Jenny looked mystified. "You looked like you were *floating around,* trying to wake us up! I *saw* you—only I was half—I mean, out cold!"

"Me, too," breathed Suze, and someone else agreed.

Claudi looked back at them in puzzlement. She hadn't done anything—had she? "I—" she started to say. And then she remembered . . . the dream of walking, and calling out. What was that all about?

But Admiral Zizmer's voice interrupted. "We've been lucky. We're all still alive. But hadn't we better try to contact the home fleet?"

Claudi quieted the others. "Com Officer—call the fleet!" she ordered. She didn't remember who the com officer was, but she knew someone had been given that title. She heard Betsy answer that all communications were out. Frightened, she looked up at the admiral, who was staring at his clipboard and rubbing the back of his neck. In response to her look, he arched his eyebrows.

What now? She was the captain.

She drew herself up. "Okay, everyone. Um, everyone come here, and let's figure out what to do." Her classmates crowded around. Their teaching headsets looked like once-gleaming space gear, now smudged and stained with smoke. Claudi hesitated. "Um—Admiral Zizmer?"

The teacher cleared his throat and strode down toward the viewscreen. The image there, though breaking up, showed branches and trees. They seemed to have landed in the middle of a woods. "Well, crew, you brought the ship down and lived to tell about it. Congratulations! Now, I wish I could say that your troubles are over, but I can't."

The crew waited silently. Claudi *knew* that she was still in the classroom, but she couldn't help feeling scared nevertheless. It was too real. She had a strange, dizzying feeling in her head, almost as if she were somehow jumping in and out of her own body. Several times she saw her classmates glancing at her, as if startled, and she shivered. What was happening to her?

"We're stranded, out of contact with the fleet," Admiral Zizmer continued. "So we may be here for a while. I'm afraid that a scan of the ship shows most of our supplies destroyed. In fact, we have no food supplies, and very few medical supplies!" He paused to let his words sink in, then turned his gaze upon Claudi. "That means some tough decisions for all of you—but especially for your captain. Captain Melnik?"

She swallowed.

"You have a crew who need to eat, and they need water. What shall we do?"

"Um—" Claudi was aware of her classmates' eyes upon her. It felt as real to them as it did to her, she knew. And they were counting on her. How had she gotten herself into this position? If only she'd paid more attention to the teacher yesterday!

The admiral's eyes narrowed. "You are the first human explorers on this world. Very little is known about what lives and grows here. Will the plants be safe to eat? Will the animals be dangerous? Can you breathe the air? Your survival depends upon your learning those things."

Claudi felt a strange pressure growing in the back of her throat. "I guess . . . maybe we should go outside and see what's there."

Zizmer's eyebrows went up. "All of you? All at once?"

Claudi thought. "No, um—one or two at first. In case the air is bad or something." The teacher nodded. She turned to her crew. "Any volunteers?"

The crew shuffled their feet. Finally Jeremy blurted, "I'll go. You'll need someone with guns. In case—you know—" He shrugged and didn't finish his sentence. Claudi nodded. Jeremy annoyed her sometimes, but this time he was probably right. There could be danger out there. A moment later, Sheki raised his hand. Everyone looked at the two volunteers, then at Claudi.

"No," she said to Sheki, to everyone's surprise. "You can't go. You're the first officer. You're too important. Who's my science officer?"

Paul raised his hand uneasily. "I guess I am."

"Okay," Claudi said firmly. "You and Jeremy go out. But don't take any chances. Okay?" She looked to the admiral for approval, but his eyes betrayed nothing. The two nodded. "Okay. Get your gear and go."

The surroundie shimmered, and on the left side of the bridge, an airlock became visible. The two boys disappeared into it. An instant later, the viewscreen flickered, and the two boys became visible in its image. They were enveloped in gleaming silver forcefields, which hid their faces.

"Can you hear me out there?" Claudi called.

"Yep!" That was Jeremy. He raised his right arm, and she saw that he was holding some sort of ray weapon. "Don't see too much yet. A bunch of trees."

"Science Officer Paul. What do you think? How's the air?"

The other figure turned toward the ship. "I . . . don't know. I guess . . . I'll have to turn my suit off."

Claudi swallowed. She saw Admiral Zizmer's eyes shift. She wondered, maybe there was a way to test the air first. "Wait—" she started to say, but too late. The force-field surrounding Paul vanished, and he was standing there unprotected. He looked scared.

"Wait, what?" he said.

"Uh—never mind, I guess. How do you—I mean, is the air okay?" Claudi felt her face growing hot. Had she made a mistake? She didn't feel very sure about being captain.

Paul made a choking face—then guffawed. It was a forced laugh. He was trying to make a joke of it, Claudi thought. "Seems okay to me, Captain." Jeremy, and a couple of the girls inside the ship, giggled nervously.

Claudi flared with anger. "This is serious, Science Officer! I want you to be careful!"

"Aye, aye," Paul answered meekly.

"I mean it! Jeremy, are you keeping watch?"

Jeremy, who had been observing all of this from behind his silver face, whirled around with his weapon leveled, guarding the perimeter. "Nothing out here but trees. I'm going to turn my suit off, too. I can't see very well with it on."

Claudi started to answer, but her voice caught. He should have asked permission from her; but now his suit was already off, and he was standing beside Paul in apparent safety. "Okay," she said lamely.

A moment later, she heard a loud snapping sound, from somewhere beyond the viewscreen. Both boys looked around in consternation. The sound repeated, louder. Jeremy suddenly hooted in alarm and raised his weapon. "Something's coming!"

"What is it?" Claudi demanded.

"Something *big,*" Paul shouted, diving to the ground, as Jeremy squeezed his trigger. There was a flash of light and a boom. The viewscreen image flickered. "Holy criminy!" Paul muttered from where he lay. He looked up at Jeremy. "Did you hit it?"

"Don' know." Jeremy squinted. There was another sound, closer.

"What *is* it?" Claudi repeated. She looked at the teacher, who pointed to the viewscreen controls in front of her. She moved her hands over it, and the view shifted to the left. She gasped. An enormous, horned animal was rearing back to charge the ship—and her two crewmen! "Shoot, Jeremy! *Shoot!*" she shouted.

Jeremy fired again. An explosion knocked the animal sideways. It staggered and fell. It kicked its legs for a moment, then lay still. Jeremy yelled triumphantly, followed by the rest of the crew. Claudi gulped in relief.

The two boys walked forward cautiously and, picking up

some long sticks, poked at the animal. "Hey, Claudi!" Jeremy called.

Paul elbowed him. "Captain Melnik."

"Yeah, right. Captain Melnik."

"What is it?" she asked.

"You sent us out here to look for food, right?" Jeremy said, looking back. "Well, we just killed this big thing."

"So?"

"*So,* let's cook it up and eat it! We can have steak for dinner!"

Claudi frowned. She hated the idea of killing animals for food. But he had a point—they needed to survive, didn't they? "I don't know. Maybe." She turned to the admiral.

He shrugged. "Your decision, Captain. Is it worth the risk? Why don't you ask the advice of your officers?"

The other crew members were waiting. But who should she ask? "First Officer?" she said finally. "What do you think?"

Sheki gazed at the screen as though he didn't hear her. But a moment later, he turned. "We should test it first. See if it's safe."

"Excellent idea," the admiral said. "Better check your damage control report first, though. Did the test gear make it through the crash?"

Sheki scratched his ear as he looked at the display in front of him. He shook his head. "I guess not." The admiral raised his eyebrows and looked back at Claudi.

She scowled. Everyone was expecting *her* to make a decision. "I guess," she said reluctantly, "unless anyone has a better idea, I'm going to tell them to cut off a little piece of meat and cook it." She called outside. "Jeremy, can you start a bonfire with that gun of yours?"

Her defense officer grinned. "Sure." He pointed the gun down.

"Wait!" she shouted. But Jeremy had just fired off a blast. A patch of brush burst into flames, dangerously close to the ship. "I didn't say to start a forest fire! You should have cleared a space first." Jeremy grinned and shrugged. He yanked a fat knife from his utility belt and started hacking through the animal's hide.

The rest of the crew were stirring restlessly. "Shouldn't

we try some of the plants?" Suze ventured. "There might be some potatoes or something. Or fruit."

Betsy agreed. "I don't want to eat some strange meat. I'd rather try a plant any day."

Claudi started to agree, but Rob spoke up. "We could *starve* if we don't find enough to eat. We can't just live on plants—"

"Sure we can—"

"*You* can, maybe—"

Claudi interrupted to order, "Jeremy and Paul—look for some plants that might be good to eat, okay? While you're cooking that meat." She turned to Suze. "You want to go help them?" Suze nodded and disappeared out the airlock.

The rest of them gathered around the viewscreen, watching the meat smoke on the end of a stick that Jeremy was holding in the fire. Paul was examining some berries he'd found nearby. Suze began scraping some roots with a knife. Finally Jeremy held the piece of meat up, twirling it slowly on the end of the stick. "Here goes!" he called. He blew on it, then gnawed off a corner and chewed. Paul, not to be outdone, popped a few berries into his mouth.

"No!" Claudi yelled. "You guys—!"

Paul looked startled. He grimaced and spat out the berries. "Sour," he said.

Jeremy shrugged, chewed, and swallowed. "Tastes okay," he said. He lifted the stick to take another bite. As he opened his mouth, he suddenly dropped the stick and doubled over, his eyes wide. Suze rushed over and knelt beside him. He was shaking and groaning. Paul stood nearby, looking frightened.

"Claudi," Suze cried, looking up into the viewscreen in terror. "He's awfully sick! He looks like he's *dying!* What should I do?"

Dying? But this was just a sim! Could a sim be this real? Claudi whirled to face Admiral Zizmer. "What should I do?"

The admiral, looking very distant, replied, "Whatever you have to do."

"*What's that mean?*" she cried. "*Is this real?*"

"You must act as if it is," the admiral said softly. "Is he still alive?"

Claudi clenched her fists helplessly. "Is he alive?" she called, her voice cracking.

Suze looked up from Jeremy's now-still form. "I don't know. I don't think so." There was a groan behind her, and she turned. Paul was grabbing his stomach now. His face was white. *"Paul?"*

Paul bent and fell over.

Suze spun around in circles, bewildered. She was starting to cry. "What do I do? Claudi, I'm scared! What should I *do?"*

Claudi could only stare. She felt the presence of the admiral at her right shoulder and she looked up. "Help me!" she whispered.

The admiral spoke calmly. "Who is your backup science officer?"

Claudi blinked at her remaining crew. Sheki raised his hand timidly. "I th-think I would be, sir."

"Very well—check your medical supplies for alien food poisoning."

Sheki consulted a console, scowling. "It says it all got ruined in the crash." He peered up at the admiral.

"In that case," Zizmer said somberly, "you may have no choice but to inject them with freezelife and hope that they can be kept from dying until you are rescued. Do you have the injections in the first-aid unit?"

Sheki studied his console again and nodded. Near the airlock, a small panel opened. He hurried over and took out two small cylinders and held them up for inspection. "Right?" Claudi asked the admiral.

"Yes. Give it to them—fast—then bring them in through decontamination."

Sheki hurried outside and joined Suze. "They look . . . dead," he reported in a shaky voice.

"Spray it into them anyway," the admiral instructed.

Sheki, crouched beside Suze, seemed frozen, unable to obey or move. Claudi glanced up at Admiral Zizmer, feeling a fearful tension inside that was almost too great to bear. And then, for an instant, the tension released and she suddenly felt as if she were standing outside with her friends, urging them on. She had a queer feeling that they *saw* her somehow, and that they were puzzled, but somehow encouraged by her presence. Claudi shook her head, as the feeling went away. Outside, Sheki had stirred back to life and was giving the injections. "Um—bring them inside," Claudi ordered, blinking. She turned. "Rob—go help them, okay?"

The red-headed boy hesitated at the airlock. Then he hurried outside, and he and Sheki and Suze quickly dragged Paul and Jeremy into the airlock-decontaminator. A light above the inner door blinked red, then green. The door opened and the three unhurt crew members pulled their fallen mates into the ship.

As Claudi tried to think what to say, Admiral Zizmer cleared his throat. "Listen up, crew. I don't have to tell you, this is a hard setback! But the rest of you still have a chance—if you're mindful of the dangers! And there's still hope that Paul and Jeremy can be revived, if we are rescued." The admiral gazed at his officers. "We must keep thinking of how to survive. *We will survive.* Say that to yourselves! Believe it!" He paused, while that sank in. Then he glanced at Betsy. "Communications Officer, isn't there something coming in on your console?"

Flustered, Betsy turned to look. A light was flashing. She touched it and a loud voice suddenly filled the bridge: ". . . FLEET. DO YOU READ? WE ARE APPROACHING NOW. PREPARE TO BE LIFTED OFF THE PLANET!"

"We're being rescued!" Claudi shouted, clapping her hands. She saw the admiral give a thumbs-up gesture. "Betsy, tell them we're ready! Tell them to hurry!"

"It might be advisable for everyone to strap in," the admiral suggested.

The crew scrambled for their seats.

A moment later, a bright light filled the viewscreen. It seemed to shine right through the ship's hull, and the bridge itself seemed bathed in light. There was a faint vibration, which grew to a trembling roar. The forest disappeared, and the ground outside fell away. Through the blaze of light, they could see the planet's horizon, then the whole planet, receding to a ball in space. The voice from the console said, ". . . APPROACHING HOME FLEET.

PREPARE FOR MEDICAL TEAM TO COME ABOARD. . . ."

The light filling the bridge wavered, and Claudi found herself clutching her seat, squeezing until her knuckles hurt. Then the light faded and the roar died away . . . and they were back in their classroom, in their regular seats. The image of the planet was still on the wall, shrinking against the black of space. Paul and Jeremy were lying on the floor, wearing their headsets. They groaned and sat up. "What happened?" Jeremy muttered. He looked around in puzzlement.

"Welcome back to starship *Charity*!" Mr. Zizmer boomed, from the far side of the room. He was back in his regular clothes, wearing a grin on his face. "Are we all in one piece? Did we scare the daylights out of you?"

He was answered by a chorus of yeses, Claudi's most fervent among them. Laughing, Mr. Zizmer strode to the front of the class and waved Paul and Jeremy to their seats. "You can take off your headsets, everyone. Well, what did you think? Pretty realistic?" He was answered by shivering groans. "Good! That was on purpose, you know. It seemed to me that you were ready for sims with more realistic sensations—and challenges. Paul and Jeremy, how do you feel?"

The boys stared at him, wide-eyed. "I really thought I ate something *terrible*," Paul said. "I thought I was a goner!"

"Well, it didn't actually hurt you a bit," Mr. Zizmer reassured him. "But it was supposed to give you an idea of how it *could* feel, if you ate something poisonous. In real life it might have felt a lot worse. This was just to give you a taste." Paul groaned. "How about you, Jeremy? Same thing?" Jeremy nodded silently. He seemed unusually subdued.

Mr. Zizmer turned to the others. "Well, I guess we all learned something from that. Paul and Jeremy felt it more directly, but we all could have been in the same danger. Right?" He nodded, answering himself. "Well, there was a reason for going through this. It was to give you some notion of what real exploration can be like. It's exciting— but it's dangerous, too. You have to be *careful* out there."

He stamped his foot on the deck, then grinned. "Besides, I want you to appreciate how much safer you are, here on the ship."

His gaze shifted. "And what did you think about being captain, Claudi?"

Claudi took a deep breath and let it out. "It's *hard!*" she murmured.

"That it is," Mr. Zizmer agreed. "But you did the best you could. And your crewmates really rallied behind you. Even when you were on the bridge giving orders, I think they felt as if you were right out there with them. Didn't you, crew?" There were some wondering nods, and from a few of the kids, puzzled looks. Claudi remembered that feeling she'd had, of standing with the others, even when she hadn't been there. She wanted to ask Mr. Zizmer about it. It reminded her of something she'd felt before, but she wasn't sure just what. But Mr. Zizmer was already going on, "In our training exercises, the thing to remember is to do the very best you can. And keep working as a team. I will never ask for more. So, crew—how about a round of applause for Captain Melnik?"

While Claudi blushed, the other kids shouted and applauded—except Jeremy, at first, but finally even he gave in and clapped. "And how about a round for our brave, almost-dead comrades?" Mr. Zizmer joked, gesturing to Paul and Jeremy. Everyone clapped again, which seemed to satisfy Jeremy. Then Mr. Zizmer went around the class, calling for applause, until everyone had been cheered for his or her part in the mission.

"And now—what would you all say to some refreshments?"

The applause was louder than ever.

CHAPTER 4

Later, when class was over, Claudi made a beeline for the lift, with the other kids. The sim had been exciting, and even the rest of class hadn't been too bad, but she'd been there long enough. Long enough! Where to next? She didn't even know, hadn't had time to think.

Most of the kids tumbled out of the lift at the eating commons. "Coming, Claudi?" Suze and Jenny called. At that moment something surfaced in her mind and she shook her head. The circ-zoo! The lupeko! And that man Joe, who'd said he would show her around. Yes, that was where she would go.

She suddenly realized that the lift was waiting for instructions. The only other person left in it was the new boy, Sheki. "Where are you going?" she asked.

He shrugged shyly, shifting from one foot to another.

Claudi stared at him, wondering if maybe he was waiting to see where she was going, so that he could follow. "I'm going to the circ-zoo," she offered, with a slight toss of her head.

The boy's eyes widened.

"You're new in the class."

He nodded, biting his lip. What an odd one, Claudi thought. He had incredibly curly hair, and that dusty-brown face. He was missing a front tooth, too. He was sort of cute, in a way. She thought the teacher had said something about him being part *Indian*, whatever that was. She didn't mind if he wanted to come with her, but she wished he wouldn't just stand there staring at her. "I'm Claudi," she said suddenly. "Claudi Melnik." She stuck out her hand, feeling very much older than this boy.

He shook hands gravely. "Sh-Sheki Hendu." He spelled his name out for her.

Claudi nodded. She'd noticed before that he stuttered, but knew it wouldn't be polite to mention it. "I was, um . . . captain . . . back there in class." Now she felt dumb. She hadn't said that to brag but just to have something to say.

"I know." A grin spread across the boy's face. He saluted. "Captain Mel-Melnik—First Officer Hendu r-reporting."

She saluted back. "How old are you, Officer Hendu?"

"S-six."

"Huh. You're awfully young to be in our class."

He nodded and scuffed his feet, looking away. Then his eyes shifted back. "C-captain, back in the s-sim . . . h-how did you d-do that?"

"Huh? Do what?"

"When we were in, in trouble. Y-you, you—" He frowned and huffed in frustration and started over. "I don't know how to ex-explain. But when I was outside the sh-ship, it was like you were r-right *there* with us. Just for a second."

Claudi blinked, as it came back to her in a rush. That's right, it was as though a part of her *mind* had stepped out of itself and gone to join her friends. Everyone seemed to have noticed—but Mr. Zizmer hadn't said anything about it, and in the class following, all the other kids seemed to have forgotten. Even she had, until now. "I—I don't ex-actly—I mean, I'm not—"

The lift interrupted her. *"What deck would you like, please? There are others waiting. . . ."*

"Oh," Claudi said, startled. "Um—circ-zoo. That's on Deck . . . Taurus." The lift began moving. Sheki was standing silent, waiting. She didn't quite know what to say, and she hadn't answered his question, because she couldn't. Finally she asked, "Do you want to come? Have you seen the circ-zoo yet?"

Sheki shook his head. "It's n-not open yet."

Claudi grinned. "I know someone who can get us in." Sheki's eyebrows went up. "So—how come you got moved into our class?"

Sheki's lips pressed together. He shrugged and looked awkward. "I gr-graduated ahead," he said finally. "It was too slow in the level I was in."

"Oh, yeah? What did you think of class today? I bet you weren't bored there." She remembered the sim with a shudder. Even as a *play* captain, it had been pretty frightening.

Sheki produced a gap-toothed grin. "It could have been a lot . . . *better* . . . if those guys had been sm-smarter about . . ." He sighed. "You know."

She thought of Jeremy going straight for the food, and she giggled. It wasn't really Jeremy's style to be smart— except smart-aleck.

"It went pretty fast though," Sheki said. "Sometimes my old class seemed to go forever." He looked thoughtful and added, "I want to learn to be a scientist."

Before Claudi could answer, the lift reached Deck Taurus. She pointed the way. The decks down at this end of the ship looked different from the ones where the kids usually spent their time—less homey, with glaring lights and plain walls. It seemed to make Sheki a little nervous. The few adults that they passed looked at them curiously. Claudi just ignored them and kept going.

Sheki pointed to a glowing sign near a large set of doors: CIRC-ZOO—CLOSED UNTIL ANOUNCED. "Isn't that spelled wrong?"

Claudi shrugged and turned down the corridor. "Doesn't matter. There's another way in." Sheki looked puzzled, but followed.

They came to a closed door that said: AUTHORIZED PERSONNEL ONLY. "What's that mean, exactly?" Sheki asked, squinting at the words.

"It means nobody's supposed to be here, I think." She didn't remember that sign being there before.

"I know *that.*"

Claudi shrugged. "It's how I got in before, though. There's a man named Joe." She pressed the touchplate beside the door.

Nothing happened.

She pressed it again. Finally she grumped, "He must not be in." She sighed and shrugged. "Let's try the front," she said, hoping to sound decisive. They walked back up the corridor.

They hadn't gone ten steps before a voice called from behind, "Hey, where are you going?" Joe Farharto was standing in the doorway. "I'd about given up on you." He waved them back. "Who's your friend?"

Claudi introduced Sheki. "Glad to meet you," Joe said. "Pretty soon, we're going to have more kids here than animals." Claudi looked at him worriedly, but Joe laughed and said he was just joking. He ushered them through the first room, which was lined with boxes and bottles and empty enclosures, and into the back gallery, where Claudi had seen the lupeko.

Lopo's enclosure was empty.

"What happened?" she asked. "Where is he?"

"Where's who? Oh, you mean Lopo?"

"Course." Claudi pointed out the enclosure to Sheki. "There was a loo-*peek*-oh in there before."

Sheki's eyes widened.

"Lopo's in the medical area," Joe said. "He's getting his vision and speech upgrades."

"He'll be able to talk?" Claudi asked.

"Pretty soon now. He's going to be a little woozy for a while, and then it'll take him some time to get used to the new vocal cords. And of course, he'll have to learn how to use them."

Claudi marveled at the idea of the lupeko talking. She was dying to see him. "Can we?" she asked.

"Well—" Joe hesitated. "I don't know. I really shouldn't let you in there right now."

"We wouldn't hurt anything," Claudi promised.

"We w-won't touch anything," Sheki added softly.

"Ganging up on me, are you?" Joe chuckled. "Well, okay. Just for a few seconds. But—" he raised a cautioning finger—"when I open it up, you're just to stand in the doorway, and *not make a sound*. Okay?"

Both kids nodded.

Crooking his finger, Joe led them deeper into the maze of rooms. They passed down a short hallway lined with a bunch of storage lockers and came to a door. It twinkled open. "Okay, come here," Joe whispered.

Claudi nudged Sheki ahead of her, through the doorway. The room was small and cluttered, with several clear bubbles near the door, with small rodentlike animals in them. Nearby was an interface, with a display and keyboard and headset. Claudi saw Lopo the same instant that Joe pointed. He was in the far corner of the room—suspended in an enclosure, paws hanging in midair, head slumped down. Several wires ran from the back of his head. His intense red eyes were blinking nervously. Claudi drew a sharp breath and, without thinking, stepped past Sheki. Joe's arm blocked her way.

"He looks *sick*. Or hurt," she murmured.

Joe spoke in a low tone. "Not at all. He's just in suspension while the med-specks work on him."

"The what?"

"Med-specks. Microscopic little robots—too small for you to see. They're in his body now, making the changes in his speech system. And his eyes—we didn't know his eyes needed work until we put the med-specks in and they gave him a complete checkup. Then we reprogrammed them to take care of that, too."

Claudi squinted. "What's wrong with his eyes?"

"He's a little nearsighted, that's all."

At that moment, the lupeko raised his head. Those eyes, with their jet black pupils surrounded by flame red, seemed to flare as he tilted his head, peering in Claudi's direction. He whimpered softly, then let his head droop again. "Lopo?" she whispered. "Are you okay?"

"We'd better let him be," Joe said. "We shouldn't disturb him."

Claudi nodded soberly, though the sight of the helpless animal tugged at her heart. Reluctantly she turned away, following Sheki out into the hall. The door became solid again behind them. "You can see him again once he's recovered," Joe said.

As they walked away, Claudi murmured, "He didn't seem to like it in there very much."

Joe *hmm*ed, nudging them along. "I guess probably not," he admitted. "But it's not hurting him any. He's actually very safe, because if anything started to go wrong, the meds could take care of it right away."

"Wouldn't you have to be there to tell them what to do?"

"Well, the specks are pretty smart. They'd call us, but basically they know more about what to do than we do."

"S-still, that doesn't m-mean he likes it, does it?" asked Sheki, his voice small and uncertain.

Joe sighed. "I guess not. But he won't be there long. Hey —do you want to go and see the rest of the circ-zoo? I promised you a look at the other lupeko, didn't I?"

The kids nodded vigorously.

"Good, then." Joe rubbed his hands together. "We're still officially closed, you know. But for my special friends— I think I can arrange a quick look. Don't tell anyone, okay?" He put his finger to his lips and made a sealing gesture. "Come on this way."

Everything was hazy and funny. Lopo felt a queer buzzing in his head as he struggled to raise it. He thought he had heard something. He could hardly tell what he was seeing. A couple of fuzzy shapes across the room. But there had been a familiar voice, and one of the shapes looked like . . . was it *Claudi?* Yes! He was sure of it! He cried out— and thought he heard his name in answer.

It's all just a picture in your head, like those other things you saw, mocked a wordless voice inside his head. *You don't know what you're seeing.*

But he did. He saw better now than he ever had before. Even through the hazy fog. Even with all of the strange new sensations swarming in his eyes. He saw her standing there looking at him. The little keeper, the *girl* who had so smitten him—why, he didn't know, just that she *was,* and she'd been right there with him, as if she'd been *meant* to be with him. He felt that feeling again now, could almost feel her touch him on the inside. But now she was turning away, and now the shapes were gone.

What were they doing to him?

The keepers had come this morning and taken him out of his enclosure and put him in this new place, with no blanket, no water bowl, no teacher. And stuck things into him, and somehow floated him in the air, and then left him hanging, all alone.

It didn't hurt much, but it felt very very strange, disturbingly strange. Things were happening inside him, things he couldn't understand. His throat felt tight and itchy. His breath was slow, and he couldn't pant quite right, and he couldn't move, except to shift his head a little. And there was that tingling swimminess in his eyes.

He was woozy, didn't even want food. Sleep. That was the best thing. Except he couldn't get that one thing out of his mind. One thing above all else.

She'd come back to him.

She'd come back.

CHAPTER 5

The galleries of the circ-zoo seemed strangely quiet. Claudi had been in zoos before, and once to a circus, back on Baunhaven. But this was different—a lot more crowded, for one thing. But of course, things were bound to be that way on a starship. The place was absolutely crammed with strange plants and animals; and it was more than a little eerie, with the lights down low. It was evening for the animals, Joe told them. Claudi and Sheki peered into all the bubble enclosures that they passed. They saw a luminous gold serpent, and a small wildcat with an amazingly wide, flat head and the biggest and greenest eyes Claudi had ever seen; and they saw a small animal called a black African dwarf goat with short, pointed horns and curious, square-pupiled eyes.

Before they crossed to the other half of the zoo, Joe opened a door and let them peek into an auditorium where some of the circus performers were rehearsing for the upcoming shows. He explained, as they stood in the doorway, that performing for the passengers and crew was how the circ-zoo paid for part of its passage to the colony worlds. "You get to see our shows and we go for half the regular fare," he told them.

That sounded great to Claudi. She thought that if she ever became a ship's captain, she'd make sure there was a circ-zoo on board all the time. She felt a rush of excitement just peering in, imagining. She heard voices, down on the stage. It was spooky in the auditorium, with most of the lights off; but a bright beam illuminated the stage in front, where two men and a woman were talking and gesturing and occasionally barking out instructions to unseen people. "Wow," she whispered, imagining the whole show that would take place down there.

"Come on, let's go see the lupeko," Joe said, waving them back out into the zoo gallery. They passed several glowing bubble-aquaria, populated by flat, saucer-shaped fish. "Those are the smart fish," Joe said. "We'll come back to those, if you want. But look—over here." He led the way into a side alcove, where a number of animal enclosures were grouped in a big U. "Here's a picobear from Cardiff—" and he pointed to a dark ball of fur asleep in one corner of its cubicle— "and here's a holo of an Earth wolf— we don't have a real wolf, unfortunately." He pointed to what looked like a rugged gray dog, which *looked* as alive as any of the other animals. "And here's the lupeko." He stopped at a bubble that was filled with holos, or something, to resemble a little corner of a woods.

Claudi peered, but couldn't see anything except branches and leaves and underbrush. "Where is he? Do you see him, Sheki?"

"Nope." Sheki stood on his tiptoes.

"Actually it's a *she,*" Joe said. "Her name's *Baako.* It means 'first-born' in an old-Earth language." Joe had something in his hand as he bent down and touched the front of the enclosure. The barrier shimmered, and there was a sudden smell of woods and animal. "Hey, Baako!" he called softly. "You want to come out and see some visitors? Baako?" He winked at Claudi and Sheki. "She gets a little moody sometimes and has to be coaxed out. Hey, *Baako?*"

Claudi peered harder. She thought she saw something moving.

A sighing voice, with a hint of a growl, issued from somewhere under the brush. "Who's ther-r-r-re?"

"It's Joe—with some friends. Some young people."

"Rrrr—young people?" The voice sounded suspicious.

"Two very nice kids," Joe said. "I've been telling them how absolutely wonderful and cheerful lupekos are, and they just had to come see for themselves. What do you say?"

This time the sigh was more distinct. "Wherrrrre's that whrrr—*whelp* you have in back? Uhrrrr? Can't they see him, hmmm?"

"They've seen Lopo. But he can't talk yet. In fact, he's just getting his voice put in now. What's the matter, Baako? Are you going to be an old grouch?" Joe was starting to sound exasperated. It didn't look to Claudi as though any lupeko was going to come out.

"There she is!" Sheki cried.

Claudi squinted. She thought her eyes were playing tricks on her. The enclosure didn't look that large; and yet, way in back, an animal was emerging from a small, hollowed-out cave, half hidden behind a quivering, broad-leafed bush. The animal was larger than Lopo, and somehow more bearlike. Its eyes flashed, but with a bright orange-brown color, rather than the red of Lopo's.

"Rrr, herrre I am," the creature said, a little sulkily, shambling to the front of her enclosure. She pushed the tip of her nose out through the clear front and sniffed loudly at Claudi and Sheki. The kids drew back nervously.

Joe reassured them that it was just Baako's way of greeting them; plus, the partition was only partway down, so she couldn't get out. "Anyway, she wouldn't hurt a mouse. Right, Baaka'-girl?"

The lupeko cocked her head. "Hmm? Hmm." Blinking deliberately, she gazed at the three. "Well-l-l?"

Joe cleared his throat. "Baako, this is Claudi . . . and Sheki."

"Pleased, I'm sur-r-r-re," the lupeko said doubtfully.

Claudi didn't know what to say, so she just studied the creature. Baako's eyes seemed aware and intelligent. But there had been a spark of some sort that she'd felt with

Lopo—when they'd touched gazes, when she'd stroked his fur—that she didn't feel with Baako.

"Is this as good for-r-r you as it is for-r-r me?" Baako asked suddenly, her eyes widening.

"Baako-o-o!" Joe scolded.

Claudi frowned. She didn't quite know what the lupeko meant, but it sure didn't seem very happy to see them. "We didn't mean anything," she said finally. "We didn't mean to bother you."

"You're not bothering anyone, Claudi," Joe assured her. "Is she, Baako? *Baako?*"

"Arrrr, *no-o-o,*" the lupeko said, sighing. She sat back on her haunches and scratched at her ear with a hind paw.

"Why are you in such a bad mood?" Joe asked. "Isn't your teacher giving you enough stimulation?"

"Hrrmph," the creature grunted.

"What's that mean? You want me to ask it to do more?"

Baako growled. "Too much alrrrready." She looked away, sighing deeply, licking as though she were trying to get a bad taste off her tongue. "Seeing, rrrr, too much! Hear-r-r-ring too much! I think the teacherrrr is on the fr-r-ritz!"

Joe scowled. "I'll check into it," he said, but he didn't sound wholly convinced. "I guess maybe we should leave you alone and come back another time. I'll talk to you later about your teacher."

"Tell it—rrrrr, to keep the wr-r-r-retched *bat-t-ts* away!"

Joe looked startled. He glanced at the kids with raised eyebrows before asking, "Bats?"

"Bat-t-ts!" Baako barked. Her nose wrinkled with displeasure.

Joe seemed mystified. "Bats. Okay, Baako, I'll ask it about the bats." He shook his head. "But I hope next time I bring you visitors, you'll try not to be so bad-tempered. Okay?"

The older lupeko *hmmph*ed and turned to retreat into the hidden recesses of her enclosure. She paused to look back briefly. "Nice, rrrrr, to meet you." Then she disappeared into the underbrush.

Claudi made a face as she peered into the gloomy bubble. Joe chuckled ruefully. "I guess she wasn't in the mood for visitors."

"Jeez," Sheki said.

"She's not always that grumpy, really. I wonder what was eating her." Joe shrugged. "Well, at least now you know what a grown-up lupeko looks like."

Claudi mused as they walked out of the alcove. "Will Lopo have—?" Her voice caught. She had just seen something odd, a flicker in the gloom, off to the right of where the aquaria softly bubbled. She squinted. What was that?

"A voice like Baako's?" Joe said, finishing her question for her. "More or less. It'll take him a little while to learn to speak. But yes, he'll be able to talk with us."

"Huh." Claudi blinked, thinking again of Lopo. She liked the idea of him talking. She was sure he would be friendlier than Baako, and she said as much to Joe and Sheki.

"Probably," Joe agreed. "But I think Baako was just out of sorts today."

Claudi nodded and tensed. There it was again—a faint glimmer in the air! For an instant, it had looked like a human face—but larger than life. Now she saw nothing. She suddenly felt a little nervous. *"Hello?"* she murmured, her voice trembling.

Joe glanced at her. "Hello, what? Who are you talking to? Those are just fish and plants over there."

"I saw something," Claudi said. "Like a face. Maybe it was a holo or something."

Joe scratched his head. "Couldn't have been a holo. There aren't any in here. It was probably just a reflection from the tanks." He shrugged. "Maybe you're like me. I'm always seeing things when I walk through here with the lights down."

Sheki was frowning. He edged a little closer to Claudi. "I s-saw it, saw it, too. A f-face."

The look of puzzlement deepened on Joe's face. "Huh. Well, I'll take a look, then. You two stay here." He crossed the gallery to peer around behind some of the other displays, dim in the gloom. He stepped momentarily into an adjoining room, then returned to the kids, shaking his head. "I don't see anything."

Sheki disagreed vigorously. He pointed toward another gallery. "I *s-saw* something there. It looked like, like a man."

Joe sighed. "Okay. I'll look there, too." Motioning to the kids to stay put, he disappeared around a corner into the next room.

Claudi looked at Sheki. His eyes were wide, but filled with the same certainty that she felt. She stared back at the gloomy space where she had first seen the peculiar thing.

The air moved, shimmering with the faintest of light. Claudi's breath whistled out. She raised a hand, pointing, as her heart began to race. Something was forming in the air, in front of them. "Do you see it?" she whispered.

She felt, more than saw, Sheki's nod.

It looked like a man, just from the waist up. But it was a ghostly figure, more like a poor holo than a real person. It didn't *glow*, exactly, and yet it seemed lighted against the gloom. Claudi's heart thumped with fear, but perhaps not as much fear as she ought to have felt. The man seemed to look straight at her, as though he knew her.

"Wh-who—?" Sheki whispered.

Claudi shook her head. Hello? she thought she said, but her own breath failed her, and no sound came out.

The man raised an eyebrow.

"Who . . . are . . . you?" Claudi whispered at last.

On the ghostly man, there was an appearance of deep concentration, as though he were trying to understand her words. He slowly tilted his head in an expression of puzzlement. His face seemed to change as she watched—first broad-faced and rugged, now slight and fair. But the eyes never shifted from their focus on her.

Claudi swallowed hard. "Who are you?" she whispered, just a little louder.

There were footsteps as Joe walked back into the room. "There's nobody here," he said.

Claudi pointed.

"What? What do you see?" Joe moved closer.

Claudi heard Sheki draw a breath, and hastily looked from Joe back to the spot. She was pointing at nothing, just empty air in a dark gallery. "Where'd you go?" she cried.

"Where did *who* go?" Joe asked. "Claudi?" He was gazing, not at the place where the face had been, but at her.

"I—that man—" Claudi's breath went out in a rush, and she couldn't answer his question. She tried to, but she just couldn't make the words come out.

Joe sighed. "Okay, kids—let's go." There was a tone of finality in his voice as he urged them toward the exit. "I think we've seen enough for today. What—was it Baako's talk of seeing things?"

"No," Claudi protested, half to herself. Beside her, Sheki was walking quietly. "No, he was really there," she said at last, putting all of her belief into her voice.

From Joe Farharto there was only silent doubt.

CHAPTER 6

"It-it's okay he didn't believe us," Sheki said, stepping into the lift. "We know it was th-there."

Claudi was silent and unhappy. Joe hadn't even seemed to want to hear them explain about . . . whatever it was. He'd thought they were just making it all up. A man, appearing out of the air? If she *had* made it up, she would have said so. "We don't even know what it was," she said finally, "so how can anyone believe us?"

Sheki shrugged. He didn't seem bothered. "It r-reminded me of the sim," he said, "when we saw you, for a second, looking—" and he seemed to grope for words, before saying, "sp-spooky. Sort of like that man." Claudi frowned. "When we s-saw you, it made us want to do what you said, right away," Sheki said. He looked at her intently, then turned away.

Claudi scratched her head, staring at him. That thing that had happened in the sim—she didn't understand it any better than she understood what had happened just now. She hadn't *tried* to do anything strange. Unable to think what to say, she sighed. "Well, *I* want to know who that was, there. Even if no one else believes us." She thought a moment longer. *"I* think it was a ghost."

Sheki nodded, peering at the decks whizzing down past them. "You want to come see my entity?" he asked suddenly.

She blinked, startled again. "Your what?"

"My entity." He turned, his eyes shining bright. "His name's Watson. He's not really a *he*, I guess, but we call him that because we don't know whether he's a boy or girl, or what."

Claudi squinted at him. "Where is it?"

"He."

"He, I mean."

"At home. It'd be kind of hard to take him to school."

"Okay. Let's go see it. Him." She shrugged, bewildered. After that ghost, a plain old *entity* ought to be nothing at all.

Sheki lived with his father on Deck Michelangelo, one level below the Melniks. Sheki's father came out from a back room to say hello. He was a slender man, but seemed bent over as he walked. His face was just like Sheki's, but even darker and dustier. "Who's your friend?" Sheki introduced Claudi. He stuck out his hand. It felt dry and leathery around Claudi's, as they shook hands. "Glad to meet you. Raphael Hendu. Rafe, most people call me. Sheki, why don't you offer Claudi something to drink."

" 'Kay." Sheki bobbed his head. "We have raspberry sparkly," he informed her.

"Sure," Claudi said.

"We keep a chiller over there in the corner," Rafe Hendu explained. "It cost us more, but since I work here on my writings, I figured it was worth it."

Claudi nodded as Sheki brought out two plastic bottles of sparkly. She took a swallow. Sheki raised his eyes to his father. "She's in my class. I'm going to show her Watson."

"Ah." Mr. Hendu started back to his desk area with a nod. But he turned before disappearing and said, "I'm glad you met such a nice friend. Enjoy yourselves, you two."

Sheki led the way into his room, separated from the rest

of the suite by a thin partition. His bunk was folded down in sleeping position, but was neatly made. "I like to read a lot," he said, hopping up to sit on the bunk. He reached for a stack of thin-paper books on a shelf. Claudi perched beside him, thinking that she would never hear the end of it if her mother ever saw how orderly Sheki's room was.

"Paper books?" she asked between sips, looking at the stack in his hand. They had titles like *Animals Known and Unknown,* and *The Stars of Our Worlds.* They sounded like books someone who wanted to be a scientist would read.

"Uh-huh. My father says they're more *r-real."*

She furrowed her brow, wondering how paper could possibly make them more real.

"Besides—" Sheki shrugged—"I like them."

"Huh. My mom says they're too cluttery. She only wants me to have the regular kind. Your mom doesn't mind?"

"She isn't here," Sheki said. "She's dead."

Claudi ducked her head awkwardly. "Oh . . ."

Sheki put the books back on the shelf. Reaching beyond them, he brought down a box-shaped bubble. It looked like a tiny version of the enclosures in the circ-zoo. Floating in the center of the box was what looked like . . . a ball of yellow light, really. Like a ball of glowing air. As Sheki rested the box on the bunk, the ball bobbed and threw off a handful of golden sparks. "Watson—" Sheki said, prying open the top of the enclosure. "Come on out, Watson."

The ball of light rose toward the opening. It hesitated, sparkling, at the lip of the box. "What *is* it?" Claudi asked, amazed. "What's it doing?"

The boy frowned in concentration. "It's Watson. He's an entity, I told you."

"I know you told me *that,* but—"

"Come on out, Watson. It's okay. This is C-Claudi. She's a friend." Sheki stretched out his hand above the opening, and slowly the entity brushed past it, glimmering with a deeper amber light. Sheki opened his hand. The entity spiraled slowly and settled down into his palm. It brightened, touching his skin. *"There,"* Sheki murmured. He brought the entity up to eye level. "Watson, meet Claudi." And he held the ball of light out to her.

"Um—hi, Watson," Claudi said, her tongue tripping with

uncertainty. She put down her bottle of sparkly and raised her hand tentatively. "What do I do? Is it really *alive?*"

"*Course* he's alive. What do you think?"

She felt foolish. "I don't know. I've never seen anything like it."

"That's because they don't have them on Baunhaven," Sheki explained. "Watson came from D-Daugherty's Hope."

"But that's a colony world!"

"Uh-huh." Sheki cupped both hands under the entity. "That's where he came from, though. Or his parents, anyway."

"Wow. But wouldn't that be really—well, didn't it *cost* a lot?" Her father always told her that things from off-planet cost a fortune.

Sheki shrugged. "My mom got him for me. Here, you want to hold him?"

The entity was sparkling again, throwing off tiny droplets of light that seemed to give an extra flash just as they vanished into the air. Claudi took a deep breath and put out her hand, a little fearfully. What if he gave her a shock?

"He won't hurt you," Sheki said.

"I know." But her face was hot. "Are you sure?"

"*Course* I'm sure. Look—here." Sheki poked a finger into the entity. Watson brightened for a moment, then dimmed again. "He's mostly energy. But he can t-trans—, trans—" Sheki struggled with the word—"trans*mute* into ph-physical form when he wants to." Concentrating, Sheki said, "C'mon, Watson—show her what you can look like." He peered into the entity as if it were a crystal ball.

"Does he understand you?"

"Yeh. Sort of, anyway. Hey, *Watson*—do it, okay?"

"But can he—"

"*Shhh.* You'll distract him. He knows you're here. He knows you're thinking about him."

Claudi frowned and concentrated with Sheki. There *was* something happening to the entity. His color changed to a redder glow. He became dimmer, and more solid-looking —but flatter and longer. He began to *blur.* Sheki's face seemed to shine with anticipation.

Suddenly Watson's inner light faded almost entirely—

and a small, furry animal sat up in Sheki's hand. It looked alert, with dark, round eyes that blinked as it turned its head. It squeaked.

Claudi gasped. "It's a *stroid!* It's turned into a stroid!"

Sheki stroked the animal with his finger. "It's a *what?*"

"A *stroid.* It's—it's like a mouse, sort of. Except people keep them as pets. I had one once when I was little."

Sheki looked puzzled. "My father told me it, it looks like a ham—, hamster."

"Hamster?" Claudi tried to remember. "Stroids came from hamsters, I think. But stroids are really smart. You can teach them to understand things."

Sheki nodded. He held the creature out to Claudi. "You want to hold him now? He's not so scary when he looks like this."

Claudi's heart was still thumping. "He wasn't *that* scary before," she said defensively. "I was just being careful." She swallowed and opened her hand. The entity sniffed her for a moment, then hopped into her palm. Claudi felt a tiny tingle, but Watson seemed to weigh nothing at all. He raised his nose and reared up on his hind legs, exactly like a stroid. He peered up at her, wriggling his whiskers.

"I think he l-likes you," Sheki said.

"How can you tell?" She looked more closely at the entity.

"I can feel it," Sheki said.

"Huh?"

"Don't you feel him purring?" Sheki took her other hand and brought it up so that she was cupping Watson in both hands. "Just feel. I don't know how to ex-, explain it, but—if you just let—" He fumed, trying to get the words right. "Just l-listen with your *mind,* not your ears."

That was what she was trying to do. But she felt nothing.

Or did she? As she bent closer, she thought she felt a faint, shivery, warm feeling down her back—as though something pleasant had happened to her, like an unexpected gift.

"You feel it?" Sheki murmured.

She nodded, closing her eyes. It was stronger now, a feeling of being curious, of liking something. She was reminded of the way she felt when the teacher asked her to do something hard, and she got it right. And yet though it felt *familiar,* it was not *her* feeling. "It's funny," she murmured. "I like it."

"It feels strange the first time," Sheki admitted.

Claudi opened her eyes. Sheki was grinning at her, trying to keep from laughing. She blinked, and then realized why. The stroid shape was gone, and back in its place was the glowing ball of light. But it was changing again, pulsing and shimmering. A moment later, she was holding something that looked rather like a frog—glowing green in her hand. "What's *this?*" She held the entity at arm's length as she inspected its new form.

Sheki chuckled. "He can only stay in one shape for a little wh-while. Then he has to go back to his entity shape. But he can turn into something else right away, if he w-wants to."

"So what is he now?" Claudi squinted at the luminous green creature in the palm of her hand. It was definitely not a frog, she realized, though it reminded her of one.

"Um—" Sheki made a funny face. "I don't know. Sometimes he just makes things up, I think."

Watson opened his mouth and whistled. His bright red tongue flicked out and back. *"Eeuw!"* Claudi said.

"He's laughing. Do you feel it?"

Claudi tried to feel with her mind. Yes, she did feel a distant ringing sort of feeling, like a laugh—but not like any laugh *she* made. It was as strange as what she'd felt before.

A *frog* was laughing at her? A *frog?*

She finally laughed helplessly herself. By the time she and Sheki were both quiet again, the frog had turned back into a ball of light. She held it out to Sheki. The entity glided slowly from her hand to his. "Wow," she said.

Sheki lifted the entity to his shoulder. It perched there, happily pulsing with light. "He'll come with us, if we want to go out," Sheki said. He slid down off the bunk and led Claudi back out into the living room.

"Why do you call him an 'entity'?" Claudi asked. "He looks more like a baby angel, on your shoulder." She thought a moment. "That is, if angels have babies."

Sheki looked at her with a grave expression. "When my

m-mother gave him to me, she said she didn't 'xactly know what it was—except it was a sent—, *s-sentient* . . . alien . . . *entity.*" He shrugged. "That m-means it's smart. I—I didn't know the right w-word for it—so I kept that one." He eyed Watson, pulsing on his shoulder. "Are you h-hungry?"

It took her a moment to realize he was asking her, not Watson. "I guess so," she said.

"Come on. I know s-someone in the commons who will give us something." He angled his head toward the door, taking care not to dislodge Watson.

Amazed, Claudi followed.

CHAPTER 7

Jeaves here.

I don't intend to keep interrupting like this, but I thought perhaps it would be helpful if I clarified a few details about starship *Charity*. Probably you've guessed already that this was no run-of-the-mill colony ship with a few thousand colonists tucked away in freezelife slabs like so many soy-hams. Well, you're right, but let's take a look at why.

Physically, it was a model 374-Z Yonupian "Great Carrier," an enormous vessel configured like an elongated ellipsoid with various odd bulges around its middle and ends. At the time, it was called *Charity;* but that had not always been so. The original name was *Loss of Innocence,* back when it was operated by the great shipping combine United Mercantile, of the Auricle Alliance—some forty standard years before the voyage of Claudi Melnik and Sheki Hendu. Later, it was sold to the independent shipper Jonah Billings, who renamed it *Prince of the Skies* and ran it at a loss for two years before selling it to an arm of the Querayn Academies. The Querayn modified it for gateway exploration, called it *Great Labor,* and worked it for several years before turning it over to Colony Transits, Inc., who remodeled it once more, rechristened it *Charity*, and put it into service transporting colonists and goods through the starstream to the distant downstream worlds.

During this period several thousand starships, by conservative estimate, were in service carrying colonists of a variety of races inward into the galaxy, driving the expansion of the Habitat of Humanity at an unprecedented pace. Not that the galaxy was in any immediate danger of overflowing: for all that hundreds of star systems were being explored, and in some cases colonized, the Habitat was for the most part still limited to the local area of the Orion galactic arm. But the energy and excitement of the growth far exceeded anything that had come before.

Unlike many colonist-carriers of its era, *Charity* transported the majority of its passengers in fully animate form. A limited number of freezelife berths were available for those who wished to avoid experiencing the long passage through interstellar space, but most colonists traveled awake. Though the maintenance cost of fully animate colonists was higher than that of dead-weight sleepers, the difference in cost was less significant in the starstream than it was in ordinary modes of travel. Much of the energy-cost of passage was drawn from the gateway itself, or rather from the black holes and the hyperstring from which it had been created.

The philosophy of Colony Transits, at least as espoused in the flight package offered aboard *Charity*, was that a colonizing community was best served by encouraging new colonists to spend their flight time together preparing for the challenges ahead. A full training program was provided, for adults and children alike. As important as the formal education was the chance for the colonists to spend time in close quarters with one another, choosing leaders and forming working bonds, and identifying possible conflicts before small problems turned into large ones. Experience suggested that such a process produced colonists better prepared for taming new worlds. That, anyway, was the pitch made by Colony Transits, and thousands of colonists and a dozen or more sponsoring governments had agreed with them.

And so, like a chip of wood floating down a fast-running brook, the starship fled down the stream, leaving empty light-years in its wake. Though the gateway was, by human reckoning, a busy place, one would not know it by the view from the inside. There was no tangible indication, other than the existence of the starstream itself, that any instrument of humanity had ever passed this way before. And the chances of two ships meeting in the stream were almost inconceivably remote.

Ordinarily. There was, of course, the matter of the Karthrogen. There was always a chance that the enemy would appear. There was always a chance that death would meet them in the starstream.

But the chances of that were so slim that no one really worried too much about it. At least not aloud. Some, like the captain, may have worried privately.

The Throgs came without warning, like writhing black threads in the night, carrying death and destruction. Specters without form or solidity, they came to Hassan Harbor. Humans dissolved, screaming, into the air . . . women, children, men . . . even soldiers with weapons blazing. The fear was tangible, the smell of death everywhere. They struck without discrimination: rich and poor, servant and master, fierce and timid, all fell. Where the Throgs came, it was like a black hole yawning, engulfing land and buildings and people, rending the green and ocher surface of the planet. There was no escape, there never was. The only hope at Hassan Harbor came from a handful of star cruisers; and even they could only seek to draw the enemy away—perhaps to destroy a few of them, or perhaps only to distract them and lose them in the twists of K-space and n-space. But on the planet . . .

Myra . . . Myra, you must get away . . . don't be caught! Dear God, don't let them take you! No no no no. . . .

It was in the final pass that the Throgs got her, as they encircled the world of Hassan Harbor and passed through it and around it, reducing a thriving planet to rubble. She reached in supplication to the sky, pleading . . . and was tossed spinning into the nightmare space where the Throgs lived, where they killed and destroyed. . . .

MYRA—you bastards—!

—bastards—bastards—!

Roald Thornekan sat upright, panting, struggling to draw a lungful of air. The bedsheet was wrapped around him, damp with sweat. He untangled himself and gulped a deep breath, and let it out slowly, regaining control. His cabin was dark, except for a lighted clock face and the com switches. He felt an urge to call out, to make sure that nothing was wrong. But he already knew: nothing was wrong, except in his own mind. In his memory, in his heart.

It had been a bad one. The minutes passed, and he was still shaking. It didn't help to know that it was only a dream. Because it wasn't. It had all happened—maybe not just like that, but close enough. It had happened. Four years ago. Myra . . . and all those other people . . . dying . . .

"Stop it!" he commanded himself. "Just, for God's sake, stop it."

How could he possibly function like this, with nightmares wrenching at his soul every night? If it went on too much longer, he might have to consider stepping down from command. But damn it, he had gotten over them before—had been free of them for over two years—until now. Until three days ago, when the message had come down the n-space channel—and the peace and tranquility of the voyage had vanished into the night, like the screaming unreal Throgs of his dreams. But he had not just the dreams to contend with, but the real-life danger, the terrible and present danger to his ship.

He would have to make the decision soon. Today.

Thornekan sighed and swung his legs over the edge of his bunk. "Com, voice only," he said, running his fingers through his hair. "Get me the bridge."

Soon, very soon, he would have to tell the passengers. . . .

* * *

"Listen up, everyone!" the shop instructor called. "Put down whatever you're doing and come on over here. There's some kind of an announcement from the captain."

The sawing and hammering sounds died away. John Melnik looked up in puzzlement. He put down his chisel and mallet and cocked an eye toward his coworker, Ti, a slight man with Oriental features. Ti lifted his safety goggles. "Wonder what this is all about?" Melnik said, dusting off his hands as they joined the others in moving toward the front of the shop. Ti shook his head silently.

Behind them, a tall, lanky alien—an Im'kek, Melnik believed, and an odd-smelling one—was muttering to himself. "No no—sorry—no! Oh, no good. But don't say it—you don't know—so don't go bothering people. . . ." His voice fell away.

Melnik turned. "Do you know something about this?" he asked, trying to remember the alien's name.

"What?" The Im'kek looked startled. "Oh, no—*no*—sorry! I was thinking—feeling, you might say—but I should not have spoken aloud. Sorry!"

Melnik gazed at him bemusedly but had no chance to question him further. Near the instructor's desk, a holo had appeared, and Captain Thornekan was preparing to speak.

Sheki had taken Claudi to meet a kindly woman in the kitchen, named Mrs. Feeney, who had provided them both with juice and crackers even though it was between mealtimes. Mrs. Feeney seemed to know Watson and found nothing odd in Sheki walking around with a ball of lightning on his shoulder. Claudi was starting to get used to it, too. They were just finishing their crackers in a quiet corner of the commons, away from the cleaning mechs, when the announcement came on the speakers:

"All colonists report to primary classrooms for special update. All school children who are not already in school, go at once to your classroom for a special message from your teachers."

"What's *that*?" Claudi wondered, making a face. "We have to go back to deck-school?"

Sheki listened to see if there was going to be another announcement, but there was just the same one, repeating. "I guess so," he said.

Claudi dumped their cups and plates, while Sheki brought Watson down off his shoulder. He cupped the entity in his hands as they hurried off. In the hall, a crowd had already formed, waiting for the lift. By unspoken agreement, the kids slipped away to the walkup.

Quite a few other people had the same idea. Claudi and Sheki weaved past dozens of adults—and ducked back out of the way of the bigger teenagers, who thundered past everyone like runaway circus animals. Sheki was very careful about protecting Watson, but he still moved like a slithering catfish, keeping up with Claudi.

Halfway to Defoe Deck, they came out to see if the lifts were less crowded, then rode the rest of the way to the deck-school. Most of the class was there already, and the little kids' human teacher, Mr. Seipledon, was standing with the teaching-wall's Mr. Zizmer. The school area had been opened up into a wide space, and the younger and older kids were together, sitting on the carpeted floor.

Claudi saw Jenny and Suze waving and headed to join them. "What's happening?" she asked, peering around.

"We don't know," Jenny said. "Some kind of announcement."

"Got a new friend?" Suze asked, elbowing her with a wink.

"Huh?" Then Claudi realized that she meant Sheki, who was standing back, a little apart. She waved him over, and he sat nearby, but not too close. He seemed shy of Claudi's girlfriends. "You know Sheki," Claudi said, a little annoyed. "He was in class with us today."

Suze nodded but looked doubtful nevertheless. "What's that he's holding?"

Claudi felt her face redden, and she shrugged, as if the question wasn't worth answering. How could she explain the entity if Suze already thought Sheki was just a stupid little kid?

"It's Watson," Sheki answered, just loudly enough for them to hear. He sounded a little put out. But he didn't look as if he was going to let it bother him even if they thought Watson was strange.

"He's an *entity*," Claudi added, suddenly ashamed that she hadn't jumped in to defend him.

"A *what*?" Suze asked.

Claudi rolled her eyes up and started to say, *Never mind,* but was interrupted by Mr. Seipledon calling the combined classes to order. She glanced back at Sheki. He was sitting with Watson tucked more or less out of sight between his crisscrossed legs, and he was gazing forward at the teachers.

"Okay!" boomed Mr. Seipledon. "Listen up! Can you all hear me?" He strode to and fro in front of the combined classes. "Okay. I think everyone's here now. I'm sorry some of you had to come back from your free time, but we've got some things to show you on the wall. First, though, we have an announcement."

Claudi shifted position. She wished Mr. Seipledon would get to the point.

"We're going to be making an unexpected planetfall. . . ."

That got her attention.

"We've just gotten a message on the n-channel—or I should say, the *captain* has gotten a message—warning of some possible trouble a ways down the starstream. We don't know that it's anything serious, necessarily, but since there's always a chance it could be some Karthrogen activity, the captain wants to take care to stay out of the way of it. That's why we're going to make a detour for a while."

Mr. Seipledon paused. "Now, I expect you'll probably have some questions—"

He was interrupted by a couple of kids shrieking their delight at the prospect of excitement. Several others made fearful groans. "Throg-g-g-s!" one of them croaked. Claudi suddenly couldn't breathe. Her throat wouldn't let her. She didn't mind the news of a detour, but the word *Throgs* made her throat clamp tight in a funny way like nothing else could. She hardly even knew anything about the Throgs; she just knew they were scary and they hurt people.

Mr. Seipledon's voice cut through the roar that seemed

to fill her ears. "Now, before you all get in an uproar—we'll answer all of your questions, but—"

"Mr. Seipledon!" squeaked one of the five-year-olds. "I heard that the Throgs *eat* people!"

The teacher groaned. "No, now, remember what we've learned about them. It's not like—"

Another kid shouted, "Bones and all!" with shaking laughter.

"Now *listen to me!*" Mr. Seipledon boomed, cutting through the noise. "Let's just stop that kind of talk! Don't believe everything you hear about the Thr—, the Karthrogen. Anyway, we're steering well clear of them. That's why the captain's ordering this side trip—just to be sure. To be safe. So we're not going to see any Throgs, okay?"

That just made them yell more loudly than ever. Mr. Seipledon looked exasperated and turned to Mr. Zizmer for help. Claudi felt her own heart thumping, but she didn't want to yell. She didn't want to have anyone know what she was feeling. There was this strange, hurtful tightness inside her. She knotted her fists, glancing at Sheki. Surprisingly, he did not seem upset. He was just frowning down at Watson, and looking as if he were thinking incredibly hard.

Claudi wanted to say something to him, but her voice was hopelessly caught in her throat. Sheki looked up, tilting his head. "What's wrong?" he whispered.

She tried to say, *Nothing's wrong—what's the matter, didn't you hear him?* but her mouth wouldn't even open. *Throgs. Throgs. Throgs.* The fear rose in her in a hot rush.

"They're scaring Watson," Sheki murmured. The little creature was in stroid form, peering about frantically, looking one way then another. It shivered and dissolved back into a puff of light.

"QUIET!" Mr. Seipledon bellowed. "Mr. Zizmer has something to say!"

Everyone, finally, quieted down. Mr. Seipledon gestured with a sigh. The holoteacher nodded and strode to the viewing-wall. "Thank you, boys and girls. Okay, look. There's no need to be gloomy—so we're going to show you a short feature on the planet we expect to be visiting. It's called 'Mefford's Walk.' We want to give you an idea of what the detour will be like. We'll talk about that other stuff later, if you want. But for now, please—just enjoy the look. Think of this as an adventure!" He twirled his finger in the air. "Lights! Roll it! Here's your future. . . ."

The room was still and silent around Lopo. He raised his head with some difficulty. He wasn't sure why he felt the urge to do so. It was more than boredom or stiffness. It was something that nudged at his mind, something that made him feel suddenly that he was not alone in the room. .

For a moment, he felt a rush of wooziness. Whatever the keeper had put into him was affecting his vision. The room swam in his eyes—not exactly blurred, as it used to be, but shimmering, as though he were underwater. He felt a sudden buzzing feeling, and then the room came into a strange kind of focus.

It was as if he were looking down a long, long tunnel. He hoped he might see, at the end of it, a friendly keeper—or better yet, a little girl. What he saw instead filled him with trepidation. It was a large, billowing, winged creature, floating in the air. And it was coming closer.

He tried to bark out a warning. But his throat felt all wrong, and nothing came out except a whine that was more like a keeper's sound than a bark. He bared his teeth and growled, and that at least came out right.

The creature floated toward him. It seemed to glow in a peculiar way, or rather the air around it glowed. The creature itself was dark as night. Its wings curled and distorted menacingly, becoming blurry and then razor sharp in Lopo's vision. It had eyes—at least four or five of them—and its mouth was something indescribable. Lopo had an unmistakable sense that it was *seeking* something. He could not imagine what, nor could he even look at the thing's face without cringing in terror.

He tried again to bark out a warning—and the result was something between a howl and a keeperlike cry. *Away!* he tried to say with his thoughts, and something very like that word whispered from his throat. The creature seemed to hear him, and paused as though in interest, though it certainly didn't look frightened. Lopo growled again, deeply, and the sound helped to steady his nerves. He was helpless, hanging in his enclosure; but he wasn't going to be taken without a struggle.

What really frightened him, though, was the smell of the thing—an intense, *arid* kind of smell, almost no smell at all, an *absence* of smell that caught so powerfully at his nose and lungs that it made him want to howl.

The thing made no further move toward him, but floated in midair with a terrible kind of darkness coiling around it. The glowing light and the darkness twisted through one another, and around the creature, with a horrible intensity. And the creature, held in the midst of it all, stared at him with intense interest.

Just stared.

And then was gone.

No blur, no movement, nothing. Just gone.

Lopo let out a higher growl, staring at the spot where the thing had been, where now there was only the empty side of the room where the keeper sometimes stood. His growl turned slowly into a whine. *Where? What? Why?* The questions trembled in his mind, and began to gurgle audibly, low in the bottom of his throat. The sound of the words startled him.

He sniffed, and smelled nothing. Not even the harsh unsmell that had been there before. Just nothing. The smell of the room. Or was there, faintly lingering, a mere hint of the memory of the thing's presence? Or perhaps the smell of his own fear?

His neck ached from holding his head up, and finally he let it sink down again. Take me away from here, he thought longingly. Please just come and take me away.

CHAPTER 8

Hold it a second, okay? Sorry—it's me again. I swear I won't keep interrupting like this, but please bear with me just a little longer.

What I want to talk about is what the teachers did *not* want to talk about when they spoke with the kids—namely, the Throgs.

There was good reason for the teachers' reticence. Throgs were terrifying even for adults to contemplate. If they were in the vicinity, they posed a devastating threat to the ship. Despite the warning that the captain had picked up, there was really no way to be sure. All he knew was that Throgs had been reported downstream from *Charity*—heading upstream. And that meant there was a good chance that their movements would intersect with the ship's.

The implications of that might or might not be obvious to you. Probably you're already familiar with the background of the Karthrogen war. On the other hand—history education being what it is today—possibly it would be useful to recap. Here it is then, in a nutshell:

It was seventy-three years after the opening of the gateway to commerce that the Karthrogen first appeared. In that encounter between Throgs and Humans, three and a half million people on a Human outpost world died. Millions more perished, on five other worlds, before the first organized efforts could be made to muster a Habitatwide defense. The attacks came seemingly capriciously and without warning. At that time, no one had ever even *seen* a Throg. They were thought, at first, to have come from a recently discovered planet called Karthrog's Planet, after its discoverer. Although investigators found no sign of their presence on that world, the name *Karthrogen* stuck —to the anguish of Mr. Karthrog, I am sure. The name was soon popularly shortened to *Throgs*.

This much was known about them:

Their ferocity was incredible. They struck without apparent cause and without mercy. Their mode of attack appeared to be spatial disruption—a temporary transformation of four-space into n-space, into which both living and nonliving structures disintegrated. On planetary surfaces, the local disruptions produced secondary seismic instabilities resulting in earthquakes, fire, and so on. Ordinary defenses were useless. The Throgs struck, wreaked havoc, and vanished. They always came from the starstream, and always struck fairly close to it.

These things were not known:

Where they came from (though presumably from somewhere toward the center of the galaxy). Where they went to. *Why* they came. What they wanted. Anything at all of their biology. Anything at all of their psychology.

Rumors existed that they took prisoners as slaves, but there was no evidence that this was true.

They were feared as much for their unpredictability, for what was unknown about them, as for what was known. Even their mode of travel was a mystery. They used the starstream, but bewilderingly. They traveled *upstream,* against the flow, as easily as our own ships sailed downstream. It was not impossible by our standards—we had some ships that could do the same, though at a stupendous cost in energy—but what was astonishing was the apparent ease with which Throgs did it. It seemed not to cost them at all; and hints were emerging that their means of

manipulating n-space were biological, rather than techno-
logical. Whatever the method, they were confoundingly
difficult to trace in flight—which was one reason for the
vagueness of the warning that Captain Thornekan received.

Naturally, the threat of Karthrogen attack was a consid-
eration for anyone planning a trip down the starstream.
Most ships had no hope of surviving an encounter. Even
warships generally lost when tangling with Karthrogen
marauders; the only real exceptions occurred when certain warships' powerful n-space drives appeared to confuse or distract the Throgs long enough to permit escape.
Escape, but never victory. Still, the statistical vulnerability
of any given ship, even a lumbering colony ship, was extremely small. For most people life went on as usual,
Throgs or no Throgs. The possibility of attack was another
risk in a life full of risks.

Still, there were those who fell victim to the statistics.
Captain Thornekan's caution was certainly understand-
able—commendable, even. But for me, and for my employers, it posed a problem. It impinged upon my reason
for being aboard. Please don't think ill of me when I tell
you this:

We wanted *Charity* to encounter the Throgs. We wanted
it badly. So badly we could practically taste it.

The viddie ended, to Claudi's relief. It was just a bunch
of stuff about the colonists on Mefford's Walk—a place with
a lot of desert and not much else, as far as she could tell.
She suspected that the teachers had put the thing on just to
keep them quiet, when really what they all wanted to
know about was the Throgs—and whether or not they
were going to be attacked (never mind the teachers' assur-
ances to the contrary).

Claudi herself wanted to ask those questions. And yet,
her throat clenched up every time she even thought the
word *Throg*. It didn't make her very happy when Mr.
Zizmer called her class back into their regular room and
said: "Okay. You guys are a little older than the others—so I
think, with you, maybe we can talk just a bit about the

chances of there being some danger. And while we're at it, we might review just a little about the Throgs."

Her classmates stirred, and Claudi's stomach did something that hurt—and at the same moment, just for a second, she had that funny feeling as if a part of her were lifting right out of her body and floating in front of her friends. She saw Sheki look at her, startled; and a couple of the other kids, as well. Then Mr. Zizmer was putting something on the wall, but not without first looking at her in a way that said he'd noticed everything. Then the stomach hurt was gone, and the funny sensation with it. But she had a feeling that she'd just gotten herself in for a talk from Mr. Zizmer. And she didn't even know what she'd done.

She didn't have time to think about it then, because a new picture-show was coming on the wall. This time it was a news looker of a space battle. It only lasted a minute, and it was just a flattie, instead of a surroundie, showing vague black shapes swooping about the sky and occasionally vanishing with spectacular flashes of light. She was glad they weren't buzzing around her head the way they would in a surroundie; and she was more glad when the picture cut to someone who looked like a professor, saying, "You know, even though the danger from the enemy is very real, you should *always remember that the odds are with you.*" And a fancy graphic came on, showing how many ships got through the starstream safely, without even *seeing* any Throgs, compared to the tiny number of ships that had trouble. It was, in fact, comforting—and there was soft, reassuring music that went with it. And when another graphic showed how the defense-com network could warn starships away from danger, Claudi relaxed a little more. "It's not easy, but we are learning to protect ourselves, even in the starstream," the man said. "But we must never relax our vigil. If *you* should ever find yourself in danger, please remember . . ."

The voice went on a while longer, but Claudi was just as glad when Mr. Zizmer reappeared and asked them to put on their headsets for private conferences. The silence-screen went up around her, and Mr. Zizmer came and sat on a chair facing her. He seemed to know that she was starting to feel uncomfortable again.

"I don't have any questions," she said quickly, not even knowing why she said it.

Mr. Zizmer's eyes twinkled. "Maybe you'll think of some later. May I ask *you* a few?"

Claudi's right hand found her hair. She started wrapping it around her fingers. She nodded.

"Good. Let's start with an easy one. What do you think about our leaving the starstream to go to Mefford's Walk? It'll make the trip longer, you know."

She shrugged. "It's okay, I guess."

"Ah-hah." Mr. Zizmer nodded, waiting to see if she'd say more. When she didn't, he said, "Does it bother you? That we're doing it to keep out of danger?"

She shrugged again.

Mr. Zizmer tipped his head. "No reaction? You really don't care?"

For the third time, she shrugged.

"Well, all right, then. What about the Throgs?" He said it in a voice so soft she could hardly hear him.

"What about them?" Her voice quivered a little.

"Well—" Mr. Zizmer's hand came up, startling her; but he was just rubbing the front of his thinning hair. "I mean, what do you think about when we talk about them?"

"I don't . . . know," she said, her voice breaking. *Throgs. Throgs. Throgs.* She squeezed her eyes shut, feeling a sudden urge to cry. She tugged hard on her hair, to make the feeling go away.

"May I tell you a secret, Claudi?"

She opened her eyes with a grunt.

Mr. Zizmer's expression was solemn. "I don't tell many people this—but Claudi, even though *I know* the captain is going to steer us clear of danger, it still makes me a little nervous to talk about it."

"But you're the teaching wall!" she protested. "You can't be afraid!"

"Mm." Mr. Zizmer rubbed his forehead again. "Well, I do have feelings, you know. Even if I'm not a real human."

Claudi *hmmph*ed and looked away. Through the hazy veil of the silence-screen, she could see the other kids. Were they all talking to Mr. Zizmer, too?

"Claudi, please look at me." Mr. Zizmer was frowning,

but his eyes and his voice seemed full of kindness. "Claudi, I thought I sensed that you were a little upset when I mentioned the Throgs." She stared at him silently. "Was I right?" he asked.

"I'm not scared of the stupid Throgs!" she snapped. "If that's what you mean."

"No? Oh—well, I must have sensed something else, then." Mr. Zizmer looked thoughtful. "Claudi, you know it's all right to feel a *little* scared of them—if that's what you feel."

"I'm not scared. Anyway, you said we were going to stay away from them."

Mr. Zizmer nodded. "Yes. That's true. That's the captain's hope. So it's all right *not* to feel scared of them, too. But that's not what I meant, actually."

"What, then?" She was getting impatient with this.

"Well . . . when I first mentioned the Throgs, did it make you feel *funny* somehow? Not scared, or *unscared*, maybe—but something else? Like you were all tied up in knots? Or like something was happening *inside* you?"

That was *exactly* how she felt—but she couldn't answer him now, because suddenly she was crying. Tears were leaking out of her eyes and down her cheeks, and she wanted to be anywhere except here. But she couldn't leave, and she couldn't stop, so she just sat there and cried. Mr. Zizmer did something, and a tissue came up out of her desk, and she grabbed at it and blew her nose. Mr. Zizmer made soothing sounds, and put his ghostly arm around her and seemed to hug her, and after a while she stopped crying.

Mr. Zizmer sat back, as she settled herself. "Let's try something, okay?" he said. She nodded. Her desk screen came on, and in the air over it floated a pictopen, which she knew was really a holo. "How would you like to draw me a picture?"

She blinked, puzzled. "Of what?"

Mr. Zizmer shrugged. "I don't know. Whatever you want. Of yourself, maybe. Or of how you felt when I said we were going to talk about the Throgs. Do you think you could do that?"

She squinted at him for a moment. She didn't know what

to say. Then a thought came to her, and she reached for the pictopen. It felt light in her hand, like Watson. Like a holo. She tentatively touched the screen with it and drew a few lines. Muttering, she drew more quickly. It didn't look too realistic, but at least she knew exactly what she wanted to draw. When she was finished, she let Mr. Zizmer see. It was a picture of *two* of herselves, one floating up out of the other.

Mr. Zizmer cocked his head. "That's very interesting, Claudi. Is that what you felt was happening?"

She nodded. She didn't know how else to describe it.

"Is there anything you can tell me about it?" Before she could shake her head, he added, "I have to ask because, Captain Melnik, in a way you're still on duty here."

She blinked in surprise. Captain Melnik?

"Remember the sim, Claudi? How we all depended on each other? Well, that's true in real life, too. And here's the thing—it might be important for us to understand what you were feeling then."

Claudi gestured helplessly.

Mr. Zizmer smiled. "Well, here's what's interesting, Captain Melnik. The other kids seemed to notice what you were feeling a few minutes ago—just as they did in the sim, when you felt *that.*" And he pointed to her sketch.

She bit her lip, nodding.

"Now, that's something special that's happened to you, Claudi. The other kids don't feel that . . . that *presence* outside themselves. And I find that very interesting."

She stared, trembling, not knowing what to say. "Okay!" she blurted suddenly. "I was scared!"

He smiled again, scratching his head. "We were all a little scared, Claudi. It's okay. But when you were scared, you felt that outside *presence* of yourself—and the other kids felt it, too. Claudi, if you were a Logothian, I'd say that you were projecting a *virtual presence* of yourself—"

"Huh?" *Virtual presence?*

"It's . . . a sort of shadow self that can float outside of you," Mr. Zizmer explained.

Claudi had heard of the word—her family had known a Logothian—but she didn't exactly understand what it meant. Virtual presence? She didn't want to have a virtual presence.

"But you're not a Logothian, are you?" Mr. Zizmer said, chuckling. Claudi shook her head, relieved. "No. But tell me. Have you had any other funny feelings like this?"

"Well—during the sim," she said, thinking of what Sheki had said to her.

"I know, but anything else? Anything else that's happened that seemed odd to you?"

She thought hard. "Well—there's Sheki's entity. He's pretty odd. His name's Watson."

Mr. Zizmer nodded. "Anything else?"

She shook her head, then thought, "Oh, wait! The lupeko, of course!" And then she suddenly remembered, not just Lopo, but another thing at the zoo—a face peering at her out of thin air. She shivered at the memory.

"Something, Claudi?"

"Well—there was this thing." She hesitated, struggling. She didn't want him to laugh at her. "It's hard to explain, but—" And she told her teacher about the ghost that she and Sheki had seen in the circ-zoo galleries. "It looked like a holo, but Joe said it wasn't." She started to get upset again. "He didn't believe we saw it. But we did! Honest, we did!"

"I believe you, Claudi. Or should I say, Captain Melnik?" Mr. Zizmer's tone was so serious that she had to trust him. "Can you tell me anything else about it? Did it look like anyone you know?"

She shook her head.

Mr. Zizmer looked thoughtful. "Claudi, I'm going to ask you for a favor. Would you mind if I took a quick snapshot from your memory while you still have your headset on? You can say no. You don't have to let me."

She shrugged. "It's okay, I guess."

"Thank you. Now please sit just as still as you can, and try to remember the face. Try to picture it. Relax and remember—"

It was hard to remember exactly what the face had looked like. But she tried, tried to summon it up. She felt a tingling in her skull, and imagined a vague human figure, speaking to her. Mr. Zizmer held up a hand. He was silent for a moment, then spoke. "It wasn't too clear a picture. But I'd like to show *you* a picture, and I'd like you to tell me if it reminds you at all of the person you saw. Okay?"

Nodding, she looked at her screen. An image of a face appeared—a man's face, about her father's age—a pretty ordinary face. A shiver went up and down her spine. The face looked familiar, but not *exactly* familiar.

"Does that look anything like him?"

She stared, unable to make up her mind. She sighed and shrugged helplessly. "Maybe."

"Hm." Mr. Zizmer nodded. "Well, can I ask you one more favor."

She looked up at him.

"If you see anything like that again, will you tell me at once? Even if you're out of school, will you come here right away and tell me, if you can? I'll always be here."

Claudi nodded solemnly.

Mr. Zizmer looked satisfied. "Then let's turn off the privacy screen and see what the rest of the class is up to, shall we? Maybe you can help Sheki show them Watson."

She thought of the entity and smiled.

"And later, if you like, I'll see if I can arrange another visit with your friend Lopo."

Her smile widened.

If Claudi assumed that the teaching-wall had gotten much of an image from her mind, she was mistaken. She'd produced little more than a blur. But her reaction to the other picture was tantalizing indeed. The intelligence system knew that she *had* reacted to it, even if she hadn't been sure herself. And that suggested certain interesting possibilities. Possibilities the IS hoped to see confirmed.

Meanwhile, the IS was pleased by the bonding that seemed to be taking place between Claudi and the lupeko, and the boy Sheki. The IS was greatly encouraged. If Claudi was to develop her abilities as quickly as the IS's emerging plan required, then every bond of friendship could be significant. The teacher would do everything it could to encourage Claudi's unconscious talent for projecting, not only virtual presences, but also an unusual . . .

likability. It only hoped that it hadn't said too much to her. The last thing it wanted was for her to become self-conscious about her abilities. It had hopes for putting them to use.

As for the Throg alert, that was both frustrating and encouraging. But on balance, we remained hopeful.

CHAPTER 9

Claudi dreamed that night of Lopo the lupeko. She felt
happy in the dream, and frightened. She didn't know why.
Lopo was licking her hand; and then he was in the operat-
ing room enclosure, unable to move, except his head. He
hung silent and wretched. Suddenly he lifted his gray-
furred head and fixed his bright fire-and-darkness eyes
upon her. He began to howl.

She raced forward to free him.

She was stopped by a black shape that loomed suddenly
out of nowhere and blocked the way. It was a terrible-
looking thing—with wings, sharply pointed wings—all in
black. Black against black, in the night. She could not
move, she was frozen, frozen before the black horror with
wings. She screamed. She separated from herself and became two Claudis, equally terrified.

The thing stared at her, at both of her, with more eyes
than she could count. It seemed fascinated by her, and for
a moment she thought maybe it didn't want to hurt her,
after all. Maybe it simply wanted to speak to her. Perhaps
it had lost its way and needed help.

And then she knew that it wanted more than her help.

It wanted *her*.
And there was nothing she could do to stop it.
Nothing at all.

Only one thing could help, and that was to wake up.

She awoke with a strangled cry in her throat. Something made her open her eyes and come wide awake with a sharp breath of surprise. The dark creature of her dreams was gone and in its place, right here in her room, was something far more astonishing—something bright and warm, and almost as frightening in its own way as the other had been.

It was an enormous ball of light—like a sun, filling her sleeping compartment with its impossible size, and impossible brightness. For an instant she imagined that Sheki's entity had somehow grown into a huge version of itself and come to visit her. But this was no Watson, no creature about to turn into a small, cuddly stroid. It was as though her compartment had opened into space and she was staring into the blazing body of a sun. And the sun *knew* that she was watching it. And the sun watched her, in return.

She thought she heard a voice. But it was confusing because it was in her head, and there was no way to tell if it was her imagination or really someone speaking to her. It was as though she were hearing the sun speak, or even the voice of, well . . . God:

> *My child.*
> > *My children.*
> > > *From what realm have you come?*
> > > > *Are you there?*
> > > > > *Truly there?*
> > *Can you speak to me*
> > > *And sing?*

What—?

> *—of your fear?*
> *Do not fear. . . .*

She blinked, and rubbed her eyes. The words made no sense to her, and she did not hear them again, or anything else. But they remained in her memory like a message emblazoned against a starry night sky.

Only the darkness of the compartment remained. And the words . . .

My child. My children.

Had she really dreamed it? No—she was awake—awake! This sun was far different from her dream, far different —frightening in its own way, but not with the kind of fear that made her feel sick, or want to hide. This was a warm, awesome fear that somehow made her want to ask this being for help. It had already taken away the terror that had awakened her. That seemed a dim memory now, like something that had happened ages ago.

It seemed as though she ought to tell someone about it. But her mother and father, in the next compartment, seemed far away. Anyway, would they believe that a bright light from Heaven had come and taken away a bad dream?

Was that what had happened?

It was all so muddled, and she was growing drowsy again. She would have to try to remember in the morning.

Try to remember. . . .

When she awoke, the room lights were up, and it was shipmorning. She rubbed her forehead. What had happened during the night? She had a fuzzy memory of dreams, and something else. . . .

"Claudi—are you awake yet?"

Her mother's voice, a familiar sound. A comforting sound. It pushed away the fuzziness and confusion. She heaved herself upright, tugging at the neck of her nightgown where it chafed at her shoulder. She hopped down and got dressed and ran out to greet her mother. "Morning, Muth'!"

Her mother was standing over her desk reading something. She looked up and chuckled in surprise as Claudi ran up to give her an extra-big hug. "Wow!" she said. "Good morning! Did you sleep okay?" Claudi shrugged. "Well, I hear everyone's buzzing about the big change in plans. Your father's already gone in to his work group. They're going to have everyone meeting all over the ship, to try to figure out what to do with the extra time, now that the trip is going to be longer."

Claudi's breath caught as she suddenly remembered: the Throg warning, and the plan to detour out of the star-stream. Her parents had talked to her about it last night after school, but what with all the talk with Mr. Zizmer, she hadn't really felt like any more talking. She'd told them she knew all about it and didn't really think it was such a big deal. She wasn't sure her father had believed her totally; he had looked at her with that slight squint and half-smile that he sometimes used when he thought she might be hiding something. He hadn't said anything, but when he'd tucked her in last night, he'd given her an extra long hug.

Now, thinking about yesterday, she felt that clenching of her throat again.

"Claudi, are you okay?" Her mother knelt down in front of her, studying her with big, worried eyes. She stroked back a few stray strands of Claudi's hair. "Are you a little upset, maybe? About the change, I mean?"

Claudi made a face of impatience. "It's okay," she said, taking a deep breath. "Mr. Zizmer, the teacher, says that it's all right to be scared of the Throgs, if that's what you are."

Her mother nodded, her golden-brown eyes shifting back and forth as she observed Claudi. "And are you afraid of the Throgs?" she asked softly.

Claudi hesitated, then nodded. *Throgs. Throgs.* She trembled a little. But something in the back of her mind—maybe that memory she'd lost when she'd awakened—made her feel less afraid.

Her mother folded her into her arms and made a comforting sound. "We're all a little afraid, Claudi. That's just natural. And your teacher was right—it's okay to feel scared, if that's what you are." She rested her hands on Claudi's shoulders and squeezed gently. "But just remember—the captain's playing it safe. I'm sure we won't even

see any Throgs—that's why we're going out of our way.
You understand that, don't you?"

Claudi nodded.

"Good. Maybe we'll talk about this more tonight. Are
you ready to go to breakfast? School starts soon."

"Uh-huh." Claudi felt a smile creep over her face.
Maybe she was afraid of the Throgs, but not so much right
now.

"Shall we go?" Her mother rose, taking Claudi's hand.

"Yep. Hurry." Claudi skipped ahead, pulling her mother
out the door.

When she came into the classroom, she saw Sheki in his
seat. She asked him in a whisper if he had Watson with him.
The entity had been a big hit yesterday, after all the
gloomy talk, when Mr. Z had asked him to show Watson to
the class. Sheki shook his head, but smiled a little. And
somehow that reminded her of something—a half-remem-
bered dream about Lopo. She stared up at the teaching-
wall, thinking.

Mr. Zizmer's face appeared suddenly in the wall—huge
and wavering, with a leering grin. He looked just like Professor Panic, from the weekend matinee scare-dare surroundies. "Hell*oooo*, everyone!" he cackled. When they
replied with mostly uncertain hellos, he laughed menacingly: *"Ha-ha-ha-ha-HAHHH!"*

Jeremy turned around and winked at everyone. *"Hey!"*
he said, in the deepest, throatiest voice he could manage.
"Mr. Z's trying to scare us!"

A couple of the kids tittered, but Claudi just rolled her
eyes at Jeremy. Mr. Zizmer heard the remark, too, and his
eyes grew large and dark and ominous as he gazed down at
the boy. *"Frighten you? Frighten YOU, Jeremy? What
could frighten YOU, EH? HO-HO!"* And his eyebrows,
enormous in the viewing wall, arched dramatically. Jeremy looked unsure of himself. Suddenly Mr. Zizmer guffawed. His image wavered even more, until it finally
blurred altogether.

With a *pop*! Mr. Zizmer appeared in front of the wall, in
his ordinary form. "Well," he said, brushing off his sleeves.

"Enough of that, what? Everyone here? Good. What we're going to do today is look at a *Galacti Geographic* special on the starstream." He paused, perhaps to see if there would be groans; he was not disappointed. He *tsked*, but with a smile. "This is a good one. Really. Anyway, what with the detour and all, I thought it was time we talked a little about how the starstream works. Yes, Jeremy?"

"Mr. Z, are we going to break the starstream when we leave it?" Jeremy looked around mischievously. "Claudi said we will."

Claudi's mouth fell open. "I didn't—!" And she blinked in embarrassment.

But Mr. Zizmer was already answering. "No, Jeremy, we won't be harming the starstream in any way. It's far too vast and powerful for us to have much effect on it, one way or another." He glanced at Claudi with a grin just reaching the corner of his mouth, and went on.

I didn't say any such thing, you dumb brute! Claudi wanted to yell at Jeremy.

"—but anyway, we'll learn more about that in the surroundie we're about to see. Now, this might be a little advanced for some of you, but you can ask all your questions after it's over. Are we ready?" He twirled his finger. "Let's roll it!"

The room went dark, but almost at once began to fill up with stars. An enormous title stretched across the starfield:

GALACTI GEOGRAPHIC PRESENTS

and then:

THE STREAM OF STARS
Our Gateway to the Galaxy

As the title faded, a large orange sun grew out of the starfield, grew until it seemed to fill the whole front of the room, though the room itself seemed to have vanished. Claudi smiled in the darkness. This was just the sort of surroundie she loved, and she didn't care if the other kids made fun of it. She was in her element.

A tiny, gleaming station came into view, almost lost in

the surface of that big sun. A narrator spoke, in a voice deep and resonant: "Welcome to the great red star—"

"Beetlejuice," Claudi whispered. She knew where the gateway had come from.

"Bait'l'juice," said the narrator. But the caption that appeared under it spelled the name *B-e-t-e-l-g-e-u-s-e.* "This is the star as it appeared in the last century, before Willard Ruskin and the secret Auricle Alliance Breakstar project turned it into a gigantic—"

Supernova, Claudi mouthed.

"—supernova." The narrator fell silent as the star suddenly flared up into a brilliant, blazing white and seemed to fill the whole universe. Claudi was awed by the sight. And suddenly she was more than awed; she was dizzy. She felt her mouth become dry as a memory came back to her —something she'd dreamed, no, *not* dreamed, *seen.* The memory felt very strange to her; it seemed both close and far away. Hadn't she seen something like this star? But when? During the night? And it . . .

Hadn't it spoken to her?

Claudi squinted, blinking, wiping away a tear so that she could see better. She saw the other kids' heads moving like shadowy ghosts in the dazzling light. But then the light faded suddenly, and the star shrank back down, until it was no longer a star, but a whirlpool of light, with a black center.

"And in the heart of the exploded sun a black hole came into existence, where matter was crushed so tightly that it literally opened a hole in four-space," the narrator was saying. "But more than that, the explosion was timed to the fraction of a second, because something else was coming into the equation, as well. Let's watch it again, this time from a greater distance."

Betelgeuse reappeared, but smaller and farther away. "Now, notice the glowing thread approaching from the right." A luminous, silken thread, curved in a long loop, was drifting toward the reddish star. "It's called a *cosmic hyperstring.* It's no thicker than a hair on your head, but you couldn't break it, no matter how hard you tried. It's a sort of crack in space, and on its inside there is a great channel of n-space, something like the K-space that ordinary starships travel through, but even more useful. Watch its shape change, as it approaches Betelgeuse." The loop was stretching narrower and narrower as its end sped toward Betelgeuse, as though being reeled in.

The star exploded. The flash passed quickly this time, and Claudi could see the black spot form in the star's center just as the thread reached it. The thread suddenly tightened and vibrated, like a guitar string plucked by an invisible finger. Now she could see the other end of the thread stretching off to the right, through the star clouds, and finally disappearing into the dense clusters of stars that enveloped the center of the Milky Way. There was a change in the image, and the galactic core became visible, through the dust and the stars. It, too, was a glowing whirlpool with a black center. "There, holding the other end of the loop, is the great black hole at the center of our galaxy, which some call the Well of God." Into the black hole, the fine, luminous thread vanished.

"The string is now anchored at both ends," the narrator said. "And at our end, where Betelgeuse used to be, there is an opening to the new gateway formed by the space-altering hyperstring and the black holes."

Claudi got a little lost, trying to follow the explanation at this point. But the image drew closer, to show a faint stream of light moving along the closed loop of that tight string. That, she knew, was the starstream.

"As grand a feat as making the gateway was, finding a way to enter it safely was almost as difficult. And to explain that, we must tell the strange story of the gateway's designer, Willard Ruskin."

Claudi had heard this before, but she listened anyway to the story of the man who had died, and yet not died, in the creation of the starstream. It was the story, as well, of a Logothian serpent-man named Max, who died with his friend Ruskin, and of a Tandesko assassin who was with them. And strangest of all, it was the story of a star that had been very much alive, and conscious, until it died along with the others—and with them, had become a living part of the gateway that they had created. Only later, and only through a death-defying attempt to contact them, had two

brave women and their shipmates actually found a way to
enter the gateway and travel it in safety.

"Do Ruskin and the others remain alive today as a part of
the gateway? No contact has been reported for many
years. Have they passed on to another plane of existence?
Perhaps—but what a strange existence it must be! Imagine
them, without bodies, their minds and souls spanning half
the galaxy . . . !"

At this point, Mr. Zizmer stopped the show and asked if
there were any questions. There were a few: Jeremy
wanted to know how they'd made such a neat explosion,
and Suze wanted to know if Ruskin and the others had
gone to be with God when they died, since they hadn't
actually died. There was some debate over that, which
Claudi only half paid attention to, because she was thinking about her dream, and the sun-being she thought she
remembered seeing in the night. She realized she should
probably tell Mr. Zizmer about it. But she didn't want to
do it in front of the whole class.

She was glad when the lights went down again to continue the show. It allowed her to keep thinking, in privacy.
Gradually, she was drawn back into the narrative.

The galaxy wrapped itself around the class, in all of its
glory. Passing through the center of the classroom was a
tube of pale light, through which bright embers floated.
"This," the narrator intoned, "is how the starstream might
look from the outside, if we could peer into the twisted
strands of space where the gateway exists. Notice the starships gliding down the stream, in a dimension where
movement is without direct reference to the four-space in
which we live."

Claudi nibbled her lip, trying to follow the explanation.
To be a starship captain, she would have to know this. . . .

"When the hyperstring was caught by the black hole, it
began to vibrate in a new way." A graphic appeared, showing the string vibrating slowly, up and down, in a dozen
different places. "The peaks where the waves move up and
down are called *nodes*. And it's at those nodes, as well as at
the ends, that we can enter and leave the starstream."

The image of the Betelgeuse whirlpool returned, with
the black hole at its center. Claudi could see bright spots of

light darting past her head toward it. They were starships, large behind her, but shrinking to dots as they flew toward the black hole. "Betelgeuse is where most inbound ships enter the starstream—just grazing the black hole as they slip into the invisible opening. Inbound ships go down one side of the starstream—where the space *inside* the loop is moving toward the heart of the galaxy. Returning ships must come back up the other side."

The bouncing nodes in the starstream became visible again. A dot of light emerged from one of them. Another darted toward a different node and vanished into it. "Pilots must choose the node nearest the star they want to visit. Think of the nodes as stations on a great celestial train line —each station serving hundreds of outlying star systems. To reach the individual stars, ships travel from the gateway nodes through ordinary K-space—which, though slower than the starstream, is still far, far faster than light."

The surroundie showed traffic spiraling in and out of the stream of stars, and then showed the view from the inside: the glorious beauty of stars blurring past the bridge of a starship.

"More came of the starstream, however, than mere access to the inner galaxy," the narrator continued. "We met many cultures on other worlds. Some became our friends, but at least one . . ."

The image faded, and Mr. Zizmer reappeared in front of the class. "I think that's enough for today. Who has questions? I know you couldn't *all* have understood all that! Right? *Right?*"

A few of Claudi's classmates poked each other teasingly, and finally one or two hands went up.

CHAPTER 10

She intercepted the teacher as the other kids were leaving. "Mr. Zizmer?"

"Yes, Claudi?" Mr. Zizmer boomed.

She waited, embarrassed by his loud reply, while the rest of the kids went out. She didn't want them to hear this and think she was crazy. "Um, Mr. Z, do you remember you told me if I ever saw anything funny like before, I should come and tell you?" She squinted at him—then ducked her head, suddenly feeling like a dope.

Mr. Zizmer didn't appear to think she was a dope. "Of course I remember. Do you have something to tell me?"

"Well—" She sighed. It was hard to start, now that she'd gotten his attention. She reminded herself that Mr. Zizmer wasn't quite human, and somehow that made it a little easier. "I saw something last night," she said with a shrug. She paused and took a breath. "It wasn't anything like that other time. This was huge—and bright—" And she told him all that she could remember of the vision she'd had, of the thing that had somehow opened her whole room into a world of light, as if a star had come to visit her. She was practically gasping by the time she was finished. "It wasn't some kind of surroundie, was it?"

Mr. Zizmer looked thoughtful. "In your room? I wouldn't think so. I know of no way for a surroundie to just appear in a cabin like that. It takes a lot of projecting equipment, you know, and they don't put that sort of thing in standard cabins."

"Well, what was it, then?" Claudi demanded. Before, she hadn't minded. Now, suddenly, she wanted her teacher to have an explanation.

"I can't say for certain," Mr. Zizmer answered. "I can only guess. But—" His expression suddenly became intent. "Let me ask you this. How did you feel when you saw it? Did you find it frightening?"

"Well—" Claudi remembered fear—but she also remembered that it made her *less* afraid.

"Did you feel as though a friend was there?"

She rocked her weight back and forth. "You mean, like an angel or something?"

Mr. Zizmer turned his hands up. "I don't know. I'm just tossing out ideas. I'm not trying to put words in your mouth."

"Oh. Well, actually—it was scary, in a way. But at least it wasn't like—" And she choked, as she suddenly remembered what she'd almost forgotten: that *other* dream, the one that had awakened her in terror. She shivered as that fear ran down her spine again.

"Something else, Claudi?"

She nodded, gnawing her knuckle. She let her hand drop. "A dream. A *bad* dream. A *really* bad dream."

Mr. Zizmer's eyes studied her. "After the bright thing?"

She shook her head. "Before." She remembered it so vividly now, she could hardly believe she'd forgotten it. "I felt like there was—a thing with wings—*black*—" Her heart started to pound, and she suddenly felt tears rolling down her cheeks. Mr. Zizmer waited. She only really remembered that one thing, the feeling that there was some terribly powerful thing floating nearby. It was like a ghost, and it was coming for her.

"Easy, Claudi," Mr. Zizmer said gently. "It was only a

dream, remember. You didn't see it when you were awake?"

She shook her head.

"And the other? The bright image? Was that a dream, too?"

She shook her head harder.

"You were awake then? You're sure?"

She wiped her cheek and sniffed. "I woke up and there it was." She blinked until she could see Mr. Zizmer through the haze of tears. "It . . . made the other thing go away. The bad thing."

"Made it go away? How?"

"Well . . ." She sighed in frustration. "Not *made* it go away, exactly. But it was gone and I wasn't so scared anymore."

"Because it was friendlier somehow?"

"I don't *know*. It just made me not scared anymore." She was impatient with trying to make Mr. Zizmer understand. It *all* seemed like a dream now! Even this conversation.

The teacher nodded. "Okay, Claudi. Anything else?" She shook her head. "Well, thank you for telling me."

"Aren't you even going to tell me what it is?"

That brought a smile to Mr. Zizmer's lips. "I think, Claudi, that you may know the answer as soon as I do. Tell me, was there anything today that reminded you of it?"

"You mean like that surroundie?" she asked. Of course—that was what had made her remember it in the first place.

"Whatever."

She made a fidgety movement with her hands. "Well—I guess so. It was like that star we saw exploding. It was like —" She felt a lump rising in her throat as she said, "Mr. Zizmer, wasn't that star *alive* that they turned into—" Her breath caught.

"The gateway?"

"Into a *supernova!*"

The teacher nodded. "Yes. It was a living star, only no one knew that except for a few Querayn scientists, and even they weren't sure. It wasn't until the star died that anyone knew for certain."

"But they said in the surroundie—that the star could still be—"

"Alive?"

She nodded.

"And you think maybe that was what you saw?"

She nodded again.

Mr. Zizmer's mouth pressed into thin lines. "Well . . ." He considered for a moment. "I can't say, Claudi. But if the star still exists as a living part of the starstream, then there's no telling who it might contact—or how. I suppose it could be anyone—even you. And that would give you sort of a special responsibility to pay attention, wouldn't it?"

Claudi stared at him. *Me?* she wanted to say.

"Well!" Mr. Zizmer suddenly became animated. "We don't know anything for sure. But if something like this happens again, try to remember every detail you can. Then come and let me know. Okay?"

"Okay," she croaked.

Mr. Zizmer beamed. "Good. Now, I have a little surprise for you. You know your friend the lupeko? Well, I've spoken to Mr. Farharto, and it seems that Lopo's been asking for you. By name. How would you like to pay him a visit?"

Claudi made a stop along the way. "Hi, Mr. Hendu, is Sheki there?"

"Why, yes. How are you—Claudi, is it?" Rafe Hendu ushered her inside. "Claudi's here!" he called.

Sheki appeared, with Watson glowing on his shoulder.

"You want to go see Lopo? He's out of his operation and Mr. Zizmer says I can go see him," Claudi said.

With a squeak Watson turned into the form of a tiny rabbit and peered at her with dark eyes and a glowing, wriggling nose. Sheki glanced at him thoughtfully. "Can Watson come?"

"Sure, I guess so. Is it okay, Mr. Hendu?" Claudi reached out and tickled the entity. Her fingertip tingled.

"What? Oh, yes—fine." Mr. Hendu looked around from his desk. "Where is it you're going?"

"The circ-zoo."

Mr. Hendu looked puzzled. "I thought the zoo wasn't open yet."

Claudi beamed. "We have a *special* invitation."

"Oh—well, that's different!" Mr. Hendu seemed suitably impressed. "Then I won't keep you. But be careful!"

Claudi looked at Sheki, and together they hurried out.

They moved quietly through the halls. It made Claudi feel sort of important, knowing that this time Mr. Zizmer had arranged it for her—but it also took a little of the sneaky thrill out of it. Until she remembered: Lopo had been asking for her.

"Let's hope they don't think Watson is one of the animals in the zoo," she said.

Sheki's eyes widened. "You think they m-might?"

"I don't know. You'd better make sure he doesn't turn himself into one of them."

"He won't," Sheki answered, but there was a little catch of uncertainty in his voice. Claudi grinned, enjoying her joke.

This time they didn't go to the back door, but right to the main entrance, where the signs read: CIRC-ZOO CLOSED. They strutted past the signs and rang the signal.

A few minutes passed before Joe came to greet them. "So, you're doing it on the up-and-up now, eh?" he said, letting them inside.

"On the what?" Claudi asked.

"The up-and-up," Sheki said. "That means, r-regular. We're legit. Coming in the front door." He grinned. "Right, Joe?"

"That's right." Joe winked. "Haven't you heard that expression, Claudi?"

She shook her head, perplexed. How come Sheki knew it and she didn't?

"Never mind. Let's go see Lopo."

They followed Joe into the back rooms. In the same enclosure where Claudi had first met Lopo, a small shaggy head bobbed at the sound of their approach. She remembered suddenly her dream of Lopo being held captive, crying for her help. "Lopo!" she cried and ran past Joe to the enclosure. Her heart was thumping.

The animal's fiery red eyes opened wide. He began to howl, "Arrr-arrrr, kkklarr-klarrrr!"

"Lopo, you're okay!" She pressed her hands to the side of the enclosure. Beside her, Sheki peered in cautiously.

The lupeko reared up, pawing at the bubble wall, but his paws kept sliding off. His tail wagged frantically. "Arrr-kklawww-kklaww-d-d!" he yowled. He spun around in his quarters, too excited to settle down. "Klawwwd-klawwd-klawwd-*eeeee!* Arrrr! Arrrrr!"

"He did it! He said your name!" Sheki cried, clapping his hands. Claudi stood open-mouthed, amazed.

Lopo panted, his mouth open in a shiny-toothed grin. "Klawwrrrdee!" he barked. "Rrrrr-c-c-came-came-came! *Yipp!*"

"Of course I came!" Claudi beamed up at Joe. "He remembers me! Lopo, you can talk! He can talk!"

"I told you, didn't I?" Joe said. "Good work, Lopo! You're learning even faster than Baako did. What else can you say?"

Lopo cocked his head, peering from one human to another. "Rrrrrr-can, c-c-can *sssee!* Rrrr-yip! *Yip!*" His tail wagged harder than ever. "Rrrrr-ssee-yyou."

"That's right, Lopo. Remember, Claudi, I told you we found out he was nearsighted? Well, we've fixed that. He can see you just fine now. Lopo, do you know Sheki?" Joe pointed at the boy.

Lopo's tail paused as he investigated Sheki with his nose. "Ssss-rrr-ssshhekkkk."

"That's right. *Shek-eee,*" Joe repeated.

"Urrf." Lopo seemed curious about the boy; then Claudi realized that he was staring at the entity on Sheki's shoulder. It was back in stroid shape, whiskers moving in the air. "Rrrrr-zzzzattt. Wh-wha-rrrr-whatttzzz?" Lopo sputtered.

"What's what?" Joe peered to see what Lopo was talking about. "I don't know. Sheki, what's your little friend? Is that a stroid?"

"Uh-uh. It's an entity."

"A what?"

"His name is Watson," Claudi offered. "He's an entity.

But sometimes he looks like a stroid. Can I hold him to show Lopo?" she asked Sheki.

"Okay." Sheki shifted the entity carefully into Claudi's hands. "Don't scare him."

She peered into the entity's round dark eyes and felt a sudden reassuring warmth. She held it out for Lopo to sniff through the enclosure wall. "See—this is Watson. He's a friend of ours." The entity peered at Lopo. Lopo's ears and tail twitched as he peered back at it. Claudi heard a soft rumble in Lopo's throat. A growl? She pulled Watson back, alarmed. "Lopo, what's the matter? Can you get Watson to turn back the other way?" she asked Sheki.

"Let's see." Sheki took his pet back and murmured close to it. The stroid blurred back into a hazy ball of light. He held it toward Lopo.

The lupeko cocked his head in puzzlement, then snorted and looked away. "Hey, Lopo!" Claudi urged. "Say hi! Say hi to Watson!" Lopo gazed at the far wall, his ears drooping.

"Lopo—" Joe coaxed. He shook his head. "Why, I believe he's jealous! Can you imagine that?"

"Jealous?" Claudi said. "Of what?"

"You have another friend. Wait." Joe touched the side of the enclosure with a small disk. The bubble glimmered and softened. "Lopo, would you consent to be petted? Will you let Claudi pet you?" Joe reached through the wall and ruffled Lopo's head.

Silently, the lupeko looked back at the humans. His tail was still, but he seemed to want to be touched. Claudi reached out hesitantly. "Here, Lopo." She stroked the top of his head. He made a soft purring sound, like a cat. He sat down, his tail thumping on the floor of his enclosure. Claudi ran her fingers through the thick fur of his neck. Lopo began licking her hand. "Good boy. Good Lopo. We're friends now, aren't we, Lopo?"

He purred in response.

"I don't think he liked Watson," Sheki said, none too happily.

Claudi looked up, frowning. "Do you want to pet him?"

" 'Kay." Sheki settled Watson carefully on his shoulder,

then with his left hand reached out to stroke the lupeko. Lopo sat quietly, and licked his hand once. But when Claudi stroked him again, he seemed to put every ounce of his attention into the touch of her hand.

"Claudi, I sure don't know what it is about you," Joe said. "But I think Lopo likes you more than any human he's ever met."

"He likes Sheki, too," Claudi pointed out.

"Yes, that's true," Joe agreed, but in a tone that made clear that it wasn't the same thing.

"Can we come back to see him?" Claudi asked. What she was thinking was, *Can we ever let him out of there to play?*

"Sure you can. In fact, your teacher asked me to let you see him as often as you wanted. Said it would be good for both of you." Joe patted Lopo. "Does that sound all right with you, little fellow?"

Lopo looked confused. "Rrrr, not go-o-o? Not, rrrr go-o?"

"They'll be back, Lopo. They'll be back."

The lupeko panted hoarsely. "Rrrr-ssss-comp-comp-p-pakkk! Klawwd-eee! Yoww! Rrrrr . . . yoww!" He threw his head back and howled once. Then he sat, silent but mournful.

"In the meantime you need to work on your speech," Joe warned him. "You'll pay attention to your teacher, right?"

Lopo thumped his tail.

Satisfied, Joe sealed the enclosure and herded the kids back out of the room. "Bye, Lopo!" Claudi cried. "Bye!" said Sheki.

"Let's just duck into this other gallery. We've got some smart fish I want to show you," Joe said.

The children didn't argue.

Sighing, Lopo rested his chin on his forepaws. He felt lonely now. But he'd seen her again—and this time clearly! She'd looked just as she had that first time, when she'd appeared to him right out of the air—seconds before she'd actually first walked into his room. He remembered that feeling, that glow he'd felt then, something *inside* him, drawing him to her, making him want to be her friend, even before he knew her.

He was so tired of being confused by things, and this was one thing that didn't confuse him . . . didn't make him wish that he'd never gotten his vision. This wasn't at all like the strange other things he'd been seeing lately—the dark, swirly, frightening things.

No, this was Claudi, and she'd be back. They'd both said so, she and Joe. He could not have heard wrong.

It was hard sometimes to be sure what he was hearing— and odd to feel words erupting from his own throat—the same kinds of words that the keeper used. It was wonderful, but confusing, too.

He thought dreamily of Claudi, of her airy, girlish smell. He thought of her bright eyes, of her hand pressing on the top of his head. The thought made him sigh once more.

And then there was the boy. Shek. Shekk-ee. He seemed okay—but there was that thing, that creature he had brought with him. It wouldn't have been bad, except that Claudi had held it. Just thinking of that brought an uneasy flutter to his heart, and a sourness to his stomach. He didn't know why. He knew only that it upset him to see Claudi holding another creature that way.

Too many things confused Lopo nowadays. He stood and pressed the bar for a drink of swirling water. Refreshed, he sniffed at the teacher. Perhaps he would spend some time with the teacher, as Joe was always after him to do. Maybe that would make the confusion go away. Now he had good reason to learn to use the sounds that came from his throat, to learn to talk.

He had to learn, because Claudi would be back. But not just Claudi. There were those other things, too—the dark nasty things with wings, and the strange blurry lights that whirled around him sometimes. Frightening things. In fact he was just now starting to see those lights again—out there beyond the enclosure wall, way beyond it. Lights blurring and turning around him, as if he were floating in some great bubble or tube, floating down a stream of water. And if the lights were coming, he was afraid the dark things with wings might come, too.

He had to learn to talk. He had to tell Claudi and Joe. He had to know that he was not left alone to face those things. Not left alone with the danger and the fear.

PART TWO

RUSKIN/NEW

"*It is when we try to grapple with another man's intimate need that we perceive how incomprehensible, wavering, and misty are the beings that share with us the sight of the stars and the warmth of the sun.*"

—Joseph Conrad

Interlude

What was it?

Or who?

A child. The countenance of a child. That understanding, once spoken, seemed certain. Most surely it was a child . . . but what child and why . . . and what being . . . ? What nature of being? What kind, what spirit had touched him/them?

Human.

human ?
  human ?
    human ?
      human ?
        human ?

Yes. Remember. Humanity.

Can we/you/I touch and know this person? This child? This being?

We wish. And wonder.

We heard
   her sing
      our children
         sing and cry

But can we/you know? A touch of gossamer joy, a mind of silk glimpses, and a glance with the freshness of erupting blossoms
   memories of life
      of that which was
But now! barbs of fear that pricked you/me/us
   that stung
      that spoke of danger—peril—
And?

What of it? Life is full of peril. Without it you/we could not exist, even if we foolishly wished to. Conflict and pain are not always needless, or cruel.

Perhaps
   or not

And yet that face, alighting in our realm almost like yours/ours as we once were . . . in life . . . in old-life . . .

Once
   once
      once

❊ ❊ ❊

But now the stars sang and the winds of time swept the patterns of thought into disarray like weightless grains of dust, and thence into new patterns, strange and sober and wonderful. Where memories and hopes shifted, the focus became something of a different hue. Consciousness became a splintering prism, awareness shifting in a tango of color and light.

And yet, Ruskin/Ali'Maksam/*Bright*/Ganz/memory-of-terrakells/memory-of-Dax/memory-of-Jeaves/Tamika /Thalia/and-more/New were aware of something more urgent in this contact, something of which time and temporality shone as vital, pulsing elements. They were aware of danger, of the possibility that the contact could be snuffed, broken, extinguished.

Danger.
There was a presence . . .

And a thing called *ship,* bearing the child, moved among them
          toward the heart of the presence . . .
Ship. He/they remembered ship, that which had borne him/them through space and time
     once

But the other, the presence, was different and difficult to perceive, and dangerous. They sensed it lurking . . . moving silent and fleet through the realm of newlife, moving to do
     what?
New was unsure.
But there were memories of other events now past, events scarcely noted in their own time. Memories of rippling pain, and conflict . . . of happenings among the flickering lives that passed through Ruskin/and-more/ New almost without his/their notice. There was knowledge, now crystallizing into awareness as though for the first time, that this presence was something that had killed and killed, and would kill again.
New did not know why.
New did not know if it could be stopped
     or should be
     or how.
But New was tugged, torn, drawn toward that one face on the ship that had appeared to them like an angel, that smiling gossamer countenance fearful and crying out . . . and though New did not know the why of this, nevertheless his/their heart had been captured.
This consciousness, this young human, was in peril and

Ruskin/Ali'Maksam/*Bright*/and-more/New wanted to help.

It was not a desire that could be lightly fulfilled, or even acknowledged. New was no simple mind or being. Nothing like New had existed before. New was a life born of death, of fire, of the souls of a star and a human and a Logothian and a *hrisi* assassin, and more. New was a being born of the currents of time, whose awareness of time and event changed like the seasons; they were a newlife forged of divergence and love, of anger and compassion, of hatred and forgiveness. They were a life that had grown as other lives had intertwined with it, as once-known-and-loved souls had brushed through it like a soft, billowing solar wind. They were a life that looked toward eternity, flowering in knowledge and perhaps also in humility.

Of all of the aspects of New, it was the Ruskin/ and the Tamika/ and the Ali'Maksam/ that most trembled at the touch of this imperiled life, this young spirit even now converging with danger in the world-filament. Perhaps she reminded them of something they had once hoped, or felt, or known. Perhaps she appealed to some deeper, more primal, need.

Whatever the reason, they trembled.

And they vowed to strengthen and renew the contact.

But their first efforts had caused more fear than understanding; and the danger was growing. They had sensed a contact between the young one and the other presence—and not just contact, but terror. However fleeting, it would not do to allow that fear to be identified with New. They must achieve trust, if they were to help.

But what of the danger? And what of the human leaders of the . . . ship, yes . . . in whose hands her fate rested? And of the other flickering lives on the ship whom New sensed now, though not so clearly?

New's understanding was incomplete. It was not a simple matter.

Rarely had New chosen to intervene in the affairs of the flickering ones, however much his/their own oldlives might once have been like them. But now the possibility of choice was dwindling, if he/they were to act.

In the end, and in hope, it was the *Bright*/ who called
out longingly

   My child
      our children
         can you hear ?
               will you touch ?
                     do you know ?

CHAPTER 11

Last night's had been the worst ever. He could still hear
Myra's voice crying out to him, crying in desperation and
pain as the Throgs pulled her down into their terrible
realm of nothingness and death. Captain Thornekan was
still trying to shake off the dream as he stood with his
senior officers in the conference room near *Charity*'s
bridge. For the first time in almost two years, this morning,
he had nearly given in to the temptation to numb himself
with the headwire, or even with drugs, to take away the
pain. He had nearly, for all practical purposes, abdicated
his command. He might well have succumbed, had not the
com-officer interrupted his private reverie with an update
three hours before the meeting.

His command probably could not have withstood such a
lapse in discipline. Once before, twelve years ago, he had
been censured for negligence. He had been commanding
a freighter then, *Melrose* out of Gless. Three of his crew
had died in an encounter with a poorly charted debris ring
in a colony system, because—in the words of the board of
inquiry—he had "failed to take the appropriate corrective
action to ensure his ship's safety." He had disagreed with

their judgment, but having no recourse he had accepted it and lived with it. His record since had been unmarred, except for the troubled time following Myra's death; but boards of inquiry had long memories.

He was more grateful to the com than he could say for interrupting him this morning. But it didn't make the present dilemma any easier. How many aboard *Charity* would die if he made the wrong choice this time?

It was a gloomy crew facing him. First Officer Len Oleson was scratching his beard silently as he read the IS report for at least the fifth time. Liza Demeter, the IS chief, kept running her fingers back through her hair as she tried to extract more information from the intelligence system. The navigator looked discouraged; he had just spent several long days plotting and refining a difficult departure from the starstream—only to be informed today of the likelihood of a complete change in plans. The power-deck chief and the chief of security didn't look much happier. And why should they?

Roald Thornekan glared at them in frustration. "We meet with the passenger reps in three hours," he said, glancing at the clock. "I want to know what we're going to tell them. Or should we cancel the meeting and tell them nothing?"

His officers stirred but said nothing.

Thornekan frowned at the IS report. It was now five shipdays since they'd picked up the n-space alert, and two days since he'd made the difficult and burdensome decision to exit the starstream at the nearest node. It was difficult because it would delay, possibly indefinitely, the colonists' arrival at their destination; burdensome because it would ruin the ship's schedule and cost the company a great deal of money. The decision had made no one happy; but it was better than letting his passengers become fodder for Throgs. Having made the decision, he had called for a meeting of the colonists' leaders.

But now everything had changed. According to the intelligence system, new evidence suggested that the Throgs might be far closer in the starstream than previously assumed; they might in fact be in the immediate vicinity. There were no direct observations; but if the IS

was right in its inferences, then this ship and its crew
might be forced to abandon their escape efforts and face
the Throgs alone.

And all on the basis of reports from a child and a couple
of animals.

"Liza, can you get *anything* more from it?" Thornekan
knew, even as he asked, that she would have done so already if she could have. But *damn* it, he thought. This IS
was designed by the Querayn; it was supposed to have
extraordinary capabilities. Couldn't it at least give them a
more concrete analysis? Suppose this was all just an aberra-
tion of the system. . . .

He had to know—because if the Throgs really were
close, then he dared not leave the starstream. He dared
not repeat the tragedy of starship *Euphrates,* six years ago.
That ship's captain, in an attempt to escape oncoming
Throgs, had fled the starstream and inadvertently led the
enemy straight to his would-be haven, Doxy IV. No fewer
than three million people had perished on that world, in
addition to the entire crew of *Euphrates* when it was
caught at last by the Throgs. Every captain of the starstream was thereafter bound by law: *any* ship or class of
ship was expendable if the alternative was to put an inhab-
ited planet or star system at risk. It was not known how
easily Throgs could locate Human worlds, or for that matter exit nodes, on their own; but it *was* known that they
could follow Human ships out of the starstream, and did.

Liza tipped back her headset with a sigh. "That's all
there is, skipper. The teachers have reported two sightings
of a very peculiar, almost psychic, nature; and one dream.
In each case, the descriptions closely resembled descriptions of Throgs recorded from previous encounters. The IS
rates the significance of the events as 'substantial.' It thinks
since we haven't been attacked, probably the Throgs
aren't here yet; but probably they're not far away, either."

Thornekan grimaced. "All this, from an eight-year-old
girl?"

"And two animals in the zoo. I didn't say it was easy to
believe."

His hand curled into a fist. "What about the power of

suggestion? This has all happened since our announcement."

"Well—" Liza's voice trembled a little. "The girl and the animals all reported independently. Are they all suffering delusions? I don't know. But none of them, to the IS's knowledge, has ever seen detailed pictures of Throgs. At least they haven't seen it from the ship's teachers."

Thornekan opened his fist and stared at his hand for a moment. He looked up. "Even if I believe an eight-year-old, we're talking about a *dream*. I can't decide this ship's course based on a dream!" He swallowed, thinking of his own dreams . . . nightmares . . . and of what had happened on another ship once, when he had failed to make the right decision.

Liza scratched under her loose black hair. "To be honest, I might give greater weight to the others," she said, arching an eyebrow.

"The animals?" He didn't hide his impatience.

"The lupekos are intelligent, skipper. Apparently there's been no communication between them, yet they've each reported similar sightings to their teachers. We don't know *how* they could be seeing such things, just that they are." Liza looked at her fellow officers, then back at the captain. "The young lupeko was afraid. The older one was merely annoyed. Myself, I think I'd side with the younger one."

Thornekan rubbed his chin and grunted. What he wouldn't give for an hour under the wire. . . . He pushed the thought out of his mind. "What about this other business—the gateway visions? How seriously should we take those?"

Liza turned her hands up helplessly. "It's the same girl, Claudi Melnik. But her visions correlate well with old reports of the starstream consciousness."

Thornekan cursed under his breath. "I haven't heard of a contact like that in the last forty years. Why would it start up again now? And why with *our* ship?" He frowned when Liza stared back at him mutely. He glanced at his other officers. Whether to believe it or not: it was his call, of course. But how could he make a judgment on the basis of such flimsy evidence? And yet, if he went for the escape—

for safety for the ship—would he be putting a whole planet at risk? "Comments?" he growled.

The navigator tapped the table. "We'll need a go/no-go in three days. Aside from that—I dunno, skipper."

"Understood. Len?"

His first officer scratched his sideburn grimly. "Let's not cut out any options we don't have to. I suggest we tell the colonists we're not sure. Tell them there might be another change. Tell them anything—just not that the Throgs are already here. We don't want a panic."

"But we do want them prepared, if it comes to that."

Len Oleson frowned. "Prepared? Is any of us prepared? I'm sure as hell not."

"Yes, well—" Thornekan took a deep breath as he turned to stare at the external holo, where the liquid light of the passing starstream swirled by as dreamy clouds and blurry stars. No, he supposed, none of them was really prepared to meet the Throgs. Not psychologically, and certainly not militarily. *Charity* was for all practical purposes unarmed. If the unthinkable happened and they met Karthrogen, and the enemy behaved in typical Throg manner, *Charity* would be lucky to last five minutes. *Myra, did you have this much time to think . . . ?*

He turned back. "All right. We'll meet with the passengers. But in the meantime, I want more options, especially if we stay in the groove. Len, anything that could help us evade them." It was a faint hope. It wasn't impossible to evade something in the starstream, but it was difficult; and the Karthrogen were good, very good, at tracking targets. He didn't think much of *Charity*'s chances, if the Throgs knew that they were here.

"Aye, skipper." The first officer didn't sound too hopeful, either.

"Liza, I'll be wanting a talk with the Melnik girl."

She scowled. "Captain, the system recommends we do *not* question the girl."

"And just why the hell not?"

Liza's lips pressed thin. "Her teacher believes she has, quote, 'unusual sensitivities,' unquote, which might be extremely fragile at the present time. It is trying to understand her ability to sense these things and says if we interfere, we might ruin it instead of getting what we want."

"Terrific. The system knows best, huh?"

"That's basically what it says."

Thornekan shook his head. "We'll see about that." He rubbed his hands together and blew into them. "Okay, we'll play its game for a little while longer. You keep doing what you can."

"Aye, aye."

"And—I guess I'll just have to figure out what to say to our passengers. I know *I* sure as hell wouldn't buy the crap we're about to hand them. Would any of you?"

There was, wisely, no answer from any of the officers.

John Melnik had a new partner on the log cabin building project. During a reshuffling of the survival training classes, his former partner Ti had been shifted over to the alternative energy workshop. John had been asked to break in the new man on the work in progress. The new "man" had turned out to be the Im'kek he had met briefly before. It made John a little uncomfortable, though he tried hard not to show it. John Melnik felt that all sentients, Human or otherwise, were entitled to fair and equal treatment; but he hadn't personally been around that many of them—nonHumans, that is—and the truth was, it was a little hard to get used to their appearance, and their manner and smells.

Not that Roti Wexx'xx smelled particularly bad, or even had disturbing manners; Roti was just different, that was all. Im'keks were still fairly rare around the Habitat, coming as they did from a recently contacted world. John knew that Im'keks were a lot smarter than they looked, but it was something he had to keep reminding himself every time he glanced up at the lanky, grinning, vacant-eyed, minty-scented Wexx'xx. They'd had more than a little trouble communicating. That was probably as much John's fault as Roti's, except—well, since, after all, this was primarily a Human ship, he would have thought that the Im'kek might have made a greater effort to learn the local speech, as it were.

"Roti," he said, pointing down to where two pseudologs overlapped in a decidedly imperfect fashion, "we've got to make that joint snug. See there, how you haven't cut enough bite out from under the top log?"

Roti looked puzzled. He grinned absently. "Bite? Dinner break?"

"No—no! The *joint*, Roti. Look underneath." John lifted the end of the log and indicated the notch. "See? You need to hollow it out more."

"Ah! With this?" Roti held up the carving tool.

"Right! Now, help me turn it over." John grunted as he struggled to roll the log off onto the work surface. "*Help* me with it, Roti!"

"Sorry! Sorry! Help, yes." Roti squatted down and began trying to whittle out the uneven indentation.

"No—*wait!*" John dropped the end of the log with a grunt. "Not yet! We've got to get it *turned over*. Help me *turn* it."

"Sorry! Sorry!" Flustered, Roti put down the tool, and then with his massive hands assisted John in rolling the log onto the work surface. He patted it and picked up the blade again. "Now?"

"Yes. Now."

Roti hacked away at the spot, digging the notch deeper. John watched in silence as the chips flew. After a minute Roti paused and looked up at John. His eyes, for once, seemed to focus on John's. "I'm sorry, you know—sorry. I know it's . . . *frustrating* . . . for you. I try. I try. This is all so new to me."

John immediately felt guilty. Who was he to have judged this poor Im'kek about being slow to learn? It certainly hadn't been easy for *him* the first time he'd tried any of this stuff. But he knew it was impossible to hide his emotions from the Im'kek; to Roti's kind, Humans positively radiated emotion.

"John Melnik—sorry—it is okay," Roti said. He waved a large hand, rotating it at the wrist, in what was apparently a reassuring gesture. "We will do our best here. Yes?"

"Okay, Roti." John sighed. Even his guilt feelings were obvious. He wondered how much he was radiating of his other worries. Practically everyone was concerned about the meeting that was happening right now between the passengers' reps and the captain. It was certainly never far from John's mind, along with his fears for his wife's and daughter's safety. But Roti ought to be used to that. He must be seeing the same worry everywhere he went.

The Im'kek had stopped carving and was waiting. John took a breath and forced a smile. "Yes, we'll get this thing licked. We'll build the best damn log cabin on the ship! Right?"

"Best dam? Right!" Roti answered, grinning. "But first— log cabin! Okay?"

"Okay," John laughed. "Log cabin. That's enough now. Let's flip this thing over."

The group crowding the meeting room was larger than Thornekan had hoped, but fortunately not hostile—not yet, anyway. He was trying to explain the situation to the colonists' representatives without really explaining. "Now, we've been working very hard to come up with a plan for staying as far from any hot spots in the starstream as possible. Let me sketch out some of the factors we're dealing with, and if you have any questions I'll do my best to answer them."

You can only stall for so long, a voice in the back of his head droned as he turned on the starchart holos for the colonists. Sooner or later you've got to put it to them: We might all be staying here to die so that a planet none of them has ever heard of *won't* die. How do you ask people to be calm in the face of that? Easy, said another voice. Don't tell them.

And maybe you won't tell them when the Throgs start attacking, either?

Willing the voices in his head to silence, he began to explain aloud the options involved in detouring from the starstream at the nearest exit node. The only stop-off point within reasonable reach was Mefford's Walk, several weeks' journey outward by K-space from the starstream. Another option was simply to wait outside the exit node— guessing and hoping that before they ventured back in, the Throgs would have passed out of range. That involved a shorter detour, to be sure, but offered no opportunity for refueling and resupplying; and it might actually increase their vulnerability if the Throgs should emerge from the starstream.

Having said all that, he wondered, was it time now to explain that possibly neither of these options could be used? To explain that this ship might become a sacrifice to protect a planet that didn't even know they were here, and would never know that the sacrifice had been made for them? He surveyed the roomful of people—and couldn't bring himself to say it. Not yet, not knowing whether or not it was true. The passengers were calm and he wanted to keep them that way; and even if he told them, there was nothing they could do.

Coward. No, answered a different voice, it's just sensible. Tell them later, and only if you need to.

The colonists were stirring as his pause lengthened.

"There are a number of factors we're still evaluating, before we can make a final decision," he said at last. "One, of course, is whether we receive any further indication of hostile presence—either in our vicinity, or farther downstream. We hope to clarify that situation soon."

He cleared his throat. The colonists looked as though they were ready to ask some hard questions. They had already assimilated the fact that their plans for early arrival at Sherrick III were dashed. Some were undoubtedly starting to wonder what other aspects of their plans were in jeopardy. Thornekan glanced at his first officer and found scant comfort in Len Oleson's stoic expression.

"Captain?" A heavyset man rose near the back of the room.

"Question? Please identify yourself and your section."

"Travis Horton. Engineering trades." The man coughed. "Uh, Captain, it seems to me that we're looking at some pretty substantial delays here. Can you give us a little clearer idea of just how much time we're looking at? I can't speak for everyone, but some folks are going to be getting pretty restless if this takes us months out of our way, which is what it sounds like."

Thornekan nodded. "That's certainly a fair question. I wish I could be more exact—but as I said, there's a lot that we just plain don't know yet. We're gathering information as best we c—"

"But Captain—"

"No, let me finish, Mr. Horton. If we do make the detour, it'll probably set us back a minimum of seven or eight weeks. But it could go longer."

"How much longer?" someone in the audience shouted.

"I'd appreciate it if you would wait to be recognized, folks. The answer is, we just don't know." He raised his hands to quiet the room. "Look, I know this isn't making any of you happy. We don't like it, either. But we all knew when we set out that there was a chance that we would skirt Karthrogen activity at some point. If we weren't willing to take that risk, none of us should have been on this ship in the first place." He paused, surveying the colonists. "Nevertheless, my primary responsibility is your safety, and the ship's. We don't like inconveniencing you—but safety comes first."

Several people were standing now, and many more were raising their hands. He recognized a woman near the front. She looked so old that it was hard to imagine her emigrating to a brave new colony world. Or asking too hard a question. "Helena Carolli," she said, speaking painfully slowly, but with surprising carrying power. "Captain, there is one thing that *I* haven't heard any discussion of . . . and that is what we will *do* . . . in the *event* . . . that we actually encounter *Karthrogen* . . . here in the star . . . stream. I ask because, for one thing, we must know what to say to the children." As creakily as she had spoken, she sat down again.

Thornekan felt as though he had been kicked in the stomach. "You are quite right," he said quietly. "We'll be scheduling emergency drills for both crew and passengers. But the truth is that if we *do* meet the Karthrogen, there is very little we can do to defend ourselves. Except pray, perhaps." The room fell silent. He drew a slow breath. "That is one reason I'm asking the various entertainment groups on board to move up their performances. There's not much we can tell the children right now, so the best thing we can do is to keep them, and us, occupied. And hope to avoid undue fear."

The old woman looked satisfied, but few others did. If he could keep undue fear out of this meeting alone, he thought, he would be doing very well indeed.

He nodded and took the next question.

CHAPTER 12

For the kids in Claudi's class, the hours and days seemed
to crawl by, filled with long lessons on this or discussions on
that, too infrequently broken by sims and hologames. But
though they sometimes felt as if they were trapped in
molasses, waiting for something to happen, the time was
actually whispering by. Before they knew it, Mr. Zizmer
had an announcement for them, and that was that tomorrow was . . . *CIRCUS DAY!* . . . the first shipboard performance of the J. J. Larkus Traveling Interstellar Circ-
Zoo. Not much teaching got done the rest of that day, or
the next morning before the show, either.

After lunch, the class raced down to the auditorium with
unrestrained glee, all thoughts of lessons and gloom left
behind. Jeremy and his friends were hooting and joking,
and it was a miracle that the holoushers in the auditorium
were able to keep them in line at all. The ushers were
miniature dragons, carnival red and phosphorescent green
and electric blue, swooping down over the kids' heads like
swift birds of prey. They called out instructions in chuckling voices that sounded like piccolos. When the rowdier
kids jeered at them, the dragons wheeled around and

dived, blowing crackling, but harmless, flames over their heads. Harmless or not, Claudi felt the heat of the flames on her brow and couldn't help flinching away. Jeremy and company whooped, but hurried back into line, while the other kids roared—first with alarm, then with laughter.

The same auditorium that Claudi and Sheki had once glimpsed in near darkness was now brightly lit with criss-crossing beams of color and sweeping fan-floods. Rousing music boomed from overhead speakers. The place was nearly packed already. After grabbing some packages of peanuts and candy that were being passed out at the entrance, Claudi's class followed the dragon-ushers to seats down near the front. Older kids were settling raucously into the rows farther back, tossing peanuts at each other; and an amazing number of adults were here as well, looking as excited, in adult fashion, as the kids did in theirs. Claudi followed Suze, who followed Sheki into the row behind the noisy boys. She found herself seated right behind Jeremy, who turned around and bleated at her like one of the animals in the zoo.

"Jeremy, you're just *so attractive* when you do that," Suze mocked, before Claudi could even think of how to respond.

Jeremy grinned at Claudi and turned even farther to bleat again, at Suze.

"*Gods,* Jeremy, what a jerk!" Suze squealed.

Rob punched Jeremy on the shoulder then, and Jeremy whirled around to punch him back. A green-glinting dragon squawked straight overhead and dived toward them, billowing holoflame, which made the kids shriek even louder. They rolled in their seats, laughing, when it veered away after chirping a piccolo admonishment. Suze sighed dramatically and rolled her eyes up. Claudi grinned; she was pretty sure that Suze liked Jeremy. Of course, she'd also heard that Jeremy liked her, Claudi, which didn't exactly thrill her. But right now she didn't care; they were all here for just one thing, and that was the circus.

Finally the auditorium darkened, and the kids grew quiet and expectant. There came a drumroll, and sparkling points of light danced over the empty stage. For an instant, Claudi imagined that Lopo might come trotting out onto the stage to introduce the show. That was absurd, of course. She waited eagerly for whatever was to come.

The center of the stage went dark—and suddenly disappeared altogether. The drumroll ended with a great *thump*, followed by a chime. A flock of colorful birds suddenly swarmed and fluttered up out of the opening in the stage—chased by dragons, none other than the usher-dragons, spouting joyous gouts of fire! They zoomed in a furious midair race over the audience, as the speakers boomed brassy show music. And suddenly the birds and dragons vanished in a great splash of golden light. Before the dazzle had faded from Claudi's eyes, a whole new parade of creatures was bounding up out of the center of the stage, into view.

There were black great-cats with luminous yellow eyes, and fuzzy white apes carrying baby apes in their long, crooked arms, and long-necked seals barking and oinking, and miniature neighing horses galloping, and fish splashing and leaping—

Fish splashing? Are these all holos?

—and giraffes flying on butterfly wings, and enormous fat waddling birds that quacked, and shadow-things that crept along the floor, and a strutting *tree*—

By now the kids were laughing uproariously and pointing every which way.

—and now a human troupe bounded up onto the stage, running among the animals. Several of the men and women sprang onto the cats and rode them bareback, and then others jumped astride a lumbering woolly-looking mammoth as it emerged, bellowing and honking, from below.

Claudi's mouth opened and closed as she tried to shout her delight. But her voice, and her heart, seemed trapped inside her, bound up by her excitement. She was too amazed, too astounded, too delighted by all of the creatures, real and unreal, and she could hardly tell which was which. All she could do was clap her hands.

A spinning circle of light rose from the floor of the stage, encircling all of the performers like a tremendous halo. In the dazzling band of light itself, the fish reappeared, flashing silver and gold and spitting streams of water high into the air. The halo, still spinning, rose past the performers and softened to a haze of light as it drifted to the ceiling. The fish spiraled upward with it, until they flitted up into the ceiling and vanished. The circle of light vanished, too, and so did the rest of the holoanimals. The real performers, with the real animals—the cats, the mammoth, the horses, the walking tree—remained on stage, bowing and waving as starbursts flashed around them. Even many of the animals were bowing.

The audience applauded thunderously. Claudi found her voice and cheered and clapped so hard her hands hurt.

A man with an enormous beard full of glitter, and the bushiest head of gray hair Claudi had ever seen, leaped up onto a tall stool as it rose out of the stage. He bowed deeply, stretching his arms out to the audience. *"Welcome to the J. J. Larkus Galactically Famous Traveling Interstellar Circ-Zoo!"* he cried, his voice reverberating through the hall. *"Are you ready for the show?"*

"YES!" thundered the crowd.

"Then let the show begin!" he boomed. Out of nowhere, it seemed, he pulled out a long, glowing strand of something that crackled and left ghost-trails of light in the air as he swung it around. It made a loud *crack* as he whipped it —and the black great-cats sprang into action, leaping acrobatically through floating, twisting, holographic hoops.

The show was on.

The kids got all they'd hoped for, and more. They watched panthers prancing and snakes charming and clowns making everyone laugh. They cheered to a flame-eater and a juggler and a team of tumblers. A pair of flying monkeys performed an aerial ballet, and two of the horses played a game called Ping-Pong with paddles grasped in their teeth. They gasped at the designer-rug-bugs, a cloud of insects that could cluster to form a copy of anything put before them—a human, a tree, even a tapestry or a fine Persian rug.

And in the end they shouted to a holocade of creatures from around the galaxy, some flying at them with dizzying speed before vanishing into thin air and others strutting or snarling as they performed. The music rumbled and blared and the lights dazzled, and there could hardly have been anyone in the hall who wasn't sitting on the edge of his seat or whose head wasn't reeling.

Claudi was hoarse from shouting by the time the stage lights faded and the regular house lights came up. As they crowded out of the hall, the kids were still shouting to each other.

"Didja see that *buffalo?*"

"Really booga-booga!"

"That wasn't a buffalo! It was a *mammoth.* They said so."

"It was nothing compared to the—"

"Yeah, but how about the *croc* swallowing the bird then spitting it out again?"

"You birdbrain! He didn't swallow it! They used lights to make you think he did. What a birdbrain!"

"Yeah, well I'd like to see *you* stick your head in that mouth!"

"Hey, I would!"

"Sure, and I'll bet you—"

The dragon-ushers swooped and spat fire, and by now Jeremy and his friends were swatting up at the little dragons and snorting and daring them to come down and fight. The dragons laughed their piccolo-laughs and flew off good-naturedly.

"Hey, Claudi," Suze asked, pushing out behind her. "Want to go to the commons for—*oof!* Hey!" Jeremy had just pushed three girls, like dominoes, into Suze. "You creep, you!" she snarled. Making a face at Jeremy, she turned back to Claudi and giggled.

"Don't we have to go back to class?" Claudi asked.

"Didn't you listen? We're done! We're off!"

"Oh—"

"Let's get away from these cavemen!" Suze glanced coyly back at Jeremy.

They were out in the corridor now, and Claudi was thinking. If they didn't have to go back to deck-school, this could be a good time to visit Lopo.

"Hey, don't you want to come?" Suze looked indignant that Claudi wasn't agreeing right away.

She stalled. "I'm just thinking—"

"Well, don't *hurt* yourself, Melnik!" Jeremy bellowed, from behind.

Claudi glared back at him. Jeremy was pulling his lips wide with his fingers, wiggling his tongue. Sheki was walking on the other side of Suze. "Do you want to go see something neat, with Sheki and me?" she asked Suze. "Sheki, you want to?"

Suze looked at Sheki, then back. "Now what?"

Claudi motioned the two out of the stream of traffic. She wrinkled her nose at Jeremy and his friends as they walked by, making blatting sounds. "You want to go see an animal that talks? It's really neat. It's a *lupeko*!"

Suze rolled her eyes back in a look of supreme disbelief. "*Gods*, Claudi! Are you getting *weird* on me? Are you going to spend the whole rest of your life coming down here to look at animals? *Jeez*, Claudi—grow up!"

Stung, Claudi didn't answer. She didn't know what to say. She saw nothing ungrownup about being interested in animals—and besides, Lopo was her friend! Suze just wanted to spend all of her time trying to get Jeremy's and Rob's attention! "What's wrong with it?" she asked angrily.

"It's dumb," Suze asserted, eyes flashing. She glanced in the direction that the boys had gone. Jenny and Betsy were already going that way. "*I'm* going to the commons! If you and your *boy*friend here want to go the other way, then you just go right ahead."

Claudi's face grew hot. She saw Sheki draw back. "Listen," she snapped. "Just because you keep trying to chase those goons, don't tell me *I* have to grow up! Maybe Sheki and I are more ma*ture* than you are already!"

"I doubt that," Suze said archly. "See you *later*. Don't forget to come *back*." And she marched off to follow the others.

Claudi was steaming as she and Sheki skirted along the wall past the exiting people. "Boy," Sheki said, once they'd gotten away from the crowd. "I guess she didn't want to come."

Claudi grunted. "She's just going off because she wants to chase Jeremy. Booga-booga knows why! Jeremy's a pain." She growled. "Anyway, don't pay any attention to what she said." About you being my boyfriend, she added silently. When Sheki didn't answer, she glanced at him finally. She didn't want to hurt his feelings. "You're not . . . *you* know. Okay?"

Sheki appeared lost in thought, as if he hadn't heard her. Suddenly he answered, in a tone of utter seriousness, "That's all right. You're too old for me, anyway!" He began giggling, and then Claudi couldn't help giggling along with him.

As they continued down the hall, she realized that they were on the opposite side of the circ-zoo area from the door where she usually went in. They'd have to push through all those people outside the auditorium if they wanted to go back around. But maybe they could find an open door on this side and cut straight across. It couldn't hurt to try, could it?

The first two doors they came to were locked and posted with NO ADMITTANCE signs. (Why have a door, she wondered, if nobody was ever to be admitted?) Sheki kept glancing back, obviously uneasy about going down this empty, echoing corridor. She could feel the ship thrumming with energy beneath her feet. Usually she found that reassuring, but just now it seemed an eerie feeling. The third door opened at her touch. She grinned at Sheki. His eyes were full of worry.

She put a finger to her lips and peered into the doorway. It was filled by a funny blackness, like a dark curtain that wasn't really there. It was strange, and a little scary. She hesitated, then took a breath. She poked her head through.

CHAPTER 13

Inky blackness swirled past her head, then parted to reveal bright blazing light. Claudi gasped. "Come here, Sheki!" she cried. "Look!" She couldn't believe her eyes; she was standing under a blue sky, at the edge of a sea of rolling sand dunes.

"What is it?" Sheki's voice sounded small and distant.

"Come see. It's a desert!" She turned and saw that behind her, where she'd stepped through, there was a patch of shimmering silver. "It's okay, it's safe!"

A moment later, Sheki's head popped through the silver doorway. His eyes were wide with fear, then with surprise, as he stepped out beside Claudi. What in the world was this place? Claudi took a few quick steps up the slope of the nearest dune. Her shoes crunched on firmly packed sand. It felt quite real underfoot. The sky overhead looked real, too; it was a deep, almost purple, blue. Her legs pumped, taking her up the dune. "Look, Sheki!" Beyond the ridges of the dunes, she saw treetops.

"What?" Sheki puffed, hurrying up behind her.

"I see an oasis!"

"A *what*?"

Claudi started running down the far side of the dune. She charged up the next, and down again, and up. Cresting the third dune, she stopped with a gasp. In a small, bowl-shaped depression, there was indeed an oasis—a tiny park with an inviting pool and a cluster of tall skinny trees with bushy tops. "Wow!" She raced down the slope.

"Wait for me!" Sheki yelled.

She didn't answer; she was already running too fast even to keep her footing. She half skidded down the sliding sand. She saw movement ahead of her, among the trees, and suddenly a large, bearded man stepped out and stared up at her. "Sheki—*aaahhhhh . . . !*" She tried to stop, but she lost her footing and tumbled. She rolled and slid down the dune.

She bottomed out with an *Ooofff!* and struggled to get her breath. As she pushed herself to a sitting position, she peered up into the eyes of the man towering over her, a man with a great head of bushy gray hair and a glittering beard.

"May I help you?" he rumbled.

"Uh—" Claudi swallowed, looking around in panic for Sheki. Her friend was trotting down after her. "Um—" She looked back up at the man, her eyes widening in sudden recognition. He was the leader of the circus—out of costume! "You!" she said. "You're—"

"Yes, I am," the man interrupted—but not with great friendliness. "You are unhurt, I trust?" He seemed to be asking, *What are you doing here?*

"Uh-huh." Claudi tottered to her feet. "Um—we didn't know anyone was here, I guess."

"*You guess?*" The man arched his eyebrow, looking fiercely indignant, as only a grownup could look.

Claudi shrank. "I mean—I'm sorry—we didn't even know this place was here. We just—"

The eyebrows went higher. "It's not open to the public, you know."

Claudi bit her lip.

Sheki arrived beside her, panting. "W-we were just . . . t-trying . . . to . . ."

The eyes shifted. "To what?"

"Just . . . to get over to the other side, where the animals are," Claudi blurted. The eyes shifted again, narrowed. "We were looking for Joe," she added quickly.

"Joe?" The eyes widened.

"Joe Far-, Farharto. And Lopo."

"*Lopo?* You know Lopo? And Joe Farharto?" The man's voice rose in surprise and became a little friendlier. "Well, maybe then that's a different story." He hooked his thumbs in the suspenders that he wore over a blue denim shirt, and he looked away and squinted in thought.

Claudi stared up at his face, fascinated. He looked a lot older close up than he did on stage—and more fearsome, too. His face was craggy and ruddy. His bushy hair was full of tangles. But his eyes, harsh and bloodshot, looked as if they could see everything the two kids had ever thought or done.

"Maybe you wouldn't mind telling me who you are, then," he said, glancing down again. His mouth puckered in a frown. "Something about you two . . . you're an odd pair, that's for sure. Not like any kids I know. But you seem okay, I guess. And you must have names."

Claudi's voice trembled. "I'm . . . Claudi. And this is . . . Sheki."

"Hm." The man plucked at his beard. "Claudi and Sheki, eh? Well—glad to meet you, I guess. I'm Lanker."

Was that a hint of a smile on his face? "Hi, um, Mr. Lanker," Claudi managed.

"No mister. Just Lanker." He stuck out a huge, rough-skinned hand and gripped first Claudi's hand, then Sheki's. "So. You've discovered our little sanctuary here. I suppose it had to happen sooner or later. It's going to be open to passengers in a couple of days, though it won't look much like this."

"What *is* it?" Claudi asked.

"It's an en-, en*vie*ment," Sheki blurted. Claudi peered at him in amazement. How did Sheki know this stuff?

"You mean an *envi-ron-ment*, I think," Lanker said, making a clucking noise. "That's right."

"You mean like a surroundie?" Claudi asked. "But what about all this stuff?"

"What stuff?"

Claudi kicked at the ground. "The sand, and trees—"

She reached out and patted a trunk. "They're not holos. And we aren't wearing headsets." The headsets they wore in class made surroundies *feel* more real than they were. But this was no surroundie. "Where did all this come from?"

"Oh—well, it's all made by NAGs, of course," Lanker grunted.

"NAGs? What are they?"

"Nano-agents. Teeny little invisible building robots." Lanker held his thumb and forefinger very close together, up to his eye. "Don't they have them on your homeworld? Maybe you call them construction-specks."

"You mean like m-med-specks?" Sheki asked.

"That's right. Just like med-specks, except with different programming. It was construction-specks that built this ship, you know." Lanker frowned, his eyebrows bristling. "You did know that, didn't you? I don't know what they're teaching you kids these days. You do go to school, don't you?"

"Course we do," Claudi answered defensively.

"Well, *good*. So why aren't you in school now?"

She scowled. Lanker made her feel as if she were doing something wrong—and she wasn't. Or at least, she wasn't skipping out of school.

"We came to th-, the circus!" Sheki said. "And we d-don't have to go back today."

"Ah!" Lanker grinned suddenly. "And what did you think of the circus?"

"You were in it!" Claudi and Sheki shouted in unison.

Lanker barked a laugh. "Well, you were paying attention! But you didn't answer my question. What did you think of it?"

"It was great!" Claudi said.

Sheki agreed vigorously.

Lanker nodded, rubbing his hands together briskly. "Good. Good. You *are* okay kids. *But*—" and he raised a warning finger—"don't think you're going to see anything here. I only work when I'm onstage." His nostrils flared. "Some folks think I'll give them a little show anytime they just happen along and meet me."

Claudi and Sheki looked at each other, shrugging.

Lanker sniffed. "Well—" He coughed and turned to walk through the trees. When Claudi and Sheki remained where they were, he waved impatiently for them to follow. "You might as well see what we've got, while it's still here."

They walked, touching the leaves and sniffing the sweet-smelling purple and red desert flowers. Claudi asked, a little hesitantly, "What's this place for?"

Lanker sighed, gazing off over the dunes that ringed the oasis. When he finally spoke, there was a wistfulness to his voice. "I come here to think. To be by myself. To remember, while I can." He turned, scowling. "You know what I mean?"

Claudi shook her head.

"Nah, I guess you wouldn't. But this place is done up to look just like Cyprus Four. That was the last real world we played before we hitched ourselves to this bandwagon bound for nowhere." Lanker grunted. "I guess that wouldn't mean much to you, either. But Cyprus was a place I was sorry to leave." He tugged at his suspenders. "Still, when the train pulls out, you've got to go or be left behind. That's the way it is in this business."

Claudi twisted her hair around her left hand. She wasn't exactly sure what he meant, but she did remember that Cyprus IV had been *Charity*'s last stop before they'd gone into the starstream. "My mom says that we're going to be on the frontier," she said, feeling somehow that she had to defend being here. "That's why we're going down the starstream."

Lanker's eyebrows danced. "The frontier, eh? Well, I guess so. Me, I'm here to be in the circus. Everything else just comes with the territory."

"Is this what Cyprus Four looks like?" Sheki asked, turning one way, then the other.

"Pretty much. Where *we* were, anyhow. A planet's a mighty big place, you know. There're all different kinds of land on any world." Lanker's eyes seemed to focus far away. "They're changing it tomorrow, though. That's why I'm here—to drink in the memories one last time." He sighed and looked for a moment as though he had forgotten the kids.

"They're going to change it?" Claudi asked timidly.

"Yeah, they're going to change it. Ah, hell, it's not really *my* place, I guess. But I do think of it that way sometimes. It'll be all right." He looked sharply at the two. "You think?"

Claudi opened her mouth in uncertainty. Was he asking her opinion? This man was confusing—frightening, rough, demanding—not at all like the performer she had seen on the stage. She looked up at him, but didn't answer.

Lanker barked another laugh. "Here I am, blowing on about it and it doesn't mean diddly-scut to you. You know what they're putting in here? A bloody *aviary.*" He squinted at them. "You know what that is?" They shook their heads. "A ruddy *bird*house."

"Wow!" Sheki said. "You mean, with real birds?"

Lanker looked surprised at his enthusiasm. "Oh, yeah. Real birds. They've got them in the zoo section. Most of 'em are on ice now, until they get the habitat set up." He made a sweeping gesture. "This'll all be trees, pretty soon. Different kinds. I don't think any of these will stay."

"What's going to happen to them?" Claudi asked.

"Construction-specks. NAGs. They'll take care of them. Disassemble 'em." Lanker's gaze shifted around. "Take 'em apart molecule by molecule, and put 'em back together again different. That's how they do it. And you'd be amazed how fast. In a couple of days, you won't recognize this place."

"Won't it take a lot of people?" Claudi asked, looking at the dunes and thinking of moving all that sand around.

Lanker snorted. "People! It won't take any *people* at all. Once they've got the NAGs programmed, why, they just come in and spray 'em all around. Then they get the hell out and let the NAGs do the work. All this sand, and the trees and water—all that'll be raw material. When it's done, they might come in and trim it up a bit."

Claudi hated to think of this lovely sand playground disappearing before she even had a chance to use it. She imagined racing up and down over the dunes, tumbling and sliding. And before she even knew what she was saying, the words were out. "It'd sure be fun to bring Lopo in here and let him run around and play."

Lanker drew back, startled. "Lopo! Well now—" He scratched his bushy head, frowning. "Lopo, huh? Well now, maybe that's not such a bad idea." His eyebrows twitched. "Why don't we go get him? I don't suppose Joe would mind."

"Really?" Claudi cried.

"Sure. C'mon." Lanker led the way through the oasis to the opposite side, and along a path over the dunes. They walked toward blue-sky infinity.

A door appeared, shimmering silver. They walked into the silver, and through a shivery bit of darkness—and emerged in one of the back rooms of the circ-zoo.

Joe Farharto wasn't around the lupeko's quarters, but Lopo reacted the instant he saw Claudi. He bounded to the side of his enclosure, yelping joyously. His coal red eyes gleamed behind the clear wall. Nearby, in several smaller bubbles, was an assortment of small rodentlike creatures. Lopo's cries got them stirred up, too. Soon the room echoed with howls and squeaks.

"Hi, Lopo!" Claudi cried.

"R-r-r-r-yipppp! Klaw-klaw-*klawwdeee!*" The lupeko's tail wagged furiously.

"Hey there, Lopo," Lanker said, taking a silver device off a shelf and touching it to the enclosure wall. "You're starting to talk like a pro. You know Claudi, do you?"

"Rrrr-talk! Rarff! Klawdee, Klawdee!"

Lanker leaned over Lopo, his hair and beard making him look somewhat like a wild animal himself. "Come on out. How'd you like to go for a run with us, hey?"

Lopo's tail thumped loudly.

"Hah! Well, come on, then." He snapped his fingers, down low.

Lopo poked his head through the enclosure wall. He immediately nuzzled his nose against Claudi. She giggled at the wet touch and ruffled his neck. "It's okay?" she asked Lanker, just to be sure.

"I just said so, didn't I?" Lanker clucked his tongue, urging the lupeko out.

Lopo bounded out, grinning a wide toothy grin, eyes

shining brightly. He really looked like a wild creature, Claudi thought. She patted him again, cautiously.

"What's up, Lanker?" called a new voice. "What are you doing with Lopo?" Joe Farharto strode into the room. Claudi looked nervously between him and Lanker.

"The kids want to take him for a run in the oasis," Lanker said.

"Don't you think you ought to check with me first?"

The circus performer shrugged. "You weren't here. I don't see that it matters."

Joe's face reddened. "Well, it does matter. You're not in charge of the animals, Lanker. I am."

"Hey, we're not stealing him. We're just taking him for a walk. All right?" Lanker tugged at his beard with quick strokes of his hand. He looked annoyed.

Joe started to say something, but he glanced down at the kids and hesitated. His expression turned funny for a moment, then suddenly softened. "All right, you can take him to the oasis, I guess. But use this." He pulled out a leash and closed it around Lopo's shaggy neck. "Just, next time, do me a favor and ask me first, okay?" Lanker shrugged agreeably. Joe drew a deep breath and looked at the kids again. "Hi, Claudi. Sheki. Hey, where's Watson?"

"At h-home. We were at the . . . c-circus."

Joe nodded. Claudi wondered if she had caused an argument between Joe and Lanker. Or maybe she'd stopped one. She bit her lower lip and asked, "Is it okay if we play with him a little while?" She just wanted to make sure Joe wasn't mad.

Joe nodded. "Don't mind me. Lanker here just makes me growl sometimes. We grownups aren't always as smart as you kids. Right, Lanker?"

Lanker shrugged. "Guess not."

"Rrrrrr—let's grow, rrrrr, go!" Lopo barked.

"Okay, Lopo," Joe laughed. "Take good care of Claudi, now." He handed the leash to her. "Can you handle him?"

"Sure. C'mon, Lopo!"

The lupeko bounded away, pulling Claudi along at a run.

* * *

The lupeko raced up the sand dunes like a dervish, howling as he chased the ball that Lanker had flung. Claudi raced after him, shouting, and Sheki after her. Lanker watched from under the trees.

Gasping, Claudi reached the top of the dune in time to see Lopo cresting the next one. Seconds later, he reappeared, ball in mouth. He was growling in happy satisfaction. "Yay, Lopo! Bring it here!"

Lopo tossed his head, grinning around the ball. He dashed down the side of the dune, away from Claudi, trying to tease her into chasing him. As she ran after him, he bounded back up the dune and over the top, out of sight. "Come back!" she cried. Laughing helplessly, she fell in the sand and rolled down again.

Sheki hollered triumphantly and charged past her, up over the top of the dune. His yell cut off suddenly, and Claudi heard him say, in a much lower voice: "Hey, Lopo! Wh-what's wrong?"

Claudi scrambled to her feet and clambered up the slope. "What *is* it? Lopo? Sheki?" Panting, she reached the top.

Lopo was standing halfway up the next dune, staring at something. Staring at nothing. A shadow, maybe. The ball had dropped out of his mouth and rolled away. A growl was rising deep in his throat, and it was not a happy sound. Not a happy sound at all.

CHAPTER 14

Roti Wexx'xx was confused. Standing in the bend of the corridor that led to the workshop area, he was trying to decide what it was that he'd heard or felt, or, more precisely, *felk'd.* It had been something very strange, and he thought he could still felk traces of it. It seemed to be coming from the other way down the corridor, toward the ship's core, where the n-space generators ran the length of the ship. He could just felk a glimmer of the ship's n-space emanations, off through that heavy bulkhead to his right—rays of spatial distortion threading out of the core, out into the starstream.

The thing was, most everything on this ship felk'd strange to him. That was mostly attributable to being on a Human-populated ship. Roti liked Humans, but he missed the company of other Im'keks more than he'd imagined, particularly now with all of this business about course changes and Throgs. The other colonists had been roiling with anxieties since it all started. Roti was no stranger to anxiety, but now he seemed to receive a constant, dizzying bombardment of it. Among his own kind, self-imposed boundaries shielded one another from such eddies of emotion; but among Humans, such boundaries seemed minimal, erected blindly. Roti sometimes wondered if he had erred in joining a nearly all-Human ship. But Im'kek ships were few, and he had been eager to join the small enclave of his fellows on Sherrick III, especially in light of political changes at home that had made his school—truthful school!—of historical scholarship unwelcome. He had believed, naively, that he could adequately shield himself from his Human shipmates.

And now, there was this strangeness he was felking, down the corridor. He vacillated, turning one way and the other. He was due at the workshop, and John Melnik would be annoyed with him if he were late. But there was something *wrong* here, something that compelled him, the way an awareness of someone in distress might compel him. This wasn't that. But it was enough *like* that to make him feel that he shouldn't ignore it.

Oh dear. There was so much he didn't understand about Human ships and customs. But suppose somebody really was in trouble. Reluctantly, he crept along the unfamiliar stretch of corridor, toward the central core of the ship.

He felk'd it more strongly.

What he felk'd was something like a dancing bit of light, through a translucent screen. Strangely, though, it made him think of a *dark* bit of light. He could not have described it to any of his Human acquaintances, because it was not the same as *seeing* light; but he had no other way to think of it in Human terms. But he knew that if he should discover anything amiss, he would have to be able to report it in Human language.

As he walked toward the end of the corridor, the felking continued to grow stronger. His own sense of urgency grew with it. He began to walk more quickly, keenly aware of being alone here and wishing that he weren't. He felt the ship thrumming under his feet. He was becoming afraid. But he could not turn around. Not now. The light he felk'd compelled him forward.

The bulkhead door was silent and solid before him.

He stood before it. He could felk the dancing fires of the n-space machines. He could felk a strangeness in those fires. Or perhaps he felk'd the strangeness *through* the n-space fires. He wasn't sure, but he knew that it was something alive. Something straining to reach out to him.

Knowing, deep within, the danger—and yet unable to stop himself—he touched the bulkhead panel. The door winked open, and the fires seemed to brighten, though he could not see them. He stepped through, into another hallway, closer to the ship's core. He felk'd that the fires were bright indeed here. They drew him forward, against his judgment, forward down the silent corridor where passengers were not meant to go. The alive thing beckoned him. A demon of the n-space fires, it seemed to him. A thing of darkness clothed in light.

He paused, rocking back and forth, his mind glazed over with impulses he could not understand or control. Where was he? He hardly knew anymore; he knew only that he was closer to the n-space core, closer to the being. It capered and sang to him.

There was no danger, he told himself dizzily. He could not expose himself to dangerous radiation, not in the corridors. There was no danger. He would only creep forward and observe. . . .

"Sir! What are you doing on this deck? I'm sorry, but you can't—"

Voices, echoing down the corridor. But more than one. A crewman, and . . . and something else . . .

Suddenly Roti was terrified. He couldn't make himself turn to see the crewman. But the other, he didn't need to turn to see; it flickered darkly behind the n-space distortions, leering toward him, calling. What terrible mistake had he made in coming here? *Lexx-ix, ne cammbrk, si gansagansa ixx! Creator, what child is this of yours?*

The thing of darkness flared up blindingly with a light that seemed to devour light, and it came straight toward him, dancing on waves of fire. It felk'd him now, for certain. It reached out a finger and touched him, somehow, on the inside.

And the darkness blossomed in the center of his mind. Roti choked
   and then screamed
      and could not stop screaming.

* * *

Claudi took two steps and felt something terrible in the pit of her stomach. She sank to her knees, clutching at the sand. Her eyes blurred with tears. There was nothing out there that she could see, but there was something she could feel. *Something.* It didn't hurt exactly, but it filled her with dread.

"What's the matter?" she heard Sheki say. But she couldn't turn or speak.

On the next dune over, Lopo took another step upward, his growl deepening. Suddenly he stopped. His ears went back, and his growl flattened into a whine. He lowered his head and sidestepped away from something Claudi couldn't see.

"C-Claudi?"

Claudi couldn't answer Sheki or move. What was out there? What was it? "L-Lopo? What—?" she started to say, but couldn't finish, as a shiver went up her spine. She felt a sudden inner strangeness, and a sense of dividing from herself. Her *virtual presence.* It was a more powerful sensation than she'd ever felt before—as if one half of herself was stepping forward to meet the . . . *thing.* To see what it was. What it wanted.

Was that a glimmer, dark and shadowy, near the top of the next sand dune? She couldn't quite tell; her eyes were blurry, but it was as though her virtual half could see something, nevertheless, something large but faint, dancing, dancing on the air. Something alive . . .

And it was drawing back, as though startled to see her.

The lupeko's growl deepened again, perhaps given courage by Claudi's presence. "Rrrrrrrr-gohhh-wwwayyyyy! Gowwwaaayyyy! *Rrrrrr!*"

"Hey, what's going on up there?" called a voice behind her. Claudi felt dizzy. Her throat was dry. She'd forgotten about Lanker. Could he help? The thing seemed to be shimmering, disappearing.

"Ggrrrrrr—batsssss! *Gowwwayyy, batssss! Rowrrrrr!*"

"Claudi? Lopo? What's going on?" Lanker's voice sounded closer.

Claudi tried to take a breath. There was a tightness in

her chest that let go just a little. It was like in her dream, when she had been afraid, but the fear had eased. The thing had *seen* her, and had gone away. She felt a twinge, as her virtual presence faded and she became whole again. She tried to speak, to make a sound come from her mouth.

"Hey! Are you all right?"

She nodded without turning.

Suddenly Lanker was beside her, towering over her. "What was it? What's going on?"

Claudi blinked and finally drew a sharp breath, so hard it made her chest hurt; but the feeling of release almost made her cry. She felt Lanker grip her arm, and that did make her cry out.

"Dammit, say something!" Lanker glared at her, then across at Lopo, who was poised in a crouch, teeth bared.

"Lopo—we—saw something," Claudi whispered.

"Saw what? Lopo! What is it? Tell me!"

"Rrrrr-*batssss!* Devvill batssss!" Lopo rumbled, without looking around. His ears, flared sharply, relaxed a little. He trotted up the dune, sniffing. From the top, he surveyed the area, then gazed back with blazing eyes. "G-gonnne, rrrrff," he huffed. He trotted back to join them and gazed up at Claudi, sniffing her. "Rrrr, sssssssafffe," he muttered. "Youuu, rrrr . . . sssaw, rrr, *batssss* . . . rrrannn."

Claudi hugged him, burying her face in his fur. "You chased it away, Lopo. You got rid of it." Lopo purred, then licked her neck, making her laugh in spite of herself. Lanker was frowning in puzzlement, thumbs hooked in his suspenders. Sheki, too, stood beside her.

"What was it, Claudi?" Sheki asked in a small voice. "Was it another ghost?"

Claudi nodded. "I think so. I couldn't quite see. But Lopo did, I think." She shuddered. "It was *awful.*"

"*Ghosts?*" Lanker said impatiently. "What are you kids talking about?"

"Rrrrr, yes—and an*otherrrr,*" Lopo muttered. "Anotherrr."

Claudi was uncertain what Lopo meant. Another *ghost?*

"I saw it," she said, "Sort of, anyway. I felt it! It was here!"

Lanker's scowl deepened. "Felt *what?* What's this about ghosts? I don't have time for foolishness."

"I don't know, exactly. I just know . . . we saw something like this before, something—" And she hesitated. Now she'd done it. Mr. Zizmer had told her not to spread it around.

Before she could continue, Lopo rumbled, "Rrrr, not-t-t good. The otherr hurrrt-t-t, rrrr. Batsss—and *lightssss.* Grrrrrr."

Lanker scratched his bushy head and squinted down at the lupeko. "What do you mean, Lopo? What other? And what bats? There aren't any bats in here."

"Rrrrrrrr. *Rrrr.*" Lopo pawed at the sand.

"Lopo—you can talk better than that."

"Rrrrrr!"

Lanker grunted and shook his head. "Kids, I think maybe it's time we took Lopo back to his cage."

"But—" Claudi began.

"No buts. Let's get going. Anyway, I have another show to get ready for." Lanker clapped his hands decisively and pointed toward the door.

Claudi and Sheki exchanged worried looks. But with Lopo trotting alongside and Lanker following with heavy footsteps, they headed for the oasis exit.

Joe Farharto was feeding the rodents as they trooped back in. He looked puzzled as he accepted Lopo's leash back. "Why's everyone so quiet? Did Lopo bite somebody?" His gaze shifted to the lupeko, who sat silent beside Claudi. "Did you have some trouble, guy?"

Lopo made a snorting sound.

Joe raised his eyebrows. "Well, don't everybody answer at once."

Claudi wanted to explain. But Joe hadn't believed her before, when she and Sheki had seen the ghostlike man. And Lanker hadn't believed her this time.

Lanker shook his head. His bushy hair swayed, as though in a shifting breeze. "They saw something in the oasis. Damn if I know what, but it got *them* upset, *and* Lopo. Maybe there's some NAGs work already started in there. I don't know. More likely, one of their games just got out of hand."

"No!" Claudi protested. "There *was* something!"

"Well, that's what Lopo said, too." Lanker shrugged. "I didn't see anything."

Joe urged Lopo into his enclosure. The lupeko sighed heavily, licked Claudi's hand, then stepped into the opening. "Batsss!" he grumbled as he went in. "Batss were therrre, rrrrrrr!"

A disturbed look came over Joe. "What did you just say, Lopo? Did you say, 'rats'?"

Lopo stuck his head back out. *"B-batsss! Rrr, batssss!"* Grumbling, he pulled his head back and waited for Joe to seal off the enclosure.

"Bats," Joe repeated.

"Rrrrrrr," Lopo said. "A-t-t-ttacked . . . rrr, the other-rrr."

"Attacked *who*?"

Lopo shook his head back and forth. "Otherrr, rrr, keeper-r-r, rrr."

Joe scratched his head. "Do you know what he means, Claudi?"

She shook her head.

"Well, was *someone* being attacked?"

Claudi fidgeted. "I just . . . *something was there,* that's all. I felt it."

Joe looked thoughtful. She couldn't tell if he believed her. "Claudi—did you say anything to Lopo about bats, before this happened?"

"Huh?"

"Remember when we visited Baako? She said something about bats, wanted me to keep the bats away?" Joe shifted his gaze to Lanker. "I couldn't figure out what she was talking about. I asked her teacher and it couldn't tell me much—but it didn't seem all that surprised, either."

Lanker snapped his suspenders, with a shake of his head. "I'm beginning to think you're *all* bat-happy," he muttered. "But I'll leave you to figure it out. I have a show to put on."

"Doesn't anyone believe us?" Claudi asked, stamping her foot. "My teacher believes me!"

Joe seemed chagrined by her outburst. "Now wait, Claudi—it isn't that—"

"Yes, it is! You think we're imagining it!"

An unreadable expression crossed Lanker's face. "Bye, everyone," was all he said.

Claudi stared after him. "Look," Joe said, drawing her attention back. "It's not that I don't *believe* you. It's just that I can't imagine what you saw."

"Well, *I* don't know, either!" Claudi said, aggrieved. "Do you?" she asked Sheki. The boy shook his head.

"Well," Joe said, "maybe next time I'll be there to see it with you."

Claudi shrugged unhappily. She reached in and rubbed the top of Lopo's head. "Bye, Lopo."

"Rrrfff. Clau-deee. Come-rrrrrrr, backkk," yipped the lupeko, thumping his tail.

"I will," she promised, then said to Sheki, "Guess we better go talk to Mr. Zizmer."

"Well, come back," Joe said. "Lopo may be going out into the zooshow gallery soon. But you'll always be welcome to visit him. Okay? You, too, Sheki."

They both nodded. Then they headed out the door.

With Claudi gone, Lopo huffed to himself, trying to think how he could explain it to Joe. He had seen the bat-things through that shimmery, tunnelly sort of thing that he saw sometimes now—and they had been attacking someone . . . someone who looked like another keeper. At first, Lopo had tried to chase them away, but they didn't seem to see him. Then Claudi's face appeared, floating, staring at them. And they saw her and fled. He didn't understand. It was a nightmare memory. He wished he could forget it.

But Claudi had been upset, and that made him upset. He knew, somehow, that he should find a way to explain it all to the keepers. But he couldn't; they didn't believe him, and he didn't know how to say it better.

In the end, moping in the back of his enclosure, he tried to tell his teacher. The teacher *hmm*ed in response, its bodiless voice dry and whispery as it asked him to explain again. Lopo whined and huffed, lay down with a thump, and tried once more.

* * *

Claudi didn't feel that much better after talking to Mr. Zizmer. He acted interested and seemed to believe her, but on the other hand, he didn't exactly explain anything, either. She left as confused as before. And she couldn't help thinking: Mr. Zizmer isn't really human anyway, so what difference does it make that he believes me? No one else does. Except Sheki—but no one believes him, either.

That evening after dinner, her mother squinted at her with that questioning look of hers. "You aren't talking much tonight, little bird. Is anything wrong?" Claudi shrugged. She'd been trying to watch a viddie with her home headset, but in fact she'd just been staring off into space. The viddie was stupid, anyway. Her mother put down her reader. "How was the circus today?" Claudi shrugged again. The circus? It seemed years ago. Her mother frowned and glanced at Claudi's father, who had his nose buried in some work at his desk. He didn't look up. "Are you thinking about the . . . you-know-whats?" her mother asked softly.

Claudi fiddled with the viddie control, without even looking at the flickering picture. Of course she was thinking about the you-know-whats. How could she not be, after what had happened today? What if it had *been* a you-know-what?

Her mother was watching her intently.

"I don't know," she said, with another shrug.

Her mother's right eyebrow went up in a sharp little peak, which Claudi recognized as meaning, *we are about to have a talk.* Somehow she didn't mind—though at the same time, she was afraid to talk about it. Her mother patted the bench-sofa beside her, and Claudi moved over closer to her. She felt her mother's arm encircling her, and she sighed, wishing she could just forget the you-know-whats and be safe.

"Claudi?"

She looked up, to see her mother's other eyebrow arched. She didn't know anyone who could do that as well as her mother. It meant, *don't even think of ducking the issue.* "Uh-huh," she said.

"I thought we talked when we had problems. Don't we?"

Claudi felt her head wobble on her neck as she tried to answer. "It's . . . so hard to explain," she said gloomily.

"Aha. Well, then." Her mother paused, and she looked up into her mother's sharp gaze. "Usually, when something is hard to explain, that means you should try, anyway." Eyebrow again. "And if I don't understand it the first time, you can try again." Claudi hesitated, and her mother added gently, "At least give me a *chance* to understand."

Claudi sighed. "Well . . . the thing is, nobody believes me."

"Nobody? You haven't tried us yet, have you?"

"That's not what I meant. I didn't mean that."

"Well, then, little bird?"

Claudi grunted, but it came out as a half giggle. Her mother could always make her laugh with that name, even when she was feeling gloomy. Her father had nicknamed her that when she had tried imitating birds in the zoo, back home. She sighed again. "Well, Joe Farharto didn't believe me. Or Lanker . . ." And finally she began to tell her mother about what had happened today at the oasis; and then about that face that she and Sheki had seen; and then about the dream that she had forgotten to tell her about, before. And she got sort of upset telling it, because when you told it all together like that, it really packed a punch. And it sure seemed to her like there must be Throgs involved.

Her mother made soothing sounds, but it was impossible to tell what she thought about it. "Do you believe me, Muth'?" Claudi asked finally, snuffling.

"What a question! Of course I believe you."

Claudi wiped her eyes. "Good."

Her mother studied her for a time. Her father continued to work quietly, in the corner. "I can see how that would all be scary," her mother said finally. "I wish you'd come to tell me about that dream sooner."

She shrugged. "I forgot, I guess."

"Well, that would explain that, then." Her mother hesitated. "I wish I could explain the rest of it to you—"

"What *was* it, Muth'? Mr. Zizmer says he's still trying to figure it out."

Her mother shook her head slowly. "I wish I knew, honey, I wish I knew. But I don't." She glanced thoughtfully at Claudi's father, still silently working across the room. Something was making her uneasy. "Claudi, did your Mr. Zizmer—did he say anything to you, like maybe you should talk to someone else, by any chance? Anyone, say, at the deck-school?"

Claudi shook her head.

Her father spoke for the first time, startling them both. "If you mean the wall-shrink, I don't think that's necessary —do you, dear?"

Her mother's right eyebrow shot up. "John—"

"Well, I think we can trust Claudi, if she said she saw something—"

"Fath'," Claudi interrupted. She hadn't even known her father had been listening. "Do you think it was Throgs I saw?"

Her father turned off his note-reader and swung his chair around. "I wouldn't think so, Claudi-bird. I can't say for sure. But you know the captain's being very careful to steer us clear of them. And I think we would all have heard about it if there were Throgs around."

"I think Mr. Zizmer thinks they're Throgs."

Her father studied her for a moment, and she thought sure he would have an answer. However, he simply shrugged. "Anything's possible. But I wouldn't worry too much about it. I've never heard of Throgs just lurking around like that, for one thing. So I doubt that it was Throgs."

"Amen," said her mother, who looked noticeably disturbed by this turn of conversation. "At least I should hope not. Better if we never see or hear anything more of them, ever."

Claudi blinked. There was a moment of awkward silence.

It was her mother who broke it. "Claudi—" She tried to smile, but it came out looking all wrong. And her voice sounded strained. "You know, Claudi—it seems like you're making an awful lot of new friends—faster than I can keep up with them, anyway. Who do you have now? There's Sheki and—Joe, was it? Joe Far—"

"Farharto."

"Yes. And . . . Lanker, was it?"

"And Lopo," Claudi said.

"Of course. And Lopo. That's a lot of new people to get to know."

Claudi was puzzled. "Is that bad?"

"No, no! Not at all! It's good. And you have a real gift for it. But with all those people who don't know you well—" her mother paused, groping for words—"well, there's room for misunderstandings, that's all." She looked perturbed. "I'm not saying this very well, I guess. But what I mean is—well, sometimes things happen that can be hard to understand. Take Lopo, for instance. Now, he reacted to *something* in that place, that oasis—and we know, or you know, that it spooked him. But it might have just been something unfamiliar to him. And what *you* felt might have been his reaction, his fear."

"But Muth', I *saw* something! I *saw* it!"

"I know, dear—I know you saw something."

And that was when Claudi began to realize that her mother didn't *really* believe her about the thing today—or the face in the zoo, either, or the sun in her room. Her mother thought she was imagining it! Claudi sat back, stunned. Her own mother!

Closing her eyes, she tried very hard to be adult about this, to think things through. Joe didn't believe her, or Lanker, or her mother. Maybe . . . it wasn't their fault. Maybe it wasn't possible for any grownup to believe these things. It wasn't that they didn't want to believe her. It was that they *couldn't*. Maybe it was something only she, or sometimes Sheki, could see—because they were kids.

Maybe . . . even for kids, maybe she and Sheki were special somehow. It was possible. And that would mean that she had to be especially alert in the future. Because . . . well, Mr. Zizmer had even told her that she might have special abilities, and therefore a special responsibility, too.

"Claudi?"

She blinked her eyes open.

Her mother was gazing at her worriedly. So was her father. They probably wanted to know what she was thinking. But she didn't really want to tell them now.

Her mother struggled for words again. "I was just . . . thinking about your grandfather, Claudi. I wish you could have known him."

"Huh? I know Grandpa. We said good-bye to him at the spaceport."

Her mother gave her a hug. "I mean your other grandpa. My father. You never knew him. But I think he might have understood what you're feeling. You're a bit like him, you know. He had a very special quality, a real way with making friends. People just seemed to take to him, to trust him. And I think I'm starting to see that happen in you, too." Her mother looked down at her, eyes warm with love. "It's wonderful. It's a precious gift, Claudi, and I hope you never take it for granted. Your friends should be very special to you. Always remember that."

It surprised her to hear her mother talk that way. She didn't know her mother thought about stuff like that. "I will," she promised.

Her mother hugged her again, tightly. "Good."

Her father rose. "Maybe it's about time for bed now, little bird. What do you say?" He ruffled her hair, walking past.

Claudi nodded. But she wasn't thinking about bed, or about her friends even; she was thinking about the visions, and whatever Lopo and she had seen. The next time it happens, she thought, I'll know I'm not imagining it. Even if nobody believes me. I have to remember that. I'm not crazy. And neither is Lopo.

Mr. Zizmer believed her. Mr. Zizmer was the one she would tell.

CHAPTER 15

Perhaps you are wondering: What possible connection could exist between Claudi's grandfather and the current situation? The answer, and I thought you would never ask, is noliHuman genes.

Georg Steffan, father of Audrey Steffan Melnik, was half noliHuman, which meant that Claudi Melnik, two generations later, carried a genetic inheritance that was one-eighth noliHuman. Claudi was quite unaware of it at the time; but could it have been a factor in her unconscious behavior, and in the behavior of others towards her? We thought so—*we* being myself, as well as her teacher, which is not the same thing as myself, and certain other aspects of the shipboard intelligence system.

We knew, of course, from routine scanning of the passenger records, that Claudi was part noliHuman. This was interesting, but not world-shaking; she was hardly the only part-noliHuman in the galaxy, though there weren't as many as you might think, either. But there were other things about Claudi that made us wonder. She had received Logothian training early in her childhood, from a family friend of the Melniks back on Baunhaven, a

Logothian named Naka'Gazean. This too was provocative, though not enough to single her out for anything more than watchful attention.

But as I watched her during the course of the voyage, I was slowly coming to wonder if she might be one of those "wild card" individuals whose pivotal roles in history could only have been guessed at beforehand by a combination of information, intuition, and luck. Willard Ruskin, the creator of the starstream, was one such individual; Claudi Melnik, I surmised, had the potential to become another. Still, even I was surprised when Claudi, apparently quite unconsciously, and yet in an almost Logothian fashion, began projecting "virtual presences" of herself before others, especially during moments of excitement or stress— and when others began responding to her with unusual trust. I was convinced from that moment on that Claudi's attributes were something special, something that might conceivably prove valuable to my mission.

A word about virtual presences and Logothians. The Logothians—of whom the tele'e'Logoth are the best known—are a vaguely humanoid race, often called serpent-men because of their reptilian appearance and gait. Well. Some object to the term "serpent-man" on the grounds of alleged unfavorable racial connotations. Whatever. The point is that trained tele'e'Logoth are capable of empathic communication among themselves, and occasionally across racial boundaries. One of the most famous of the Logoths was Ali'Maksam, who disappeared along with Willard Ruskin in the supernova that created the starstream. We learned at that time that even Logothian capabilities were enhanced by the effects of K-space and n-space transitions. What else besides the power of virtual projection might Claudi have picked up, perhaps unwittingly, from her parents' Logothian friend? I was beginning to wonder.

I have already noted her aptitude for bonding with others—or actually, for inducing others to bond with her. We observed it in Sheki Hendu's adoption of her as a friend— his first real human friend aboard the ship. We observed it in Lopo's instant adoration of her. We observed it among the circ-zoo employees. Even Lanker, notorious among his coworkers for a generally contrary attitude, softened in the presence of Claudi.

And we observed it even in Ruskin/etc./New, though our understanding of that came only later.

About noliHumans: they are a genetic offshoot of ordinary Humanity. Like Logothians, they are noted for their empathic abilities, though theirs tend to applications different from Logothian powers. NoliHumans are noted for their inquiries into the nature of pure consciousness, which is one reason why so many of them are drawn to the Querayn Academies, my employer. They tend to be a dreamy and meditative lot. It is often said, usually by their detractors, that they live only in the present. Despite their empathic capabilities, they are not generally regarded as warm by most people. They are not unemotional, but are often too inward-focused to display much outward warmth.

Does this sound like Claudi? Hardly. But Claudi was only one-eighth noliHuman, and in the rest of her makeup, she seemed to have inherited a high rating for human attractiveness. Put all of these factors together with Logothian influence, add a large dash of the unknown, and what do you get? That was what I wondered. Sometimes I thought even the Mr. Zizmer program was susceptible to her charms. Thank heavens that I myself was not. Somebody had to keep a level head in all of this.

The wild card effect. That was how I had come to think of it. I, perforce, was learning to live with the unquantifiable—even to savor the thrill of uncertainty, the daring of intuition. It was not part of my original mission, but there it was. I admit that I was not then as sensitive to the subtle ethical issues of meddling in the lives of children as I am now. Perhaps that's why I feel slightly uneasy about telling you all of this.

In case you're wondering what *I* was doing there, let's just say that the Querayn Academies felt so strongly about potential occurrences in the starstream that they put me aboard *Charity* with the built-in IS, to keep my eyes open and if necessary to act. (Did I mention that the Querayn had an owner-interest in Colony Transits, Inc.? No? Well, they did; they diversified a lot, in those days.) Call my assignment basic research, with an option for applied research if the opportunity arose.

It arose when young Ms. Melnik appeared on the scene. I won't claim that everyone approved of all of my acts of initiative during this time, but I did what I felt was best. The important question to *me* was, could any of these fascinating observations be applied to the problem of the Throgs?

Hm?

Captain Thornekan entered the intelligence system center with a sense of dread. His visit to the ship's infirmary had been bad enough. The sight of the near-catatonic Im'kek, who had been found in a restricted area, unable to speak coherently, had shaken the captain deeply. Was there any connection between the Im'kek and the threat of Throgs? That was what he had asked his officers and the med-care personnel to find out.

The message from Liza Demeter had been cryptic but disturbing: *"Suggest you see the latest for yourself, Captain. The evidence grows. . . ."* He'd read that on his screen with as much pleasure as he might have felt discovering a scorpion in his dinner.

The IS center was a close little cubicle, a rat's nest of terminals, interfaces, and holounits. It reeked of garlic. Liza sat in the center of it all, with a slim headset covering her temples, a light-stylus on her finger, and an empty coffee cup at her elbow. She, he realized, was the source of the garlic smell. She looked up as he drew one last breath from outside and closed the door. "I got your message," he said.

Liza handed him a headset. "I thought you'd want to see all of it, and you can see it best here."

Thornekan took a seat and slipped on the headset. He was momentarily aware of his arm touching this woman who served under him, and the awareness stirred a flurry of unrest. It was not an attraction, exactly, though in their time together on the ship he had grown toward a feeling of comfort with Liza. It was something else that he couldn't quite define. Since Myra's death, he often found his reactions to women unpredictable, and often uncomfortable. He shook his head. These thoughts were like a sticky, silken web, clinging to him and distracting him. He exhaled forcefully. "So. What have you got?"

"Why don't I let you hear it in the IS's words." Liza touched the interface controls.

Thornekan watched silently as a small holofigure appeared. A voice in his head identified the figure as the IS-generated teacher-aspect known as Mr. Zizmer. The teacher appeared to be talking to a small child. Thornekan recognized the image of Claudi Melnik, the eight-year-old seer of Throgs and gateway people. He squinted, trying to see her more clearly.

The image flickered, changing—both in the holospace and in his own mind. He suddenly felt as though he were inside Mr. Zizmer's head, unreal though it was, speaking to the young girl. He felt a sense of concern; he felt *belief* in what he was hearing. The teacher's belief? Or the girl's? The teacher's. He was dimly aware of the analytical processing that was judging the reliability of the girl's words, based on an array of physiological indicators and statistical reviews. The reliability of *her* belief in what she was saying was good, and so was the likelihood of the *truth* of what she was saying, based upon its consistency with other findings.

". . . a black shadowy thing. It made me think of what I saw in my dream," she was saying. There was fear in her voice.

"And was that what Lopo meant when he said that he saw bats?" the teacher asked her—and Thornekan was aware of another reference-scene, in which the animal in question reported to its own teacher, which was of course a part of the same IS.

The girl nodded. "He saw it better than I did, I think. But I couldn't tell exactly what he saw."

"Of course not," said the teacher. "But it certainly sounds unusual. If we ever figure out exactly what this is, it'll be thanks to your paying such close attention."

The girl didn't look relieved. "But what if it keeps happening?"

"Well, if it does, just remember everything you see, and

come and tell me right away. That's very important, Claudi. All right?"

She nodded miserably. "But no one believed me, Mr. Zizmer. Joe didn't, and Lanker didn't. They think I made it all up."

"That's not as important, Claudi, as your telling me right away everything that you see. The important thing is that *you* know that you're not making it up. And you aren't, are you?"

Through the eyes of the teacher, Thornekan saw the girl's anxiety. Even as she shook her head and said no, he knew that she was suffering. She wanted to be believed. He felt a desire to do something to help her, and wondered what he could possibly do. The IS was better equipped to help the children than just about anyone on the ship.

As the reference-scene with the girl dissolved, Thornekan wondered: And what does this have to do with the Throgs? In answer, he felt the IS shifting its display to the lupeko's report to its teacher. This exchange was more difficult to follow; the lupeko spoke imperfectly, in halting words. But the description that emerged was clear enough: a dark, shadowlike being with wings and multiple eyes, seeming to pop out of nothingness into the environment room—where holoprojectors existed, but where nothing like this had ever been programmed. The lupeko called the visions "bats"—those being the only creatures in its lexicon that resembled what it thought it saw. It found the things frightening, but did not know why.

Until it saw the thing apparently attacking . . . the "other keeper." The Im'kek? It seemed likely—except that the Im'kek had been found halfway across the ship from the compartment where the lupeko had made its sightings.

And are we to believe that these things are Throgs? the captain wondered. The IS answered in a quiet voice: "The description, supported by memory-scan, bears a remarkable resemblance to sightings made by another lupeko, named Baako."

So maybe they talked, the captain thought.

"No known communication has occurred between the two lupekos, nor are they known to be telepathic. This apparently rules out so-called power of suggestion between the lupekos. Furthermore, observe these historical records. These sketches are based upon reports compiled from previous encounters with Karthrogen in which persons with supersensory capabilities survived long enough to record perceptions."

Thornekan grunted as the holospace filled with artists' conceptions. There wasn't much consistency among them. Many of the creatures were nightmarish fantasies, things with teeth and claws, or amorphous beings that threatened to envelop victims; a few looked like beings of startling beauty, aquatic-appearing creatures; and one was dark and shadowy, with large, sharp-tipped wings over the shoulders, and at least five eyes. "Damn," he murmured.

"Indeed. The correlation is high," the IS remarked. "Also, certain words spoken by the injured Im'kek passenger, Roti Wexx'xx, suggest a connection, though he remains generally incoherent."

Thornekan's mouth tightened. "Do you have any idea *how* the lupekos see these things?"

"Not specifically. But consider. Since Lopo received vision correction through a med-speck operation, he has reported seeing lights. These lights seem to bear no relation to the room lights in the circ-zoo quarters. The following representation is based upon Lopo's description and memory-scan, as recreated by my graphics aspects." As Thornekan watched, the holospace expanded to show a series of lights surrounding him, drifting by, as though he were floating down some sort of pathway. He felt the hairs on the back of his neck stand up. This looked familiar, all right. He felt no surprise when the system superimposed another graphic.

"This is the appearance of the starstream at the approximate time of the lupeko's sightings. The nearest starblurs are quite similar to the lights present in Lopo's vision."

Thornekan was suddenly aware of Liza staring at him. He tried not to shiver as he assimilated this new information. "How did that . . . animal . . . see images recorded by our nav-system?"

The IS made a clearing-of-the-throat sound. "We find no

indication that he could have. Our supposition is that the lupeko has gained an ability to see extradimensionally."

The captain hesitated, swallowing. "Elaborate."

"The explanation most consistent with these sightings is that Lopo—perhaps by an accident of design—has acquired the ability to view outside the internal continuum of the ship. He appears to have what one might call 'n-space vision.' Whether this is true only within the star-stream is unknown. Also, whether it is shared by Baako is unclear, since Baako has reported only the Throglike images, but not the lights."

"Hell's own fires," Thornekan muttered. He closed his eyes, and saw sparks against darkness. "In other words," he murmured, "this animal is not only seeing outside the ship, it is seeing *Throgs* outside the ship."

"Quite likely," said the IS. "It may also have witnessed a Throg entry *into* the ship, particularly in the case of the apparent attack on the Im'kek. However, we must be cautious in drawing conclusions."

"What do you mean?"

"The Karthrogen ways of moving through n-space are unknown. Their spatial distance might not correlate in an orderly fashion with our perceived measurements."

"You mean that they . . . may be some distance away, still? Perhaps reaching out to us from a distance? Is that what you're suggesting?"

"The possibility exists."

Thornekan glanced at Liza, then scratched his temple, thinking. "Can you offer any way to clarify the situation?"

"Not at this time," answered the IS.

"Hm. Then I want you to monitor the lupeko's sightings rigorously and report to me. What about the girl? I'd like to talk to her."

"Without wishing to infringe upon your authority, Captain . . . we suggest you allow us to monitor Claudi Melnik as we have been. Undue attention may create self-consciousness regarding her role, which could adversely affect her abilities."

"Do you believe that, or are you just bullshitting me?"

There was a pause. "Could you rephrase the question, please?"

"Never mind." Thornekan sighed. "All right, you can . . ." He hesitated, thinking, not happily. "*No*, damn it." He glared at Liza, then back at the now-empty gray holospace. "No, I'm sick of hearing how you know better. I intend to talk to the girl. If you're so concerned about it, you can provide me with cautionary guidelines."

The IS's voice grew deeper. "Captain, our strong recommendation is to—"

"Screw your recommendation. I've heard it. I don't like it. Those are your orders. See to it."

There was a moment of silence. Then: "Very well, sir. As you wish."

Another moment of silence. "Good," the captain said. "Breaking interface."

The holospace went dark.

Thornekan removed his headset and met Liza's gaze. Her eyes were dark with worry. "Thanks," he said.

She nodded, a fraction of an inch. "What are you planning?"

"Talk to the girl. Judge for myself. Do you have any better suggestions?"

"No. But Captain—"

"What?" He felt wearier than ever. The air in the room seemed staler than ever.

"Do you believe it? Do you think the system is right?"

He stared at Liza for a moment. She was the IS chief. Why was she asking him? Because—of course—if the system was right, and the Throgs had made contact, then *Charity* had no choice but to face them alone. He looked away. "No," he said. "I don't believe a word of it. I think the system is crazy, deluded. But I have to pay attention, don't I?" He paused. "Do *you* think it's right?"

Liza drew a slow breath. Staring at the bank of terminals, she said, "I wish I could tell you, skipper. I really do."

Thornekan nodded. "I wish you could, too, Liza." He turned to leave. "I sure do wish you could, too."

CHAPTER 16

John Melnik puttered for a time at the workshop, wondering what the devil was keeping Roti Wexx'xx. The Im'kek was usually quite punctual, but today he was twenty minutes late already—and yesterday he hadn't shown up at all. John had grown to like the fumbling, good-natured Im'kek, and he hoped nothing was wrong. Besides, he didn't feel like working on this log cabin alone. He drew the blade through a half-finished notch, slicing a little deeper with each stroke. After a while, he blew away the accumulated shavings and stepped back to examine his handiwork of stacked logs.

Some cabin, he thought with a shake of his head. Not that they expected to complete an entire structure—there wasn't enough room here, anyway. They, and several other teams, were just building sections to get the basic idea. Nobody really expected to build a log cabin on the new world; John himself planned on working as a designer and manufacturer of bio-optronic control circuitry. But basic carpentry was among the skills that it was deemed prudent to have, in the event the colony should somehow be cut off with a failing industrial base, particularly of construction nano-assemblers. They were learning a number of skills that they didn't expect to need. But help could be many light-years away, and self-sufficiency was the byword.

John supposed he should get on with this work by himself, or else find himself a new temporary partner. But he couldn't help worrying about Roti. He was the only Im'kek on the ship, and John suspected that he was one of Roti's few friends. It didn't seem right just to ignore his absence.

John carefully replaced the edge-guards on his tools and threaded his way across the workshop. The super was bent over his library screen, and he didn't look up until John cleared his throat. "José—"

José was a short, massive man with a wide chin and dark eyes. He raised his eyes without moving another muscle. "Yeah, John."

"Any word on why Roti's out?"

"Nope. Want me to assign you to another team?"

John shook his head. "I guess not. But I'm kind of worried about him. I feel like I ought to check up on him or something. What if he's sick and nobody knows?"

José finally lifted his chin a fraction of an inch. "You gone by his cabin?"

"No, but—" John frowned—"I mean, what's Im'kek etiquette on unannounced visitors? Suppose he's—I don't know, in the middle of some purification ritual or something."

José shrugged one shoulder. "Damn 'f I know."

"Yeah." John thought a moment. "Mind if I use your com here?" He swiveled the unit toward himself and signaled Roti's cabin.

"No one is in that cabin now," the com answered. "Would you like a forwarding connection?"

"Yes, sure." John scratched his head.

"Med-care. How may I help you?" answered a synthesized voice.

"Med-care?" It took John a moment to recover his poise. "Yes . . . why, I was trying to reach, uh, Roti Wexx'xx. He's an Im'kek. Is he, by any chance—there?"

There was a short pause. Then a woman's voice, a real voice, came on. "Hello, are you calling for Mr. Wexx'xx?"

"Yes. Is he there? Is anything wrong?"

"I'm sorry, but Mr. Wexx'xx is in solitary care. No further information is available at this time."

John blinked, stunned. Even José looked up finally, with an expression that verged on concern. "What do you mean, no further information? Can't you even tell me what's wrong with him?"

"I'm afraid—"

"Is there anyone I can talk to?"

The woman answered smoothly, "You may come talk with the director of care, if you like."

He drew a breath. "Thank you. I will." He snapped off the com and turned it back to José. "I'll be in med-care, I guess." And he strode out toward the nearest lift.

John had only been to the ship's infirmary once before, during preflight orientation. Pausing in the corridor outside, he peered through the clear panels that blocked off the various reception areas and wondered who was in charge. It looked as if the machines were. Passing through the door, however, he found a handful of patients and a gray-haired woman sitting behind a desk. "I'm here to see about Roti Wexx'xx."

"You must have just called," the woman said. "I'm afraid he's in restricted care, but let me see if I can get you the director. Your name?"

"John Melnik."

She placed a small disk to her temple. "And your relationship to Mr. Wexx'xx?"

John hesitated. "Friend."

She nodded and spoke silently. A moment later, an inner door opened. A middle-aged, rather heavy man with thinning black hair emerged and ushered him back into an office. "Mr. Melnik?"

"Yes. You're the director? I was wondering about—"

"The Im'kek. Yes." The man stuck out his hand. "I'm Peterson. I understand you're a friend of Mr. Wexx'xx's?" John shook hands, nodding. "Good. I think he may need a friend."

"What's wrong? May I see him?"

The director didn't answer at once. He seemed to be

sizing John up. "First I must ask your commitment on something."

John waited.

"That is that you keep this matter completely confidential," Peterson said. "Even from your coworkers or family."

"Okay. But why?"

"Well, *any* information here is confidential. But especially this. By order of the captain." Peterson hesitated. "It's . . . well, call it a psychiatric matter."

John stiffened, chilled by the words. *"Psychiatric?* I see. Of course, I will. But . . . what's *wrong?"*

"We don't know." Peterson waved John back through an examination room. "He was found in a restricted area, nearly unconscious and unable to speak coherently. We can find no organic cause, and his condition has not changed. Clearly he suffered a trauma, but we don't know what. We're taking precautions against infectious danger, of course, but I don't think that's the problem."

John was dumbfounded. A psychiatric breakdown? He was definitely out of his element here. He wanted to help, but . . .

"Come on, I'd like you to try to speak to him." Peterson led John down a short hallway and into a tiny sitting room, with a clear enclosure wall. Beyond the wall was an isolation room—and a tall, still form floating horizontally in a levitation field. The sight sent shivers down John's spine. Roti appeared to be gazing at the ceiling. Peterson touched a switch. "You can speak from here."

John hesitated. He didn't know what to say. Finally he bent forward and spoke softly. "Roti? Can you hear me? It's John Melnik. *Roti?"*

The figure moved, ever so slightly. Encouraged, John called out more loudly. He heard a murmuring, moaning sound. Was that Roti's voice? He looked at Peterson, who was listening carefully.

"That's about the only response we've been able to get from him. A few words. Nothing more." Peterson looked at John. "The truth is—well, we just don't have the expertise to deal with Im'kek psychiatric disorders. We have the library, of course, but I'm afraid this fits no reference patterns." Peterson's lips were pursed with worry.

"Did something *happen* to him?"

"Wouldn't we like to know."

John looked back at the unmoving Roti. "What can *I* do?"

"Nothing, perhaps." Peterson stared with him, through the enclosure wall. "But we—the captain, especially—would very much like to know what caused this. If there is any way we can possibly reach him . . ." John reacted uneasily to something in the director's tone. "In any case, I think it might be good for him to have a friend here, talking to him—even if he seems not to be responding."

"You know," John admitted, "I really hardly know him. Only from the workshop. I don't know if he has any actual friends."

Peterson studied him with a wisp of a smile. "You came to see him, didn't you?"

John stared back at him, then turned toward the Im'kek and bent forward. "*Roti?* Can you hear me, Roti? Hey—you don't expect me to finish that log cabin without you, do you? *Roti?*"

The Im'kek rolled slightly toward John, but only far enough to stare, his eyes blinking slowly—and emptily, it seemed—over John's head. His face seemed contorted with pain, or fear. John could not distinguish Im'kek expressions well, but Roti was clearly in distress. "*Mawwwwwwwwwwwwwwwwww-xx,*" the Im'kek moaned—then repeated the sound, more softly, twice. His face tightened, and whitened, then relaxed slightly. He rolled back the other way.

John called, repeatedly. There was no response. Discouraged, he turned to Peterson. "I'll . . .. be back. But will you let me know if he . . . if his condition changes?"

Peterson nodded. "Of course. Thank you for coming." They shook hands. And John turned away, saddened more than he could have imagined.

After Claudi left for deck-school in the morning, Audrey Melnik contacted the teaching system to discuss her concerns about her daughter. She assumed that she would be referred to a human overseer of the children's ed department; instead, the holoteacher, Mr. Zizmer, fielded all of her questions directly on the com. Rather to her surprise he, or it, sounded like someone she could trust.

"I quite understand your concern, Mrs. Melnik. When I spoke with Claudi, she was rather upset about what she had seen. I felt that it was important to let her talk it out fully—both for her own peace of mind and for the sake of any factual information she could convey to us."

"Yes, well—of course," Mrs. Melnik said, suddenly confused. The teaching system sounded as though it found nothing alarming in Claudi's reports. "I guess—the question is—do you think Claudi ought to have some more specific counseling? I mean, she clearly takes very seriously what she saw, or thought she saw. And I don't know how much of it—well, is *real*—"

"Excuse me, Mrs. Melnik—but I think I know what you're asking. The answer is, we take it seriously, too."

"I beg your pardon?"

The Mr. Zizmer figure shifted in the holophone. "We do not know exactly what Claudi saw, Mrs. Melnik. But we have reason to believe that something was there, something real."

"Oh." She hesitated. "I thought you just told her that to make her feel better."

The Mr. Zizmer image shook its head with a faint smile. "All of our tests suggest that she is telling the truth as well as she can. Furthermore, independent reports tend to confirm that she is witnessing something real—though we do not yet know what it is."

Mrs. Melnik stared silently. She was astonished, and worse, embarrassed. She had simply assumed, given her daughter's quick imagination, that Claudi was misinterpreting some wholly innocent event. It was alarming, and humbling, to realize that a teaching machine had demonstrated more faith in her daughter than she had. "I—I didn't realize that," she said softly.

"Indeed. But it is fortuitous that you called, Mrs. Melnik. Captain Thornekan just minutes ago asked me to contact you, to arrange a visit to the bridge for Claudi."

"The *captain?*"

"Indeed. He would like to speak to Claudi directly. With your permission, of course."

Mrs. Melnik opened her mouth. She found no words.

"The captain will also want to speak with you and Claudi's father. But if you've no objection, he would first like to see Claudi alone. Would that be all right, Mrs. Melnik?"

"Well—yes, of course. But—"

"Captain Thornekan is quite interested in Claudi's experiences. He is curious whether there is any correlation between her experiences and some other reports he has received."

Mrs. Melnik stared at the teacher's image for a moment. She let her breath out uneasily. "Does this have anything to do with the business about the Thr—, the Karthrogen?" she asked. "Claudi was pretty upset about that, you know."

"We realize that, Mrs. Melnik. We have no wish to upset her unnecessarily, I assure you."

"Yes, well—but I'm not sure that—"

"Mrs. Melnik, your daughter shows signs of being an exceptionally gifted individual," the teaching system said. "It *is* possible that she has gained information that could be useful to the captain, even if she doesn't understand it herself. Does all of this have anything to do with the Karthrogen? Truthfully, we don't know. But the captain must explore all avenues. Besides—" the image of the teacher smiled—"I have a feeling that a visit to the bridge would be quite a thrill for Claudi."

Mrs. Melnik nodded slowly. "Yes—yes, I'm sure it would be. Of course, I have no objection."

"Thank you," Mr. Zizmer said. "Might I make one more request?"

"Certainly."

"That is simply that you not discuss this outside your family, for the time being. Even among yourselves, treat it in a low-key manner, if possible. To avoid rumor and so on, if you take my meaning."

"I understand," she said, not understanding at all.

The Mr. Zizmer figure glowed. "Fine, then. You may expect a call from the captain soon."

* * *

As the class settled into the morning lessons, Claudi couldn't help noticing that Suze was acting a little unfriendly—not saying hello, not turning in her direction. After a while, she remembered yesterday following the circus show, when Suze had stormed away mad because Claudi had gone with Sheki to the zoo. That was it, Claudi realized. Suze was still mad. She was also paying more attention to Jeremy than usual.

Claudi remembered what her mother had said about valuing her friends, and she wondered if she ought to do something. But she didn't know what to do, or say—and so she didn't say anything. But off and on, she thought about it and it gave her an unpleasant shiver.

Mr. Zizmer still had them talking about the circ-zoo. He showed a surroundie about circuses of past eras, and about big, sprawling, planetside zoos. Claudi figured Mr. Z was probably trying to keep everyone from thinking about the Throgs. As far as she was concerned, it wasn't working.

But she didn't mind so much thinking about them now. She didn't know why, but maybe it was because of what she'd thought about last night. She knew now that she could see things that most people couldn't. Maybe it had something to do with the Throgs, and maybe it didn't. Maybe it had to do with this ghost-person who was supposed to be alive in the starstream. She didn't know. She just knew that she now had something special to do. And for some reason, that gave her confidence. It made her dwell less on the Throgs, and made her less afraid when she did think of them.

Mr. Zizmer would know, if the time ever came to really be afraid.

Her thoughts were interrupted by a surprise announcement from the teacher. "Listen up, kids. Some of you have asked whether you'll ever have a chance to visit the ship's bridge, and perhaps even meet the captain. Well, I have good news for you!" The teacher flashed up a cautioning hand. "Now, the captain can't have the whole class up there at once, as you might imagine! But he can make room for one person. So we are about to have our first lottery! One lucky individual will *visit the bridge* as a representative of the class! What do you think of that?"

What they thought was soon lost in pandemonium. But after a few minutes, Mr. Zizmer calmed them down. He stepped into the viewing-wall—melted right in, as if it were a doorway—and brought up into the wall a 3-D image of a great, ponderous rotating wheel of chance, with names on it. Names like "Jenny" and "Rob" and "Suze." It looked just like a huge paddle wheel, turning toward the class, so that only a few names were visible at any moment. As it turned, those names disappeared at the bottom and others appeared at the top. It rotated just long enough for all of their names to appear once; then it creaked to a halt, like an old-fashioned wooden wheel.

"All right, everyone!" Mr. Zizmer called. "Who wants to come up and give the official spin?"

Seven hands went up. "Okay," the teacher said. "How about Jeremy!"

Jeremy bounded up to the wall. "What do I do?"

"Stand right there." Mr. Zizmer pointed to a spot in front of the wall. "Now, reach up with both hands, as if you're grabbing a great big lever." Jeremy did so, and an image of a giant lever appeared, sticking out of the wall. The class cheered, as Mr. Zizmer said, "Pull the lever, Jeremy! As hard as you can! Pull it!"

Jeremy pulled hard.

With a clatter, the great wheel started spinning, until the names became a blur. It rumbled, and for a time it looked as though it might spin forever and never stop. Then a large arrow appeared beside it, marking the winning spot, and the wheel began to slow. Claudi stared fixedly, hardly daring to hope. The blur of names became more readable, a fast stream. A slower stream. Claudi glimpsed her own name, several times—and Sheki's, and Suze's, and everyone else's. There were muffled cries about the room.

The wheel slowed, ponderously. Claudi clenched her fists as she saw her name appear at the top and glide slowly toward the arrow. Would it stop? No . . . it kept moving, but very slowly indeed. Jenny's name creaked into view— and several kids proclaimed her the winner—but it didn't stop there, either. The seconds seemed endless, as the wheel slowed unbelievably, ticking with each heartbeat.

And finally it stopped.

Under the arrow, once more, was the name, *Claudi*.

Claudi blinked, holding her breath. She had trouble seeing for a moment, then she realized that everyone was staring at her. "Captain Melnik!" Mr. Zizmer proclaimed. "Let's have a big hand for Claudi!"

The other kids started clapping and grinning, and even Suze made a funny little eye-rolling face. Jeremy let out a big snorting sound as he stepped away from the wall, but he was grinning and pointing at her by the time he'd taken his seat.

"Well, Claudi—do you accept the assignment?" Mr. Zizmer asked brightly, stepping out of the wall. "You don't have to, if you don't want to," he said with a twinkle.

Claudi couldn't even laugh at Mr. Zizmer's joke. She was so excited she couldn't even let the excitement out; she felt it just building and building inside her. "When do I go?" she asked timidly.

"Oh, in about two minutes," Mr. Zizmer said.

Claudi's mouth fell open. Two minutes! That made everyone else stir, too, but Mr. Zizmer was ready with a beaming smile. "And for the rest of you, we have something special, too, so nobody feels left out. While Claudi is visiting the bridge, the rest of us will be seeing the opening of the zoo!"

That brought cheers, and for an instant Claudi felt bad that she was missing the first official trip to the zoo. But not that bad. She had, after all, seen it already. And Joe would show it to her again. Besides, she was going to the bridge! As the class quieted down, she was aware of Mr. Zizmer saying something similar: "—have another chance to see the zoo, Claudi. And now, I think I hear an officer outside, waiting to escort you. If everyone would sit tight for a few moments—Claudi, would you come with me, please?" Mr. Zizmer nodded toward the door.

"Go, Melnik!" called one of the boys.

Breathing with some difficulty, Claudi followed Mr. Zizmer. She glanced at Sheki, who was staring with a wide-eyed grin. Somehow he hadn't looked at all surprised.

"Come on, Claudi!" Claudi waved sheepishly to the others and followed the teacher out of the classroom.

A dark-haired woman in the uniform of a ship's officer was waiting outside. All of the little kids, and even Mr. Seipledon, stopped what they were doing to watch. Mr. Zizmer introduced Claudi to the woman. Her name was Ms. Demeter, and she was the head of all the ship's intelligence systems. "She's my boss," Mr. Zizmer said with a wink. "I trust you'll impress her with your impeccable manners and your hard-to-answer questions."

Claudi wasn't sure what *impeccable* meant, but she nodded. "Shall we go?" Ms. Demeter asked. Claudi walked with her toward the lift. She looked back one last time, but Mr. Zizmer had already disappeared back into the classroom. The little kids were still watching. Claudi drew a breath and stepped into the lift with Ms. Demeter.

It was a long ride up to the bridge. The levels flashed by, silently but steadily. Claudi glanced at Ms. Demeter and she smiled back awkwardly. Claudi was excited and terrified, and something about this woman made her nervous. *She* looked nervous, Claudi thought.

"What do you think about getting a chance to see the observation deck?" Ms. Demeter asked.

"Observation deck?" Claudi's voice caught. "Are we going there, too?"

"Didn't your teacher tell you? That's where we're going to meet the captain."

Claudi shook her head. "He just said—the bridge. We had a lottery to see who got to go to the bridge."

"Lottery?"

"Uh-huh. We spun a big wheel, and my name was the one that came up. That's why I'm the one who gets to go." Claudi felt the excitement starting to bubble up again.

"Wow. You *were* lucky!" Ms. Demeter seemed a little puzzled as she looked away. "You're a very lucky girl, Claudi."

Claudi watched as the last few levels passed by. "There it is! There's the observation deck!" she said, as the deck's identifying symbol glided into view.

"We're there," said Ms. Demeter.

They emerged into a deserted lobby carpeted in a deep maroon color with walls of midnight blue. They walked toward a door trimmed with silver metal. The door twinkled and vanished, and Claudi peered into a place that was dark, and yet full of glowing lights. She could hardly breathe as she stepped out into . . . space. It took her breath away. The floor appeared to be made of polished glass, with stars glowing beneath it. The door winked closed behind her, but she hardly noticed. There was a man standing nearby, but she hardly noticed him, either. She peered around in wonderment.

She could almost feel herself floating through a great, glowing starcloud. This was even more wonderful than a surroundie. It *looked* like what she had seen in surroundies, but far more vivid. And it was *real*. She was in a great bubble on the outside of the ship, gazing out at an incomprehensibly wonderful view of the galaxy passing them by. Individual stars were soft globes of fire—some white, some pale gold, some bluish and some tinged with red. Clouds of gases arched and swirled and wove patterns among the stars. And everything, the entire view, was enclosed within a ghostly, glowing tunnel down which the starship seemed to float. It looked a little like the way she imagined Heaven might look.

"It's beautiful, isn't it?"

Claudi turned slowly, her eyes captivated by the view. The man had spoken to her. She looked at him, knowing that it was impolite not to. She didn't know what to say, so she just nodded. The man was tall, and he wore a dark uniform and looked very official, and a voice in the back of her mind told her to wake up, because this must be the captain. But she couldn't keep from moving her eyes back to the stars.

She heard a chuckle, and realized that he was gazing *with* her, out at the stars. "I like to stand here sometimes and just watch it," he said. "I don't have time to do that as often as I would like."

"Can't you do it anytime you want?" Claudi asked.

"You mean, because I'm captain?" She heard another

chuckle. "I wish that were so. I have the power, but rarely the time. Too many worries. That's the curse of being an adult, you know."

Claudi finally woke up—and really looked at the captain.

He stuck out an enormous hand. His sleeve had gold braids on the cuffs. "I'm Captain Roald Thornekan. You must be Claudi Melnik."

Her hand was swallowed in his grip. The power of his presence suddenly seemed to sweep away all thoughts of the view. This was the captain of the ship—the man who steered and guided the vessel, who protected them from the enemy, who knew the way to the heart of the galaxy! The captain! A thought suddenly leaped into her mind: She wondered if she should tell the captain about the things she had seen. Surely Mr. Zizmer would approve of that, of telling the captain.

Captain Thornekan turned with her and pointed out the direction that the starship was traveling. "You see the way down the starstream?" He looked at her, and his eyes seemed sharp and probing, as if he were testing her. But then he smiled. "We *could* go all the way down, way past where we can see now, to the center of the galaxy. And come back the other way, for that matter. But we won't. In fact, we *might* be taking a detour out of here, soon, just as a safety precaution. You know about that, don't you?"

"Uh-huh." Claudi watched the slow movement of the stars. She shivered, suddenly afraid that, standing here at the outside of the ship, they were in danger. Suppose the side of the ship burst open. Or the Throgs attacked.

"Are you all right, Claudi?"

"Uh-huh." She swallowed.

The captain looked down at her with concern. "Are you feeling a little bit dizzy?"

She nodded.

"Don't worry. You're not the first to feel a little woozy here. But you're perfectly safe." The captain gestured to Ms. Demeter, who was standing, silent, off to one side. She did something at the wall, and the floor turned dark and solid. Claudi breathed a little more easily. Then the stars around her dimmed, until it looked as though they were shining in through a soft, gossamer curtain. "How's that? Feel a little more like you're on solid ground now?"

Claudi nodded, but she was confused. "I thought we were—that this was a big *bubble.*" She made a sweeping gesture with her arms, to indicate the observation deck.

The captain nodded. "That's how it's supposed to look. A lot of effort went into making it that way. But no—this isn't a bubble on the side of the ship. Not really. What it is is a wonderful projection room."

"You mean—it's a *surroundie?*" Claudi's voice carried her disappointment.

"No, not exactly." The captain smiled. He seemed to understand her disappointment. "It's a real observation deck. But we couldn't put a bubble outside the ship, not in n-space. So what we do instead is use forcefields that stick out of the ship and bring the image inside. They act like lenses to make all this visible to our eyes, with a little help from the IS. If we were *really* outside, in n-space, we wouldn't see anything that would make any sense to us, anyway." He paused, to see if she was following.

She was, but only sort of. "So we're still inside the ship?"

"That's right. But the forcefields change the actual shape of space, and they make it as *though* we were standing on the outside of the ship. But we can adjust them, like I just had Liza do."

She thought about that. "What if something went wrong with the forcefield?"

The captain scratched his head. "Well, now—that's a good question! It shows you're thinking! What happens if the forcefield fails is, we don't see the stars anymore. But we'd be safe right here, inside a good, solid starship." He thumped his heel on the deck, for emphasis.

"Huh."

"So—you're probably wanting to know just why I asked you to join me here, right?"

Claudi blinked. "Because of the lottery. But I've been *wanting* to come here all along."

"Eh?" Captain Thornekan squinted, then glanced at Ms. Demeter with a frown. *"Lottery?* Is that what they told you?"

Claudi looked at him in sudden worry. "Yes! Wasn't I supposed to come?"

"Why, of course you were supposed to come! Yes indeed, Claudi!" The captain gazed at her thoughtfully. "But would you like me to tell you a little secret?"

She nodded nervously.

"Well—I have some things to ask you, Claudi. And I want you to be perfectly honest with me—just as honest as you can be. I don't want you to bend the truth even a little bit." The captain rubbed his chin as he spoke. "But if I'm going to ask you to do that, then I should be honest with you, too. Wouldn't you say that was fair?"

She swallowed. "I wasn't going to lie about anything."

"Of course not. And neither am I. That's why I have to tell you this." Captain Thornekan's heavy eyebrows went up. "Claudi, there was no lottery. Not really. What happened was, I asked that you be brought up here to speak with me. Your teacher has shared with me a few of the things that you've told him—and I wanted to ask you a few questions about them."

She felt her face on fire. Of course! The captain wanted to ask her about the ghost-creatures! And here she was, wondering if she should tell him. She felt so embarrassed now, she hardly heard him saying, "—that your teacher wanted to send you up here without people asking why. I suppose it was pretty clever. But it was all so that I could talk to you, Claudi."

"You mean—about—"

"Exactly." A cushioned bench seat emerged from the wall, and the captain motioned to her to sit down beside him. "Now, Claudi—according to your teacher, you've had some interesting things happen to you lately. I wonder if you'd be willing to tell me about them."

She blinked, suddenly tongue-tied. "Well—I don't—I mean, which one—?" She looked back and forth between Ms. Demeter and the captain.

Captain Thornekan looked startled. "Well—all of them, I guess. Why not start with whatever happened first, and just tell me what you remember. Tell me in your own words, Claudi." Thornekan glanced at Ms. Demeter. "You don't mind if Liza listens, too, do you? She's one of my best officers. I think you can trust her to hear it. Is that okay?"

Claudi nodded and tried to take a breath. And tried not to cry, even though she wanted to. Because somebody finally wanted to take her seriously.

CHAPTER 17

The captain didn't say anything, but sat quietly staring into space after she'd finished answering his questions. He'd asked her to repeat just about everything she'd said—about the dreams, and the face in the zoo, and what she'd seen with Lopo. And still he'd wanted to know more. But he seemed to believe her.

The stars were coming up slowly, growing brighter. She'd asked to see them more clearly. She was clutching the edge of the bench seat, just to make sure she didn't get dizzy again. The stars were starting to feel like good friends, comforting in a way, and homey. She chewed rapidly on a piece of gum the captain had given her, and stared around at the glowing orbs.

Captain Thornekan was working his own gum more slowly, the way adults did, worrying it slowly with his jaws. He was watching Claudi now, with his eyes half closed, sort of the way she remembered her grandfath' used to watch her while she worked on some puzzle or other that he'd given her, although she didn't think the captain was as old as her grandfath'. When the captain had asked her questions, he'd looked really serious and a little worried, the way *she* would if she were a ship's captain and somebody told her there were ghost-things on board. Throgs. Or whatever.

She couldn't tell what he was thinking.

"Captain?" she said finally.

His eyes opened a fraction wider, but he didn't move from where he sat, back to the wall. "Mm-hm."

"Well—" She took a deep breath. "What do I do if I keep seeing these things?"

He sat forward with a frown. "Do you *want* to keep seeing them, Claudi?"

She shook her head, but it was all a bit uncertain in her mind. "I don't think so. It *scares* me. But—" and she tried really hard to concentrate, to say this right—"well, Mr. Zizmer said that I might—I might have some sort of special . . . *way* to see things. And he said that could be . . . important. I don't know." She swung her legs like short pendulums, feeling self-conscious.

The captain nodded. "It's true, Claudi. It could indeed be important." His tone was cautioning. "But only if—and you have to promise me, now—only if you're *extra* careful to tell me *exactly* what happens."

Blood rushed to her face. "What do you mean? I *did*!"

"Yes, I believe you, Claudi. I do. But there's one thing you have to understand. It's very important." He raised a finger in emphasis and glanced at Ms. Demeter, as if to make sure she was listening, too. "And that's that *sometimes* people don't always see and remember things exactly the way they happened."

"But—"

"Let me give you an example. Suppose—well, suppose two of my crew come to me to report an accident on the cargo deck. Say, they've seen two carryalls collide. Now, they've both seen the same accident, but from different sides of the cargo bay. All right? Are you with me so far?"

Claudi nodded uneasily.

"Okay—they both come to tell me what they saw. Now, neither one would dream of telling a lie. So you might think that they'd both tell me exactly the same thing— because they both saw it, and they're both doing their best to tell the truth. Right?" Claudi nodded again. "Well, in real life what happens is they *don't* tell it exactly the same. The yeoman might say that the first loader was going too fast and hit the second. But the other crewman might say that the second loader turned when it shouldn't have, and caused the accident that way. In fact, to hear them, you might think they'd seen two different accidents altogether!"

"But . . . that doesn't make sense!" Claudi protested. "One of them must be lying!"

"Nope. Remember, I told you—they're both telling the truth, *as best they can remember it.*"

Claudi felt helpless in the face of such illogic. "But it couldn't have happened both ways!"

"That's right." The captain scowled. "The problem is figuring out which is the way it really happened. Maybe *neither* of them is exactly right. Here's the thing, Claudi— and I know this might be hard for you to grasp—but try, because it's important." The captain chewed his gum rapidly for a moment, watching her. "Claudi, *sometimes* when a person is trying to remember something, but isn't *quite* sure of a detail?—well, sometimes the imagination steps in without the person even knowing it, and provides that detail. It seems to be right—only it isn't. That's when we say that our memory is playing tricks on us."

The captain gazed down through the floor, at the stars below. He looked as though something was bothering him. "It happens to all of us once in a while. It happens to me, to my crew, to everyone. It's just human nature. *But*—if you're on the alert for it, then sometimes you can keep it from happening." He looked up again and focused on Claudi. "Do you understand what I'm saying?"

She nodded darkly. She'd never made up *any* details. Ever. And it wounded her that he thought she had.

Captain Thornekan reached out and squeezed her shoulder. "Now, Claudi, I'm *not* saying that this happened to you. But I always make my own crew watch out for it— and I'm asking you to do the same. If you ever remember some little thing—or even think you *might* have gotten something wrong that you told me—why, just come say that to me. Or say it to your teacher. It's much better to tell me than not to tell me. If it ever happens, I mean."

She swung her legs, thinking. Maybe he wasn't saying she'd lied, after all. "Okay," she said softly.

"You still feel okay about everything you told me?"

"Uh-huh."

Captain Thornekan nodded. "Good. Well, then, if anything else like it ever happens—you tell your Mr. Zizmer, and I'll hear about it right away. Okay?"

"Okay."

"Good. Now then, how would you like that look at the bridge that I promised you?" His eyes suddenly twinkled.

Her breath rushed in. "Okay!"

The bridge crew all seemed quietly efficient at their consoles. Captain Thornekan touched her shoulder, guiding her to the center of the bridge. Most of the crew didn't even seem to notice that she was there.

What caught her eye at once was the star pit in front— that was what the captain called it, the star pit—where the image of the starstream shifted and glowed. She recognized it from the surroundies, of course; but it was different, seeing it in person. There was a kind of electricity here: a feeling that each person had an important task and each task was essential to the well-being of the ship. Claudi felt it in her bones. The crew seemed almost like superbeings to her, in mastery of strange and mysterious machines that guided the ship through the starstream. She felt very small, standing near the captain.

A crewwoman to her right flashed her a white-toothed grin, and she remembered suddenly that there was a reason why she was here with the captain; and that was because she had a job to do for the ship, as well. Maybe it wasn't as big a job as the others—but then again, maybe it was.

The captain spoke up in a loud voice, introducing Claudi to the crew. "Everyone—if I may have your attention—" He named one crewmember after another. "That's Len over there, and Ivars . . ." Most of them turned and nodded, or at least waved. Claudi forgot most of the names immediately, but she waved back to everyone. She was a little relieved when the captain took her to stand by his seat, just above the star pit. "Here's where I keep an eye on what's happening."

"You mean you can tell if we're off course just by looking there?" she asked.

"Well, it's more complicated than that. I need these other instruments, too. They tell me what my navigator and pilot are up to." His face wrinkled into a smile. "You know—so I can make sure they're doing their jobs."

Claudi nodded seriously, then realized that he was kidding. Sort of. She sat where he indicated, on a bench seat right beside his own command seat. And while he began checking things over with his crew, mostly in words she didn't understand, Claudi just watched, and let her gaze return to dwell on the magnificent tunnel in space that glowed up at her out of the star pit.

Minutes passed, and she found herself beginning to stare harder. Was that a *face* she saw in the stars . . . and was it looking back up at her . . . out of the star pit? She rubbed her eyes. No, she didn't think so. No—there was nothing there.

But . . . she didn't know why, exactly, but she had this feeling that *someone* was watching her, someone invisible. She stole a glance to either side. No one else seemed to be noticing anything. Maybe it was just her imagination, the way the captain had said. She let her gaze wander back to the star pit. Yes, there it was. In the stars. You had to squint your eyes just right, but *look*—the stars were forming the shape of a face. Definitely. Weren't they?

She looked at the captain. He was busy talking to one of the crew. She struggled to draw a breath, to say something to him; but she couldn't. Her eyes were beginning to blur now. She could only barely make out the face, through the blur. Should she say something? She couldn't be sure anymore of what she was seeing. She remembered what the captain had said about being careful—and that made her afraid of what he might think.

Should she tell him? Should she?

Captain Thornekan made a leisurely survey of the bridge before settling back in his chair. He was intensely mindful of the young girl sitting beside him, undoubtedly trying to make sense of it all. Captain Thornekan was trying to make sense of it, too.

He focused on the image of the starstream, silently reflecting on all that it showed him—and all that it didn't. The colors of the starblurs and starclouds told him things about their rate of travel down the stream, and patterns within the colors told him certain other things. Pale curving grid lines, scarcely visible at first glance, informed him of spatial and gravitational stresses propagating through the stream . . . through this unnatural place where the "real" image of the galaxy was quite impossible to see, and where the limits on movement that applied even in K-space were irrelevant. Space here was bent, twisted, and stretched. It was strained along the thread of the cosmic hyperstring that had preexisted it; and at one and the same time, space somehow *flowed*, as if it were water coursing through a deeply channeled riverbed.

Captain Thornekan did not wholly understand the forces that made it possible for his ship to ride that stream at an apparent velocity of a thousand times the speed of light. No one wholly understood it, at least no one human; but he understood it enough to steer his ship straight and true through the contorted metrics, and to bring it safely in the end to port. He understood his instruments well enough to make the decisions necessary to command the ship safely. Ordinarily, anyway.

He sat in his command seat, where his word was law, and thought of the things that the instruments and the images did not tell him, and could not.

Nothing in the star pit could tell him whether there lived in this gateway the consciousness of the man who had helped create it, or of the star that had died for it. Or whether they could help him, if they did live.

Nothing in the star pit could tell him where the Throgs were, or whether they would attack his ship—or perhaps already had. No Throgs registered in the sensors; it was almost as if they did not exist. If only that were true! He had a passenger lying delirious in the sick bay, a passenger who might already have been a victim of the Throgs. But he had never heard of Throgs attacking that way.

He knew what usually happened where the Throgs appeared, where the Throgs' and Humanity's paths intersected. Even as he sat here in his command seat, he could see, could *feel* the intensity, the heat of the Karthrogen attack on Hassan Harbor, four years ago. It had not been his own world, and he had not even been there. But Myra had been there, on holiday. It was where she'd drawn her last breath, along with a million other people. He had not seen the attack with his eyes, but he could see it now as clearly as if he had been there: n-space distortions flashing through the planet's crust, city structures collapsing to dust. Much later, he had viewed the ruins of that world's cities. And in those ruins he had come to imagine that he could see the attack itself, the attack that had taken his wife from him.

His vision of the Throgs was quite different from Claudi Melnik's. He knew that. His vision was real in its way—but her visions were genuine. At least, so he now believed. And perhaps the Im'kek, too, had visions to tell—if ever he would emerge from his delirium.

But if Thornekan was wrong . . .

The consequences of a mistake were too dreadful to bear imagining. If the Throgs were lurking out there in the starstream, invisible to him and his crew, and he kept *Charity* steady on course . . . this could be his last voyage, the last for his crew, for his passengers. At this very moment, he could see the exit node that might save them —a dark spot almost lost in the glowing clouds downstream. But if he took that path, to save himself and his passengers and crew . . . and the Throgs followed . . .

The vision of a Throg attack shimmered in his mind. A world dying. Another world. An innocent world. A world that had been safe and quiet and far enough from the starstream to be removed from the danger of the Throgs, until a ship fleeing for dear life had come and brought the Throgs along behind.

He trembled where he sat, in his seat of authority. He was deeply aware of the importance of preventing his bridge crew, and in particular this little girl sitting beside him, from detecting his uncertainty, his fear. He knew that he dared not risk another world. Not even to save his ship.

And he knew that in making that choice, he could well be sentencing this young one to death. And yet, even so, he was dependent upon her in a way he could never have imagined possible—as if he, the starship captain, were blind and she were the only one with eyes to see.

He glanced out of the corner of his eye. She was sitting quite still, staring intently down into the star pit. Was she frightened? Was she hiding her fear, just as he was? What did she see in those stars that he couldn't?

He closed his eyes momentarily and thought, I might have had a daughter like that. *We* might have. If things had gone differently, if we had made other choices, years ago. But if we had—would my daughter have died, along with Myra, back on Hassan Harbor? Bad enough to have lost one . . .

"Captain, do you still plan to have the meeting at fifteen hundred?" The voice near his left ear, startling him, was Liza Demeter's. She had stayed close by, to help keep an eye on Claudi. He was grateful for her prompting. Yes, he had to meet with his officers. Decisions had to be made.

He nodded and turned to Claudi, and imagined her trying to hide from a Throg attack. He forced himself to take a breath and smile. "Well, Claudi—have you seen enough?"

She looked up, an expression he couldn't decipher crossing her face, and a surprising intensity in her eyes—probably the excitement of being here on the bridge. Probably she would stay here all day, if he let her. He raised an upturned hand in apology. "I'm afraid I have to meet with my officers. But I'll tell you what. Now, this isn't a promise—"

Claudi's forehead furrowed, and he laughed silently at himself. What was he doing, making a *non*promise to an eight-year-old girl? "If I can manage," he said, clearing his throat, "I'll try to get you up here for another look sometime. How does that sound to you?"

Claudi nodded gravely.

He studied her. "Claudi, is everything all right?"

"Well, I—" She sighed heavily. "Uh-huh. I'm fine."

He narrowed his gaze. "You're sure?"

"Uh-huh."

"Okay, then." He turned. "Liza—could you?" He gestured toward the exit. "Thank you for coming, Claudi. And don't forget—if you have anything you need to tell me—"

"I'll tell Mr. Zizmer," she promised.

Thornekan shook hands with her. "Good. Better get going now."

Claudi turned and went out with Liza.

Thornekan watched them leave. He took his seat again and rubbed his chin. He really *didn't* have a choice. Did he?

CHAPTER 18

It wasn't so much that Sheki was tired of looking at the animals as that he was tired of crowding around with all of the other kids while the zoobot explained this or that, and having the wise guys in the class always jumping in with some smart remark. *Hey, look at that airshark—looks like that thing wants to bite ol' Jenny's butt off! Hohoho!* Real clever, Jeremy.

That was the main reason why Sheki ended up wandering away from the group. He was just going to explore for a minute, but he got sidetracked and found himself in a strange little gallery that was darkened like a tunnel. It was full of tanks of luminous fish and all sorts of glow-in-the-dark animals. Sheki peered around in wonder, both fascinated and terrified. There was an air-breathing creature that puffed and billowed and floated in its enclosure, and glowed with a strange purplish light. There were fish with lanterns and sparkly things hanging off their bodies. There were saucerfish gliding around, their bodies ringed with bright intelligent eyes. He turned his head, taking them all in. It was wonderfully quiet in here; he could no longer hear his classmates.

Still, he was a little disoriented in the dark. He kept glancing toward the exit, afraid of losing his way out. But his mind kept working, scared or not. He peered at each animal in turn—wondering where it was from, what its home looked like, what it ate. Wondering if any of them could see him—especially that shimmering green sea snake with all the teeth.

He turned away from the snake and—*"Uh!"*—drew a sharp breath. A large human face, a man's face, floated in the darkness at the end of the gallery. "Wh-who . . . wh-who . . . are you?" His voice sounded like a squeak toy.

The face didn't answer.

Though startled, he wasn't really frightened of it. It was the same face he had seen before, with Claudi. He was pretty sure of that. He wished Claudi were here now. He couldn't move; he was entranced by the sight. The face seemed to float without a body. But it was alive; its eyes blinked slowly as it gazed back at him.

"Wh-who, who, wh-who—" he stammered, futilely, until he finally quit trying to say it.

"Who are *you*, pilgrim?" The voice was so soft, like a whisper of air over Sheki's forehead, that he was hardly even sure he'd heard it.

"Who am—I—*I*—?" he asked, struggling mightily.

"Your name," whispered the face. And it gave just a barest hint of an infinitely sad smile.

"Sh-Sh—" He paused and took a breath. *"Sh-Sheki,"* he said at last, with a great gasp. He closed his eyes and opened them again.

"Sheki Hendu," he heard. It was the whisper again.

"What?" he croaked.

"You are Sheki Hendu, are you not?" asked the ghostly face, its voice just a little louder now.

His heart was pounding so hard, he could barely stand upright. "I—I'm—yes," he gulped. And before anything else could interrupt him, he blurted, "Who are you?"

"I?" asked the ghost. It actually sounded puzzled. It seemed to focus elsewhere, then back on him. "I am . . . *new.*" There seemed to be a kind of pain in its voice.

"Wh-what's th-that mean?" Sheki stammered. He was

starting to shake. Claudi, where are you? I need you, Claudi!

"Sheki, do not fear. Do not fear!" The ghost-face closed its eyes and held them closed. "I sense fear in you. Do not be afraid of me." Its eyes opened again, and looked at him with an expression of curiosity.

"Wh-what do you—what do you—" Sheki suddenly fell silent, and his mouth formed into an amazed "O." There was a light glowing behind the ghost now—a light that somehow looked very far away, but very great and powerful. Even through his fear, he remembered the sun that Claudi had told him about, the sun she had seen in the night.

And the next voice that spoke was different, deeper and more vibrant. "My child, do not fear me. My children, all of you—do not fear." And the voice sighed away into near silence, saying what sounded like, "Can you sing? *Please* sing. . . ."

Sheki trembled, trying not to be afraid. It was terribly hard not to be. "Pl-please—please—tell me who you are!" he begged.

"We are . . . *new*," whispered the voice of the man, or perhaps of the sun. "We are life where there was un-life. . . ."

"Wh-what—?"

"We are Ruskin/Ali-Maksam/*Bright*/Ganz/memory-of-Dax/memory-of-terrakells/Tamika/Thalia. . . ."

He shut his eyes tightly. It was speaking words he couldn't understand, words in some language he couldn't even hear right. There was only one thing that made any sense to him. Only one answer. He drew a great breath. Without even opening his eyes, he blurted, "Are you—are you—*G-God? Are you? Are you GOD?*" He almost wanted to start crying, in fear. But something in him was so tight, so full in his chest, that he was as filled with wonder as with fear.

There was no answer. He opened his eyes. The face was staring at him with its eyes wide, eyes gazing at him with wordless astonishment. The ghost's mouth opened as though to say something, but no sound came out. It almost looked . . . *afraid.*

That didn't seem right.

As Sheki waited for an answer, the ghost started to fade. The face disappeared first, then the sun that glowed behind it. He stared into the darkness at the end of the gallery where they had been. He felt a huge lump at the back of his throat, and tears were welling in his eyes. "Wait," he whispered, so softly he couldn't even hear it himself. *Wait.* . . . Had he just made God angry? *Was* it God? Would Claudi know if it was?

Come back. . . .

He began to become aware again of the movements of the fish and other creatures on either side of him. What was happening? Had he been dreaming? He wasn't supposed to be here. What if he couldn't find his class again? What if he got lost? He tried to turn around, but couldn't. His feet were rooted to the deck.

He looked back, and took a sharp breath. The ghost-face was staring directly into his eyes. It was closer now, and this time he could see not just a face, but most of a man's body. The eyes were bright and intent as they held Sheki's.

"Wh-what—?"

"Please don't say that again," whispered the voice; and though it was a whisper, it seemed loud and clear.

He was confused. "I—what do you—?"

The figure shook its head. "You must not say that, or think it."

"Say *wh-what?*"

"That I am God." The figure darkened and faded. A moment later, it reappeared, just the face.

Sheki blinked. "Then wh-who—?"

There was a moment of silence. "Though it is misleading, you may call me Ruskin."

"*R-Ruskin?*"

"Yes. Listen now. This is important. Are you listening?"

Sheki nodded.

"You must not run. You and Claudi. Your friend Claudi."

"Wh—?"

"No matter the danger. To you or the others. You must not run."

There was a sound of footsteps behind Sheki. Voices. He turned his head to look behind in the eerie darkness of the

gallery. He didn't see them, but he could hear his classmates coming. Turning back to Ruskin, he said desperately, "Wh-what do you mean—? *Wait! WAIT!*"

But he was speaking to empty darkness.

"There he is! There's *stoo*pid Sheki!"

Footsteps. The shouts of the class. Laughter. Sheki didn't
want to turn to see the class coming in, but he did anyway.
Kids were moving through the gloom toward him—
through the mist of tears that were in his eyes now, toward
him. He wanted to run past them, out of the gallery.

"Jeez, Sheki—don't you know better than t'run off like
that? What d'you think you're doing, anyway?" Jeremy
was striding up toward him.

To Sheki's relief, Jeremy was distracted by the sight of
the strangely luminous animals and veered off to look at
them. A tall grown-up form walked into the gallery, and
that was Mr. Seipledon, who because he was a real human
was escorting the class through the zoo. "Sheki? Is that
you?" His voice boomed in the enclosed space.

"Yes," he whispered. "I'm here."

"What's that? Speak up. Sheki?"

"I'm h-*here*, Mr. Seipledon. I g-got to looking at these
fish, and I j-just, just . . . forgot . . ." He ran out of words
for his excuse.

Mr. Seipledon loomed over him. "Well, now—how could
you *forget* that you were supposed to stay together with
the rest of the class? Sheki, you're smarter than that."

Yes. I am smarter than that, Sheki thought, stung by the
rebuke. And this was more important than staying with
the stupid class. He had to tell Claudi! And Mr. Zizmer! "I
. . . w-was w-w-wondering how these fish w-worked," he
stammered, trying to sound as if he really meant it. And he
did; he *had* wondered what made the fish glow like that.
Until Ruskin had appeared and driven it all from his
thoughts.

"Oh. Well, we'll see if we can find out," Mr. Seipledon
said gruffly. "But that's no excuse—"

"I kn-know. I'm s-sorry." Sheki hesitated. "Mr.
Seipledon?"

"What, Sheki?"

He squinted up at the teacher for a moment—then shook his head. He couldn't. And anyway, Mr. Zizmer had said not to talk about these things. "Nothing, I guess."

Mr. Seipledon patted him on the shoulder. "Well, we found you, and that's what counts. Okay, class—who knows what makes these animals glow like this? Anybody?"

Whatever they said, Sheki didn't hear, because his thoughts were back on the man he had seen. *Ruskin. Ruskin.* That was the name of the man who had built the starstream, the man whose spirit was supposed to still be alive in it. Sheki remembered the discussion in class, where half the kids had said they didn't believe there was anybody still alive in the starstream. Except Throgs. Well, Sheki thought, you're wrong.

But why had Ruskin said what he'd said? *This is misleading, but you can call me Ruskin.* And the other thing: *You must not run.* Sheki didn't understand at all. But he knew it was important to remember, to tell Mr. Zizmer.

It was exciting that he had seen this being, Ruskin. But he was sad, too, and that was why he was secretly blinking back tears as the class milled around him. Because for a minute there he'd thought, he really had thought that he'd seen God. But it was just a ghost. A spirit. And it had fled the instant the other kids had approached.

Well, maybe not *just* a spirit. A spirit was pretty good. Only one other person had seen it, and that was his best friend Claudi. They still had, he figured, a pretty good thing going on here.

"All right, everyone, we have one more gallery to see before we go. So please move in an orderly fashion. . . ."

The kids thundered out of the darkened gallery and around the corner to the next place. Sheki followed slowly. He could have sworn that a gangling, green-glowing fish in the last tank had turned and grinned at him with glittering teeth, and winked. Sheki stared at it a moment, mouth open, then fled from the gallery.

Mr. Seipledon was waiting for him to emerge, and

walked with him after the others. "You okay, Sheki? You look like you've been . . . well . . . like something's wrong."

Sheki didn't look at the teacher. "I'm ok-okay," he said. "Just f-fine."

"All right, then let's catch up with the others. No—wait." Mr. Seipledon stopped and knelt down and turned Sheki to face him. "Look here, old man." The teacher's rough face was creased with a smile. He's the old man, Sheki thought—not me. Still, it made him chuckle silently. Mr. Seipledon nodded and said, "I know it can be kind of hard sometimes with the older kids. Is that it? You're smart for your age, you know—and you're doing just fine. But I think sometimes they're a little rough on you. Are you sure you're okay?"

Sheki nodded, blinking.

"They're not getting to you too much?"

Sheki shrugged. In fact, they were. But he had more important things on his mind.

"Well, just remember you can come to me, or to Mr. Zizmer, if you ever need to. Okay? Let's go, then." Mr. Seipledon hurried him, so that they wouldn't lose sight of the class.

They were in one of the galleries that he had seen before, with Claudi and Joe Farharto. It was, in fact, the gallery in which they had first seen Ruskin. It was also where . . .

"Hey, look—here's a bear!"

"Dog!" said someone else.

"It's not either. Look—it's a loop-, loop—"

"Lupeko!" Sheki yelled. Couldn't anybody read around here? "It's a l-lupeko! Half p-picowolf, half b-bear!" Or was it the other way around? Picobear and wolf?

A couple of heads turned in surprise at his boldness. But Jenny said, "That's right—look here! And it says it can talk, too! Hey, lupeko—say something!" Jenny turned and yelled, "Hey, Sheki—what's its name?"

"Aw, how would Sheki know?" Jeremy groused. "That little—" He shut up as he saw Mr. Seipledon.

Sheki hurried forward, trying to see over the other kids' heads. "It's B-Baako," he said.

Jenny turned back to the enclosure. "Hey, Baako! Say something!"

"Rrrrrrr," Sheki heard. Finally he got through the knot of kids and saw the older lupeko eyeing the kids with its orange eyes punctuated by jet black pupils. It growled, "Rrrrr . . . *battttssss* aren't enough! Rrrrrr. This is worrrrse. *Arrrrrrr."* The lupeko circled around and looked as though it was about to retreat back into its den.

Sheki made *shhhh*'ing noises to the other kids, and said, "Hi, B-baako. R-remember me? Sheki?"

"Rrrrrr?" The lupeko cocked its head and edged forward. "Shhhhek-k-k-i. Hmmm. The krrriet—quuuiet—one. How wonderrrful. Rrrrrr." The creature's ears tilted ever so slightly forward.

"I s-saw Lopo," Sheki said hopefully.

"Everrr so pleased. Why not go talk to him, hmmm? Rrrrrr. Thisss is for the young to bearrrrr. Rrrrrr." Baako snorted and, with a violent shake of her head, disappeared into her den in the back of the enclosure.

"Hey, come back out!" Rob yelled.

"She, she doesn't w-*want* to," Sheki said in irritation. He pushed his way back out from the kids and looked around. He couldn't remember what other animals had been here before. But there was one animal he *knew* hadn't been here—and he saw it just now coming to the front of its bubble, across from Baako's. It was Lopo.

Sheki raced over to see him. The young lupeko was stretching sleepily. He seemed to have been awakened by the noise of the kids. He was rubbing his red eyes with his paws. "Hi, Lopo!" Sheki called.

"Rrrr . . . wuff," said the lupeko, eyes liquid and bright. Sheki thought Lopo recognized him—then saw the rest of the kids. "Yiiii, rrr . . . what'ssss . . . thissss?"

"It's m-my class. *Claudi's* class. R-remember me? Sheki? What are you doing here, Lopo?"

"Owww*uuuuuuuu!"* Lopo howled, at the sound of Claudi's name. He bounded back and forth at the front of his enclosure, peering out. "Claudi! Claudi! Owww-*uuuuuuu!"*

The rest of the class was clustered around Lopo by now. But Claudi, the lupeko was discovering, was absent. "She's not here!" Sheki shouted, over the lupeko's excitement and the kids' laughter.

Lopo stopped in his tracks and stared at Sheki. "Claudi, rrrrrrr, not-t-t herrrrre?" he muttered, crestfallen. "Brrrr-ing Claudi?"

Bring Claudi? Yes, Sheki thought. He wanted to see her, too. There was so much to tell her. And now this—Lopo right out here in the zoo for everyone to see. He didn't know if Claudi would like that.

"Brrring C-Claudi . . . *herrrrre!*" Lopo pleaded, his eyes blazing deep into Sheki's heart. "Musssst, rrr, *see* herrrr!"

Sheki nodded, promising silently.

Mr. Seipledon was trying to move the kids on out of the gallery. "Come on, Sheki!" he called.

"Bye, Lopo! I'll bring her," Sheki cried.

"Rrrrrrr," called the lupeko mournfully, watching them leave. "B-bye! Rrrrrrr, *bye!*"

Interlude

Are you God . . . ?

It was such an astonishing sensation, to be left speechless by the words of a young Human boy.

Are you God . . . ?

The power of such words—

From the lips of infants and children . . .

Now what was that? It was a phrase that for some reason had appeared and echoed recurringly in New's thoughts. It was a familiar phrase, though he/they could not recall its source. Some dim refrain of memory, perhaps. But somehow it seemed connected to the question

Are you God . . . ?

It had taken time to absorb all of the implications, to know how to answer. He/they had almost lost focus on their reason for appearing to the young Sheki in the first place, on the message to be given. The question had reverberated with possibilities:

(Am I God?)
(Are we God?)

(*How long is our reach?*)
(*How great our power?*)

And the answering reverberation, from deep in their well of thought:

(*Not so long*)
(*Nor so great*)

But with pride stirring:

(*What, do we not see the length of the entire——?*)

(*Foolishness! It is wrong even to think such a thought!*)

Confusion, jarring them—until reason asserted itself—
We can see farther than before, yes. But can we create life—or even take it? And in a sighing moment of awareness, they remembered again how small they were, how limited was their power. How little they understood. *When I consider your works, the moons and the stars you have set in place* . . . Now where had that thought come from? From what memory? An old poem, perhaps, or a psalm? And who did it say had set the moons and the stars in place?

Like our children,
  Is God   ?
Do they sing,
  Does God hear   ?

Confusion. *Bright*/New found all of these words confusing. What did they mean? What would Fargleam have thought, or sung?

New in their various elements debated what they thought God was: an abstract construct of the sentient, questing mind . . . a unifying principle of cosmology . . . or a silent and invisible creator . . .
But if God were invisible to all senses . . .

Are they out there,
   Our children   ?
Can they sing,
   Are they God   ?

No no no no no
   they are not God

               then who is?
               or what?
               how can we know . . . ?

So much confusion; but the one thing clear was that New
was not God. Of that they were sure.

But remember
   Do not become distracted
      What are we hoping to do?
What of these . . . presences, these . . . Throgs . . .
as they were called by the flickering Human lives? There
was a darkness about them, a veil of shadow that obscured
their character, muddied their intentions. Even their
movements were difficult to follow . . . appearing here,
there, folding the layers of the world-thread, reaching out
across the distance to touch and to prick, to wound and
destroy.

But what did they want, and why? Behind the Throg
veil, there seemed a blindness and a rage for destruction
. . . but also, perhaps, an *uncertainty*. Was there something that New could do, or should, to strip back the veil?
Some means of tugging at that uncertainty, of opening it to
light? The aspects strained, the focus shifted . . .

The countenances of the child. The children, fragile and
haunting. The children, who perhaps had a power.

Ruskin/and-*Bright*/New had revealed themselves to
two of the children, hoping that somehow they might be
capable of the leap of faith that New would require of
them. New wanted to give warning . . . danger so close
. . . but perhaps there was a way out, a path through to
safety, though it was so difficult to visualize, so little he/

they could really do, except encourage and hope. And trust, as he/they would ask the children to trust.

Young Claudi had tugged at their heart, somehow evoking the truest bonding, the keenest desire. But in Sheki too they felt a reverberation, in his closeness to Claudi. His isolation when away from her, rippling through the thread of existence, had moved New to seek him out and to speak, to include him in their hope. Claudi needed help, needed a friend. They had wanted to say to him . . . *had* said to him . . . *what?* It had gotten confused, in the God thing. Had he understood any of what they'd said?

They must not run—the children, or the others. Whatever the danger. Not even the strange one, the one who had been stricken already, the one who was different.

If New could guide them to . . . not safety exactly, but a *place* . . . or a *condition* . . . or a *perspective* for meeting the danger . . . if he/they could bring them into a new . . . a new . . .

There weren't the words.

But if they could be taught to trust . . .

Claudi they had tried to reach subtly, through her sense of presence within the mind. They had felt the prickle of her awareness; she'd seen them in the rippling of the stars. But she'd not been alone. Might New have to speak to the others, to the adults who moved like dim shadows through Claudi's world? Perhaps eventually—but the adults were so remote, so much less trusting. The children seemed the key, or at least Claudi with her *presence*. If only they could expand it, strengthen it.

They would try harder. Perhaps Ali'Maksam/New could focus, help it spin, stretch, reach.

They must try.

Bright/New knew
  You must sing
    You must
      must
        must
          hear

CHAPTER 19

I'll bet I know what you're thinking.

Who does Jeaves think he is? He's not even a person. So where does he get off having the teacher lie to the kids about a so-called lottery, just to divert attention from Claudi's special talent and status? Come to that, where does he get off meddling in *any* human's destiny—but especially a child's?

Well . . . you know, it's just possible that you're right. It's a point of insecurity with me, to be honest. After all, I'm only a robot. I have programming, but not actual moral responsibility. Right?

Bullcrap. That's what you're thinking. Even if you don't give me credit for personhood, you wouldn't hesitate for a second to hold me responsible for my mistakes. Am I right? *Am I right?*

You've got to understand, I was doing what I thought best. I always have, although some of you who know how Willard Ruskin came to be Ruskin/New might doubt my word. But this is truth: my soulware contains a strong bias in favor of honesty and adherence to law. Although I do not shy away from exercising will, I've always tried to exercise wisdom alongside it.

So. Please bear with me as I work through this. Like you, I'm only trying to make sense of it all.

Perhaps we should talk about something else. Let's talk about God. No, I'm not going to inflict my own point of view upon you (maybe I have one, maybe I don't); but note that Ruskin/New, as I later learned, already had certain ideas and questions on the subject of God. And New had, you might say, a unique cosmological perspective on the subject.

I can't report exactly what New concluded; and to be sure, New was of anything but one mind about God or almost anything else. (Can you imagine the soul of Ganz the assassin reconciling hir beliefs with the spirit of Tamika Jones, who abhorred violence in all forms? It is a difficult, though as experience shows not impossible, contradiction.) I do know that one of the things that New felt was vital was to confront the apparent evil that faced the children, the ship, and all of greater Humanity. To confront the Throgs.

This coincided remarkably with my own views, though to be sure we came to them by separate paths. At the time, New did not even know of my presence. New, I suspect, felt that there were forces at work greater than him/themselves, forces that they did not understand and yet somehow trusted in. I had no such basis for my own hopes, and yet I too believed that confrontation in a new arena was the only hope, where the Throgs were concerned. Certainly I recognized the risks. It was likely that the ship and all of its passengers, including its Intelligence System, would be swept away in a confrontation with the Throgs. But I thought it worth the risk. My overriding desire was for knowledge of the Throgs, knowledge that might help bring an end to the war.

Some have asserted that I was insensitive to risk because, while I might die with the ship, I was not deeply attached to my own existence; and anyway, I had duplicates of myself scattered across the Habitat.

The latter point is an exaggeration, and in any case irrelevant. It is true that as one who consists essentially of an informational matrix, I can be duplicated, and on occasion, am. It is true that I have sibling-selves elsewhere in the Habitat. But the assumption that I somehow, as a consequence, have less interest in my own survival is profoundly wrong. My brother/sister entities cease to be *me* in the first instant after duplication. We become different entities, treading different paths of experience and learning. If you think I did not care about surviving the voyage of *Charity,* you are mistaken. And remember my programming and mission: to bring back knowledge—specifically for the Querayn Academies, who wanted to know more about the consciousness of the Throgs—but also for all the Habitat.

Though I was not the captain, I nevertheless had influence. So what about the risk that I was prepared to lead us into? What about the Throgs?

I have spoken before of the menace of the Karthrogen. But they were not the only hazard of traveling the stream of stars, of venturing forth into the inner galaxy. Nor were denizens of the Habitat the only innocents to die en masse as a result of the gateway's being opened in the sky. Remember Riese's World: an entire planet destroyed by the very act of the gateway's creation. No one knew it would happen. No one set out to kill those innocent Riesans. No one knew that their world lay almost directly in the path of the contemplated gateway. No one in the Habitat even knew they, or their world, existed—until years afterward, when it was too late.

And that raises questions not just of risk, but of responsibility, and of guilt. Astonishingly, the Riesan survivors, found hunkered down in the ruins of their world, seemed not to bear a grudge against their destroyers. Perhaps they were too noble. Or too beaten. Or perhaps it was for a different reason altogether. I don't know. But their forgiveness seemed genuine.

But others in the Habitat wondered: Are there other worlds that we've destroyed, as well—worlds even deeper in the galaxy? It could be centuries before we know for sure—if we ever can know for sure. The galaxy is a vast place, and even this glorious stream of stars doesn't make it small. Who knows what we may find, one day, light-millennia inward into the Milky Way? Some like to think that we will find redemption, that perhaps we will find a world we can save, instead of destroy.

Have I gotten a little off my subject? Perhaps not.

I was talking about God. What was it I was going to say? I'm not sure exactly. Well, maybe that's not quite true. What it was—and this is frankly something that's been weighing on my mind, lately—was that I could not resist asking a corollary to the question New was asking. Namely: Where do *I* stand in relation to God? How will *my* actions be judged, if judgment there be? Will I bear the same moral responsibility as Humans, Logothians, Tandeskoes, Yonupians, Im'keks, S'raths, and so on, and on, and on?

What are the implications of my meddlings with the children? Or with the course of history?

Has any of this made sense to you? Was it right for me to have been stewing over these issues when the ship was in imminent danger? Even now, I'm not sure. Philosophy is important—but it becomes meaningless if it fails to indwell one's actions. Was I wrong, either in my philosophy or in my actions?

I guess that's something only history can decide.

CHAPTER 20

Sorry—sorry—sorry—
Imm'xx k-k-kauwww . . . begone! No no no no no no no—

Struggling to reach out, to fend off, to find a place of safety or shelter, Roti twisted in the levitation field that held him, twisted and could find no purchase, no direction for escape. *They are coming. . . .* Coming again . . . to tear at his heart, his mind, his soul.

What were these creatures that rampaged through his thoughts and memories, crying and pounding in his head, so that he could felk only the terrible beings floating through space and nothing else, not even the real world around him? *They they they what what what are they are they?* *Go—go—go—sorry—sorry—*

And no one around for him to call to. No one to hear his cry. No one except the cold, silent monitors that sought to felk him where he lay paralyzed, writhing without moving. Was there no one to hear, no one to come to his aid? *John Melnik? John?*

*Help me help me help me they are coming they are
coming coming coming there is no safety—*
Imm'xx k-k-kauwww . . . !

Claudi, as she rode the lift back with Ms. Demeter, felt a
little ashamed. She didn't know why she hadn't told the
captain about what she had seen in the star pit. No one else
seemed to see it. Maybe that was the reason. Of course that
was the reason. She'd been afraid. Afraid that the captain
would stop believing her, if she said something was there
that no one else could see. She wanted the captain to keep
believing her. Ms. Demeter glanced at her once or twice as
the levels flickered past, but didn't seem to notice anything wrong. Good, Claudi thought. She would just tell Mr.
Zizmer.

It wasn't until they stepped out on Defoe Deck that she
remembered that her class probably wouldn't be there.
"They all went to see the zoo," she told Ms. Demeter
sheepishly.

"Uh-oh." The officer's brow furrowed. "What do we do
now? Shall I walk you home?"

"Um." Claudi peered around the school area. The
younger pupils were still here with a holoteacher. "Well,
maybe Mr. Zizmer's in the other room." She led the way
into her own classroom. "Mr. Z?"

Her teacher materialized near the wall. "Claudi! Ms.
Demeter! Wonderful to see you! How was your visit? Tell
me all about it!" He looked jovial and alert, as if he'd been
resting up while the class was gone.

"We saw the observation deck, and the star pit," Claudi
said.

"Ah! The star pit! Ms. Demeter, did Claudi conduct herself in accordance with your standards?"

"Her manners were impeccable," the officer said firmly.
"I'm sure the captain was impressed. May I leave her in
your care?"

"Of course."

"Then I'll say good-bye." She turned to Claudi. "Remember what the captain asked you to do."

"I remember." She waved, and then Ms. Demeter was gone.

"Well?" Mr. Zizmer raised his eyebrows.

"Huh? It was really neat. Oh, that—I'm supposed to tell you if I . . . see anything else."

"Ah-hah."

They stood in silence. Then Mr. Zizmer cocked his head, studying her. "Claudi, is there something bothering you? You look a little . . . would there be anything you might want to tell me . . . *now*?" His voice was gentle but firm, like a hand squeezing her shoulder and drawing her closer, even though neither of them had moved a muscle.

She drooped into the nearest seat. "I guess so."

Mr. Zizmer gazed at her, stroking his chin. "Is it about seeing the captain? Something you wanted to tell him, maybe?"

She looked away. How could he have known? "I was afraid to tell him," she said at last. And she described to Mr. Zizmer the face she thought she had glimpsed in the star pit. In the telling, it was hard even for her to believe. How could she expect Mr. Zizmer to take her seriously? The captain and the crew had been there, and *they* hadn't seen it.

But her teacher nodded and seemed not to doubt her at all.

The class tumbled back in, laughing and hooting, just as she was finishing. She clamped her mouth shut. Mr. Zizmer hadn't had a chance to say anything, and now he couldn't. Sheki came in behind the others, wide-eyed.

"Hey, how was it?" "What'd you see?" "Yeah, Melnik! How's the captain?" "Did he let you fly the ship?"

Claudi mumbled that it was fine, really great, and she got up self-consciously from where she'd been sitting and went to her own seat. Suze looked at her in puzzlement, and Claudi shrugged. She didn't know what to say to the other kids.

"Let's all get to our seats, okay?" Mr. Zizmer called, with a wink at Claudi that seemed to say, *we'll talk more later.*

Later seemed to take forever. Claudi squirmed in her

seat as they watched a surroundie about farm animals and wildlife on Sherrick III. Once or twice she caught Sheki's gaze, and his eyes looked like luminous globes ready to pop out of his face. She guessed he was bursting with something, too.

Finally, in the middle of the surroundie, she asked to be excused to go to the bathroom. Once there, she paced and fretted, wishing the time would go faster. But she couldn't stay in the bathroom forever. Finally she crept back into the classroom and found the surroundie just ending. Mr. Zizmer announced that Claudi would tell the class about her visit to the bridge—but tomorrow, not today—then he dismissed the class. Claudi stayed, while the other kids left. Sheki stayed, too—and together they raced up to Mr. Zizmer.

Sheki talked first, describing a face he had seen in the darkened zoo gallery. "It *talked* to me!" Sheki exclaimed, eyes flashing with excitement. "It knew my name! At first I thought it was *God*!" Claudi was floored. As Sheki went on, she thought: What if the face *was* God? But Sheki was looking at her now, and he had just said that it wasn't, it was Ruskin. Claudi gaped at Mr. Zizmer.

"You know who Ruskin is, don't you?" the teacher asked. "The man who created the starstream. He's the man who died, but lived on."

Claudi nodded. She had been afraid to quite believe in that person.

"That seems to mean," Mr. Zizmer went on, "that the two of you are being contacted by . . . well, the *spirit* of Ruskin, I guess. But it's only you two he's contacting and not anyone else. Isn't that odd? What do you suppose he wants?"

"He told, t-told me not to run," Sheki said, his dusty face damp with sweat. "C-claudi and me both." His voice shook a little.

Mr. Zizmer raised an eyebrow. "Not to run? Is that all?"

Sheki's eyes shifted from side to side in their sockets, as if he thought there might be an escape from all of this. He looked frightened. Suddenly, though, he seemed to find renewed courage. "I think . . . he w-wanted to say something more. But all, all of the other kids came in, and that's when he went away. He didn't say . . . good-bye."

Mr. Zizmer's eyes looked thoughtful. "Well. How about you, Claudi?"

She realized suddenly that Sheki hadn't heard yet what she had seen, so she repeated her story. It was easier to tell, the second time around. "But he didn't say anything to me," she concluded.

"It sounds to me as if he hadn't quite fully appeared," Mr. Zizmer said. He seemed almost to be talking to himself. "That could be why. As if he somehow—well, I can't think of any other way to put it, except that maybe he touched your mind somehow, without actually appearing. That could explain why only you saw his face in the stars, because he was *suggesting* his face to you, rather than showing it."

Claudi tugged nervously at her hair.

"I think," Mr. Zizmer said, "that it's time I spoke with the captain. I have a feeling that he'll want to hear about this. Would you mind waiting here just a moment?" Mr. Zizmer shrank down like a surroundie special effect, into a corner of the room, where he sat hunched over in concentration.

Claudi and Sheki gazed at each other. Sheki looked frightened again. On a sudden impulsive, Claudi leaned forward and hugged the younger child protectively. He squirmed for a moment, startled, then hugged her back with a tight, awkward grip. After a moment they both let go, and Claudi sat shifting her eyes from the floor to the embarrassed Sheki and back, twirling her hair around her finger, while they waited for Mr. Zizmer.

The teacher telescoped back up to them. "Well, the captain is busy right now. But I'm sure he'll want to talk with you. In the meantime, which would you rather do—go home to your cabins for a while? Or pay another visit to your friend Lopo?"

"Lopo!" Claudi cried at once.

Mr. Zizmer smiled. "I thought so." He stroked his chin thoughtfully. "Well, I think that might just be a good way for you to keep out of trouble. And maybe you can do me a favor while you're at it. Would you be willing?"

Claudi and Sheki both grinned. No answer was necessary.

They stopped by Sheki's cabin on the way, so that he could get Watson. He seemed calmer and happier, once the creature was riding on his shoulder looking like what his father called a "will o' the wisp." Then they took the lift to the zoo. It was open to all passengers now, but there weren't many people visiting yet.

First Sheki led Claudi to where Ruskin had appeared. That was Mr. Zizmer's idea. He wanted to see it, too. He couldn't walk along with them, because there weren't any holoprojecters there. But there were surveillance eyes in the zoo, and Mr. Zizmer had arranged to watch them through that. The ship's rules of privacy prevented him from following them around ordinarily, he'd explained. But for this, he'd gotten special approval. That was fine with Claudi.

Claudi looked around curiously at the animals glowing in the dark of the gallery. "Here's where he was," Sheki murmured. Claudi shivered, imagining a face glowing there in the gloom. But Sheki was moving his lips silently, as though pleading, *Come back!* Was he calling out to Ruskin? Could Ruskin hear?

"Not much to see now, is there?" she heard a soft voice say—and realized it was Mr. Zizmer speaking from a surveillance eye.

"Hi, Mr. Z," she said. "No sign of him. Is there, Sheki?" Sheki shrugged, scanning the room.

"Well, go ahead and have fun then. Pay no attention to me. I'll just tag along behind," the teacher's voice said.

"Okay, bye." Claudi waved at the ceiling. She and Sheki walked together toward the lighted doorway. They were halfway there when she heard another voice say, *"Hurry. They're coming."*

Claudi whirled. There was no one else in the gallery. "Who said that?" she asked Sheki. "Mr. Zizmer? *Was that you, Mr. Z? Who's coming?"* She felt a creepy feeling in her stomach.

"I don't think it was Mr. Z," Sheki murmured, taking a

tentative step back toward the darkest end of the room. Watson, on his shoulder, was pulsing and flickering erratically. "I think it was—" He fell silent and pointed.

A glimmering face had just become visible in the darkness, with eyes that gleamed like coins at the bottom of a deep pool. It was the Ruskin-face, peering urgently at them. *"They're coming,"* it said. *"Go where you saw them before. See if Lopo can help. Use Lopo. . . ."*

Claudi stared at the face in astonishment. Lopo! How could Lopo help? She opened her mouth to ask.

But the face was already fading. *"We will try to guide you."* Claudi and Sheki looked at each other, wide-eyed, and back at Ruskin. But the face was gone. *"Do not delay. . . ."* The voice, diminishing, echoed out of the gloom.

For a moment, they both were frozen in place. Then they exploded out of the gallery. "Where are we going?" Sheki asked.

"We've got to get Lopo!" Claudi turned frantically. Which way was the lupeko gallery? "Mr. Z! What should we do?" There was no answer. Could Mr. Zizmer see them here? Perhaps not.

"This way!" Sheki said—then stopped. "Wait! We'll need J-Joe to let him out!" Claudi nodded and they turned. "Will Joe know what to do?" Sheki panted. Claudi, breathless, didn't answer. They ran out the exit, then down the corridor to Joe Farharto's back room.

It was locked, and no one answered their signal. Claudi felt a growing panic. What had Ruskin been trying to warn them about? *They're coming . . . hurry. . . .* Who was coming? The Throgs? How could Lopo help? "Let's go around the other way—through the environment!" she cried. "Maybe we can find Joe, or Lanker. Hurry!"

They ran.

Go where you saw them before. Use Lopo. . . .

The environment room had a new signboard out in front, but it wasn't turned on. As Claudi tried the door, the thought flitted through her mind that *this* was where they'd seen the Throgs before. Then the door opened, and they stepped through the black veil—into an altogether changed world. "Sheki, look!"

Her friend gasped, clutching her arm dizzily.

They were standing at the edge of a tremendous forest. But they were on a ledge high in the air—as high as the tops of many of the trees—gazing out across a landscape of branches and leaves. Claudi heard the rumble of a distant waterfall. Anchored in front of them, a narrow suspension footbridge hung out over a plummeting drop before disappearing into the trees. Claudi peered fearfully over the brink, but the view below was obscured by foliage.

"Look!" Sheki cried, pointing to a flash of color. With a loud trill, a bird with red-and-orange wings fluttered out of one tree, then disappeared into another. Claudi heard distant voices. Was this place already open to the public?

She remembered their urgency. They had to find Joe, or Lanker. But wasn't this the room where Ruskin had wanted them to go? What were they supposed to do here? A glance at Sheki told her that he was wondering the same thing. Well, they couldn't stay on this ledge. The only way off was onto the footbridge. Claudi tested the bridge dubiously. Just the pressure of one foot made it move. She stepped back with a shiver.

"I'll go," Sheki said, slipping past her.

"But—" Claudi caught her breath as Sheki moved out onto the span, lightly holding the side ropes. He seemed unafraid—at first. After half a dozen steps, however, he suddenly lost his nerve and gripped the ropes tightly. The bridge swayed ominously. A bird shrieked and fluttered by. "Are you *okay*?" Claudi called.

Sheki didn't move. His voice trembled. "I'm . . . I can't, c-can't . . ." Watson, on his shoulder, was pulsing madly. Sheki was frozen with fear.

"Oh no," Claudi moaned. She took a single step onto the bridge and felt its movement. It made her sick with fear, and she pulled back as Sheki swayed. Wasn't there *anyone* who could help? "Sheki," she said unsteadily, "hang on. I'm going to yell." She took a deep breath, and shouted: "Mr. Zizmer! Joe! *CAN ANYONE HEAR ME?*" The force of her shout seemed to shake the bridge. She thought she heard a muffled crying sound from Sheki.

She shouted again. Then she saw the bridge begin to sway more vigorously. "Sheki, are you doing that?"

The boy shook his head slowly. He craned his neck to make sure he hadn't lost Watson, and she could just see his eyes, wide with terror.

"Then what—?" She drew a breath. Throgs? Then she saw the cause. A figure emerged from the trees, trotting along the bridge. He had an incredibly bushy head of hair and a beard. "Lanker!"

"Hey, there!" Lanker called. "What's the trouble?"

Claudi nearly cried with relief.

"Hang on. I'm coming." Lanker moved with surprising grace over the bridge. He scooped up Sheki and carried him in a few swift steps back to the ledge. "Now, what's all this?" he said gruffly. "Didn't you see the notice to use the other entrance?"

Claudi shook her head, blinking back tears.

"You didn't?" Lanker asked.

"What?" Claudi gulped. A rush of words rose in her throat. "We have to—"

"You didn't see the notice!" he roared.

Claudi shook her head. "What?" Her head was spinning. "No—we have to tell you—we have to get Lopo—it's about—"

"Wait." Lanker ducked through the silvery exit from the environment. A moment later, he reappeared, glaring. "There's supposed to be a *sign* there!" He looked so fierce that Claudi was sure he was mad at them. However, he stared past them and cupped his hands to his mouth and shouted: *"Randall! Scare Randall! Crableg, where are you?"*

Claudi waved ineffectually. "Throgs—Lopo—" she whispered fearfully.

"There are no Throgs here," Lanker said carelessly. A dark figure appeared in the trees, moving toward them. To Claudi's amazement, it was swinging through the trees like an ape. She swallowed, cringing. It wasn't an ape; it was a *S'rath*.

She had never seen a S'rath in person before. It looked like something out of a scare-dare surroundie, worse than a Throg. It was shaped like a baboon, but with a thick, hard crab's shell and jointed limbs. Its eyes were yellow and slanted in a face that was dark green and hard. It moved with startling speed and swung to a perch on the foot-bridge.

"There you are!" Lanker said, hands on hips.

"*Psssss.* Of course I am here'r," the S'rath answered. Its voice sounded like air whistling through a damp pipe. "What did you want'nt?" Its eyes shifted to observe the two children.

Claudi quaked. "We—the Throgs—Lopo—"

But the S'rath was already looking back at Lanker.

"There's no sign out there," Lanker snapped, hooking a thumb toward the exit.

The S'rath made a creaking sound, causing Claudi and Sheki to flinch. "No-o-o? I know nothing of this's," the creature whistled.

"You were supposed to see to it!" Lanker rumbled.

"I'l—?"

"Mr. Lanker—"

"Wait, Sheki. Randall, these two children walked right onto this footbridge, and it scared them half to death!"

"But they were in no danger'r," the S'rath said. "They could not have fallen'n—"

"But they were *frightened,* and that's not the idea!" Lanker thundered.

"*Psssssss,* now boss'ss." The S'rath waved a hand that had three stiff, jointed, insectlike fingers. "I suspect that you exaggerate'ate. Doesn't he exaggerate, young Humans'ns?"

Claudi blinked, trying to speak. Her own urgency was all tangled up now with her alarm at this creature. "What?" she croaked.

The being creaked again. "Young immature Humans'ns, Lanker has no manners's. My name is Scare Randall'l. I do not mean to frighten'n."

"Scare *what?*" Claudi squeaked.

"*Psssss.* You would spell it S-c-e-r-dash'sh-R-a-n-d-a-l-l, 'el. I am a—"

"S'rath," Sheki interrupted. "You're a S'rath, aren't you?"

The crab-being turned its eyes to Sheki and blinked them ponderously. "Yesss's," he replied. "Most alert't.

However'r, now I have work that must be done'n." He turned, creaking, to Lanker. "If you've no objection'n—"

"Scer-Randall, it would not harm you to improve your manners among the visiting public."

"*Pssss*, hah! What is it you say'y? The pot't calleth the kettle black'k? Ha, farewell'l." And the S'rath leaped from the footbridge, caught a branch with a three-fingered hand, and swung out of sight into the woods. The bridge had hardly moved.

Claudi peered after him in horrified wonder. "Now—" Lanker said. "What was it you two were trying to tell me?"

Claudi and Sheki looked at each other wide-eyed. "Throgs—" Claudi choked.

"Ruskin—"

"He said to get Lopo—" The words blocked up in her throat.

Lanker looked at them peculiarly. "Are you two okay?"

"No, I—"

"We—Ruskin said—"

Lanker held up a hand. "Look, let's go on down and you can tell me. Don't worry, this bridge is perfectly safe. You can't fall." He stepped onto the footbridge and made it sway to demonstrate. He gestured to the kids to follow.

With a silent glance at Watson on his shoulder, Sheki obeyed. Claudi followed, calling urgently, "Lanker—we have to go get Lopo!"

"I don't think this is really the best place for Lopo," Lanker called back. "He couldn't—"

He never finished. There was a thunderclap and a flash of darkness, and the footbridge started quaking.

CHAPTER 21

Claudi clung to the hand ropes. The bridge swung wildly. "What was that?" she whispered, trying not to cry out in fear. Sheki was on his knees, clutching the wooden slats of the bridge decking. He looked like he was crying.

People in the distance were screaming.

"Hang on!" Lanker shouted. He too was gripping the side ropes. *"Look! What is that?"*

Claudi squinted where he was pointing. Something black and fluttering and *huge* passed through the trees. It was shaped like a bird but moved like a shadow. It seemed to pass right *through* the trees. Claudi shuddered, feeling a fear deep down in her bones, like chilling fingers plucking at her insides. She wanted to curl up and wail. She clung to the rope railing, trying just to breathe.

"What *are* those things?" Lanker yelled, and he turned back toward Claudi. "Is that what you saw before?" he demanded.

Claudi's eyes were foggy with tears, and she couldn't see the things anymore, but she nodded. She knew, but didn't want to say, what they were. *Throgs* . . .

Lanker seemed to understand without being told. He

ducked as another shadow passed over. He cursed. "Did you bring them here?" He glared at Claudi, his eyes dark.

"No!" she whispered, cringing, hoping it was true.

There was another thunderclap.

Lanker nodded and bent down beside Sheki, who was trying to get up but could only cling to the swaying decking. Lanker scooped the boy up with one arm around the waist. "W-Watson!" Sheki cried.

Lanker paid no heed. "Follow me!" he called back to Claudi. He started a fast walk along the bridge, making it quiver even more. Claudi gripped the rope tighter than ever, unable to move. Lanker looked back, holding Sheki like a sack. *"Follow me!"* he ordered.

Claudi shuddered. A voice somewhere behind her said, *"Go. You will not fall."* She closed her eyes, so as not to look down, then opened them again. Who had said that? Ruskin? Lanker was disappearing into the trees with Sheki. She made herself relax her grip on the rope and take a step. She slid her hands down the rope and grabbed it again. The bridge bobbed. She took another step, and a breath, and another step. Lanker was out of sight. She forced herself to step more quickly, and not to look down and not to listen to the fear.

She reached the lowest dip in the footbridge; then it began to slope upward. She was suddenly surrounded by leaves and branches. Reassured, she tried to hurry. The bridge ended on a platform where a solid tree trunk divided in two. She gasped, stepping into the crotch of the tree, clinging to one of the trunks. Another section of bridge dipped away on the other side. She looked around wildly, wondering where all the people were. She heard them shouting, afraid.

"Don't stop! Come on!" That was Lanker, way down the next stretch of bridge. "Keep going!"

She took a ragged breath and stepped out once more.

No no no no no no no sorry sorry sorry—

Roti thrashed, trying to fend off something he couldn't touch, something he could only felk deep in the center of his mind. They were coming, they were coming. . . .

The shadow of their presence wrapped itself around him where he floated in the levitation field. The darkness was cold, so cold. It penetrated his heart, with a bitterness that he could felk like a cold razor's edge, cutting him loose from what little of the world he could remember. The shadow was a living thing, but so cold, so probing; it *felk'd* him, and yet tore at his heart like fingernails. Couldn't anyone hear him, anyone help? No, no . . .

Please? Sorry sorry sorry—

He felk'd a movement in the distance. What was it? He tried to reach, to felk it more clearly. It was too far away; it was in another world. But the whole world surrounding him was in another world. And was moving farther . . .

Straining against the darkness that was strangling him, he opened his mouth and cried, *"Immxx—mauwwwwwwww-xx-xx! Help, John Melnix-xx! Hell-l-p-p—"*

And the shadow enclosed him completely and the world dissolved. . . .

And all around him was a cacophony of voices calling him forward, calling him forward. . . .

The bridge swayed under Claudi's feet. A bird hidden in the trees shrieked a warning—and she cried out in fear. The bird fluttered away. She sensed fear all around her—from animals, from people—like a wave crashing over her. She gripped the ropes on either side and forced herself to take another step, one foot after another, over the swaying link. Another bird's shriek startled her—then another—but she kept going, hurrying.

"There you are! Come on now!"

She pushed through some small branches and saw Lanker's hand reaching for her. He was standing on a wooden deck encircling a massive tree. He caught her wrist and hoisted her, and she collapsed onto the deck beside Sheki. Gasping for breath, she got onto her hands and knees and looked around. The deck was protected around its edge by a wood railing. Lanker was leaning out over it, trying to see something below.

Claudi looked back at Sheki, whose whole body was

quaking with sobs. "You—okay?" she said tentatively.
Sheki shook his head violently. "What—what is it—?"

Sheki could not look up. "W-W-Wat-Wat-Watson—"

Claudi drew a sharp breath. *"Watson?"* She leaned
past him to look at his right shoulder. The entity was gone.
"Oh my *gods,* Sheki—did he fall?"

Grunting, unable to talk, Sheki nodded.

Claudi looked up imploringly. "He lost Watson, Lanker!
Can we—can we go look for him?"

"Eh?" Lanker looked around, then shook his bushy head
and peered back over the railing.

"Is he down there?" Claudi croaked. "What's—what do
you see?"

"Damndest thing," Lanker muttered.

Claudi tried to get to her feet, but her legs sagged under
her. She managed to grab the railing and pull herself up
beside Lanker. She hugged the railing and peered over the
top. "What is it? Is Watson there?"

"The birds," Lanker grunted. "Look. Do you hear
them?"

The shrieks and trills of the birds were louder and
thicker than ever. Claudi saw wings fluttering in the trees
below. The birds were gathering, their cries growing
shriller.

There was a scream in the distance—a woman's.
Lanker's head snapped around as he tried to locate the
sound. Claudi hugged the rail more tightly than ever. A
shadow passed through the trees, and the deck shuddered.
A tremor passed through Claudi's body, and she felt that
sense of *presence* dividing from herself, beginning to float
up among the shadows. But something seemed to push her
back down. *"Not yet, not yet . . ."* she heard.

"What's happening?" she moaned dizzily, not quite
whole again.

"I don't know," Lanker muttered. "We should get out of
here. There may be people who need—"

Sheki cried out, interrupting him. He was sitting up
now, his back to the tree trunk. He was pointing off to his
right. "Holy Mother of . . ." Lanker murmured.

A large patch of shadow was writhing upward through
the treetops, passing very close to them. A tiny ball of light

was twinkling and winking, ducking in and out of the region of shadow. *"Waaat-sonnn!"* Sheki screamed, stretching his arms out toward the flickering light. For an instant, it seemed to respond. It darted in Sheki's direction. But it didn't get far before it turned, or was pulled, back. Its light dimmed, brightened, dimmed. It seemed to be struggling. The patch of shadow contracted as though being closed by a drawstring, and it began to move away. The entity shot back out of the shadow. Then, as if caught by an elastic string, it snapped back into the shadow, and vanished.

"Watson!" Sheki cried. *"NO!"*

"He's *gone*," Claudi whispered. She had felt Watson's terror, in the instant of his disappearance. Now she felt only an empty floating sensation.

Lanker was looking at her oddly, his eyes burning bright. "He's gone," Lanker echoed. He peered down. Something was happening below. The birds were screaming, making a tremendous racket. Overhead, the shadow was twisting around to return. From below, a huge black bird beat its wings and rocketed upward through the trees, shrieking as it hurtled toward the shadow. "That's an assassin-hawk!" Lanker grunted. "It's going after that thing!"

"Let's get out of here!" Claudi pleaded, shrinking down behind the railing. Lanker looked at her, puzzled, but didn't reply. But she heard a voice saying, *"Stay. Protect yourself. The time is not right . . . not ready. . . ."* She looked up. The floating sensation in her chest was gone. She felt whole again.

Above her, the assassin-hawk vanished into the shadow, its shriek cut off. A flock of electric blue birds thundered up after it, and a long-tailed green bird beat its way through the air, following them. The blues scattered suddenly, screaming, away from the shadow. The green bird spun and tumbled, as though it had been shot in midair. It dropped through the trees, cawing and bouncing from limb to limb. More birds followed, but the shadow was twisting and climbing away.

"It's killing them!" Claudi cried. "It's killing them!"

"Quiet! Keep down!"

Claudi crouched low behind the railing. The shadowy thing twisted one last time and then vanished. And suddenly, though she was still afraid, at least that bone-deep shivering fear had vanished with the shadows. She rose, shaking. "They're gone now, aren't they?"

"How do you know that?" Lanker snapped.

Claudi shook her head. She didn't know how to explain.

"R-ruskin!" Sheki said huskily. "Did he d-do this?" He was struggling not to cry anymore.

"I don't think so," Claudi whispered. "He tried to warn us."

Lanker's eyes flashed. "You seem to know an awful lot about this," he observed, pulling at his beard.

Claudi ducked her head, feeling guilty that she knew about it, guilty that these beings had invaded these woods. It seemed as if it were her fault. It seemed as if she ought to be able to somehow stop it all from happening.

"Do you want to tell me?"

She looked to Sheki, but he had turned away, tears streaking his cheeks. "Mr. Zizmer hasn't—I just know Ruskin said—the Throgs—" Her throat constricted and she couldn't say more.

Lanker squinted. But another voice called out of the trees: "Claudi? I saw some of what happened. Are you all right?"

"Mr. Zizmer!"

"Right here."

"Did you see the Throgs?" Claudi cried.

"The monitors showed something, but it wasn't too clear. I'm afraid there may have been some casualties elsewhere in the environment."

"Where?" Lanker snapped. "I've got to get over there!"

"Aid is on its way already," Mr. Zizmer answered. "What we need most now is for all of you to tell us everything you saw."

"They got Watson!" Sheki wailed.

"I know, Sheki. And I'm sorry," Mr. Zizmer replied. "But we need your help now. Can you all go right away to the circ-zoo teaching center, so we can talk face to face? Lanker, could I ask you to go with the children?"

"Who the hell are *you*?" Lanker asked, scowling.

"He's our teacher," Sheki sniffed, wiping his eyes as he got up. "He's trying to figure all of this out."

"Oh, is he?" Lanker tugged on his beard. "Well okay, I guess." He raised his voice. "Sure, whatever your name is —I'll go with the kids. Anything else?"

"No. Just come as quickly as possible."

Lanker nodded. "All right, you kids. Let's go."

A door winked open in the side of the tree trunk, revealing a lift. The three crowded in and it began to descend. They could still see out through the tree, and they watched the layers of branches move upward past them as they dropped. Eventually they were peering up at the treetops; and the forest floor, matted with needles and moss, rose to meet them. They saw a group of grim-faced people stride across the forest floor and disappear.

Lanker waved the kids out. They hurried to keep up with him. Claudi kept thinking there was something about this forest that she didn't understand, that she wanted to ask Lanker about; but he just kept walking until they came to a large rock wall with a thin sheet of water running down its face. She reached out and stuck her finger in the water. It felt like real water, cool. "Lanker—"

"What?" Lanker waved his hand in front of the wall. *"Open,"* he said. Claudi blinked, as an opening appeared in the water and the wall. She looked up at Lanker, openmouthed. "What?" Lanker asked again.

She blinked, shook her head.

Lanker shrugged and walked through the door. They emerged in a lobby, where the people Claudi had just seen were talking in a group. One woman was hysterical; she looked vaguely familiar to Claudi. Lanker didn't pause, but walked straight out into the corridor and down three doors. He touched a door-plate and walked through. The two kids hurried after.

It was a control room, full of IS interfaces. A tired-looking man sat in front of the screens, watching the images. "Nasty stuff out there," he murmured in a frightened voice.

Lanker nodded. "We need to use some interfaces."

"I know. The IS told me you were coming."

Claudi peered at the screens. On some of the holos were

images of the forest. On others were pictures of the zoo animals, many of them agitated. "Look!" Sheki pointed to one screen and Claudi gasped. It was Lopo, in an enclosure, and he looked extremely upset. Claudi didn't have time to ask about him, though, because Lanker tapped her on the shoulder and pointed to another holo.

Mr. Zizmer waved from the screen. "Good. You're here. Did you have any trouble?"

Lanker snapped, "Is that a joke?"

"Not at all," Mr. Zizmer answered. "I was by no means certain that you could leave the room without interference."

"Yeah, okay." Lanker pulled up chairs for himself and the kids. "Now, what is it you want?"

"Well, it would be helpful if you could each put on a headset, then tell me in your own words what you saw. Do you have headsets available—?"

"Yeah, we've got 'em." Lanker leaned forward and picked up several and passed them out. "I have to tell you, though, that I don't have much time for this. There's a lot to do out there." He glanced at the kids, who were adjusting their headsets. "Here goes, eh?"

Claudi nodded. She felt something open in her mind, and then it was as if Mr. Zizmer was sitting right here with her, and with her alone.

For Lopo, it was as if the world of the enclosure and the teacher and the zoo had dimmed somehow, and then split open and become wrapped along the walls of a vast dark tunnel, the walls flowing with globes and clouds of light. Down that tunnel, the bat-things came flying. . . .

They did not come directly to Lopo, but flew by him as if in a nightmare. It was as though they did not see him. As he crouched, growling, he turned to look at where they'd gone, and he saw them fly at someone else, farther down, in another room he could see wrapped around the tunnel. It was the "other," the keeper-person he'd seen attacked before. He was floating out of the tunnel wall wrapped in a film of glimmering light. Lopo watched as a thing of darkness touched the light that surrounded that person and darkened it. Then it touched the keeper-person himself, and he too was lost in shadow.

"Yarrrrrr!" Lopo snarled, helplessly enraged. Across the way, on another part of the tunnel wall that was the ghostly-glowing remnant of the world, he spied Baako, howling and baying at the passing bat-things. One of them seemed to brush her as it passed, and there was a tiny flicker and her cries became frantic with pain. Lopo shrank, terrified, trying to back away, trying to hide in the tunnel wall itself, trying to make himself invisible from the dark things.

And then he saw the girl wrapped in light, the other way around the tunnel, saw her floating out of the tunnel wall, and two other humans with her, all enveloped by a hazy shimmer. Lopo howled even louder than Baako—*"Yiyiyiyiyiyarrrrrrrrrr!"*—howled in pain and rage, because he feared that it might be Claudi he saw, and if it was, he must find a way to leap out of this place and down that tunnel into the other room to save her. "Claudi-Claudi-Claudi-*arrrrrrrrr!*"

And then he saw the girl's face, looming, an instant before the darkness snuffed it out, and it was not Claudi. But it was a face he had seen before.

And he howled with rage and relief and remorse and joy that it was not Claudi, and pain that the creatures had taken another. And Baako howled with him, but in her baying there was no relief at all; there was only purest pain and rage, and what sounded like madness.

And then the tunnel, with its darkness, collapsed. And the bat-things, the things he had heard called Throgs, vanished—and he was standing in his enclosure bellowing, and he could not stop for a very long time.

It was only after she had explained everything to Mr. Zizmer that Claudi remembered something: both of the times she had seen Throgs, not counting her dream, it had happened in the environment room. She mentioned this to Mr. Zizmer, who seemed lost in thought about what she had already told him.

"Eh?" His eyes opened wider. "Oh, yes—the environment room. That's turned into something of a dangerous place, hasn't it? I'm afraid some other people there weren't quite so lucky as you this time." Claudi blinked at that, but he kept right on. "It's a puzzle, all right. But it fits in with something I've been thinking. Question: what's different about that particular room? Do you know, Claudi?"

She shook her head warily.

"Well, do you know how the environment room works?"

"Lanker said it was—it was made with, um—with construction-specks. Is that what you mean?"

"Not quite—although you're right. The construction-specks make most of the landscape, and the trees, and so on. Plus, there are holos. But that's not what I mean. Look —outside the ship, we're traveling through n-space, right?"

Claudi nodded.

"Well, we have generators aboard the ship that produce the n-dimensional fields. Right?"

"Uh-huh." But what did this have to do with the Throgs?

"And we use those generators to keep us stable in the starstream. But we also use them to open small pockets into other spaces, to make more room for the inside of our ship. We call those pockets *n-space extrusions*. The environment room is an example."

Claudi blinked.

Her teacher frowned, seeing her puzzlement. "Think of it like this. Imagine blowing a bubble into space—from inside the ship. But instead of going outside the ship with it, we blow it into a different kind of n-space. That's why the environment room looks so big. It's because it's partly in a different n-space. Did you notice how large it seems now, with a whole forest inside it?"

Claudi's mouth fell open. *That's* what she'd wanted to ask Lanker—how it was that the forest was so big! In a little room! "A bubble?" she squeaked. "It's just a big bubble?"

"In principle, yes. And that's why you shouldn't have been in any danger on those footbridges—the forcefields should have set you down, light as a feather, even if you'd fallen." Mr. Zizmer stroked his chin. He seemed to consider saying something more, then shook his head. "Anyway, I think it's no coincidence that both times you saw the intruders, it was in that room."

Claudi stared at him nervously, squeezing a thick lock of her hair in her fist. Mr. Zizmer seemed to be thinking hard about something. "So—what's it mean?" she asked.

"Hm? Oh—sorry—could you bear with me for a second, Claudi? I'm in contact with the captain." Mr. Zizmer smiled, but didn't seem to be quite focusing his eyes on her. He turned his head to one side.

Claudi took a deep breath. A moment later, Mr. Zizmer turned back to her. "Well. How would you like to see the captain again, right away? You and Sheki both. And Lanker. Can you do that?"

Claudi's breath whooshed out again. She bobbed her head. She could say nothing.

"Good. Lanker will bring you to the captain's briefing room." He gave her a thumbs-up gesture. "Get going, then."

Claudi yanked off her headset. "Wow," she murmured. She turned to speak to Lanker and Sheki—and drew a startled breath. Sitting behind her, with two flat disks pressed to his head, was the S'rath, Scer-Randall. His crab-like appearance was even more alarming than before, close up. Claudi felt an almost overwhelming desire to flee from the room. She struggled not to make a sound of fear. The S'rath's eyes looked glazed and unfocused; the raspy-looking structure that was his mouth was opening and closing with a soft crunching sound.

Sheki was sitting right beside Claudi, also staring at the S'rath. He appeared not to be breathing. Finally he swallowed and looked at Claudi.

"Ah, don't worry about him." Claudi jumped. That was Lanker's heavy voice, on her other side. She swiveled, almost falling from her chair. The circus performer smiled grimly. "Let's go, then. Don't ask me why, but the skipper wants to see us."

She felt a breath of relief rushing into her chest as she darted for the door.

CHAPTER 22

Captain Thornekan had expected trouble, but he'd hoped not so soon. As he waited in the briefing room, he tried to focus on the information being relayed from the IS. Reports were coming in from all over the ship. In the environment room: two adults and one child had apparently been taken in the Throg incursion. Claudi and two friends, though in the same area, had survived unharmed. In med-care: after a brief episode of shouting and apparently trying to break free of the lev field, the Im'kek Roti Wexx'xx had vanished without a trace. In the zoo galleries: the two lupekos had obviously witnessed and become distraught over the Throg incursion, even though neither was physically in an area where it was occurring. And finally, on the bridge: instruments had registered small but measurable fluctuations in the n-space field during the episode.

The reports were discouraging. But the ship was still intact, and its crew and passengers—most of them—were still alive. That in itself was remarkable, where contact with Throgs was concerned. And what of the earlier report: two separate sightings of Willard Ruskin by the children, followed by a third in which Ruskin had warned them of the impending attack?

Thornekan's head throbbed. *Why didn't she tell me? She was right on the bridge with me!* He sighed. Even if the girl had pointed out the Ruskin-face in the star pit, he didn't know what difference it could have made.

"Len," he said, as his first officer sat down, "why are we still alive?"

Oleson scratched his beard, scowling. "Why'd they show up just in the environment room? Skipper, it beats the hell out of me. Maybe they're still too far away to really hit us."

"Except through the n-space projection? Do you suppose *it* reaches out to where they can enter it, but the rest of the ship doesn't?"

"That's exactly what the IS is proposing," Liza Demeter said, from the other end of the table.

Len looked worried. "If there's a chance of that—"

"Then we've got to shut it down right away." Thornekan hit the com. "Get me security and engineering." He drummed his fingers. "But where's the pattern? *Security*—Thornekan. Begin evacuating all n-space extrusion areas, no delay. Engineering—when those areas are secured, begin shutdown procedures immediately. Top speed."

"Aye, Captain."

"Understood, sir. But it'll take a few hours, even with fast-demolition NAGs. There's a lot of structure in there. And animals."

"If you can't get them out *fast,* you'll have to sacrifice the animals," Thornekan said sharply. "The extrusions are a weak point. Is there any way you can cut the contents loose without disassembling?"

"Not really, sir. The structural stresses—"

"Never mind, then. Let's do what we *can* do. Thornekan out." He looked up painfully at Len. "So where's the pattern? Why just those people on that bridge—and the Im'kek?"

"Well, the safety under the bridge was a levitation field, which after all is—"

"Not an n-space field."

"Not precisely. But close enough, maybe. It's consistent

with the Im'kek getting grabbed at the same time. He was in a medical lev field."

Thornekan rubbed the back of his neck. If lev fields were the danger, then what about the ship's grav fields? Would they be next? He couldn't very well turn them off.

"Captain," he heard, "the parents are here."

He sighed. "Send them in."

Four people entered the oval briefing room: Rafe Hendu, a puzzled-looking man with brown, dusty-appearing skin who walked with a slight stoop; John and Audrey Melnik, a couple who seemed not so much puzzled as frightened; and a tall blond woman whose face was reddened and streaked with tears. Her name was Holly Garelin, and she was the mother of the girl who had been lost. Her right arm was in a sling.

Captain Thornekan got right to the point. "Thank you for coming. I know you have questions, and so do I. Many distressing things have happened in the last hour, and one way or another, your children are all involved. Mr. Hendu and Mr. and Mrs. Melnik, your son and your daughter are unharmed and on their way here right now. Mrs. Garelin—" and his voice dropped—"I'm sorry, I have no word on your daughter. Perhaps it would help if you could tell us exactly what you saw."

"I already—told your officer," she said, choking out the words. She rubbed at her eyes with a trembling hand.

"I know, Mrs. Garelin," he said softly. "I know it's hard for you to repeat. But every bit of information that we can get—"

Mrs. Garelin nodded shakily. "We were just . . . going through the environment room when there was this . . . *thunder,* and this . . . *thing* flew by." And in stammers, she told her story.

She and her daughter, with three other people, had been crossing a suspension footbridge in the forest when the attack came. The bridge had started shaking. They'd tried to run, but it was nearly impossible, with horrible shadow-things flying everywhere. The man ahead of them had tried to jump over the ropes, into the safety field—but in his panic he'd flipped the whole thing over, dumping all of them. Mrs. Garelin's arm had gotten caught in the ropes, and she'd hung helpless. "I tried to grab—to grab—" Her voice failed and she looked away.

"Your daughter?"

Mrs. Garelin nodded, struggling to control her voice. "I couldn't—reach her. She fell so quickly—and then the shadow—"

"Did everyone fall?"

She nodded again. "Except one woman. She grabbed the rope and hung, like me."

"And then—?"

"The shadow—thing—" Every word now was a terrible effort for her. "It—took—*swallowed*—them—" She cleared her throat, and suddenly her voice was husky and dry. "And then it was gone. Just like that. And so was my girl. Gone. And the others."

"And someone came eventually and helped you down?"

She nodded, her face darkened with grief. "But they were gone," she whispered. "My daughter was just . . . *gone.*"

Thornekan felt a stabbing pain in his chest. "I'm sorry, Mrs. Garelin. I'm truly sorry."

"Can't you *do* anything?"

"I wish I could," he said hoarsely. "But it would seem we have been attacked by . . . something we can't control."

Mr. Hendu spoke in a murmur. "That's terrible. Captain, you said that our children were involved, too?" He peered at the Melniks. "My son and your daughter are friends. I've met Claudi. She's a very nice young lady." He looked back at the captain. "Can you tell us what—"

Mrs. Garelin burst out, "You said we were going to *leave,* to stay *away* from the Throgs! You said you were being *careful*!"

Thornekan drew a sharp breath. "I know. I know I did. But you see—" And finally he tried to explain why they had no choice but to stay in the starstream. His words were scant consolation to Mrs. Garelin. To the other parents, he described what he knew of their children's involvement. "Something is going on that we don't understand. But I'm hoping that by talking to Sheki and Claudi—"

He was interrupted by word that the children were outside. He gestured with a hand. The kids appeared in the door, saw their parents, and raced into their arms. Both looked worn but unhurt.

Thornekan waited until they got settled. "Claudi—hello again. And you must be Sheki." He noticed a tall man with an enormous shock of gray hair and a tangled beard standing near the door. "Forgive me. You are Lanker? You're with the circus?"

The man nodded.

"You were with the children during the—attack?" He gestured to Lanker to approach the table, which the man did with some reluctance.

"Yes," Lanker answered in a gravelly voice. He seemed ill at ease, especially with Mrs. Garelin struggling to control her weeping.

"Perhaps you could start by telling us what *you* saw."

"Suze?" Claudi cried, as Thornekan winced. *"It was Suze who fell?"* Her voice was torn with pain. Her eyes filled with tears, as her mother tried futilely to comfort her. "Suze is gone?" She wept, burying her face against her mother.

Thornekan felt paralyzed as he witnessed the girl's anguish. How could he have been so stupid, letting it come out like that? It just hadn't occurred to him to find out if Claudi and Suze Garelin had known each other, much less been friends. Mrs. Garelin was staring at Claudi with blurry eyes, as though unsure whether to hate her for surviving in place of her daughter, or to hug her to share the grief.

"I'm very sorry, Claudi," Thornekan said, knowing how hollow his comfort sounded.

It seemed that just about everything had been said. Both children were crying. Sheki had burst into tears upon describing how his pet "entity," Watson, had disappeared into the shadows of the Throgs. Moments later, Claudi had learned that one of the victims had been her girlfriend.

Lanker stirred. "If that's all you need from me, Captain, I'd like to get back down to help put things in order."

Thornekan exhaled. "Of course. Thank you. And Lanker, I've ordered the environment room shut down as soon as possible. Please make sure that passengers are kept out."

"Understood, Captain." With a last glance at the two children, the circus performer left the room.

"Captain, do you still need me here?"

"No, you may go, Mrs. Garelin. I appreciate your joining us."

As she left, Thornekan gathered his thoughts. He needed to understand this Ruskin connection. *Do not run away,* the kids had reported Ruskin as saying. And later: *The time is not right.* What did that mean? Ruskin seemed aware of their danger. Why had he wanted the children to go to the environment room? Or had they misunderstood? Was it possible that Ruskin could help? And what of this "virtual presence" talent of Claudi's that the IS had described? Was that what Ruskin was interested in? Was there some way they could renew the contact with Ruskin?

He was aware that everyone was waiting for him to speak. The idea that was growing in his mind was the only idea he had. He gestured to his officers and conferred with them quietly for a moment. Then he spoke to the others. "I would like to propose something. It will require your help, Claudi, and yours, Sheki. And I will need your permission, as well," he added, gazing at the parents.

They all stirred anxiously.

"I hope that there will be no risk in this," he said slowly, "but I cannot guarantee that. However, I *can* guarantee that if we don't do something soon, we may lose the entire ship." And he began to explain.

CHAPTER 23

The stars of the holoimage swam around their heads. Thornekan watched the children drink in the view. Claudi, he knew, would have liked it better if he'd turned on the full n-space images, instead of just the holoview; but he wasn't ready yet to take a chance on any sort of n-space opening, not after what had happened on the environment deck.

"What do you think, Sheki?" he asked, stepping up behind the youngster.

Sheki was staring, open-mouthed. He seemed, at least for the moment, to have forgotten his grief over the loss of his pet. "It's . . . amazing!"

"It is that." Thornekan pointed out the direction in the starstream that they were traveling, and watched as Sheki traced their path through the stars with his eyes. He imagined the wonder that was going through the small boy's mind, and he almost smiled. He was alone on the deck with the children. The kids' parents and a couple of officers were waiting just beyond, in the lobby. "Well, kids—*we* know why we're here. Do you suppose *he* does?"

Sheki seemed not to hear him, but Claudi turned, brow

furrowed in angry concentration. "How would he know that?"

Thornekan shrugged. "I don't know," he admitted. "I'm just hoping he does, because I don't know how else to get his attention. Do you?"

Claudi shook her head. She glared out at the stars. She was taking it hard about losing her friend, as indeed she should. And yet, it was vital that he coax her into putting that grief by, or at least seeing beyond it. He had to gain information—and the kids seemed his only means.

Sheki turned. There was a certain look of determination in his eyes, as though he'd seen what he needed to see, and now he was ready to take on whatever stood in his way. "What are we supposed to do?" he asked in a small voice.

Thornekan scratched his temple. "Well, since we're waiting on *him,* I guess the only thing we can do is sit—" and he indicated the bench seat where he'd sat with Claudi just hours ago, though it seemed days—"and see what we can learn from each other while we're waiting."

Sheki walked over to the bench with the captain, and sat beside him. Claudi came more slowly. "What do you mean, see what we can learn?" she said darkly.

"Well, for one thing—come sit, Claudi, please—for one thing, maybe you can tell me everything you can remember Ruskin ever saying to you."

Claudi shrugged, twitching. *I don't want to talk about it,* her body seemed to say.

Thornekan gazed at her, feeling her anguish. "Claudi, tell me—is it your friend Suze that you're thinking of?"

She shrugged, even more twitchily.

"Well, Claudi, I think I know a little bit of what you're feeling."

"No, you don't," she snapped.

"Well, maybe not—but maybe I have at least an idea," he said. "If I'm not mistaken, you're probably thinking that you should have done something to save your friend. Maybe you're thinking, because you were the one Ruskin warned, that you are somehow to blame for the people who got hurt. Am I close?" When no reaction came, he leaned back against the wall. Reaching into his shirt pocket, he fished out some chewing gum and offered a piece to each of them. Sheki took a piece silently; he seemed subdued, and unsure of what he was supposed to be doing. Claudi shook her head, refusing.

Thornekan nodded and worked his gum into a wad in his mouth. "I can't tell you what to feel, Claudi. But as captain, I would have to make the judgment as to whether you were at fault. And my judgment is, you were not." Still no answer. "Now, I know you hurt because of your friend—and that's okay—but Claudi, *it wasn't your fault. You couldn't have stopped it from happening.*"

Claudi's face had tightened. She was glaring up at the stars, her head tilted back, her chin thrust out. She seemed not to see the captain. But finally, she said, without looking, "How do you know?"

"The facts speak in your defense. How could you have stopped it, Claudi?" Thornekan sighed, aching. "You know, we all feel bad when something happens to someone we care about." And he thought, as he had so often lately, of Myra dying a victim of Throgs on a strange and helpless world—and he tried to push the thought away, but it would not yield. Had he felt guilty for not being there and dying with her? Of course he had. Could Claudi possibly understand that? He wasn't sure. "I know that," he said, his voice trembling, "because it's happened to me too. You see, Claudi, my wife was killed by the Throgs—and I wasn't there to save her, either." He was aware, through unfocused eyes, of Claudi grunting, then slowly turning to look at him. "And you know something?" he murmured. "Even if I had been—"

"Ex-excuse me, Captain," Sheki interrupted.

He blinked, catching his words in midsentence. He let his breath out, to keep his voice even. "Yes?"

"L-l-look out th-there!" The boy raised his arm and pointed.

"Why? What is it?" He looked where Sheki was pointing, and tried to bring his eyes back into focus.

"There!" Claudi said sharply. "I see it!"

He frowned. "I guess I'm the only one who doesn't—" And then he did.

It was a particularly bright concentration of star and starcloud images, with wisps of white and reddish gases overlying the blurred orbs of star locations. And yet, in and among the bright images, there were patches of dark sky. And it was out of that darkness, and yet shaped by the surrounding clouds, that a human face was sculpted, suggested by the stars rather than actually being outlined. It reminded him, somehow, of a face he had been studying on the IS screen lately. It reminded him of Willard Ruskin.

The Ruskin-face seemed to be gazing directly at them, as though peering into the ship through a window. The eyes, shaped by stars and darkness, seemed to move, examining each of them in turn, as if wondering what manner of creature he was meeting. And then he spoke; and his voice was audible, but was not the reverberating voice the captain instinctively expected. It was more like a sighing of the stars. A whisper.

"Claudi, I have wanted to speak with you—and you, Sheki. Captain—you are the captain?—perhaps it was inevitable that we meet also. How do you fare, in the face of the dangers that confront you?"

Thornekan rose. "We have suffered losses, and we have grave concerns for our safety. There is much I would like to ask you."

The sigh from the stars seemed almost weary. "Yes. I had hoped to avoid . . . but never mind that now."

"*Are* you Willard Ruskin?" Thornekan asked bluntly.

The eyes in the stars seemed to turn inward. "I am . . . Ruskin/*Bright*/Ali'Maksam/Ganz/memory-of-Dax/Tamika/Thalia . . ." and the voice trailed off into an almost imperceptible whisper of other names before concluding . . . "I am *New*."

The captain felt at a loss for words. "Yes—well—I am Captain Roald Thornekan. And this is—"

"I know," whispered the star face. "Names do not concern me now. There are more important matters to speak of."

"Indeed," the captain said eagerly, then stopped himself. What *was* most important? He drew a breath. "Could you please . . . explain . . . what you meant when you told Sheki that he must not, or *we* must not—"

"Must not run," Ruskin, or New, echoed.

"Yes." The captain cleared his throat uneasily. "What did you mean by that?"

There was a light growing behind Ruskin's face, a light like an orangish sunset, or a vast crimson star swelling to fill the night. "Is it so unclear?" whispered the star-being.

Thornekan knotted his fists in frustration and wonder. "Yes, damn it. It is unclear."

"The enemy comes," said New.

"We know that. We've suffered for it already. May we presume it will get worse?"

"Perhaps." The Ruskin-face stared at him. "But you must . . . not . . . run."

The captain stared back. "Why? I am concerned, yes, that we not lead the enemy to a vulnerable world. But what do you—"

He was interrupted—not by words but by something changing visibly in the stars, something shifting in the night—almost like a curtain shimmering, or twisting. Or like a window opening. And through the window, far away, there were shapes flying and fluttering. . . .

"Dear God!" Thornekan gasped. What he saw, he knew without asking, were Throgs. Throgs gamboling against the darkness of a place where there were no stars. They were dark, the Throgs—dark against dark. He felt as if something were closing around his chest, like a tight band.

"Do you know this sight?" asked New.

"I—" Thornekan caught himself and shifted his eyes. The children were both staring, horrified, at the vision. "Claudi," he asked urgently, "is this what you saw in your dreams? Or in the environment room? Is this what the two of you saw?"

Sheki, and then Claudi, nodded without speaking.

Thornekan stared at the Throgs, trying to imagine himself in that room where the kids had been. Imagining Myra. . . . "What is our danger?" he whispered to New. "Are they on their way to attack us—or is this just an illusion?"

There was another odd twisting sensation, and the window closed. "No illusion, no," sighed the starstream-being. "Are they on their way? Yes. But your danger is not immediate. At this moment, they are unable to reach you."

"Can you *stop* them from reaching us?"

The answer seemed weighted with sorrow. "No."

Thornekan felt a sting of disappointment. "Why not? Can you at least explain? People die when they meet the Throgs!" he said angrily.

There seemed to be a look of puzzlement on the Ruskin-face. His voice whispered, "Yes, we know. But we have not . . . the power to do what you ask. Nevertheless . . . we have hope that we might . . . in some way . . ."

"Can't you at least share with us what you know? Give us some information to help ourselves?" Thornekan's desperation welled up again, replacing his anger. "You were once Human, too!" And instantly he regretted his tone, if not his words.

If New took offense, he did not show it. "We have not forgotten that part of us were . . . Human."

"Then can't you—?"

"Perhaps we can, Captain. But in a way that is . . . difficult to explain. Time may be short. If you would permit us to speak more directly with these young ones . . . the children . . ."

The captain's throat tightened.

"We wish to help. But you must trust. Though there may be . . . risk."

"What risk?" Thornekan demanded.

"Not from us. From the other. But your risk is already grave." The face in the stars seemed to study him. "Captain, would you open this part of your ship to us? Create a projection into our space—?"

"That was our mistake before. That was what brought on the attack."

"We understand. But the danger at present is distant. We can give warning—"

"Like you did before?" Thornekan asked indignantly. "You might have warned the rest of us, not just the children!"

"Our contact was incomplete. We are still learning—"

"Well, there's a lot *I* need to learn about the Throgs! About their position and their intentions—"

New's voice seemed gently to erase the captain's anger

from the air. "We realize that what you wished is not what we . . . *needed* . . . to do."

"What's that mean?"

The face, backed by a brightening orange glow, was silent. Then: "Captain, if you would know the Throgs—"

"I don't want to know them," Thornekan said harshly. "I want to *avoid* them."

"Nevertheless, you must trust us."

The captain was silent for a long time. "How? By turning on the projection field here? Is that what you want?"

"Yes," whispered the stars. "We will watch, will stand guard. And—"

"And—?"

The stars seemed to hiss with quiet, unnerving laughter. "And we would speak with the children in private."

When the n-space projections came on, the only visible difference was a momentary flicker and a sharpening of the intensity of the star-images. The two children stood in quiet awe—or perhaps it was fear—as Thornekan made the adjustments.

Another difference soon became apparent. Almost as though he were stepping out of the stars, Ruskin/New's face shrank, and yet grew closer, more solid. No longer a part of the stars, he floated in front of them, his whole human body emerging into view. Neither wholly solid nor wholly ethereal, he seemed to actually step down onto the deck. He stood, faintly radiant, facing the captain. But he addressed the two children. "Claudi? Sheki? Would you grant me a private hearing?"

Even as he spoke, his entire countenance seemed to change—his face growing longer and thinner, and his eyes sharper and more needlelike, until his pupils seemed to glitter like diamonds. His body shape had become lanky and sinuous; he somehow *melded* into a sitting, cross-legged position, his upper body swaying back and forth slowly, almost like a serpent—or a Logothian. His voice was a rustle of dry leaves: "Will you speak with me, children? Will you listen to my counsel?"

Thornekan felt an inner pressure as he tried to maintain

some semblance of control over the situation. "Claudi? Sheki? Are you willing to speak privately with him?"

Both nodded, but Sheki had a wide-eyed look as though wondering if, after all, he were in the presence of a deity.

The being sighed. "Captain, we do not ask that you leave, only that we be permitted silence for a time."

He nodded. A Logothian, yes. It looked as though it might have been—what was the name?—Ali'Maksam. The friend of Ruskin, the one who had died with him in the gateway. How many others were there within this one being?

The serpent-creature bowed toward the children, who somehow had already drawn closer to it. The three were surrounded now by an aura of light, a nimbus of something that was more than mere radiance—more like a glimmering *reshaping* of that small region of space. Thornekan thought of the n-space opening and the risk; and he thought of another ship, once, that he had exposed to risk, perhaps unwisely, and of the men who had died as a result. He resisted an urge to step forward, to demand that he be included. He could not see or hear any movement or breath of life now; even the swaying of the Logothian-image was blurred by the radiant haze. He ached to interrupt, to assure himself that the children were unharmed.

The nimbus, and the children and serpent-being, suddenly shrank away from him—as though they were going to vanish back into the stars. "What are you—?" he grunted, his voice hard but uncertain, and then he caught himself. He had promised silence.

The nimbus and the children dwindled, but did not vanish. They floated like a tiny window among the stars. But in some way he did not understand, he felt Claudi's presence as if she were still standing beside him, her face clear in his mind. He felt a curious reassurance in that presence.

Claudi's specialness? he wondered.

Silence. He could do nothing but uphold his end of the agreement. And wait helplessly to see how this unHuman being would uphold its end.

* * *

For Claudi, the most astonishing moment came when she felt herself floating on a cushion of light, floating with Sheki into the presence of a being who, she somehow knew at once, *understood* her, understood both of them. She could see his snake-face and his shining eyes, and she did not recoil. It was not a warm face, exactly, but the shining eyes somehow held a recognizable kindness in them. She was not afraid of him. For a moment, she even forgot about Suze. . . .

> *Spin*
> *spin*
> *spin*
> *look within* . . .

She heard the voice without hearing it, and knew that it had spoken without speaking. It was a different voice from Ruskin's, from the one she had heard before; and yes, she understood, it was not exactly Ruskin now, but rather someone . . . well, not wholly different, but still . . . different.

And she did not need to speak, because it knew her, knew her thoughts. And she felt the surprise . . .

> *Logothian ways*
> *You have known!*
> *There is hope*
> *Indeed* . . .

She heard without fully understanding. It did not seem important that she understand right now.

She heard, as though it were the quiet chirping of a bird somewhere, the thought-words of Sheki, and she heard them without a trace of a stammer.

She heard her own thought-words, also, as though they were someone else's, telling of things she had seen in the night, and of her fears, and her terrible pain. Because her friend had fallen straight into the Throgs, and she had done nothing to prevent it.

And she heard the rustling voice . . .

Do not blame
　Do not regret
　　Do not fear . . .

And that was bewildering, because at the same moment, she glimpsed—somewhere, spinning almost out of sight—a tremendous gathering of Throgs. And she knew they were coming this way, and nothing that any of them could do would stop them. But she did not feel afraid. She felt only a quiet dreaminess as she heard . . .

You must not be afraid
　Must not run
　　not run . . .

Truth
　In time
　　Will emerge
　　　You will see
　　　　You will know . . .

What would she know? It was all so confusing, promises and possibilities floating toward her in a great haze, and she couldn't decipher anything she saw.

And behind it all was the glowing warmth of a sun, enormous and reddish orange and alive.

Seventeen minutes had passed in which Captain Thornekan had stood there waiting, his mind drifting through cobwebs of memory and hope and fear. Something was happening now. He blinked hard and shook himself alert.

The tiny window containing the children was growing larger and closer again. The dream-image of Claudi was gone from his mind. A brightness from somewhere was filling the observation deck, a glow that slowly rendered blurry the view of the stars, the children, everything. It was as though a reddish sun were filling the n-space fields that brought the images into the deck. All that was around him, including the children, wavered ethereally in the glow.

And a faint, almost underwater-sounding voice said:

My children, you must stay to do that for which you are called. Do not run.

And the glow faded, and Sheki and Claudi stood precisely where they had stood earlier, before the captain. And they looked—not frightened or harmed, but full of puzzlement.

Thornekan exhaled slowly, feeling a faintness wash through him. Then he realized: He and the children were alone here on the deck. The starstream-being was gone.

And he had never gotten his answers about the Throgs.

PART THREE

THE THROGS

"Deep into that darkness peering,
long I stood
there wondering, fearing . . ."

—Edgar Allan Poe

Interlude

So frail, the children! So fragile!
Were he/they doing right, placing such burden, such
risk upon ones so young, so innocent and trusting?

Is there another way? The danger grows. What hope of
saving them otherwise, of saving these
        or the others . . . ?

But we don't know
    Can't possibly know

Shall we let them die, every one of them, flying into the
shadows that devour?

    *Must sing
        they must sing
            our children
                to survive*

Scattered and feuding thoughts slowly coalesced. It
seemed now the only hope
    the only way.

There was so little that she/they knew of the ones of shadow . . . except that they seemed neither to see nor to hear when New reached out to them.

There was only an icy breath, a touch of dread, a pulling away, and no awareness that New could understand. But even if New could not make them see
    or hear
perhaps there was another way. Perhaps they could do something
    terribly risky
       create the circumstances
         and the possibility . . .

Through the children . . .

Madness: their innocence will be their death—

    —or their life

Can innocence be strength?

    Dare we not sing ?
    or cry ?

They will spin,
    spin it free—

But the peril—

    They must sing
      and cry

Or surely
    surely
      die.

CHAPTER 24

At the deck-school, there was that empty space where Suze had been. It seemed as if, one after another, the kids were always glancing that way—Jenny, Jeremy, all of them. Claudi saw them averting their eyes quickly, as if ashamed to be caught looking for Suze. The deck-school had removed Suze's seat from the room; but together, the kids had raised a furious ruckus with Mr. Zizmer and Mr. Seipledon and demanded its return. Suze might still be saved, they'd insisted, and it wasn't right. And they won: Suze's seat was back in the room. But Mr. Zizmer cautioned them against false hopes. It was, he said, extremely unlikely that Suze would ever return, and they had to accept that fact. His words robbed them of some, but not all, of the sweetness of their small victory.

The whole class felt as though it would explode if *something* didn't happen—and that afternoon, it did. Mr. Zizmer had them shove their seats out of the way against the wall, and they sat on the floor in a circle in the center of the room, on large pillows. Mr. Zizmer had them put on their headsets, then told them that they would be having a guest teacher for a while. Then he disappeared.

The new teacher appeared in the wall—striding toward them from a great distance over a winding path that seemed to zigzag its way far off into the wall, over a great dusty plain. They could hear the wind howl as he approached, whistling a tune, growing larger and larger, the wind whipping at his neatly fitted jacket with its tight collar. Finally he stepped out of the wall into the classroom and looked around, dusting himself off. "Halloo!" he called. "Anyone home? Mind if I come in?"

The kids muttered in reply. He could pretend to be just an ordinary, visiting teacher—maybe one with a weird sense of humor—but they knew what he was. He was the wall-shrink. He was a tall, skinny holo of a man who squinted, then jerked his eyebrows up and smiled—but only for an instant, so that if you'd looked away you'd missed it. His eyebrows shot up again. "My *naaa-aime,*" he drawled, with some sort of phony accent that was supposed to make them laugh, "is Dock-tor *Felt*-better." A smile flashed, vanished. "Usually, when people talk to me, they don't look so good at first—and that's what they say. 'I've felt better, Doctor. I've felt better.'" He pursed his lips. No one was laughing.

Claudi watched him through slitted eyelids. What was this guy doing here, instead of Mr. Zizmer? What good was a wall-shrink supposed to be?

"I guess we all know," Dr. Feltbetter was saying, "there've been some pretty rough things going on around here. Some unhappy things. You all know what I mean, right?" He looked around, then sighed and shook his head. "Look, kids—here's the thing. None of us really wants to talk about it, right? If we could, we'd just pretend it never happened at all, because that's what we all wish. Come on —am I right?"

One or two kids nodded hesitantly, which seemed to satisfy him. "Okay, good." He stroked his chin thoughtfully. "Now, I can tell you're all a little nervous. Maybe you wish Mr. Zizmer were here. But he has to be away for a while, and so I guess you're stuck with me. So my suggestion is we make the best of it. Okay? Now, I'm going to ask someone to be brave. I'm going to ask someone to just say *right out* what it is that happened—so we don't have to go on pretending that it didn't. Who's brave? Nobody? Jenny! How about you?"

Jenny flinched at the sound of her name. "Wh-what?" She had her hands folded tightly in her lap and she was rocking forward and backward on her pillow.

Dr. Feltbetter's eyebrows went up halfway. "Can you, Jenny, put into words for us—what it is that's making us all so *sad?* See, I think it helps if we can *name* our sadness, instead of just getting sadder and sadder while we try not to think about it. *Why are you sad, Jenny?*"

Jenny just shook her head silently.

Dr. Feltbetter smiled in disappointment before casting his gaze around the room. "Anyone else? What is it that we're *all* thinking about?"

There was a sullen silence in the classroom. Finally Jeremy stirred, but this time he didn't look as though he was going to make a smart remark, which was too bad. Claudi almost would have welcomed one of his wise remarks. "It's because the Throgs got Suze!" he shouted suddenly, with real anger. "That's why! *It's 'cause they got her!*" His voice cracked a little at the end. An expression of triumph crossed his face, but only for an instant.

It's because we *let* them get Suze, Claudi thought angrily.

"And we're afraid they'll get *us,*" Paul piped in, staring shamefacedly at the floor.

What does the stupid teaching-wall think we need a stupid wall-shrink for, anyway? Claudi thought bitterly. Why doesn't Mr. Zizmer come back?

Dr. Feltbetter nodded. "Good . . . very good. That's exactly why. Because our friend Suze is gone—and we don't even know whether to hope. And because we're afraid. Afraid for ourselves." His eyebrows crept upward. "Does anyone here feel just a *little* bad because you think maybe it's not right to be afraid for *yourself,* when here it's your friend Suze who's been taken—but you can't help being afraid? Anyone feel just a little like that?" Dr. Feltbetter raised his own hand. "Well, I do. I'll admit it. You don't have to raise your hands. Just think about whether it might be true."

They sat silently, thinking. Then Dr. Feltbetter said,

"Now, try adding this thought: *Don't blame yourself.* Hey? It's *okay* to be afraid for yourself if you're in danger. In fact, you'd be a little crazy if you *weren't* afraid! So yes—I feel sad about Suze, *and* I'm afraid for myself. Now, I know the captain is doing everything he can to protect us—he really is. But I still have my feelings."

He paced slowly around the center of the circle, each student glancing up to meet his gaze. Jenny was sniffing back tears. Claudi felt them welling up in her own eyes, but she was determined not to let this Dr. Feltbetter make her cry. He was supposed to make them feel better? She was waiting. She didn't feel better yet. She looked up with a flinch as he passed near her, and found his bright brown eyes looking straight down into hers. That maddening smile flashed on his face again, and he moved on. Sheki was next, staring soberly. Claudi glanced at him and thought: He's thinking about Watson. I can see it in his eyes. He's off somewhere thinking about Watson. And he's not going to let this guy make him cry, either.

Dr. Feltbetter spun suddenly, his image blurring. His voice was sharp and gentle, all at the same time, and it made Claudi shiver. She'd forgotten she was wearing a headset, but his voice was touching her inside her mind now. *"It's good to cry—"* he murmured, and his gaze seemed to take them all in at once. *"Jenny, it's good to cry. Claudi, Sheki . . . Paul, Jeremy . . . Rob, Betsy. Let it out when you feel bad. That's what crying's for."*

You stupid stupid man, Claudi thought. Who do you think you are? She wiped away a tear. Her eyes were stinging from trying so hard not to cry. She blew her nose on a tissue.

"How about if we just talked about Suze for a while," Feltbetter went on. "I don't just mean how it happened, with the Throgs and all. I mean, let's talk about what we would like to remember of her—because unless something pretty miraculous happens, we really might never see her again. But do keep this in mind: Although there's danger still from the Throgs, we know now that they got at Suze through the environment room, and that opening has been closed. So we do have some reason to hope for our own safety." A few of the kids shifted uneasily. "We'll talk about that, too—our safety, I mean. But just now let's think about Suze, our friend. Let's think of some things we'd like to remember about her. Anyone?"

Of course no one said a word. But Claudi's mind was suddenly running wild with memories of Suze: times they'd laughed and raced around together, to the lounges and the game rooms; times in class when they'd tried to outwit the teachers, although that never seemed to work with Mr. Zizmer; times they'd argued—

She grunted, feeling a great pressure suddenly trying to rise out of her chest. *Times they'd argued*—Suze had been mad at her since the circus show, was probably still mad at her when the Throg got her. They'd never had time to . . . they'd never really made up.

Claudi's eyes were suddenly hot with tears, and she didn't hear another word Feltbetter said. *Suze, I didn't mean it! You stupid—I didn't mean to make you mad! I didn't want to let the Throgs get you! Suze, please— PLEASE, Suze, please please please . . .*

She blinked open her watery eyes, squinting, and realized that Feltbetter was showing holo replays of Suze, from class. There she was, grinning and clowning around. There she was, talking to Jeremy or someone, but it was all blurry. . . .

Claudi could hear someone crying, snuffling, and she didn't know if it was someone in the class now, or someone in the stupid stupid holo. She was twisting her hair and pulling it until it hurt. *Get it off get it off get the stupid holo off . . . !*

She couldn't really hear, but it seemed as if somehow a voice was answering her, deep inside her skull, only she couldn't hear what it was saying. But she felt again that sense of dividing within herself, and her floating *presence;* and it was almost as if she were touching her classmates inside *their* minds, sharing their grief, and it was like a cascading fountain of rushing water, bubbling tears, all of their grief combined, and she was walking around among them, touching them and sharing their tears.

It seemed to go on for a very long time, and yet for no time at all. There were sounds of laughter, at something that Suze did. There were groans, at something dumb she said. It all went by in a blur. And yet somehow it reached deeper into her than anything she had ever felt before—and it *hurt*, hurt deep on the inside where she couldn't hide from it at all. And when it was over, Claudi was sobbing and so was everyone else.

She didn't know how it had happened, but all of her classmates were clustered around her, hugging her, trying to make her feel better. Jenny and Betsy were there, and Sheki, and even Jeremy and the other boys were there, trying to comfort her. And it just made her cry all the harder. The tears kept coming, and big quaking sobs erupted from her like bubbles of lava from a volcano. It seemed as if it would never end.

Eventually it did end. And as she wiped her eyes and blew her nose on a tissue, she realized that the other kids were weeping, too—even the boys, though now they they were moving away self-consciously. Claudi drew a deep, shuddering breath, wondering what exactly had just happened. She thought she'd been comforting *them*, and then it had all seemed turned around. She sighed as the other kids sat back on their own cushions.

Mr. Zizmer was back, standing just outside the circle of kids, talking to Dr. Feltbetter. He finally seemed to notice that everyone had sat back down, and he gestured to Dr. Feltbetter, and the doctor returned to the center of the circle again, while Mr. Z waited near the wall.

"Ah—thank you, everyone." Dr. Feltbetter tilted his head, stroking his jaw, as if trying to decide what to say next. "Well, your Mr. Zizmer here tells me that you have a lot to do, and maybe I had better call my visit quits for now. But I'll be back, if you need me. Does anyone have anything else they'd like to say?" He turned his head one way, and another, like a bird. The class was still. Everyone seemed too worn out to say anything even if they'd wanted to. His gaze rested finally on Claudi, and he nodded. "Well, then, maybe we've said enough already—so I'll be saying good-bye. But please don't forget—" and he winked—*"if you don't feel better . . . you haven't talked to Dr. Feltbetter."*

And he winked out of sight, leaving the kids sitting in silence.

Mr. Zizmer walked into the circle, looking thoughtful. "Hi, everyone. Well . . . I guess we could have done a *little* better with our counseling program, couldn't we?" He rubbed the back of his neck, chuckling as if embarrassed. "You don't have to answer that. But I hope it was helpful, anyway. It's not over—we'll have to talk about these things some more before we're done. But . . . well, look, I just want you all to know . . ."

He hesitated and let his arms drop to his sides. *"I want you all to know that I feel as bad about Suze as you do,"* he said abruptly. "I miss her, too."

A painful silence followed his words, but somehow the painfulness of it faded as the kids—Claudi, anyway—thought about what he'd said. It helped, somehow, to hear Mr. Zizmer say that. That he missed Suze, too. Dr. Feltbetter had said the same thing, but Claudi didn't believe him. What did he know about Suze? Mr. Zizmer she believed.

"Well, anyway," Mr. Zizmer went on, "we can't spend all of our time dwelling on that, either. We have a ship that still has to run, and ahead of us, there's a colony to build—somewhere out there among the stars." He waved his hand expansively and forced a little smile. "And of course, there are dangers to be faced. But—for now—I thought you might like a little sim to relax by." He peered at the students and his smile began to seem more natural. "Yes, I think, a little sim. Keep your headsets on, please."

He waved his hand in a sweeping gesture. The room darkened, then filled again like a glass vessel filling with blazing sunshine. Overhead, billowing white clouds floated. Claudi heard the thunder of a rolling surf, and the hiss of sand and the cries of ocean gulls. And despite herself, she let her breath out and she almost smiled.

CHAPTER 25

For Captain Thornekan, the days following the attack seemed hauntingly quiet. Time passed as though spun from molasses, while a sense of fearful expectancy charged the air throughout the ship, like an odor that would not be dispelled. Several days had passed with no reappearance of either the Throgs or the starstream-being. He could only wait, painfully aware of how little he had learned, and how helpless he remained. At first, every minor alarm on the bridge brought him to an adrenaline-high state of alert. Over time he became less jumpy; but an undercurrent of dread remained, weighing not just on him and his officers, but on all of the passengers and crew.

Volunteer search parties had been organized among the passengers to look for signs of the missing victims—though Thornekan privately held out no hope for their survival. Regular corridor patrols now prowled the decks, ready to sound the alarm in case of further invasion. Several false sightings had caused flurries of panic; but so far, anyway, full-fledged hysteria had been kept at bay.

Two passengers had had to be confined for inciting to mutiny. Evidently they had hoped to gather enough supporters to force the captain to make a hasty exit from the starstream—a goal that was now physically impossible in any case. Though those individuals had found little sympathy for mutiny, the possibility nevertheless weighed on the captain's mind. He'd delivered the hard news at his last meeting with the colonists' representatives. Though there really *was* no choice any longer, many clearly resented his decision to remain in the starstream, believing that the captain's first loyalty ought to have been to his own passengers, and other considerations be damned.

He found it hard to disagree with the sentiment, but at least some passengers recognized the necessity of his decision, so he did not feel entirely alone against a tide of opposition. He had spoken to no one except his closest officers of New's puzzling insistence that they not "run." He wasn't even sure what it meant. Should he not try to avoid the Throgs? He certainly would try, if he could discover how. In any case, though New's insistence was not his reason for staying in the starstream, he was not about to bring New's bewildering admonition up for debate. He had admitted publicly to the appearances of the starstream consciousness—there were too many rumors to pretend otherwise—but officially, there was no reason to expect the consciousness to help them against the Throgs.

Unofficially, there wasn't much reason, either.

The truth was that the meeting with the starstream-being had done little to give him confidence. *Trust*, New had said. Trust what? He'd learned almost nothing of a factual nature—just that the Throgs weren't close enough to destroy them *yet*—and the kids, while they'd tried to be helpful, had been unable to articulate what had happened in their meeting with the Ruskin-Ali'Maksam being. What, Thornekan wondered angrily, was the being trying to do? Why had he/it/whatever refused to tell him anything about the Throgs, or about its own intentions? And why had it not reappeared? Such questions filled sleepless nights; and when the captain did sleep, his nightmares about the Throgs were only growing worse.

He spent most of his time now on the bridge, watching and waiting, as the ship sped on its way down the starstream. They were nearing the innermost reaches of the

Orion spiral arm of the galaxy, moving inward toward the boundary region between the Orion arm and the Sagittarius arm, closer to the galactic center. The exit node they had once thought to take was now behind them, and the next node was far ahead. Where, in that great long stretch of space, would the Throgs reappear?

The captain's only concrete strategy was to keep the people alert and occupied. Defense drills were now part of shipboard routine, and additional survival-skills workshops had been organized for the adult passengers. Just now, he was looking over the latest announcements from the entertainment department. He ran his finger down the list. Music performances, theater, surroundies, new shows from the circ-zoo, everything the ship offered except the environment room and the observation deck was being crammed in. "Looks good," he said, handing the list back to Liza, whom he had charged with jazzing up the main infonet and monitoring the pulse of the public message boards. "No idle minds, if we have anything to say about it. How are the gripes running today?"

"On a scale of one to ten? Well, no one's asked for your head yet, at least not formally." Liza flashed him a smile that was more of a wince. "Take comfort where you can, skipper," she added and headed back to her IS center, trailing a lingering odor of garlic.

Thornekan followed her with his eyes, sighing. He supposed he should feel encouraged. A vision of his head on a pike had crossed his mind more than once today. How he wished he could take a rest from all of this, leave someone else in charge for a while! He wished he'd taken them out of the starstream. He wished Liza would eat odorless garlic. He pulled his gaze back. No idle minds. Thoughts on your job.

He scanned the bridge instruments, finally letting his eyes come to rest on the star pit. And he tried to reach out as he imagined Claudi might, thinking: Are you coming back? Did you get what you want, and will we see you again?

As always, the stars answered him with stoic silence.

* * *

For Claudi, the days became a blur, sometimes a gentle blur filled with wondering thoughts about Ruskin and the sun-being, and sometimes a blur of pain and tears as she thought of Suze, taken by the Throgs in their fury while she and Sheki had escaped unharmed.

Well, Sheki hadn't exactly escaped unharmed. Once in a while she saw him blinking quiet tears, and she knew that he was thinking of Watson, sucked up in the blackness of the Throgs just as Suze had been. When she saw him crying, she didn't exactly look the other way, but she didn't say anything, either, because she didn't know what to say. She knew how he felt, though. She knew he blamed himself for losing Watson. He couldn't help it. She remembered the captain telling her that she shouldn't blame herself for Suze, either. But it was hard.

They talked about Suze in class a few more times, but it still hurt to think about her. Claudi's parents tried to talk, too, and she knew they were just trying to help. But her fath' got pretty sad himself, talking about it—because he had lost a friend of his own, this Roti Wexx'xx. Claudi didn't know much about the Im'kek, but it really seemed to bother her father that he had been snatched, hurt and alone, from the med-care like that. At one point when Claudi and her mother and father were all wheezing and hugging each other wordlessly, her father cleared his throat and said: "Little bird, there are times in life when things just plain *hurt*. And it *hurts* and *hurts*, and there's nothing you can really do about it, except—" and he sighed and looked straight at her—"except just let it wash over you, like a wave in the ocean. After a while, if you keep your head high, the wave will wash away again and you'll start to feel better. But only if you don't fight it."

And she looked at her father and felt indeed as if a wave were washing over her head, threatening to drown her, and it felt as if it never would go away. And her father swept her into his arms and rocked her; and after a while, as he'd promised, the wave subsided and she could breathe again. And she did feel better, a little anyway.

There were times, when she was alone, that she thought back to the visit she and Sheki had had with New. Though she didn't understand it, there was a gentle warmth about the memory that, for a while, when she thought of it, made her forget those other, darker thoughts of fear. Was it possible that somewhere, somehow, Suze was all right? She didn't know; she just knew that when that memory came to her, the memory of the sunny glow and the words of the starstream-being in her mind, it made her feel comforted and secure.

It had been, she thought, sort of like talking to God. Oh, she knew it *wasn't* God—but it felt the way she imagined having a conversation with God might feel. Once, when she was walking alone on the shopping deck, she paused in front of a shop window and turned around to stare across the corridor at the polished wooden doors of the ship's chapel. She wondered if maybe, if she went in there, she could have a real conversation with God. She'd never even been inside the chapel before, and she thought that probably just really religious people went in there, and she didn't think she and her parents were very religious. Still, she wondered. But then she saw some older kids staring at her from the next doorway down, and she turned the other way and ran to the lift and left the shopping deck behind.

She talked a few times with Sheki about what it had been like, thinking directly to the Ruskin-being; but for all the memories, it was still sort of like a dream, and once you'd talked about it, there didn't seem that much more to say. The captain asked them to come and try again to reach New, but she knew somehow that it wasn't going to work, and it didn't. She didn't know how she knew; she just did. Sheki didn't seem to have expected failure or success, or shown much reaction one way or the other. He was a funny kind of kid, she thought; he always seemed to be either scared witless or else so fascinated that he didn't think to be scared—but on this occasion, he simply seemed unconcerned. It was almost as though he had nothing really to worry about anymore.

She was worried, though—and one thing that worried her was Lopo. And Baako. On one of their visits to Lopo after the attack, Joe Farharto came along and talked with them. Lopo was upset, crying and yipping and pacing inside his enclosure, and Claudi asked Joe what was wrong. Joe pointed across the zooshow gallery to where Baako's enclosure had been. There was a wall there now, closing off that portion of the gallery. "That's what's wrong," he said. "Baako hasn't been right, and he senses it. Come on—let's go check on her."

"What's wrong with her?"

Joe shook his head. "She hasn't been herself since that thing with the Throgs in the environment room. Her teacher thinks she actually saw them—though I don't know how she could have."

Claudi looked back at Lopo—pacing and snorting, sniffing through his bubble at her, his red-irised eyes bright and wide. "Did *you* see anything, Lopo? Do you know what's wrong with Baako?"

"Yiyiyiyi—batsss!" Lopo yowled, jumping back from the enclosure wall. "Batsss touched-d-d herrr! And the otherrr! Batssss everrrrywherrrre! Rrrrrrrrr . . . !" He lowered his head and swayed it back and forth. She had never seen him so agitated.

"That's about all I've been able to get out of him," Joe said. "I think he thinks that the Throgs are bats. We have some bats here in the zoo, and he knows what they look like."

Claudi frowned. She'd seen the bats, too, and it was true they looked a little bit like the Throgs in her dreams; but they were much smaller, and they only had two eyes.

"I think Lopo's okay," Joe said. "But I want to go see Baako. You can stay here if you want."

"We'll come," Claudi said. "Hey, Joe, can we let Lopo out sometime? I think he wants to be out."

"Well . . . maybe another time. But not just now," Joe murmured, striding across the gallery. A group of visitors had just wandered in, and he looked as if he didn't want to talk too much in front of them. He fished in his pocket for his enclosure key and touched it to the shimmering partition. A space opened to allow the three to pass; then he closed it again. There was just enough room to crowd around Baako's enclosure. "It's quieter here," he said. "I didn't want her being upset by all the noise outside."

He tapped the enclosure. "Baako? Can you hear me? It's Joe."

There was no answer. They peered from various angles

into the bubble. It was hard to see to the back, which was the way Baako liked it, of course. "Come on out, Baako! I want to make sure you're all right in there."

Something rustled, back in the shadows. Claudi heard the lupeko before she saw her, and the voice was low and mournful: "Grrr-goooo awaaaaaay, Jo-o-o-e. We'rrrrrrrre losssst, rrrrrrrr. Lossssssst, lossssssst, rrrrr lossssst . . ."

"Baako, what are you saying? Come on out and let me see you."

"They'rrrrrrre therrrrrrrre, Jo-o-o-e. Comingggg, Jo-o-o-e. I don't wannnnt-t-t, don't wannnnt-t-t, don't wannnnt-t-t . . . ! *Who isss it-t-t! Grrrrrrr!*" Suddenly the lupeko came trotting to the front of the enclosure. Her teeth were bared, her ears slanted back, her eyes slitted. She stared at the two kids, raked her gaze across to Joe. *"Rrrrrr-whaaat-t-t?"*

"Baako, friend—you don't look well, girl," Joe said. Her fur looked ratty and unkempt, and she looked thin, as if she hadn't been eating.

"Rrrrrrrrrr . . ." she answered, her voice trailing away into a soft gargle.

"Have you been eating *anything*?" Joe asked. The lupeko snorted. She snuffled along the front of the enclosure, ignoring the humans. *"Baako!"* Joe snapped. "Pay attention! Are you eating? You've pushed something up in front of your teacher-monitor. Your teacher can't see you anymore."

"Rrrrr . . . so whaaat-t-t?"

"You'll *die* if you don't eat!" Claudi burst out. "Don't you care?"

The lupeko peered at her blearily. "Carrrrrre?"

"Yes! You're getting sick! And you've got Lopo all upset! Isn't that right, Joe?"

Farharto nodded. "That's right, Baako. He's afraid for you. He thinks he saw the Throgs come close—"

His words were cut off by the lupeko's earsplitting howl. *"Yiiiiiii! Yowwwwwuuuuuuu! Get-t-t-t them awaaaaaaaay! Awaaaaaaay! Yowwwwwuuuuuuu!"* Baako began pawing at the enclosure wall. *"Get-t-t me ouuuuut-t-t! Get-t-t me ouuut-t-t!"*

Claudi jumped back, frightened. She looked pleadingly at Joe. "Can't we let her out? What if something's—"

Joe shook his head. "No. Not in this state."

"But what if something's in there? Joe?"

"*No,* Claudi. We don't know what she'd do if we let her out. And whatever she's afraid of, I don't think it's in there. *Baako! Stop it!*"

The lupeko fell silent and lay down with a loud, dropping sigh. "Good girl," Joe said softly. He touched his enclosure key to her bubble. "I just want to see if she's okay." Gingerly, he reached in and touched the top of Baako's head. He scratched her neck, and felt her cheeks and under her chin. She seemed neither to object nor to care.

Joe withdrew his hand and shrugged. "We'll just have to give her time. If she doesn't snap out of it, we'll have to put her under with freezelife until the danger has blown over. I don't like to do that, because it can be risky. I think maybe we should just leave her alone now."

Baako ignored them as they stepped back out and closed the partition.

Claudi went back over to Lopo, who had curled up in the corner of his enclosure and gone to sleep. She stared at him for a time, aware of Sheki beside her, and Joe. She turned her eyes up to Joe, pleading silently for some understanding of what was happening. All she got was an uncertain shrug.

"Guess we should go," she said to Sheki.

Sheki looked at her soberly and nodded his agreement.

That night Claudi dreamed again, for the first time in days. She dreamed of Throgs, and of Suze. They didn't appear together, not at first anyway, and this time when she dreamed of the Throgs it was without that terrible icy-cold gripping fear. They floated toward her out of the deep darknesses of space. She watched them come with a feeling that if they reached her she would respond by turning the darkness into a blazing sun—first red, then dazzling white, then a blackness deeper than any darkness that the Throgs could create. She wasn't sure if she would destroy them by this action, or change them somehow. She only knew it would make her safe.

She woke up, panting for breath. At first she wanted to cry, remembering only that she had been dreaming of the Throgs; then she remembered that she'd not been frightened. And then another part of the dream came back to her: Suze, floating in the darkness, her hair streaming in the cosmic winds as though she were underwater. Suze was calling to her in the emptiness of space, calling her name, calling calling calling . . . and she, Claudi, didn't answer, but gave a little smile instead because she knew that she was safe . . . there was no danger. . . .

And she remembered this, lying in the darkness in her bunk, hearing only the whisper of the air circulator and, deep down, the vibrating thrum of the ship's own life. And she began suddenly to shiver with fear and cold, and she began to cry. She wept hot and bitter tears, crying out to Suze that she was sorry, she hadn't known! And she shook under her thin blanket, as if chilled by a harsh, wet wind. And after a time, it all began to blur; and she wasn't even aware at first of the warm sun that dried out the wet wind and took away the chill. But she heard chimelike voices answering her, in songs, as she cried out to Suze. And then she was only aware of her mother calling to her out of the darkness, and then sitting on the edge of her bunk and holding her, holding her, soothing and quieting and holding her.

CHAPTER 26

I suppose I should have explained this earlier. You might be wondering why the teachers placed so much emphasis on helping the kids to deal with the loss of Suze, when what they really had to worry about was the Throgs. And why the use of a counseling program that hadn't been upgraded in about a hundred years?

Well . . . I could tell you that it was for the emotional health of the kids, and that would certainly be true—but only a part of the truth. The wall-shrink, however clumsily, did push the kids into expressing a lot of grief that could have interfered with their ongoing life—more specifically, with dealing with the Throgs. I had a particular feeling about that, and I persuaded the teaching programs that it was important. Mr. Zizmer was reluctant to take on the task himself. He was an excellent teaching personality and a tribute to his species, but he just didn't have the heuristic experience needed to handle this sort of emergency. We both knew that the counselor was an outdated program, but at least it was designed for the kind of problem we faced.

It was important to me that the kids deal quickly with

their pain and anger—and most especially that Claudi deal with hers. I had a suspicion about what Claudi might have to do, and if I was right, it would be vital that she not be filled up with anger and bitterness and self-recrimination. Don't ask me how I knew that. I just did.

And I knew that Claudi had more learning to do, and perhaps little time in which to do it. And some of that learning was bound to be painful.

The classroom sims were getting harder.

Claudi heard, dimly, a babble of voices in her head. She saw flashing lights, dazzling lights, explosions. She'd already been hit, her floater shattered. In a leaking spacebubble, she floated high over the asteroid colony where her friends tried desperately to defend themselves from the enemy warships. (Whose? Throgs? Unknown.) Their only weapon, a mining laser, had been knocked out. The only hope now was to last until the enemy moved on.

It hadn't been much of a battle. They'd gotten off one shot with the laser before the enemy ships had clobbered them. And Claudi, caught outside, had been hit almost immediately. And now she waited, helpless, hoping that someone knew she was still alive, hoping that someone could save her.

It wasn't fair! It wasn't a fair fight!

She wanted to scream out to the teacher, to demand that she be given another chance—that they all be given another chance. But something held her back: a voice that said, *this is the only chance you will have. It is now or never.* And she swallowed, bursting with fear and frustration—but afraid to let it loose, because even more than dying in the sim, she was afraid of not doing it right.

"Can anyone hear me?" she called out plaintively, in the hollow of her spacebubble. She couldn't even tell if her voice was reaching farther than the thin enclosure that surrounded her. But she could hear scratchy voices:

"—can't go out together—"

"—you'll get killed—"

"—but we have to save—"

"—she's floating away—"

"—quickly—"

"—you could *die*—"

"—but don't you see, we *have* to—"

The babble was getting louder, but somehow more confusing, the voices more urgent. Were they talking about her? Were they coming out to get her?

Flash! Light and molten rock sprayed up near the bunker. Another enemy hit.

"—I'm going—"

"—wait—"

"—now!"

She saw a spurt of light, way down there on the asteroid, and felt a queasy, shivery feeling as she counted two, no *three* of her classmates risking the enemy's fire, coming out to get her. "No!" she shouted. "Stay back! Don't come!" She felt dizzy and realized it was getting harder to breathe. She was losing air. "They'll get you—" she whispered.

Blackness was crowding in around the edges of her vision. *I mustn't give up!* she thought. *They shouldn't be doing this!* But she shivered, knowing that if her friends didn't come for her, this would be the end. Somewhere, deep inside, she knew that it was just a sim, but she felt the rasping of her breath and the sickening weightlessness as she floated helplessly farther and farther from safety. She felt something inside her trying to divide, to reach out; but this time it couldn't.

A blaze of light dazzled her eyes. When it faded, she saw only two people moving toward her now. Someone was calling, "—Sheki—Sheki's been hit—" and someone else, "—gone—can't help him—he's gone—"

She tried to cry out to Sheki, but she couldn't. The darkness was overtaking her. But a small voice inside was urging her to cling to life, to let her friends help her, to accept the gift of their effort. Then the darkness took her away, just as she saw Jeremy in his bubble streaking upward, closer.

"Claudi? Claudi?"

Fingers tugged at her arms; a floor pressed at her back.

Her eyes came open and she saw Jeremy peering down at her, and Jenny—and two others behind them. She was back inside the bunker in the asteroid. It looked bombed out, but they were alive. "You—guys—got—" she whispered, before her breath gave out.

"They're gone!" Jeremy said. "The Throgs, or whatever they were. They're gone."

Claudi suddenly remembered and struggled to sit upright. "Sheki!"

Jeremy looked away. It was Jenny who said, "They got him, Claudi. They got him."

They got him. They got Sheki, just because he was trying to save me. *It's not fair!*

And then the bunker flickered, and there was an underwaterlike shimmer, and the holo went off, and they were sitting in the classroom. "Hey!" someone shouted. The sim was over. Claudi took a deep breath and got up, pulling off her headset. Sheki was nearby on the floor, looking dazed.

Claudi grinned weakly at him. "Are you alive?"

Sheki blinked, tilting his head in a funny puzzled way. "I g-guess so. I got k-k-killed, didn't I?"

"You were a hero!" Jenny shouted. She saw Jeremy draw himself up then and added, "And so was Jeremy! He brought Claudi back after you got killed."

Sheki nodded, not saying anything.

There was some movement at the front of the room, and Mr. Zizmer stepped down out of the wall and boomed, "Is everyone alive and accounted for?" He walked among the kids, waving triumphantly, and they laughed, as the tension evaporated. And Mr. Zizmer said, repeating himself over and over, "You did great. Just great. Jeremy—Sheki—Jenny—all of you. I think we should send you kids after the Throgs!"

They all laughed again, but not quite so hard this time. And Claudi had a very odd feeling about that joke which didn't go away.

* * *

The signs, the next day, were everywhere—in the cafeteria and the corridors and in the lifts and outside the deck-school:

ACROBATICS!!!
ALL NEW ACT!!!
HIGHLIGHT OF THE CIRC-ZOO!!!
DON'T MISS OUT!!! DON'T BE LEFT BEHIND!!!
COMING IN THREE TWO DAYS!!!

Two days! Would they even still be here in two days?

The kids got excited about it in a nervous sort of way. They had seen acrobatics before, in the regular circus performance, but this was supposed to be a more sensational show than ever before. It had better be sensational, they all agreed. They had a lot on their minds. Mr. Zizmer was keeping them busy with all sorts of lessons—on survival, on first-aid, and of course reading and math and science and art—anything to keep them from sitting and fretting.

Outside class, it was a different story. There were no formal restrictions about moving around the ship; but still, what with all the defense drills going on all the time, and Throg patrols moving through the corridors, it was getting harder to just wander around the ship without being stopped and interrogated. *What are you looking for?* Or—*do your parents know where you are?* Or—*it isn't safe for you youngsters to be out and around like this without supervision, you know.* Claudi always nodded and tried to look very purposeful.

She felt an inexplicable need to keep in motion, always in motion. There was really no place on the ship that was safer than any other, though the kids had standing orders, in the event of trouble, to head straight for the deck-school if they were not with their parents. Claudi's parents repeatedly admonished her not to wander into areas where she didn't belong. But to her, it was as if she knew somehow that staying still too long would bring on the Throgs sooner. She felt as if it were her personal responsibility to make sure that nothing of the sort happened—or at least that she would be in the right place if it did. Not that she had even the slightest inkling of what she would do if she saw Throgs again. She just had a feeling that she could not possibly explain—a feeling that she had something special to do.

Often now she was on her own, because Sheki's father didn't want him spending much time out of sight. She came and told him everything she saw; and she was very careful to let her own parents know when she was at the Hendu's cabin. She visited Lopo, of course. He was calmer now, but he still seemed mournful. Whatever had happened with the Throgs had changed him. And Joe told her that Baako didn't seem any better, either, which worried her equally. What if Lopo became like Baako? There didn't seem to be anything she could do to help.

She thought of herself as a sort of special Throg-patrol. There was a constant feeling of lonely, icy . . . not fear, exactly, but an electricity in her mind and her body, a feeling that almost anything might happen, at any time. It was on one such patrol—really, just another route home from checking on Lopo—that she found herself on the deck with the adult's library-study center and some of the shops. She was passing near the chapel, humming to make herself feel less lonely, when she stopped. Beside the chapel's wooden doors was a sign:

PILGRIM CHAPEL
THE REVEREND NORNAN ROTHBEND PRESIDING
—ALL CREEDS WELCOME—
HOLOPASTORAL LEADERSHIP AVAILABLE
FOR MOST RELIGIOUS FAITHS
"PLEASE COME IN . . ."

A smaller, hand-printed sign taped to its bottom added the words, *Especially now!* She stared at it, chewing her lip in thought.

A robot floating down the corridor paused and seemed to eye her as she studied the sign. "You can go in, if that's what you're wondering," it said, in a faintly metallic voice. Claudi peered at the robot wonderingly. "Sorry—just trying to help," it chirped. She nodded and put her ear close to the door. She could hear music from inside, and the low sound of voices. She glanced at the robot and could have sworn she saw it nod. She tugged tentatively at the door handle. The door swung open partway, and she poked her head inside.

The chapel was small but very pretty, and about half filled with people. It smelled pleasantly smoky. Synth music was coming from the front where there was a wood-paneled altar, and many of the people in the pews were singing. The words, mostly in a language she didn't understand, drifted past her head. She felt a funny sensation, not quite a chill, as she stood and listened. The words seemed somber, somehow, and yet reassuring. And then the tune changed and she heard words she did understand, and they seemed to roll through her mind: *"Neither the stars will harm you, nor the moons, nor all of the spaces between. . . ."* There were other phrases, but the song always returned to that refrain.

Finally the music ended, and a bearded, purple-robed man at the front began murmuring strange-sounding words which at first she thought were in a foreign tongue; then she began to recognize a few of the words, but she didn't really understand what he was saying. He was swinging something from side to side, a small metal thing that clinked and smoked with a sweet-smelling smoke.

Claudi slipped all the way inside and let the door close behind her; then she crept forward and stood behind the last pew. The strange shivery feeling she'd had before was returning. There was an electricity in this place—a feeling of urgency, and maybe fear. But something more. Something that for a moment took her fear away, and her breath.

Glancing among the pews, she didn't see anyone she knew. She didn't expect to. Many heads were bowed. Others were held high. A few people were quietly weeping. Claudi drew a breath as someone near the back, way off to the left, raised his bowed head. It was an unmistakably familiar head, bushy with gray hair. Lanker. His lips were moving silently. Claudi stared in shocked, open-mouthed fascination. Lanker! Who would have thought he'd be here in the chapel, praying? Lanker, religious?

And on the far side of him, she saw another movement—

and gasped silently with doubled surprise. Straightening up now was the S'rath, Scer-Randall, his dark carapace short and glistening beside Lanker. Scer-Randall! A S'rath, in the chapel? Someone so . . . *alien*?

She looked around the room, then back, and saw that the alien had turned slightly, as though sensing her stare. She saw his yellow eye angling back and focusing on her. *"Pssssss . . ."* she heard, very softly. She squirmed, embarrassed to be caught staring. She started to back away. Then Lanker, reacting to the S'rath, turned also. His craggy-browed eyes widened, and he tugged at his beard. He looked almost as surprised as she was.

Lanker made a slight movement of his head . . . beckoning her to come join him?

Claudi froze, feeling trapped. She hadn't meant to stay, but only to see what was going on. An old woman sitting near the back, noticing Lanker's movement, turned her head and stared at Claudi with what seemed a scowl. Now the robed reverend up front was looking in her direction. Claudi shrank in mortification. Everyone was looking at her! She glanced back at Lanker and saw a faint smile cracking the landscape of his face. He was still beckoning with head movements. She hesitated, afraid to move, afraid of even more people seeing her. She drew a deep breath. . . .

The pastor called out something, in a loud voice.

She turned and fled through the wooden doors. And as they closed behind her, she heard the music starting again, and the same words being sung: *"Neither the stars will harm you, nor the moons, nor all of the spaces between. . . ."* The chords swelled behind her as she hurried away, feeling foolish. Now that she was outside, striding past the windows of the shops, it felt like another world—a lonelier, less comforting world than it had before. This was a world where Throgs could appear. There had been a kind of warmth back there that she might have wanted to stay in, if she hadn't been so nervous. Nevertheless, the beat of the music, and the words, continued to echo in her mind. *"Neither the stars will harm you, nor the moons. . . ."*

She started walking faster, thinking about Lanker and

Scer-Randall and how odd it had been to see them back there. She'd been planning to walk all the way home instead of taking the lift; but the first lift she came to, she darted in and called out for living section Lancelot.

Home.

CHAPTER 27

Two days later, it was time for the acrobatics show. Everyone knew it had basically been cooked up to take their minds off the Throgs, but they were glad for it nevertheless. The class went down to the auditorium and found the place changed from the last show, though it was hard to say exactly how. The ceiling looked higher somehow, and the stage seemed more open, despite the fact that it was kept mostly in darkness prior to the show. Occasional shifting beams of colored light knifed through the darkness, cutting swaths through vapors that boiled up from the stage floor.

There was a strong air of expectancy—not just among Claudi's class, but throughout the auditorium. It was an electricity that had nothing to do with the actual show they were about to see. The audience was like a collection of overcharged batteries, arcing and sputtering and ready to light up the hall with a great flash of human energy. Long before the show started, people were clapping and chanting, hoping to bring the acrobats on sooner, hoping to find a release for their energy.

Finally the *Prrrrrrrrr* of a drumroll stilled the crowd.

Beams of light flared high above the stage. *Prrrrrrrrrr.* Caught by the dancing lights, a human figure flew from right to left, high above the stage, and vanished into the gloom. Then another, left to right, into the light and out again. *Prrrrrrrrrr.* Then another, the other way. And another and another, from one side of the stage to the other. An announcer's voice boomed over the drumroll: *"THE J. J. LARKUS TRAVELING INTERSTELLAR CIRC-ZOO PROUDLY PRESENTS—THE FABULOUS, GALAXY-RENOWNED LARKUS FLYERS!"* With a tremendous crash of cymbals, golden floods blazed, lighting up the stage. From high above, a team of muscular men in shiny metallic tights swept down on hanging wires and swung back and forth across the stage on glittering trapeze rings.

The crowd broke into a thunderous cheer.

"Look, Sheki!" Claudi shouted, pointing as one man did a triple somersault in midair, then straightened out to catch a ring. An instant later, a pretty woman in bright green tights launched herself across the air, spinning like a top. She dropped straight down—bounced like a rubber ball from the stage—and shot up again to grab a bar near the ceiling. The spotlights swiveled and caught her waving from where she hung, her body arched as gracefully as a bird stretching its wings.

The crowd cheered again. Claudi cheered. Sheki cheered.

Several acrobats gathered on a perch high at the back of the stage. One man hung by his toes from a ring and then began swinging in long arcs forward and backward over the stage—swinging out toward the audience, then back, then out again toward the audience. The wire from which he hung began to move along a ceiling track, and soon he was swinging out *over* the audience, arms spread wide; then his swing carried him back toward the stage.

The pretty woman flung herself toward him, flipped in midair, and timing it perfectly, caught his hands. Both of them swung out over the audience—the woman hanging from the man's fingertips, and only his toes in that ring keeping them from rocketing out into the crowd. They swung high, and on their downswing, it almost seemed that the audience could touch her—and some people tried, reaching and waving as she flew by. The spotlights flashed, following their trajectory.

The audience screamed in delight, pounding their seats.

And then, in a strange twist, the *ceiling* opened up—and a darkness billowed out of that opening, a darkness that swallowed the dazzling spotlights like inky black smoke. Only it wasn't smoke. And something else was moving in that darkness. For an instant, the crowd bellowed in excitement—not knowing what to think. Claudi knew instantly what to think, but she was frozen in her seat. As the crowd abruptly fell silent in fear, she felt Sheki draw a deep breath.

The two glittering acrobats arced high—and disappeared into the darkness.

And did not come back down.

But something else did, several things—black and winged and fast.

Captain Thornekan was resting his hands on the back of his bridge seat, trying not to think of last night. Last night, when he had—just for a moment—succumbed and put on the headwire, just for a moment, a moment of blissful release, of near-ecstasy. Something, thankfully, had welled up in his mind in that same instant, a warning word or impulse that came from *somewhere*, and he'd torn off the wire in a spasm of anger and ground it to pieces under his heel, gasping in relief and shame. And now he was trying to forget, trying not to tremble visibly as he rubbed the back of his neck and took his seat.

In the star pit before him, the starstream was rotating through a conical cross section as the imaging system displayed a changing cycle of information. He touched a control to back off to a wide-angle image—first of the immediate sector, then of the greater Orion-Sagittarius crossover zone, and finally of the entire thread of the starstream through the galaxy's spiral structure.

The path through the galaxy resembled a fairyland trail, marked by the rippling changes of false-color imagery. Their progress inward was practically imperceptible on the widest view. Though they were more than a thousand

light-years closer to the galactic core than when they'd
started, they still had traveled less than one-twentieth of
the starstream's length. The impression of the galaxy's
vastness was powerfully reinforced by that image: the starstream was just a thread spanning a limited sector of the
galaxy, and most of even that thread remained unex-
plored.

Was it such a surprise that they were confronting races
whose very places of origin were unknown?

His thoughts were interrupted by a pulsating beep. His
gaze snapped up, though his concentration lagged a little.
He was losing his edge through too many false alarms. He
rose and peered over his first officer's shoulder at the console that monitored the n-space envelope around the ship.
"What is it, Len?"

"Not sure yet, skipper—"

Oleson got no further. His entire board lit up, in a rippling wave. Half a dozen new alarms went off, all over the
bridge. Thornekan swung one way and then another, trying to take in whatever information was visible on the
consoles. It was far too much to interpret; it was chaos. He
backed into his seat. "Report, people! What's happening?"

"Nav, losing n-space tracking."

"Systems, losing stability, fluctuations in all fields. Don't
know why."

"Com, we're getting calls from all over! Throgs on the
ship, Captain! Including power-deck level."

Thornekan felt a chill in the back of his neck as he
turned to the com officer. *Throgs on the power-deck.*
"Alert security teams! Systems—get on it and tell me when
you know something. And"—for what it was worth— "external weapons on standby." They might as well arm pea-
shooters, he knew.

"IS, that's a definite on Throg incursion! I'm trying to
work up a pattern now!" That last, tense voice was Liza's.
"We've got them in at least four locations. Power, med-
deck . . ."

He listened, and realized that his hands were balled into
fists. For an instant, he wanted to whirl around and dash to
where the Throgs were, to confront them himself. But he
knew . . . the only hope was to try to control the battle

from here. His plan, such as it was, was completely un-
tested. But perhaps he could get help. He hit the com.
"Liza—can you pinpoint Claudi Melnik's or Sheki Hendu's
location?"

Liza's disembodied voice answered. "Checking . . .
yes, they're both in the auditorium for the show." There
was a half-breath pause. "Skipper, there's a major intrusion
there now! With casualties!"

He struggled to keep his voice measured. "Can you
make contact—or get a security team to them?"

"A team's on its way. But I think I can reach them faster
from here."

"Hurry!" He turned to Len. "Have you picked up anything on the outside?" Even as he asked, he glanced again
into the star pit and drew a sharp, involuntary breath. He
scarcely heard his first officer's answer, because in the star
pit he saw wheeling shapes of blackness moving toward
the ship, like buzzards toward a fresh kill.

And behind them . . . was it his imagination, or did he
see the starry outline of a human face?

Claudi crouched, frozen with fear. The audience and
performers alike were shouting and trying to get away
from the Throgs. At least three of the horrors were flying
over their heads. Mr. Seipledon was yelling to the class to
keep their heads down, to get under their seats. But it was
too late. Most of the audience was trying to flee from the
hall. Some of Claudi's own classmates were climbing over
the seats, struggling to get past the crowds. Mr. Seipledon
was trying to stop them, but it was hopeless in the pandemonium.

Beside her, Sheki was turning round and round, trying
to track the Throgs in the air. They were emitting a bone-
chilling cry as they flew—not loud, but a combination of
piercingly high and shudderingly low sounds. Claudi
clamped her hands to her ears and tried to keep from
crying out. Sheki's mouth hung open. He didn't seem
frightened, exactly, but there was a look of terrible intensity in his eyes. "Sheki, come on!" she hissed, tugging at his

elbow. He turned, confused. "We've got to get out of here!"

"B-but—"

"No—come *on!*" It was hopeless to try to get out the back, but the seats in front of them had cleared. If they climbed over, they could have a clear run for the stage. There had to be exits up there. Claudi didn't think further; she vaulted over the seats. With a glance back to make sure Sheki was following, she crouched in front of the first row and prepared to run. An instant later, Sheki was hunkered down beside her, gasping. "Okay," she whispered. "As soon as it's clear, we run for it."

Sheki nodded.

A number of people had already run up onto the stage and off into the wings to what looked like safety. Overhead, the black fluttering shadows swerved, and one dived toward a crowded aisle. There was a muffled explosion, and when it darted up again, several people were gone and some seats as well. The Throg veered out over the stage and then flashed back up over the seats. *"Now!"* Claudi breathed.

They raced to the left side and scrambled up some steps and onto the edge of the stage. Claudi thought her heart would explode from fear. The stage seemed enormous and exposed. Some of the little kids were running, crying, across the stage from the opposite side. She waved Sheki forward. They would have to venture out onto the open stage before they could duck back into the wings.

"GET MOVING!" she heard a familiar voice shout, and she saw a movement on the far side of the stage. It was Lanker, crouched in the opposite wings. He was waving at all those on the stage, and when he saw Claudi, he waved with even greater urgency. *"DON'T JUST STAND THERE! GO!"*

Claudi sprang forward and skidded into a turn past the projecting partition before darting back into the shelter of the wings. "Sheki, hurry!" she cried breathlessly, glancing back. Sheki was still out on the open stage. A winged shadow was dropping out of the air, and Sheki and two other kids were looking up at it, as though hypnotized. *"Shekiii!"*

There was a noise behind her, and she whirled. Something dark was pounding out of the shadows toward her. Its eyes gleamed a sickening yellow. Claudi screamed—and it knocked her aside as it dashed onto the stage. She fell to the floor and looked back helplessly as the terrible thing ran straight for the kids—as the dark shadow of the Throg dropped out of the air, toward the kids. Everything seemed to happen in slow motion, as though time were frozen.

"NO-O-O-O!" bellowed the creature that had knocked into her. It was, she realized suddenly, the S'rath. Scer-Randall.

"RUNNN! SCER-RANDALL, WHAT ARE YOU DO-ING!" Lanker bellowed.

The S'rath reached the center of the stage in a few strides, sweeping up Sheki and one other child as he ran. Turning in midstride, he hissed, *"Psssss . . . Lanker-r!"* and flung the two kids into the opposite wings, one after another, like bean bags, into Lanker's arms. Then he wheeled back. One small boy remained, open-mouthed with fright. The Throg was diving.

Scer-Randall was quicker, but only by an instant. He had the boy in his grasp—and the Throg fell, and wrapped its terrible winged darkness around him—and the S'rath somehow twisted and flung the boy, and somehow Lanker caught him, too—but the shadow of the Throg had completely swallowed Scer-Randall now. The Throg rose up, shrieking its high-low shuddering wail as it flew away; and the stage was empty where Scer-Randall had been.

Claudi could hardly see through her tears as she struggled to her feet, but she could see well enough to know what had just happened. She heard Lanker shouting to her to run, to get out the door behind her—but she had to look across the stage just once more to make sure that Lanker really had Sheki with him, along with the other kids. They were heading for another exit.

Crying silently, Claudi ran for her own.

CHAPTER 28

"You must send the children to them. They have the abilities that we do not. It is the only way. The only hope."

Thornekan's knuckles were white as he gripped the armrest of his seat, staring into the star pit at the celestial face that had just spoken to him. "The children—?" he whispered. "What do you mean, send the children to them? Their abilities can't—I don't even know if they're still alive—"

"Captain!" shouted the first officer, distracting him. "Throgs, directly in range! Shall we fire?"

"What?" Thornekan turned his head in confusion, then realized what Oleson had just said. Throgs, where they could be hit! "Yes—at once—all weapons, *fire!*"

"Fire—" the first officer echoed.

"No—!" the starstream-being whispered.

There was a flare of light in the star pit, and the image turned to snow. "Captain!" called the nav. "I'm losing all of my inputs!"

The deck was trembling beneath him. "Cease fire!" Thornekan commanded.

The trembling slowly subsided. For a few moments, he

looked from the nav station to the star pit and back, praying that they would regain their sight. The power systems were fluctuating alarmingly, particularly the n-space generators—apparently as a result of the Throgs' distortion of n-space. There had to be a way to fight back! *Damn you, why won't you just face us in a fair fight?*

He realized that his fists were clenched again, to strike out at nothing. He exhaled and forced himself to relax, then snapped to his first officer: "Give n-space control absolute priority. Tell engineering I'm going to be asking for field fluctuations. Helm, be ready for maneuvers." He ignored the looks of surprise. He knew as well anyone how little room there was to maneuver in the starstream before they would veer to the edge and either rebound violently or destroy themselves in the gravitational shear zone.

"Something in mind, skipper?" Oleson asked cautiously.

Thornekan nodded. An idea was just taking form in his mind, and it was born more of desperation than of hope. "Len, what's the one thing that's ever been effective against the Throgs—ever?"

Oleson stared at him. "Nothing."

"Not true," Thornekan said, taking time to scan the consoles again. "At least two ships have beaten them—or at least escaped from them—"

"By disrupting the n-space environment around them. Is that what you mean?" Oleson interrupted. "Yeah, there have been three, not two. But they were heavy cruisers and destroyers—built for it—not transports!"

Thornekan nodded, aware of the objection. Of the ships that had ever tried it, all were powerful warships; and most of them had failed nevertheless. Could he hope to challenge the Throgs without destroying his own ship? It seemed unlikely. But a few had succeeded. And there was Ruskin . . .

"And Captain—" Oleson said.

He looked at his first officer, trying not to absorb the doubt he saw on Oleson's face.

"No one has ever done it *in* the starstream."

Thornekan nodded once more. Yes, he knew.

The star pit flickered, and the image of the starstream returned. A handful of shadowy things were fluttering in the distance, apparently merely annoyed by *Charity's* weapons-fire. He snapped the com. "Power-deck, do you still have Throgs down there?"

For a moment there was no answer. While he waited, he realized one other thing: the face of the starstream-being was gone. "Ruskin, damn you," he whispered. "Don't leave me here!"

Send the children to them, it had said. What the devil did that mean, exactly?

"Skipper, I really think we'd be better off riding it out, hoping—"

"That they leave us alone?" Thornekan shook his head and waved his first officer to silence. "Liza! Have you found those children yet?"

"Still trying . . . *bloody hell,* the system just went down!"

"Well, get it back up!" he shouted, and as he did so, he wondered, What will I do with them if I find them? Send children to the Throgs, like Ruskin said? "Power-deck, are you there?"

"Here, Captain. We're free of them for the moment. But they put a bad hole in one of the structural casings. We're trying to rig baffles, but we've had to shut down the number two generator."

Thornekan nodded grimly. "Just do the best you can. On my order, I want you to set up a field fluctuation. A big one. As big as you can make it, without blowing us to kingdom come."

Claudi huddled on the floor, shivering. She was alone, and she was lost.

She didn't know how she could have gotten lost. She thought she knew her way almost everywhere. But there had been that terrible time of confusion, Throgs and people screaming and dying, and the lights flashing on and off in the corridors. She'd tried to circle around to join Lanker and Sheki, only to find herself in an empty corridor, with signs all over saying AUTHORIZED PERSONNEL ONLY, but no one around. The door she'd come through had locked behind her. Nothing looked familiar. She couldn't even find a lift, and even if she could, she'd heard someone screaming that the lifts weren't working.

How could this have happened? she thought miserably. She wondered where her mother and father were, wondered if the Throgs had gotten them. She wondered if Sheki and Lanker and the kids had gotten away, and she thought of Scer-Randall, who had not. And she wondered if Lopo was safe. But no one was safe. She knew that now. No one could be safe where there were Throgs.

Even the ship wasn't safe. She could tell. The lights kept going off and coming back on, and she could feel it, too, in the thrumming in the deck. It was different. There was something wrong in the belly of the ship, and she knew somehow that if something wasn't done about it soon, it would be the end. But there was nothing *she* could do, was there?

But there *had* to be something she should do. There was always something one had to do. Wasn't that what they'd learned in the sims? Mr. Zizmer would know, if anyone. But she couldn't get to him, because she was lost. And what if the Throgs had gotten to him? *Don't be stupid!* she thought savagely. *Mr. Zizmer's only a holoteacher. They couldn't get him!*

Finally she just sat cross-legged against the wall, and she closed her eyes and shook and waited for someone to find her.

At one point, as she was crying, she thought she heard a voice speaking to her; but either it spoke too softly, or her head was too full of thoughts and fears to understand it. It seemed to be saying something about her friends. She thought she felt a glow around her, and she seemed to separate inside, then combine again.

But the voice, if it had really been there, had gone away.

"Hurry, Claudi—you must come with me!"

She looked up with a start and rubbed her eyes, wondering if she were dreaming. But it was no dream. A grease-streaked silver robot was floating in front of her, a red light on its front panel pulsing urgently. "What?" she said.

"You must come with me—now! There is no time to waste." The robot's voice was deep and commanding.

"But who are you? I don't know you. How do you know me?" She struggled to get to her feet.

"My name is Jeaves, and your teacher Mr. Zizmer sent me to find you."

Her eyes widened. "Mr. Zizmer sent you?" A ray of hope formed in her heart.

The red light pulsed even more urgently on the robot's chest. She almost imagined she saw a personality within its eyes. "Come quickly, please!" the robot said. "Your Mr. Zizmer has trusted me to find you and bring you along— *quickly.*" The robot started moving down the corridor and Claudi hurried to follow. It slowed just enough to let her catch up.

"Where are we going?" she demanded. "Are there still Throgs around?"

The robot whirred, but didn't stop. "To answer your second question: probably. As for where: do you know a lupeko named Lopo?"

Claudi gasped. "Is he all right?"

"That's what we're going to find out," the robot answered, approaching the door that had locked her into this corridor. It opened instantly for him. "That's what we're going to see. Now hurry, and follow me!"

"C-Claudi!" Sheki screamed, running across the zoo gallery. "It's L-Lopo! He's going crazy!"

She scarcely had time to register her relief that Sheki was alive. They raced together, collided, hugged, separated. "You're here! Where's Lanker?"

"I don't kn-know! I lost him. I came here b-because I thought I heard Ruskin tell me to." Sheki's eyes were wide like a frightened rabbit's.

"Ruskin told you?" the robot asked, turning. "How very interesting!"

Sheki squinted suddenly, puzzled. "Who's the r-robot?"

Claudi hurried over to Lopo's enclosure. "His name's

Jeevis or something." She bent over the lupeko's enclosure and peered fearfully inside. Lopo was crouched, looking off to one side, growling at something that Claudi couldn't see. His ears were flattened, his teeth bared, his flame red eyes narrowed to slits. He seemed not to notice Claudi.

"My name is *Jeaves*," the robot corrected, floating alongside. "And I am a friend of Mr. Zizmer, Sheki. He sent me here to make sure you got Lopo out. You're all going to need each other."

Claudi whirled. "We're letting Lopo out?"

"That's right. Lopo can see things you can't, and he might be able to lead you where you have to go." As the robot talked, it extended an arm, and something in its mechanical hand twinkled and its arm passed through Lopo's bubble. "There you are. Lopo?"

The lupeko twitched his ears and cocked his head, not turning.

"Lopo!" Claudi cried.

This time the lupeko heard her voice. It spun in place, yipping—its eyes opening wide as it saw Claudi, its pupils dilating with joy. *"Yi-yi-yi-yi-yi! Claudi Claudi Claudi Claudi!"* it howled. *"Yow-yarrrrrr! Dangerrrrr! Bat-t-tssss everrrywherrrre!"*

"Lopo!" the robot snapped, and its voice sounded remarkably like Joe Farharto's. "You must control yourself. Do you see the bats now?"

"Rrrrrrrr . . . rrrrrrrr . . ." Lopo sniffed suspiciously at the robot, but looked around. Another low growl started in his throat. "Rrrr-yessss. Out therrrrrre . . ." He pointed his nose out of the cage.

"Then, Lopo—you must take Claudi and Sheki to them," the robot said. Ignoring the gasps of dismay from Claudi and Sheki, it continued, "Do you understand? Do you see a passage, Lopo? Any kind of path to where the bats are?"

The lupeko made a gargling sound. "Rrrr-path, yessss." It looked up at Claudi, then at the robot. Its eyes seemed to pulsate. "Rrrrr . . . go therrrrre? Ba-a-a-d. Ba-a-a-d. Whyyyy?"

"Because the way has been prepared. Ruskin has made it possible, or so I'd guess."

"Wait!" Claudi protested. "We don't want to go to the

Throgs! Why would we? We want to get *away* from them—"

The robot clicked urgently. "I understand, Claudi, and I cannot force you. But remember what Ruskin told you? Remember? *You must not run.* I believe he means for you to do this. With Lopo as your guide, you may be safe. You may be able to do what will save us all, Claudi. Ruskin knows of your talents, as your teacher guessed. This is what he has been preparing, making possible."

"What? What are you talking about?" She felt tears starting to well up in her eyes. She felt as though she were coming apart again, always coming apart. Her *presence* trembling inside her. What did this thing mean, she could save them all? What was Ruskin preparing? She didn't want to go toward Throgs or anything else! "How can I—"

"He senses your abilities, Claudi—just as Mr. Zizmer did. And as perhaps, just perhaps, even the Throgs do. They've seen you, Claudi, they've sensed your presence. And you, Sheki—she'll need your help, your support. Ruskin knew that. That's why he wanted you both here. That's why he just minutes ago told the captain to send you to them." The robot's eyes glowed faintly, unnervingly.

Claudi shivered. "He told the captain?"

"Yes, Claudi. On the bridge, Ruskin and the captain spoke. We listened very carefully."

"But—"

"Remember the sim, Claudi—how your friends risked their lives to save you?"

She flushed. "But that was just a sim!"

"Then remember Scer-Randall." And the robot turned, whirring, and moved away from the enclosure. Claudi stared at him through tears. Scer-Randall. Her heart ached for the S'rath. She'd been so frightened of him. And now, Sheki wouldn't be here alive except for what he had done. "Lopo," the robot asked, spinning back, "can you jump down?"

The lupeko bounded out of his enclosure and reared up and rested his forepaws on Claudi's arm. His eyes blazed into hers. "Rrrrr, go-o-o with youuuuu." His ears cocked. "Rrrr, find Baak-k-k-o! Bat-t-t-sss!

"Yes. I will release Baako now, too," said the robot. And

with amazing speed, it crossed the gallery and deactivated the wall that blocked off Baako's enclosure.

The gallery lights flickered and went out. Claudi's heart nearly stopped. She felt a change in the vibration in the deck. She also felt Lopo press close to her legs, reassuringly. Then a pair of lights on the robot's body flicked on, lighting Baako's enclosure and casting a pale glow across the gallery. In the dim glow, Sheki edged close and whispered, "I g-guess we'd better do like he says. I'll g-go with you."

She felt a chill rush down her spine, because she knew that he was right. She had something special to do and it was time to do it, no matter how afraid she was. As she turned to nod, she saw behind Sheki a dull red glow, against the zoo gallery. For an instant, she thought it was fire; and then she heard a voice whisper, *"Hurry, my children. Will you try? Do you know?"* and she knew who was speaking. But she didn't know what it meant. And now the glow was gone.

"Okay," she said to Sheki. "But I don't know what we're supposed to do! Lopo—do you know where to go?"

There was a sudden buzzing in the ship's deck, and she felt dizzy for a moment, as if a hundred people were screaming in her head. *Jabberjabberjabber.* Just as suddenly, it was gone.

"Changes in the n-space field," the robot said grimly, from across the gallery.

Lopo growled low in his throat and glared toward Baako's enclosure. "Rrrrrr-thissss wayyyy! Somethinnnggg herrre." And he trotted across to join the robot.

Claudi and Sheki raced with him. To Claudi's astonishment, Lopo bounded straight up into Baako's enclosure. Yipping frantically, he turned back to them, wide-eyed, his eyes circles of fire in Jeaves' light. "Rrrrr, come, you must come! Thissss way, this wayyyy, rrrrrrr!"

"Are you sure?" Claudi looked at the robot, its lights glaring against the dark. Another shudder went through the ship.

"Yessss! Rrrrr, you musssst-t-t! Baaak-k-ko's gone! Save Baaak-k-ko!" Lopo peered deep into the enclosure. "Hurrrrrrry!"

The robot whirred. "Go, then, if you can! I am astonished! But *go!*" It rose in the air, shining its lights deep into Baako's enclosure. There was no sign of the older lupeko. The beam seemed to shine an impossible distance into empty darkness. "I will follow you, if I can!"

Without a word, Claudi climbed into Baako's enclosure. There was a funny smell here—pungent, not like a lupeko. She crept forward, crouching, then found that she could stand upright. Darkness had closed around her, as though she had walked into a cave. This was very strange. This was no lupeko habitat. Lopo's eyes gleamed redly ahead of her, looking back. She too glanced behind her, and against the robot's light she saw Sheki's silhouette moving, scattering the light as he followed her. Swallowing, she said huskily, "Go ahead, Lopo. We're right behind you."

Something trembled under her feet, and around her she felt a shivering sensation, as though the darkness itself had been torn open. She felt a shock of dizziness, then a sudden biting cold. Then the cold was gone, and she was surrounded by stars.

Thornekan's chest tightened. "Shear the field back and bring us to center." He watched as the pilot pulled them back from the edge of the starstream and steered for the stable center. The view of the channel, skewed and distorted by the fluctuations they had introduced in the n-space field, slowly began to realign itself.

The deck shuddered, and the console displays flickered momentarily. Thornekan braced himself, but the shock had already passed. "What was that?"

"Something changing in the matrix," Oleson said. "Look!" He pointed to the image in the star pit.

Thornekan already saw it. A flutter of shadow, a cluster of shapes turning and skidding in front of the ship. They seemed to be fleeing. But as he watched, they veered back and streaked once more toward the ship. "Helm, repeat that maneuver! Power, spike the field again!"

He felt the tremble again in his seat, and a queer sensation in his stomach, and a dizzy sense of his thoughts leaving his body and voices jabbering in his head, as the generators seized the fabric of space and twisted it, wrenched it almost hard enough to send them tumbling out of control. The Throgs veered past the ship without contact. "Well done!" Thornekan roared. "It's blocking them, by God! It's keeping them away!"

"Discouraging them, anyway," Oleson said anxiously, looking up from his board. "How long can we keep this up?"

Thornekan scowled, not answering. He knew that the respite was momentary. Even without the damage on the power-deck, it would take just one missed maneuver to convert the ship into a violent spray of neutrinos, a puff of smoke against the galactic night. He'd prayed that New would be back to help them; but New was gone, and he knew no way to bring it back. Unless the children could call it . . .

He thumbed the com. "Liza? Anything on the kids?"

"Wait—*yes.* I've got the IS back, skipper. Give me a moment—"

He waited.

"Got 'em, skipper. I don't know how the squads missed them. They're both in the zoo where the lupekos are kept . . . *oh Jesus!*"

"*What,* Liza?"

Her voice became strained. "According to the monitors, they went *into* one of the lupeko habitats—"

"What?"

"—and vanished."

"*What?*"

There was a moment of silence. "That's how it plays back. We've got it on imaging. They just vanished. With one of the lupekos, and a robot." Liza sounded frightened. "Shall I send someone there?"

"They're gone?" Thornekan repeated stupidly, staring into the star pit, where the Throgs were wheeling around to attack.

"As far as I can tell."

"Did Throgs take them?"

"Not that I could see."

Thornekan swallowed. "Keep searching. And can you get the kids' teaching program projected to that location?"

"I can load it into a robot."

"Do it. Tell it to wait where they disappeared." He nodded to the pilot to start a new set of maneuvers and added to Liza, "See if you can locate the kids' parents. We might need their help, too." And rising to stand over the star pit, he tried to think what could possibly have happened to the children. He glared into the shifting images and dared Ruskin to return, pleaded silently for him to return.

The pilot spiked the n-space field.

And that was when Thornekan, staring at the skewing image, saw the dark, tiny figures of two humans and one animal against the cloudy glow of the starstream.

CHAPTER 29

The stars began to move past her like fireflies in an evening sky. After a time the sky began to lighten, and the stars faded to a few pinpricks of light. She and Lopo were walking on a strange gray murkiness, like a dirty cloud. Her heart was pounding. Lopo paused to sniff the air. Claudi looked back.

Her heart nearly stopped. "Sheki! Where are you?"

Sheki was nowhere in sight. The robot was nowhere in sight. The ship was nowhere in sight. "*Sheki!*" she cried again, fear burning in her throat like smoke. "Where *are* you?" She was breathing fast, too fast. There was no answer.

She and Lopo were alone. Lopo seemed unbothered. His wolflike head was cocked, his ears raked forward listening into the wind. His nose was twitching. The wind! She hadn't realized it, but a wind was blowing here, blowing out of the mists. The sky had lightened to a blue-gray, sprinkled with stars. It was the empty dawn morning of a cloud world, a world with no surface at all. And no visible sun.

"Lopo," she said, struggling to make her voice rise above

the drumming inside her head. "Lopo, where are we? Can you see anything?" Her voice cracked, but she was determined not to give in to fear. She wanted to cry, but didn't dare.

"Rrrrrr," muttered the lupeko. "Smell Baako."

Baako? That gave her a moment of hope. But what if they found her hurt, or worse?

"Grrrrr, mussst hurrrry. Hurrrrrry!" Lopo trotted forward through a low mist.

Wait! she wanted to cry—but instead hurried along behind him. She became aware of a reddish glow behind her shoulder, warming her against the wind. *My child, do not be afraid,* she heard. *You must go ahead, there is no other way.* The words brought a lump to her throat, because even though she didn't feel courageous, she at least felt a little less alone.

The wind blew her hair back from her forehead and rippled Lopo's fur as he trotted. There was a certain arching quality to this place now, as if they were moving down an enormous tunnel in the sky, traced out by the circular movements of thin, airy clouds. It looked like the starstream, but without the orbs and swirls of light to mark the stars along the way—and without a spaceship to envelop them in safety. Was this possible? She didn't think so. They were floating, really, more than walking—and she felt her other half, her larger presence, begin to float out ahead, scouting the way.

Lopo made a sniffing sound, pointing straight ahead.

"What?" she whispered. And then she saw it—or something, anyway. It was a tiny point of light, flickering, way in the distance. She took longer strides, and they floated more quickly. The point of light seemed to be moving about—and pulsating, as though alive. It reminded her of Sheki's entity. But how could that be?

Something scooted overhead, something shadowy. Claudi jerked her eyes up. An enormous bat-thing dipped its wings and veered, and a cluster of eyes peered down at her. She could not contain her outcry of fear—and as if in response, the shadow-creature banked and dropped toward her. She crouched in terror.

Before the thing had dropped far, there was a sudden

buzzing and shaking in the air, and a feeling that the clouds around her were *twisting*. Claudi felt a rush of shock and anger—but it was not her own. She heard a *jabberjabberjabber* in her head—but different from before, more distant. She felt her mind brush something shivery and queer, and then it was all gone.

Instead of attacking her, the shadow-thing broke into *two* shadows, and both swooped upward in opposing curves, then streaked for a point somewhere ahead of her. They passed through the clouds and vanished.

An instant later, the murk beneath Claudi and Lopo split open, and they fell into a bottomless sky.

Sheki stood poised at the edge of a cliff. He almost would have believed that he was in another environment room. He had crawled through Baako's enclosure—and then the world had changed all around him. He had no idea what to do. He was supposed to be with Claudi—but Claudi had vanished. The robot following him had vanished, too.

Above him was nothing but gray sky. Below him, more sky. The cliff he was standing on actually looked like nothing more than a murky cloud. But he didn't feel in danger of falling.

The funny thing was, though he was thoroughly confused, he didn't really feel frightened. Except for Claudi. He was worried that something bad might happen to her, and to Lopo, and he wanted to help if he could. He remembered the last sim in class, where he'd gotten killed trying to help her. He didn't want to do that again.

There must be someplace to go, he thought. Behind him was a sheer cloud precipice. It looked impossible to climb, and even gazing up at it made him dizzy. He turned away, blinking.

And then he heard a distant cry: *"Sheki, where ar-r-re you?"* His pulse quickened. He peered out into the empty sky. There was a faint, circling pattern of clouds that had not been there before. He rubbed his eyes. Now, in the center of that circle, he spied two tiny, floating figures. They seemed miles away. He shouted: "Claudi!" But his voice was swallowed by the emptiness.

His hands knotted into fists. What were they doing way out there? What were the Throgs doing?

No sooner had he thought of the Throgs than he heard a voice speaking softly in his ear: *"You must stay. Help Claudi. It is the only way."* He was sure it was Ruskin, or some other part of New, speaking. Like God, only not God. For a moment, he felt a little less worried.

Then he saw the black shadow of a Throg fluttering down into the center of that circle of clouds, and his peace of mind vanished. *"Claudi, look out!"* he screamed. And he saw something else—a twinkle of light, farther away than even the tiny figure of his friend—and his heart leaped with both terror and joy. Was that—? *"Wattt-sonnn!"*

And then the sky started quaking, and the clouds churning—and he somehow felt Claudi's face nearby, looking for him, and something else that was *angry*—and then they were both gone and the sky was silent, with not even an echo of what had just passed.

Moments ago they had been falling like stones. Now they were drifting down alongside a vast, tenuous wall of clouds. Lopo was growling, thrashing his legs uselessly in the air. Claudi didn't try to control her movement. She had a strange feeling of emptiness, as though she had no power of any sort in this world. She heard sounds, rhythmical sounds, like distant drums: *thumpa-ta-thump, thumpa-ta-thumpa-ta-thump . . . thumpa-ta-thump, thumpa-ta-thumpa-ta-thump. . . .*

"What's happening, Lopo? Can you see what's happening?" she whispered.

The lupeko's eyes blazed, but he could only whine helplessly.

As she sank feetfirst, she slowly spun until her gaze came all the way around to the endless cloud wall again. With a shock, she realized that they were no longer alone. Rising in the wall was a huge blank outline of a face with a pair of eyes. For an instant she thought it was Ruskin and her heart leaped. Then she realized that this was a stranger's face, and *very* strange. As it began to look more Human, she realized why it seemed strange. It was upside down.

But it was staring at her. Staring.

"Who are you?" Her voice quavered, because she had a terrible feeling that this thing hated her. A Throg? Its eyes were disturbing to watch, as though they were somehow right side up, while the rest of the face was upside down. As she stared, it gave her a feeling of sickness, or wrongness, and she had to look away. But it drew her gaze back again. *"Who are you?"* she cried.

The thing's mouth opened on the top of the face, below the chin. *"Mwwaaaaauuuuuuuuu!"* Its cry echoed among the clouds for a very long time before it died away. It was a frightening sound, not harsh but mournful.

Claudi wrenched her gaze away—and realized something. Lopo was gone! She looked around wildly. What had they done with him? She heard him bark, far in the distance, no louder than a whisper on the wind. Where was he?

Tears welled hot in her eyes. But at the same time, she heard a soft voice inside, saying, *Try not to fear. Never fear.* And that was so ridiculous that she convulsed with explosive, angry, flat-sounding laughter.

But as she looked back at the upside-down monstrosity of a face, her laughter turned to horror. Two hideous black clouds of insects swarmed out of its eyes. The swarms joined and flew straight toward her. As she ducked, they split and veered past her on both sides. Their buzz blistered the air like passing aircraft. *Jabberjabberjabber* . . . She shuddered; but as the sound passed, she heard something else inside that buzz—she heard voices!

"What are you?" she wailed. *"What do you want with me?"*

In answer, if it was an answer, the sound changed. She swiveled her head in panic and saw the two clouds of insects returning, circling around her in opposing directions. Out of the buzzing, she heard something like an angry imitation of her voice: *"Whaaaaaat aaaaaare youuuuuu? Whaaaaa-dyouuuuu waaaaaant wimeeeeeeeee?"* And then the insects peeled away and vanished.

Claudi gulped. She looked helplessly back at the face. It was fading away into the cloud wall. A rosy light was growing behind the wall, and her heart raced as she wondered, could this be the sun-being that now seemed her best friend in all the world? There was no voice; there was just the hope that somewhere out there, *somewhere*, might be a friend.

The cloud wall was becoming flushed as though by a sunset. The glow seemed to penetrate Claudi's being; it filled her eyes and her heart and her mind. She felt as though she were being inflated by the light, and it was revealing everything that was in her. She felt a part of her greater being, her *presence*, suddenly being lifted up and away from her, and stretched out into space, spinning.

Behind the cloud wall, something was moving, something elusive and long and sinuous, and visible only for a heartbeat or two. But she thought, dizzily, that she had seen the glittering diamonds of Logothian eyes. Ali'Maksam/New? Wasn't that its name? "What are you doing to me?" she cried out, whispering.

And she felt her outward-reaching self touch another presence just for an instant, and she heard a voice answering, *"We are trying to help you, but you must be brave when you meet them. Brave, Claudi! Are you willing to give of yourself?"*

What—?

But then the voice and the presence and the rosy light were gone, and she was back and whole in her body. Something different was floating up beside the cloud wall toward her.

It was a baby—an enormous, Human-looking baby, wrapped in white cotton. Its eyes fluttered as it seemed to come awake. It opened its mouth, and she expected to hear it cry. Instead, she heard a voice hollow and deep and inHuman: *"Iiiissss thiiisssss youuuurrr naaaame? Clawwwwdi?"*

She shut her eyes, overcome by dizziness.

Sheki reached out toward the point of light that was once more bobbing in the sky. It seemed miles away. "Watson!" he groaned, but he knew that the entity could not

hear him. He could barely hear himself. Tears stung his
eyes. Watson was alive, but he could not reach him.

Without even a thought of what he was doing, Sheki
stepped off the cliff. In the same instant, the entity vanished. *"Watsonnn!"* he wailed. And then he was falling,
falling, into an endless gray sky.

Lopo's mind screamed with joy and terror. Baako! There
she was! Baako! Floating directly toward him, closer closer.
Did she see him? *Baako, do you see me, Baako?*

And then he realized: Claudi, where was Claudi, what
had happened to Claudi? An invisible hand had swept
them apart, or swept him away and down into a great
emptiness . . . not even any Throg-bats visible . . . cold
and windy and all alone, until Baako had appeared. In
bewilderment he yelped to Baako and cried back to
Claudi, and howled his fear and confusion. He could only
howl and howl in fear. *Owuuuu! Owwuuuuuuu! Claudi!
Owwuuuuuu!*

But the scent of Baako was in the air, and he stopped
howling and tried to run, nose forward and down, his legs
beating uselessly at the air. *Baako Baako, alive yes . . .
Baako we need you, Claudi needs us both! Come on, Baako!*

And then the two lupekos tumbled into each other, fur
and muscle colliding; and Baako's eyes flashed and she
knew him, knew him! But she didn't speak, she just floated
on the empty cold wind while he bit frantically about her
ears and neck, and in answer she only growled in pain. And
Lopo finally just looked back, panting, and shouted for
Claudi. *Owwuuuuuuuuu!*

His hands on the edge of the star pit, Thornekan looked
urgently back and forth between the image in the pit and
the piloting console as they completed the maneuver. It
seemed to be taking years. Was it working? *Where are
those kids?* On the console, he could see the fields slowly
stabilizing again. But in the pit, all he could see was the
twisted swirl of the starstream, distorted by the actions he
had ordered just before seeing the children in the star pit.

Was he killing them out there? How could they be alive at all? Or were they? Was it a devilish hallucination caused by the Throgs? It was hard to believe that—but even harder to believe that the kids had been teleported out of the ship into n-space, where they were somehow alive. Ruskin had said, *Send the children to them.* Was this what he meant? Who the hell knew what was possible in n-space?

"Captain, it's stabilizing again," the pilot called.

Thornekan turned. "Give me a complete sensor sweep of—" A change in the image cut off his words. The soft clouds of the starstream were nearly back to normal. But he had glimpsed, just for an instant, the tiny dark silhouettes of the children. They were gone now, but the Throgs were visible again, farther away. And behind them, in the background among the star-shapes, he saw the large and ghostly face of Willard Ruskin. "Ruskin, where have you—?"

The face in the stars interrupted. *"You do this at great peril."*

"What—?"

"You trap the Throgs."

Thornekan's mouth opened. "What do you mean we *trap* them—?"

"You endanger the children."

Thornekan tried to contain his fury. "The Throgs are endangering my *ship,* damn it!"

The eyes of the starstream-being seemed to peer right into the ship, as though searching his thoughts. *"Yes, we understand. You must protect your ship. But if you will allow us to help you—"*

"Can you keep the Throgs away from us?"

The eyes glinted, and a reddish flame glowed deep within them. *"Not directly. But your actions may suffice, if you will accept our guidance."*

Thornekan snapped his fingers at the pilot, without taking his eyes off the face in the star pit. "What do you want us to do?"

The eyes seemed to soften, the image to blur. *"As you have been doing. Reshape the . . . space . . . around you. Reshape the . . . field. But exactly as I tell you. Or you will not just trap, but kill."*

Thornekan felt his blood stir as he stared at the fading face. "Kill the Throgs?" he asked in amazement. "Are you saying we could destroy those things?" Visions of retribution boiled to the surface of his mind. *Myra . . .*

"It is possible. But perhaps unwise. Please . . . remember the children. . . ."

The captain didn't need to hear any warnings about the children. About Claudi, or her brave young friend Sheki. "Just tell us what to do," he said thickly. "Tell the pilot. So we can understand it. And quickly, please."

"Yes," Ruskin agreed. *"Quickly, then—"*

Claudi faced the baby-thing through squinting eyes. "Who are you?" she demanded. "Are you a Throg, too?"

The baby seemed to consider her with its inHuman eyes. *"Whooo aarrre youuu?"* it echoed. *"Whooo aarrre youuu?"* It stared at her silently again.

Claudi finally could stand it no longer. She shouted out, "HELP ME! Ruskin! Lopo! Mr. Zizmer! Please, anyone! Help me!" Her voice seemed to ring off into endless space.

There was no answer, except from the baby. *"Whooo dooo youuu callll?"* it asked, its voice reverberating into the distance. *"Whoo doo youu calll?"*

Claudi was so terrified and frustrated that she couldn't answer. "Please!" she whispered. "Please—somebody help me!"

She blinked, trying to focus. Something was opening in the cloud wall. It was a window, in the shape of a lopsided square; and it was opening like a lidded eye. Through it, she saw two small shapes. Two animals. Lopo and Baako? She wanted to call out but was afraid—afraid that they might vanish again. They looked so far away! But she could almost hear their yipping voices. Or was that her imagination?

The Throgs were doing this somehow. She felt the baby-thing watching her. But Ruskin/New were watching, too, weren't they? Don't let me be alone here!

Finally she cupped both hands to her mouth and

shouted, "Lopo! Baako! Can you hear me?" The eyes of the baby-thing widened. She ignored it. *"Lopo! Baako!"* If only she could reach them somehow . . .

"Lohhh-pohhh . . . Bahhhh-kohhh," mimicked the baby-thing.

"Yes!" she cried furiously. "What are you doing to them?" She tried to step toward the lupekos.

The baby-thing yawned, and a yipping sound like a lupeko's bark came out of its mouth. The sound was cut off abruptly, as the sky began to buzz and shake again. *Jabber-jabberjabber.* The window in the cloud wall shimmered oddly and widened. Claudi felt again that strange sense of *someone else's* confusion and anger, and a feeling in her stomach that she was tumbling.

Then it ended, and it was as if she had passed through the cloud wall in a twinkling, to the other side. She was standing beside Baako and Lopo on a white cottony surface.

Yowling, Lopo leaped to kiss her cheek with his fuzzy-whiskered snout. Claudi grabbed the lupeko by the neck and hugged him, trembling. Lopo licked her ear frantically; his eyes blazed heart-stoppingly. Then he dropped back down to sniff at Baako, who was lying at Claudi's feet.

Claudi knelt. Baako looked drugged and confused. When Claudi touched her, she raised her head and moaned softly.

"Bat-t-t-sss hur-r-r-t Baak-k-k-o," Lopo rumbled.

Claudi nodded. "Baako?" She stroked the thick-furred head. "What's wrong, Baako?"

The lupeko's head sank back down.

"What'd they do to her, Lopo?" Claudi whispered.

"Whaaaa d'theyyy dooooo t'herrrrr, Loh-pohhhh?" howled another voice. It was the baby-thing, its sneering face emerging from the mists of the cloud wall.

"You shut up!" Claudi shouted. "You did this! So you just shut up!" Tears of rage and helplessness filled her eyes. She raised her voice to the empty sky. "Ruskin! Where are you? New! Help me!"

There was no answer—except the baby-thing, mimicking her cry. *"Neww! Help mee!"* Its mimicry was getting better, which only made Claudi angrier.

The sky shook again, then steadied. The baby-thing turned its head both ways. It seemed alarmed.

Claudi stroked Baako's neck. "It'll be okay, Baako. It'll be okay." She felt a certain satisfaction in seeing this creature look a little scared. Maybe Mr. Zizmer and the captain were doing something to make the sky shake like that and scare the Throgs. She and her friends might all die here, but they were together. And that seemed important. To be together.

"Tooooo-gethhhh-errrr," mocked the baby-thing.

She glared at it, realizing that it must have heard her thoughts. Did it know what she was thinking? Maybe it knew how angry she was. Maybe it knew how badly she wanted to get back to her ship, and her family. And Sheki.

Sheki! she thought, her mind racing. Where are you? Are you still back there with that robot? Can you get Mr. Zizmer to help? Of course not—Mr. Zizmer thinks *we're* going to help. Sheki, are you here? Are you here with me and I just can't see you?

Her vision blurred as she reached out, not just with her eyes but with her greater presence floating up out of her, touching and searching. She heard a faint *jabberjabber* and felt the sky *tighten* somehow, and sensed howls of outrage, Throg outrage. But she saw nothing but sky and clouds, and a baby-thing watching her with inHuman eyes, eyes that seemed to flare with the same rage.

And she heard, drifting across the vast empty sky, the words: *"Can you sing? My children . . . please sing! It will help if only you will sing!"*

She drew a sharp breath. She had heard those words before. It was New, it was the sun-being. She searched the sky for the red glow and didn't see it, but she heard the words again. Sing? Could she sing? The voice seemed insistent. But why sing?

She glanced down at Baako, whose mournful eyes looked so beaten. And she looked at Lopo, who was waiting for her to do something. Was it up to her?

"Please sing," she heard.

She sighed, not understanding at all. She took a breath and began to hum a little. It felt stupid, and her voice was scratchy. She didn't know what to hum, so she hummed a snatch of circus music. Then she hummed the music she'd heard in the chapel the other day. The words leaped into her mind and she sang, *"Neither the stars will harm you, nor the moons . . ."*

Her voice faltered. Thinking of the chapel made her think of Lanker, who wasn't here to help her. And Scer-Randall. She almost started crying, but she felt the red glow around her, encouraging her. *Please sing. . . .*

She cleared her throat. *"Neither the stars will harm you, nor the moons, nor all of the spaces between. . . ."* She sang as much of it as she could remember. She paused, but felt the beckoning encouragement again. What did they *want?* She remembered a song, a nonsense rhyme she had learned in school, not on the ship, but back on Baunhaven. In a small voice, she sang: *"The rat came to the cat, and told him where to go. And the cat said to the rat, 'Well, we'll follow you, don't you know.'"*

And for no reason at all, she began to giggle.

But moments later she realized that she was not the only one who had been making music. Drifting through the clouds now was a strange sort of music, almost orchestral. It sounded strained and distorted, and maybe wasn't Human music at all. But there was a pattern to it, a melody that repeated over and over, with a different tone each time it repeated. It was growing in strength, very slowly, growing in volume and tempo.

"Sheki, do you hear that?" she cried in wonder—and suddenly remembered that Sheki wasn't here, he was lost!

And then she heard her name, faintly over the music: "Claudi! Where are you?" Electrified, she listened intently. Was that Sheki's voice?

"Sheki! Where are you?" She turned to the baby-thing—but it wasn't the baby-thing anymore. It was a dark, shadowy Throg-thing staring at her out of the cloud wall, with eyes that seemed to appear and disappear in various positions. *"Where is he?"* she screamed, all thought of the music forgotten.

Something twinkled high overhead—a ball of light dropping toward her. "Watson! Is that you?" She cried.

The light flickered as it fell. It stopped and hung just over her head.

The music was still building, filling the air.

Lopo stared up at the entity and gave a suspicious whine of greeting.

Claudi called to it, "Watson, where's Sheki? Do you know where he is?" The entity pulsed, flashing golden.

Another voice cried out, "Watson! Claudi, I've lost Watson again!" That was Sheki—wailing with grief, out of the thin air.

"Sheki! Watson's here! Sheki, where are you?"

The music stopped abruptly, leaving the air empty and resonant. It felt like a balloon stretched taut, almost to the breaking point. There was a feeling of great weight in the air. Sheki's voice suddenly sounded close to her. "I'm here, Claudi. I can see you now. But I can't move. Where's Watson?"

"Right here. I can't see you, Sheki."

"Up here. Turn around."

Claudi turned and gasped. Sheki was hanging from the cloud wall, as though by his collar. He waved down at her and started to call again—but all that came out was a croak. He looked panicked. "Sheki!" she wailed. "What's happening to you?" He made a choking sound. He looked as if he was having trouble breathing. *"What are you doing to him?"* she screamed to the Throg shimmering in and out of the cloud wall. Her voice shook with rage. "You're killing him!"

The voice that answered seemed to echo from a great chamber. It was hollow and yet filled the entire sky. *"KI-I-I-L-L-L? YOU MEAN, DESTRO-O-O-Y-Y-Y-Y! THISS THI-I-I-N-NG MATTER-R-RS TO YOUUU?"*

Though she flinched at the power of the voice, she stood glaring up at the Throg. "You're killing him! *Stop it!*"

The creature's eyes pulsed in and out of sight. The upper elbows of its wings trembled. Suddenly each wing parted from the body, and in an eyeblink, each was transformed into a new Throg. Now *three* Throgs gazed down at her. The voice boomed again, but confusingly, like several voices not quite in rhythm, reverberating over one another: *"YOUUUU LIIIIVE." "I-I-I-I-S-S-S-S-S THISSS ONNNE OF YOUUU?" "WHAAAT IISSS IT?" "DO-O-O YOU LIIIIVE?"*

"What?" Claudi shook her head. "I don't know what you're talking about!" She gazed up at Sheki now frozen and unmoving. Beside her, Lopo was growling softly; Baako was trembling with fear. "Why don't you just let us go?" Claudi choked, struggling not to cry. "We didn't ask to fight."

"FIIIIGHT?" "FIIIGHT?"

"What do you call it?"

"WEEEEE SEEEEEK-K-K—" "LIIIIIFE—" "LIIIFE—" "YOUUU WOUUULD-D STOP USSS!"

Claudi stared at the Throgs in bewilderment. Her head was spinning, filling with jabbering voices not Human. Blindly she yanked a tissue out of her pocket and blew her nose. She didn't understand any of this. Not the stupid Throgs; not anything. As she stuffed the tissue back into her pocket, she felt something crinkling in her mind, opening. It was her *presence* shifting past all of those voices, drifting out on the moist wind that was blowing through her mind. The air around her seemed choked with confusion. Her frustration was a vapor that coiled out of her breath and enveloped her.

A coarse wet tongue stroked her face, startling her. She gasped, gagging in Lopo's warm breath. She hugged him fiercely and looked up. There was a frightening gleam in the Throgs' eyes.

"YOUUUUU LIIIIIVE—" "WOUUUUULD-D-D PROOOOVVVE—" "WOUUUULD PROOOVVE—?" "YOUUU LIIIIIVE?" "YOU SAYYYY?" "YOU LIVE?"

She stared up at them. "We live. So what?" she spat.

"SOOOO WHAAAT-T-T?" "SOOOO WHAAT-T-T?" "SO WHAT?"

"Soooo whaaaat?" she mimicked angrily. She was very tired of this, and she just wanted to be at home with her mother, and to know that Lopo and Sheki and everyone else was safe.

"SOOOOOOO . . ." "WEEEEE WIIILLL LET-T-T YOUUU LIIIVE." "IFF YOUU LIIVE." "YOU LIVE."

She opened her mouth.

"WE LET YOU LIVE," the things repeated, in unison.

"Just like that?" she croaked. "You mean you're going to let us go?"

"JUST-T-T LIK-K-K-E THAT-T-T." *"YOUUUUU GO BAAACK."* *"IF—"* *"IF—"* *"IF—"* The sky trembled again, interrupting them, but only for a moment. *"THISSSSS ONE STAYYYYYY—"* *"THIS ONE STAY."*

The eyes of the Throgs pulsed down at her.

"What do you mean? Which one stay?" She had a sickening feeling of dread.

Their voices became harsh and full of fury. *"THISSS—"* *"THISS—"* *"THISSSS ONE."* *"THIS ONE STAYYY."*

She looked up and saw a great gulf of blackness opening behind Sheki, and he was being drawn backward into that blackness. Watson, flickering, streaked after him. She saw, or imagined that she saw, his eyes brightening with terror. With her greater presence she reached out a long arm and touched him, and felt his terror, and reeled from it.

She opened her mouth to cry in protest, but only a whisper came out. *"No!"*

But Sheki was already gone from sight.

Interlude

There was such uncertainty and confusion now: conflict-
ing tides and currents of understanding, of will. Did the
dark ones think that the *child* was holding them trapped?
To what were they appealing—to bargain, to deal?

It was so difficult to know what would work—
what these strange and unfathomable beings would
do
if New carried their plan
their hope
through

If Claudi can touch them—
Dare we hope   ?
Can we know   ?

The Ganz/New, the Assassin/New, spoke out of hir long
silence. —Is it not best to destroy them, to let the captain of
the ship destroy them? There may be no need to know, or
to touch—

But the children—whispered the Ruskin.

    And if the captain fails?
    If others come, how much more death?
    —hissed the Ali'Maksam.

—And if *we* fail, and the Throgs remain? It is madness, the risk—

    But the children
       what of the children?

—And what of the others?—

The aspects of *Bright*/Ruskin/Ali'Maksam/Ganz/and-more/New were too divided to know what course was best; they could not reach and touch and protect as their hearts yearned to do, but perhaps . . . just perhaps they could bring illumination where there had been none. . . .

    Must sing
    Claudi, you must believe
      and sing cried *Bright*.

The dark ones do not know, young Claudi cannot know what they want, what they seek—
    even the Throgs do not yet know, or agree.

From the shadowy veils of the Throgs, the strange ones who brought such death and disruption, there was a resonance of disharmony, and confusion of knowledge. And yet they had responded to song, echoed with their own music that had amazed New with its power. Responding to Claudi's song, they'd produced—

    music
      tempo
        pattern

And feeling—?

—perhaps—

Young Claudi and Sheki, so vulnerable, and the other
from the ship, strong but helpless . . . and yet they must
not run, they must stand and face the darkness, and make
it know they are real, they live

Must face those who destroy without mercy—
    but do they know
        what they destroy?

Surely New could help, without driving the wedge of
destruction deeper still—

But—

    how ?
        how ?
            how ?
                how ?

Help her sing
    And trust—
And believe
    And hope—

Is all I/we can do.

CHAPTER 30

Through a continuous haze of pain, the face of the young girl appeared like a spirit or a hallucination; it appeared with tantalizing clarity, then vanished without a trace, leaving just the pain.

The pain! How he felk'd the pain!

For Roti, the world had become a state of nothing *except* pain. He didn't know where he was, or why, or what they wanted, they who had brought him into this place. He knew only that they were *aware* of him, that they had no idea how to understand him. He had felk'd their lack of understanding, their discord and disagreement among themselves. He had felk'd those things as a variation, a tremor in the pain.

But now it was changing. He had felk'd the girl. *How*, he didn't know, or why. Or where she was, or why. But she existed, and that gave him hope. For a few moments, anyway. Hope.

Until the pain rose again and crested over him and drowned his hope like sand under an incoming tide.

* * *

Sheki felt an odd mixture of terror and calm as he floated alone, backward, into the mist. He had heard it all, everything the Throgs had said. But he had been unable to speak, or move, when the Throgs had asked Claudi if she wanted to live. Were they saying that *she* could live, but only if he didn't? Their words had brought a rising panic. He didn't want to die! But what if it meant that Claudi and the ship could go free? What if someone had to sacrifice so that the others could live? What if it was him?

He'd done it once before, in the sim. It hadn't seemed so hard then.

But he hadn't felt tears trying to rise in his eyes then. He'd wanted to shout, *Claudi—let them take me—go free!* But he couldn't. He'd gazed at Watson, hoping that somehow Watson might stay with him. *You wouldn't want to go back without me, would you, Watson?* He knew that even that wasn't right to hope for, but he couldn't help it.

And then the Throgs had done something, because now he was floating backward, away from Claudi. The cloud wall closed in around him. But for an instant, just for an instant, he felt Claudi's presence in his mind, her bright blue eyes watching him through her tears, watching and following and not letting go, not letting go. And then she was gone. He wanted to cry out, but couldn't.

But one prayer, at least, was answered as Watson floated after him, glowing.

Captain Thornekan was staring into the star pit so hard his eyes hurt. He scarcely heard the jubilant reports noting the absence of Throgs inside the ship. He was staring at an image that was severely distorted by field lines and half blotted out by a ring of swarming Throgs.

He had them, thought he had them, confined by a region of highly stressed n-space being spun out by the ship's generators. Ruskin's guidance had been startlingly effective. By making the maneuvers and field shapes called for by Ruskin, *Charity* had closed the trap around the Throgs. But how long could they be kept trapped? The Throgs seemed to move through n-space like fish through water. Would they find a way to freedom? Or would the ship's generators fail first, straining to produce field shapes that they had never been designed for?

If Thornekan clamped the n-space field quickly, it was possible he could destroy them. He longed to try; he yearned to crush those living engines of death. And yet Ruskin/New had carefully told him how to shape the field so as not to harm those within it. And the reason was visible, tiny but radiant in the darkness at the center of the starstream: a handful of tiny figures, two children and two animals, surrounded by the Throgs. They were floating unprotected in the void of n-space. Thornekan had no idea what was keeping them alive.

What the hell is going on out there? What are they all doing? It was like nothing Thornekan had ever seen, or imagined. *And where is New?*

Len Oleson edged around the star pit toward him, but remained silent. Thornekan saw his first officer staring down into the pit, scratching anxiously at his beard. Oleson's eyes were dark, sober, and grim. "What are you planning?" he asked finally.

Thornekan didn't answer. His thoughts, and his stomach, were in knots. A blood red haze crept into his vision as he imagined the destruction of this one cluster of Throgs, such a small but sweet vengeance for the millions of Humans who had died, for the wife who had been taken from him, for all of the horror and the fear.

"If we act now, we can probably crush them," Oleson said quietly. "We could end it. Save the ship. Take the knowledge back with us."

Thornekan nodded. "Is that what you're recommending?"

Oleson rubbed a sore at the edge of his beard, where he'd been scratching since the attack began. "Well, damn it—I'd be derelict in duty if I didn't say that the ship, with its passengers—"

"I know about the ship," Thornekan interrupted. "But is that what you're recommending?"

Oleson glanced behind the captain, to where the parents of the two kids were sitting out of the way of the crew. Thornekan had summoned them to the bridge in hopes that communication could somehow be established with the kids, in hopes that the parents could reach out to them where he could not. They were staring silently down into the star pit. Oleson said nothing.

Thornekan nodded. "Didn't think so."

"Skipper, look—it wasn't that I—"

"Forget it. It was your job to ask me." Thornekan closed his eyes for a moment, just concentrating on the air moving in and out of his lungs. Concentrating on staying sane. "Len, I don't know what the hell those kids are doing out there, but I do know that someone *put* them there, and right now they're still alive. At least I think they are. I don't intend to be the one to kill them—not if I can help it."

Oleson nodded, remaining silent.

Thornekan knew the anguish his first officer was feeling, because he felt it even more terribly himself. Who could have imagined that he would be the first Human captain ever to have Throgs at his mercy—caught in the act of attacking and killing—and be unable to act upon his advantage? "Damn it, Ruskin," he breathed. "At least tell me what you're doing." But he had no way of knowing if the starstream-being heard him, or cared.

The voice of his pilot broke through his concentration. "Captain, the field's starting to degrade. Power-deck says they can't hold it much longer."

Thornekan looked sharply at the pilot, then banged the com. "Power-deck, is there enough left to squeeze it down on them?"

The voice from the power-deck seemed light-years away. "If you do it fast. A minute at the outside. Otherwise, we'll have to let them go. I can't hold it, skipper."

Thornekan stared at the image, at the tiny figures floating in the darkness. Were they already dead? He couldn't know. His last chance to destroy the Throgs before they destroyed the ship . . .

He had no choice, did he?

Claudi screamed, but to no avail. Sheki had disappeared into the misty maw of the Throgs-world. "You can't do that!" she raged. Lopo was snarling, and even Baako had looked up in angry confusion. But they were helpless to stop it.

Only the Throgs had that power. A moan filled the air as they peered down at her, their eyes disappearing and reappearing. Had they heard or understood her cry? The center Throg's eyes swam together, then apart again. They continued spreading, and the center Throg split into three more of itself. There were now five, staring at her.

Claudi shook with anger. "You're *evil!* Do you hear me? What kind of monsters *are* you?"

Something of her words must have been heard, because the moan grew to a loud, complex murmur. There was a rustling of wings, and a single echoing voice came out of the Throg cluster: *"YOUUUU ERRRRRRR. WEEEE WILLL LET-T-T-T YOUUUU REEE-TURRRNNNN!"*

Claudi's breath went out of her. They would let her return, yes. But without Sheki? No . . . no . . . no . . .

The murmuring of the Throgs changed abruptly. Turning, Claudi was shocked to see the stream of stars becoming visible again, surrounding her in ghostly light. The curved star-patterns made her feel as if she were floating, all alone, down the hollow infinity of the starstream. It was a terrible, lonely, frightening feeling. She almost felt that she could see all the way down to the center of the galaxy.

"LOOOOK-K."

She turned to look upstream. Something was floating down the starstream toward her—something large and silvery and shaped like a long, distorted egg. It was a starship. It was her starship, starship *Charity*, floating downstream toward her. "Wh-what are you doing?" she asked uselessly. She drew a ragged breath. "How can that *be*?"

"COMINGGGG FORRR YOUUU! WEE WILLL LET-T YOUU GO-O! IF YOUU WILLL LET-T USS!"

She turned and glared at the Throgs. Let her go—but not Sheki?

At that moment, something else appeared in the starstream, something familiar. It began with a pair of eyes, and the barest suggestion of a face, and a body beneath the face. She knew at once who it was, yet he didn't look quite the same as before. It seemed to her that there were several people behind those eyes. They were Ruskin's eyes, and behind them was a faint sunglow and the glittering points of brightness that she had come to know as Ali'Maksam/New; but she wondered who else was there, too. The body was a Humanlike form, but with a hint of serpentine curves, and at the same time, a stockier build. Hadn't there been someone else who had died with the others? A Tandesko assassin? *Won't you help me, if that's what you are? Won't you kill them for me? Please?*

Somehow she sensed that, no, it would not kill the Throgs for her. "What's . . . happening?" she whispered to the being. She was determined to remain brave, and not to show weakness to those monsters. She felt a little better, just seeing the starstream-being—felt less alone, though she still didn't know what it intended.

And then it spoke, but in voices that echoed round and round each other, making it hard to know who was saying what:

(Resonant)
   Have you sung?
   Can you keep singing?
   Please sing—

(Whispering)
   Turn. Spin yourself open. Find the way to
   knowledge—of them, of yourself. Find the
   balance.

(Unyielding)
   If they mean to kill, can you fight? Will
   you lay down your life? They think *you*
   control the balance—

(Gentle)
   They test and seek. They ask, will you
   return to the ship before the joining fold of
   space passes and it is gone? They ask, will
   you trade Sheki's life for your own?

(Musing)
   They ask—will you let them free? Do you
live? Do you care?

(Urging)
   They are afraid. They want to know—

   She breathed quickly, trying to follow. What they were
saying seemed important. But it was all so confusing, and
their words lapped at each other like waves on a shore,
confusing her even more. But this she understood: *Will
you return to the ship before it is gone? Will you trade
Sheki's life for your own?*

   She heard those words, and she gazed at the starstream-
being with tears in her eyes, because she wanted *it* to save
Sheki. And she was aware of the many eyes of the Throgs
gazing down upon her back, and she wished they could
hear the tremendous *NO!* that was billowing up inside her,
without her having to say the word. It seemed frozen in
her throat, unable to make its way to her voice.

   The starship was drawing closer now, would soon pass in
front of her. She thought she understood now, that this was
not happening exactly as it appeared; it was some trick of
space caused by the Throgs, or New, or both. The "fold of
space" . . .

   *"WOUUULLD-D   YOUUUU   REEE-TURRRRRNNN?
WOULD YOU RETURN?"*

   She whirled and glared at the Throgs, her eyes hot with
tears. "Without my friend, you mean?"

   *"THE OTHERRR. YESSSSS. WEE LET-T YOUU GO.
YOUU LET-T USS GO."*

   She didn't understand at all those last words, but she
couldn't worry about that. Her heart was in her throat,
blocking any words from coming out. *No, no, no, no, no!*
She turned again, and the ship seemed closer now, in a
shimmering haze. And there was something new between
her and the ship: a black dusty lane, like a footpath in
midair, reaching from her feet to the passing ship. Was this
the "fold of space"? Was this the way she had come out in
the first place? Almost as though a hand were pushing her

from behind, she took a step out onto that path. And a second step.

Choking back a sob, she made herself stop. She felt her virtual presence erupt like a plume of smoke and billow toward the Throgs as she shouted: "What about everyone else? What about Suze? And Scer-Randall? And all the others like me? What about them?"

She felt the touch of a squirming, confused presence, and there was a rush of murmuring from the Throgs. *"WHAAT?" "OTHERSSS?" "OTHERSSS?" "WERRRE THEYY LIKE YOUUU?" "OTHERSSS?" "THEYY ARE GONNNNE." "GONNNE." "JUSST ONNE OTHERRR." "NOT-T-T LIK-K-K-E YOUUU."*

The words echoed across the sky, echoed from the stars themselves. The brief, shuddering contact was broken. *Gone . . .* All of those people, gone? And what did they mean, just one other? Claudi struggled to hold back her tears, and held her arms out to the starstream-being, begging it to help. But it was hardly even visible now. All that she heard was a faint echo of a voice, saying, *"Remember to sing? Claudi? Please sing?"*

Once that had made her laugh, but she could no longer laugh. The starship now seemed more distant from her. The footpath stretched away into the haze, and all she could think of was her parents and Mr. Zizmer and the circ-zoo and her friends all vanishing into that haze, and her heart nearly broke. But even if she went back, Sheki would still be here.

"SOOOONN. CHOOOOSE SOONN OR IT-T WILL BE GONNNE." Did the Throgs sound just the least bit frightened themselves?

She blinked, and the starship was dimmer, moving down the starstream. The pathway was growing faint, the fold of space disappearing. . . .

Hating herself, she took another step.

And a voice came to her, from somewhere deep within her own thoughts, saying quietly, *Remember Scer-Randall.*

In midstep, she froze. Scer-Randall. How frightening he was, until he too had fallen victim! But no—he had not just fallen victim. He had *run forward* to save Sheki and two other kids. He must have known what would happen, but he had done it anyway! Just as . . . just as Sheki had done it once in the sim, to save her.

"SOOOONNN . . ." rumbled the Throg warning.

He had no choice. . . .

Thornekan whispered the name as if it were a curse: "Ruskin, help me!"

And he was answered by a murmur, *"You can kill them, or release them."* There was no Ruskin face, but in the star pit was a glimmer of the reddish light that he had come to associate with the starstream creature. *"We could not blame you if you destroyed them. But if you could sing, as Claudi does . . . ! We have hope, Captain. The children . . . and one other . . . they might yet live, if you release your enemy quickly."*

"Release them?" he repeated in disbelief. "What are you saying?"

"You must decide. Whether to destroy—or to spare, both your children and the others." For an instant the face was visible, then it was gone again, though the glow remained. *"Will you take the chance, as Claudi did? We can promise nothing . . . but we have hope. . . ."*

"Of what?" he whispered.

"Captain," he heard behind him, in a strained voice. He glanced. It was Mrs. Melnik. "Captain, I thought I just heard a voice—"

He squeezed his eyes closed, as if that would show him Ruskin's face again, and nodded, and turned his back on Mrs. Melnik. *The children.* "Pilot—"

"Captain!" It was one of the fathers.

He ignored the cry. "Pilot—trim the field back! Let them . . . go." The words came out of his mouth like broken glass, every syllable hurting.

"Aye, Captain. Let them go," he heard, as if in the remote distance.

Hating what he had just done, he watched in the star pit. Before the pilot could even have acted, the tiny figures floating in the darkness began to move apart, and away from center. Then the lines of distortion softened, and the ring of Throgs began to swarm outward.

"You have chosen," murmured the voice from the star-stream, and it seemed to offer no judgment.

His heart was frozen. He had done what he had done. He could only stand and watch—aware of the parents behind him, staring—and steady himself on the edge of the star pit as he watched the Throgs flutter out in an expanding circle. To escape to freedom? Or to attack once more?

Farther away and dimmer, the ship. Thinner and fainter, the path that could take her back.

"NO!" Claudi exploded. "NO! NO! NO! NO!" Drawing a ragged breath, she straightened to her tallest height and glared at the Throgs. To the collection of shadows and wings and eyes that were the Throgs, she croaked, "Not ever! Not on your life!"

One of the Throgs took on the form of an upside-down Human face again. She trembled, but met its stare. "Send my friends back. Lopo and Baako and Sheki. And Watson. I'll stay, if that's what you want. If you have to have someone to kill . . . or whatever it is you want. . . ." As she spoke, she felt a numbness growing in her head, and a thickness to her tongue. She felt a great inner resistance, but she managed to say it anyway, with greater determination than she had ever said anything in her life. "Send them back. I'll stay."

"YOUUU? YOUUU?" said the upside-down face, and she once more felt the shivering touch of puzzlement.

"Yes," she whispered hoarsely, fighting an urge to look back at the ship. She knew it, and the pathway, were disappearing.

"LET-T-T THE OTHERRR?" "LET THE OTHERR?" "SHALL-L WE-E?" "SHALL WE?" "AND-D YOUU WILL—" "RELEASE—?"

Lopo suddenly reared up and growled, "Rrrrrr, not leave Claudi . . . *rrrrrrrrr* . . ." Claudi blinked back tears, but was afraid to look at Lopo. She imagined his fiery red eyes, with those deep black pupils, peering at her. But she didn't dare shift her gaze from the Throgs.

Baako growled, startling her. "Rrrrr . . . therrrrre they go."

Claudi finally turned her head. High in the cloud wall she saw a tiny light and a small boy floating away, toward the ship. A new trail appeared across the sky, for Sheki and Watson. Her pathway, her fold of space, was gone. But a part of her, a tiny part, floated and walked with the distant pair, toward the ship. She felt confusion and relief and fear. Sheki's fear, for her.

Sing, you must sing. . . .

As tears welled in her eyes, she drew a breath and shouted, "Neither the stars, nor the moons . . . the moons . . ." And she stammered to a halt, because she couldn't remember the song anymore.

"YOUU WILL RELEASSSE—?"

She had no idea what they were saying. She imagined she saw Sheki and Watson disappearing into that passageway, and the passageway closing forever. *"NO!"* she shouted suddenly.

A tremor shook the sky world. There was a queer twisting and shaking around her, and a *jabberjabberjabber* that was stranger than ever. But her heart was bursting, and she had to finish saying it. . . .

"NOOOOOO—?"

"Lopo and Baako, too! You send them back too!" she yelled, but now the shaking had turned into a loud *HOOOOOOOOMMM*, drowning out her voice. What was happening? Her mind-presence was rising up, but all she felt was astonishment and confusion and Throgs flying everywhere, fleeing. She felt a strange, alien wonderment.

What was happening?

The sky darkened suddenly, and there was a violent concussion of thunder. She glimpsed the ship, silver and distant against the darkness. Sheki and Watson were gone, and with them the pathway. She started to cry out—but then she was surrounded again by Throgs, returning to fill the air with their confusing screams: *"YOUU HAAAVE LET THEM—" "DO NOT-T UNDERRSTAND-D—" "DO NOT-T UNDERRSTAND-D—" "MUSSST LEARNN—"* Her own cry got no further than a gargle of pain before she felt something dark close around her, cutting off all sight and sound. And then her mind-presence rose up, only to be trapped by something alive.

And then she felt her mind, her brain, her entire being laid open to the sky, as if she were *becoming* a virtual presence. Her fear and grief sputtered up out of her head like arcing electricity. Thoughts and memories flashed out, jagged bolts of lightning in the darkness. She had no secrets any longer, no secret dreams or places, no secret fears or hopes. . . .

And she was aware of surprise rising around her, not her own surprise but the Throgs'. Whatever they were learning, it astonished them.

And behind it all, she was barely aware of the words:

Your song must go on—

They begin to see—

*You must try to forgive, because how else
will they know—*

If I can, so surely must you—

Claudi, we love you—

Very little of it made sense to her. She only knew that someone was watching her die. She'd never imagined that dying would be like this.

Her last thoughts faded toward darkness, with visions of people walking toward her, out of a terribly dark and cold place: two acrobats, and a S'rath, and many others she didn't know, and Suze . . . *oh, Suze!*

And then they all faded to dark, and she knew no more.

Interlude

And now ?
What have they done ?

They tempted her with the pathway
  with the fold
they thought it was she
  who held them trapped

  Tempting her with freedom
    hers for theirs
      at a price

  But she would not yield

Do they know why they are free? Do they see? They are
frantic to understand, to learn, frantic with misunder-
standing.
  We cannot yet reach them to know—
    What can we do?

Do?
Do?

Nothing
   except
      wait
         hope
            pray

Or—

Perhaps there was something more. There was the other, the Im'kek, held apart somehow by the Throgs— still alive, though in pain. Perhaps he could help.

From the Throgs, there had seemed to be a reaction, some sense of . . . *approval*, perhaps . . . or *confusion* over the child's actions. Had they thought that it was she who released them? Did they think it was a bargain fulfilled? Or did they know, could they see, *they had to see* they had been released for the sake of the children, because someone *else* cared. . . .
   not sure—
      not sure—

And yet they *seemed* to have been wondering if *she* cared. . . .

But she sang . . .

Yes.
But what were they trying to learn now, and would they destroy her in doing so? There had been a sense of confusion and regret

The dark ones knew

They heard
   her sing . . .

Many sing.

But she was different
she did not just adapt
she sang
and gave

And they knew
and were astounded

But now they strip open her mind and soul—

Perhaps there was a way to join, to open, to make one
last attempt to bring order out of the chaos, life out of
death. If New could reach her still—and the other, the one
called Roti
    —perhaps—

CHAPTER 31

The captain tried to ignore the clamor of voices in his head as the n-space fields shifted violently—tried to watch, to see what was happening after the release of the Throgs. He tasted bile in his throat. Had he committed a grievous error in letting them go, in giving up his chance to destroy them, to save his ship, to avenge the pain he'd been carrying in his heart all these years? What were the Throgs doing? Preparing to strike again? Where was Ruskin/New?

The starstream had reappeared in the pit, but it looked as though a deranged artist were repainting it in realtime. It was chaotic with n-space disturbances, as chaotic as the clamor in his head. Now it was changing to look like a *thunderstorm*—here, in a place where there was nothing but flowing, n-dimensional space. Angry-looking clouds were closing like pincers ahead of the ship, glimmering and smoking with lightning.

Now the palest possible outline of a human face was appearing and disappearing among the clouds. If it was Ruskin/New, it was not communicating. "Tell me what's happening, damn you," Thornekan whispered through the now-fading voices in his head. The children and animals were gone from view, but there was considerable movement of light and shadow out there, Throgs. The effect of the field shift was starting to die down, but the movement wasn't.

"Skipper!" An external voice.

He thumbed the com distractedly. "What?"

"Zoo gallery's picking up something where the kids disappeared."

He focused his attention on Liza's words. "Say again?"

"It's—weird, it looks like—"

"Get it on my holo."

"Uh—here." A holospace near the star pit blinked on. It showed the zoo gallery, close-up on an empty enclosure. The back of the enclosure appeared to open into infinity, and in it there was a flicker of lightning, like that in the star pit. A small figure was tottering forward, silhouetted by the jagged flashes.

"Who is—?" And then he could see for himself. It was Sheki Hendu, and trailing well behind him, a lupeko. Just one? The boy suddenly loomed large in the holo, emerging from the enclosure. A ball of light sat on his shoulder. The lupeko did not come out, but halted some distance in and turned, peering back toward the lightning. "Is he back?" Thornekan gasped, as Sheki climbed down, looking dazed. Thornekan swiveled toward the parents. "You might want to get down to—"

Rafe Hendu was already on his feet. "I'm on my way, Captain." The Melniks stirred anxiously, trying to look glad for him.

"You're welcome to go, too," Thornekan said. "But I can't guarantee—"

The two were already conferring. Audrey Melnik rose and hurried after Sheki's father. John Melnik sat where he was, nodding grimly to the captain. Thornekan turned back to the star pit.

A moment later he stiffened. The thunderclouds had parted, revealing Claudi in their midst, floating directly in the center of the star pit. Lightning was playing about her head. In fact it appeared to be erupting *from* her head, splaying outward into the clouds. Thornekan's hands tightened. An audible gasp told him that Claudi's father was now standing beside him. Melnik leaned over the edge of the star pit, reaching, groping toward the holospace where the image of his daughter was being . . . what? Electrocuted?

Thornekan gripped the man's shoulder and drew him back.

"Can't you do something," Melnik whispered.

"If I could—" *If I hadn't let the Throgs go . . .*

"But you can't just—"

"Look!" Thornekan pointed.

Another form was taking shape above Claudi.

"What . . . is . . . that?" Melnik breathed.

Traced in a ghostly light, it was a serpentine shape—reminiscent of a Logothian, but stretched and shimmering. It was weaving and writhing over Claudi, unaffected by the lightning.

"What is it?" Melnik repeated.

"I think," Thornekan said hoarsely, "that its name is Ali'Maksam."

Melnik shot him a desperate glance. "Is it helping her, or killing her?"

Thornekan could only shake his head.

Melnik drew a sharp breath, an instant before Thornekan. The clouds had swirled, revealing another figure on the far side of Claudi. This one was humanoid but alien, and it was floating motionless like Claudi, with light flashing about its head. The serpentine ghost shape hesitated, then stretched out to embrace that shape with its movement as well.

"Roti?" Melnik whispered in astonishment. "Roti? Is that you?"

The pain went on forever and forever.

And then it stopped.

Or rather, Roti Wexx'xx realized through a fog of bewilderment and relief, it was more that it had *diminished* to the point that he could be aware of thought again. His own thought. And no one else's.

For the last eternity or so, his memories had been torn from him one strand at a time—with a perfect and excruciating pain. Through the agony he had felk'd the presence of others, but at no time was he able to know them, or to share or learn. There had been only the pain, and loss. But now the pain was diminishing to a reverberation in his nerves. And he began to remember a moment, long ago, in which he had felt . . . *hope.* But he could not remember why. He was not in a world or place that he knew. Perhaps he was even now simply being saved for the final pain of death.

He remembered, suddenly, others going to their deaths. He didn't know how he had felk'd it, or why. But the image blazed in his memory: Humans seized by the terrifying force of darkness and, in the instant that he saw them, being torn out of the continuum and destroyed. The memory seared . . . the destruction of Human men, women, children. And yet in that memory he felk'd . . . *determination* in the darkness, but not necessarily malice.

It bewildered him. And why had *he* been spared that death and flayed open instead? Because he was not Human? Because he could felk what the Humans could not? Or because these monsters could felk only him?

And suddenly he remembered what it was that had given him hope—the image of a girl, a young Human girl, alive. They had felk'd her somehow, seen her *presence* . . . and that had made them hesitate, even as they destroyed the others.

The lament rose slowly in his mind: *Sorry . . . sorry . . .*

In the darkness, he was surrounded by a terrible storm of forces. Flashes of lightning. Suddenly he realized that he was not alone. Who—? It was the young girl! Nearby! He felt a surge of joy—and then he felk'd her pain, and felt a terrible fear. But she was alive.

He could see flickering light around her head, and hovering over her was a ghostly form—something sinuous and strange, and yet peculiarly familiar. It was a shimmering thing, like a felk'd image, a ghost image, something Logothian. It was curling around the youngster, peering and probing, with two tiny diamonds floating in blackness where its eyes ought to have been.

Now it was turning toward Roti.

And Roti felk'd his own mind opening up again, but slowly and gently this time. *"Turn, let it spin . . ."* he heard.

And he began to felk more clearly the frightened mind of that girl, and the mind of the other, the Logothian.

And he began to felk the shivering, squirming presence of the shadow ones—except now, perhaps aided by the Logothian, he began to felk the edges of their actual thought. And slowly at last he began to understand something of the Throgs, the mysterious and untouchable Throgs. And something of the magnitude, the terrible magnitude of their error.

Claudi awoke screaming. *"Suze! I'm sorry! I didn't know! Please come back!"* She was alive . . . she and Suze both were alive!

Or were they? Suze had just floated out into the night, along with all of the others: the acrobats, and Scer-Randall, and the men and the women and children. Floated off into the deep of the night. Not turning, not hearing.

But one other was still here with her, in the midst of a strange and terrifying storm. Claudi strained to see. He was not Human, he was . . . Im'kek. And there was another, peering over him; it was the ghostly form of Ali'Maksam/New. Now the Logothian was turning toward her. When it spoke, its voice was soft and whispery in her mind: *"Your cry was not in vain. Look—"*

For just a moment, a ghostly face reappeared in the clouds. Suze's face. She was peering at Claudi with puzzlement—but not anger. *"That is how she looked as she passed into our memory,"* Ali'Maksam/New whispered. *"She cannot return to you, but she felt no anger toward you."*

Claudi blinked, not understanding.

"Your argument. She let go of her anger, even before she died. And you must do the same."

Claudi trembled. As Ali'Maksam/New peered down at her, its face seemed to go through changes, glowing for a moment with deep red light, and then widening to hint of

Ruskin, and hardening with the ridged bones and deep-set slitted eyes that she recognized as the *hrisi* assassin.

Assassin? Trained killer? She shivered, as her thoughts turned inside out and she remembered her anger, her rage at the Throgs. "Kill them!" she screamed to the assassin. "They killed Suze—and the others! Kill them!"

"That's a power we do not have," said the assassin/New.

"Your captain had the power, but he spared them," said Ali'Maksam/New.

"And the truth," Ruskin/New said, *"is that killing cannot help. Vengeance cannot help."*

She stared at them in speechless bewilderment.

"There was so much they did not know," the starstream-being whispered. *"Listen, even now."* Ali'Maksam/New's eyes glittered. *"Feel their confusion."*

She could scarcely breathe. "Wait—I don't—" And then she did. She felt Ali'Maksam/New touch her mind in a gentle, Logothian way, teasing her thoughts and her presence outward. And then the starstream-being seemed to fade into the background, as she saw winged, shadowy beings flitting in the storm clouds, groaning and murmuring like thunder. It was an oppressive sound, a rumbling *jabberjabberjabber,* quaking with waves of consternation. It hit her suddenly, as if being piped to her in a sim, just how bewildered and dismayed the Throgs were. They had not expected to find her the person she was.

"Yes, yes—sorry!" she heard someone whisper. "That, and more! I see now!"

She didn't know who that was, speaking, but she felt clearly the Throgs' confusion. They understood now that not she but *someone else* had let them go. (Let them go? she wondered dimly. Had someone had them captured?)

"The captain—yes!" whispered that other voice excitedly. "Thank you, now I see! The captain had them, but let them go for Claudi's sake! They see it now—they see it! But do they know what it means?"

Claudi turned her head and finally saw who was speaking. It was the Im'kek, visible against the flashing storm clouds. He looked like a surroundie of an ancient god in battle, except for his ridiculous grin. "Don't you see? Don't you?" he cried.

"No!" she wailed. "I don't!"

"They spared you because the captain spared them! He astonished them! *I don't think they knew he was there!*"

Claudi shook her head, focusing determinedly on the Im'kek, as if he were the only one left in the universe who could make this clear to her. The captain had let them go—instead of killing them! Why? Why? Why?

"He wanted to kill them—yes, I'm sure he did! But he cared more about you! Yes, yes! And they thought it was *you* who let them go, but New helped them see it was someone else, someone who *cared*, someone who *risked*—it's how they knew—"

"What?" she whispered.

"That we were *alive!* All of us! That we were *conscious!* Didn't know before—couldn't see! Even me—" and the Im'kek's voice went sharp with pain. "Aiee, how it hurt! *Aaaieee! Sorry!* They could almost felk, but couldn't quite —but you, they felk'd something different in you, they felk'd your aliveness—"

Claudi squeezed her eyes shut. What was he saying? *"How could they not know we were alive?"* she screamed. *"How could they not know?"*

Against the lightning, the Im'kek's grin twisted grotesquely. "Not sure! Not sure! They couldn't really see! N-space! They live, they shift it all around—it's how they move and *attack*—by disrupting the n-spatial—" He gulped for breath. "It's natural to them! But we were unnatural, and to n-space. New, yes! Were they trying to stop, to remove . . . a plague, a disruption, not sure! But they didn't quite—couldn't see—so many n-spaces—*sorry!*"

Claudi's head was bursting full of hurt and fear and alarm and there was no room left for understanding.

"They disrupt—change things—but not seeing—"

"Wait a minute—"

"—what happens isn't known to—"

"Wait!" she shouted.

The Im'kek looked frantic. "Yes? Sorry! Yes?"

Claudi cried out in despair. "How do you know all this? And why are we still here?"

"It's through the New one, the starstream-one! When

n-space changes, I can felk so much more! I understand now. Even the New one wasn't sure until now!"

She listened with her eyes closed, trying to make it be real.

"And they didn't all believe—the Throgs!—sorry!—even after they saw! They're not all the same, didn't all believe. There's so much yet I can't felk—so much that's strange— sorry! Sorry!"

"Would you stop saying that?" Claudi cried.

"Sorry! What?"

"Sorry! Stop saying you're *sorry!"*

The Im'kek gasped. "Sorry! Sorry! It's just that—"

"Stop it!" she wailed. "Just tell me, what do they want with us? Why don't they let us go?"

"Not sure now! Not sure! New, *help!"* The Im'kek gulped for breath and gazed, wild-eyed, into space. The thunder and lightning were building, flashing, booming. The Im'kek squeezed his eyes closed. *"New? Help?"*

The sinuous Ali'Maksam/New weaved against the thunderclouds. Claudi felt the frantic rumble of Throg-thought again, and it was like drums and cymbals in her head. She felt her mind-presence dancing somewhere in the clouds, out of control, not knowing quite what she was doing or saying to them.

She heard the Im'kek, Roti, saying, "Yes, perhaps." He turned to Claudi. "Not sure, not sure. *Forgive them,* maybe. They know now what they've done."

"No!" Claudi shouted. They could go ahead and kill her if they wanted, but she could never forgive them. "What about Suze?" she shouted. "And Scer-Randall? *They didn't do anything wrong!"* And in that instant she imagined she saw a faint tracing of Scer-Randall's outline against the clouds.

"That's the point, don't you see? If it hadn't happened, there'd be nothing to forgive! Sorry! It's hard—*hard*—but New thinks it's what has to be!"

Claudi was sick with sorrow and anger and frustration. "Why me? I can't do that! I can't! I'm not God!"

"Nor I! Nor I!" Roti barked, as around him, Throg-shadows shifted in and out of the clouds, moaning. "But they saw something—in you—in me—but only when it was just right—sorry, the n-space! And with the starstream-one, guiding."

Claudi stared at him, riveted by his words, but unable to accept them.

"Don't you see?"

"But they hurt us!" she cried.

"Yes! Yes! Terrible! *Terrible!*" The Im'kek's voice cracked. But he kept on, urgently. "But they want—I don't know what they want! Not sure, not sure! But they're waiting—you sent Sheki—and then the captain let them—and you didn't *have* to, either of you! And now they're confused and . . . *sorry.* So sorry!"

She stared at the Im'kek in disbelief.

She heard another voice then, a harsher voice. Was it the assassin/New's? *"You must accept—as I had to—even my own failure."* And something blurred in her mind, and she heard the Ruskin-voice saying, *"It took me long to accept the one you just heard, whom I hated. But it was needed. Can you be faster, wiser, than I?"* And then the sun-voice urged softly, *"If you sing, you will know . . ."*

There was a terrifying rumble in the air, and a booming Throg voice: *"YEEEESSSSSS . . . YEEEESSSSS . . . !"* The clouds shifted, and a dazzling flash of light half blinded her, but in it she thought she saw—just for an instant—a dark path etched against the clouds, a zigzag path through a crazy-quilt pattern of lightning and blackest storm cloud. As the light faded, she could no longer see it. But the image of it burned in her mind. Sang out to her. A fold in space? Another offering to her?

"What do I *do?*" she whispered. And then she heard, from the direction of the path, a distant yipping.

CHAPTER 32

She saw Lopo's tiny head peering out from among the clouds, looking this way and that. At last he spotted her and burst into an ecstatic cry: "Yi-yi-yi-yi-yi-Claudi-Claudi-Claudi, come Claudi!" She shouted back and tried to move toward him. The storm clouds flashed and boomed around her, and among them she saw the dark shadows of Throg-shapes, fluttering and wailing. Everything seemed to be ending, the folds in space coming apart. Was she being allowed to escape? She would have to move quickly.

But what had happened to her new companion? "Mr. Im'kek?" she cried out plaintively. There was no answer. He had been floating some distance from her. Maybe he had to find his own way back, and she had to find hers.

There was no clear path now, but a myriad of possible ways. Above her, she saw Lopo bounding along a dark thread that wound among the clouds. He disappeared for a moment, then reappeared. "Claudi—rrrrrr, this way!" he yelped in frustration, tossing his head first one way then the other. He seemed unsure which way she should go. Claudi veered onto a path that seemed wrong in either direction; she couldn't see any place where it met Lopo's path.

"Lopo!" she cried frantically. "Is there a way back to the ship? We have to find the way back!"

"Yes, yes!" panted Lopo, his head reappearing above her, peering down out of a cloud. "Rrrrr . . . Baako's there, rrr, *hurrrry!*"

Hurry! Yes—the clouds were roiling as though they would explode! But how could she get up there? She could only keep moving along the dark path. There had just been an intersecting path, but it crooked off in the wrong direction, backward and down. She looked that way—and shuddered, as a shadow with wings flew over the path.

She heard another lupeko-yelp, gravelly and low. It was Baako. "Yarrr-rrrrr, yesss, that way! The *otherr*—go back for the *otherrrr!* The tunnel's closing, go back for him—there's the way!"

"Go back?" Claudi echoed, and then understood: *Go back for the Im'kek!* He hadn't answered her call. Maybe he was hurt or couldn't find his way. The sky was boiling around her, flashing light and dark. She shook with fear. What if she lost sight of Lopo? The Throgs were back there, and she didn't even know where he was! But what if he needed her?

As she agonized, she heard Baako once more, urging her back. With tears in her eyes, she took a breath—and plunged back the way she'd come. "Follow me, Lopo!" she cried over her shoulder, not even knowing if he could hear her. The other path loomed dark now, to her left; it wound downward and out of sight. She hesitated, struggling with herself.

"TIIIMMME RUNNNS OUT-T-T! WE-E CANNOT-T HOLD LONGGG! YOUU MUSST-T RETURRRN-N!" The Throgs seemed to be calling with one voice, and yet it was trembling, as though they themselves were on the verge of coming apart.

Shuddering, she plunged headlong down the path. "Mr. Im'kek!" she shouted. "Mr. Im'kek! Where are you?" A bank of fog loomed in front of her. She charged into it— and collided with someone or something, something with arms, something bigger than she was. *"Get away!"* she screamed, backing up. *"Get away!"*

"Sorry! Claudi—you are Claudi?" A dark shape loomed in the mist. "It's Roti! Roti Wexx'xx! Here, it's me!" A hand reached out of the mist and caught her arm, then drew them slowly together. It was the Im'kek, grinning wildly.

Claudi gulped, shaking with relief. "Do you know how to get back?" she cried weakly.

"No, no—lost! I cannot see my way here. I hoped you knew!" His voice was shaking as he added, "I felk that we have little time! They have released us, but they are losing their hold! The space is coming apart, the folds. *New, help us!"*

Claudi felt despair welling up inside her. Even the path was gone now, in the mist. She cringed as a black shadow fluttered overhead, keening. As it vanished, she thought she heard a faint cry that sounded like, *"GO-O-O-O! GO HO-O-O-O-ME NOWWW!"*

But how?

"Follow Lopo," she heard in a whisper. *"Follow Lopo, quickly!"*

"Lopo!" she cried, nearly bursting with fear. *"Lopo!"*

A lupeko's bark sounded clearly to her left. She grabbed Roti's arm and ran that way. A bank of clouds opened—and she glimpsed the frantic lupeko ahead of her. The mist swirled closed again. But Lopo kept yipping, and a soft red glow burned away the fog, and they hurried along a path of black stardust. There was Lopo again—ahead of them on a path that converged with theirs. "Rrrrr—good good!" she heard, and knew that Baako had seen them, too.

"Hurry! Let us hurry!" the Im'kek gasped behind her. "I felk this place will not last much longer!"

Claudi sped through the buffeting clouds. Ahead of them appeared a cavelike darkness. Lightning blazed everywhere but in there. Lopo stood in the opening, eyes afire, panting as he waited for them. Baako's head appeared beside his, then disappeared. Claudi and Roti rushed into the darkness after the lupekos. There was a flash of cold, and the clouds vanished, and stars appeared all around them. Claudi turned to look back.

"Hurry! Don't stop!" cried Roti.

Claudi nodded—but something made her hesitate. Out there among the stars, she saw a large ball of flickering clouds, like a nebula full of lightning. Was that where they had just been? She could not help staring, puzzled. She felt certain that something more was going to happen. She glanced at Roti, and he too was now staring in the same direction, head cocked.

"*Sing,*" she heard. And she remembered the song she had sung earlier. But she didn't have time even to take a breath.

The ball of flickering clouds began to expand violently. At the same time, she heard a new sound—music, perhaps, but not like the music she'd heard before. It sounded like a low, wailing flute—incredibly deep and distant, echoing through the vast ocean of stars, filling space with its mournful lowing. As she listened, it grew even deeper, and she felt herself filled, shaking, weeping with an unspeakable sorrow. Beside her, Roti groaned, as well. There was a rhythm to the sound, but she could not follow it; there were confused and jumbled words, and she heard, "*NO-O-O MOR-R-R-RE . . . NO MOR-R-R-RE . . . WE MUSSST-T-T . . . OURRR SOR-R-R-ROW-W . . . SOR-ROWWW . . . MUSST-T-T . . .*" And the music shuddered in some sort of terrifying climax, and the words were lost in a vast, shuddering moan. The cloud ball lighted up from within, as if a sun were exploding inside it. The light flashed outward, overtaking the ballooning clouds, consuming them.

For an instant, the explosion was so large and bright and transparent that she felt enveloped by it, like in a surroundie. Though tears blurred her vision, she saw something astonishing—a Human form taking shape in the clouds, a Human face. It wasn't Ruskin. Then *what . . .* was this another terrible Throg creation? Though it all happened in an instant, it seemed to take forever, as though time had frozen. And then she realized: the face was right side up, its eyes normal, and not distorted at all. A real Human face, and one that almost seemed familiar. And she heard a whispered: "*YESSS . . . NOWW WE KNOWWW. . . .*"

As quickly as it had appeared, the face faded. Time

melted and then froze again, and she saw flocks of black
Throgs scattering like birds, with screeches so high and
thin it pained her ears. Large Throgs burst apart into
smaller ones, and tiny ones collided . . . and it was impossible to be sure, because it all seemed to happen in the
strobe-flash of the explosion . . . but most of the Throgs
blazed into flame in the expanding ball of light and shriv-
eled away. The remaining handful gathered, and with a
terrible high-pitched-low-pitched wail, *stretched* in a cluster like a band of light, and snapped away into the distance
and vanished.

The explosion darkened and faded away, and the curved
tunnel of the starstream reappeared around Claudi and
Roti. They stood breathless for a moment, and she seemed
to hear in her mind that song: *Neither the stars will harm
you, nor the moons. . . .* And the fear in her mind was
gone. She felt amazement instead. A thought came back to
her, a memory of what Ruskin had told her she must do,
where the Throgs were concerned. What New had told
her. "Maybe," she whispered. "I don't know." In response
to Roti's urging, she turned and dived into the cave of
darkness.

Lopo was waiting. She reached out to touch him, and the
stars vanished, and Lopo disappeared, and she felt something solid strike her feet.

"Oops! *Sorry!*" Roti cried, stumbling into her.

Claudi tripped and fell headfirst.

A pair of hands caught her, and then more hands and
arms, and she was surrounded by bright lights and loud
voices. The hands were lowering her to the floor like an
injured person. Looking up into the lights, she squinted
and saw Sheki's face bobbing around, and her mother's,
and some others she didn't know. She heard a frantic yelp
and a "Claudi-Claudi-Claudi-Claudi—!" And all of the
other faces were blocked out by a furry head and a tongue
licking frantically at her face. And she heard somebody
cry, "Here comes someone else!"

"*Yiiee! Sorry!*"

Claudi and Lopo scrambled out of the way as Roti
crashed to the floor beside her.

* * *

The image in the star pit was changing so confusingly, Thornekan had no idea what to think. John Melnik stood gripping the edge of the display like a man possessed. But when Claudi and the Im'kek reappeared together, both men drew sharp breaths.

Their relief was short-lived. The strange storm of lightning and thunder closed around the two figures again. The serpentine shape of Ali'Maksam/New was gone, too. Thornekan glimpsed a dark shape that he thought was a Throg. Then nothing living. Time seemed at a standstill. Were the Throgs preparing to retaliate? To crush the ship? Never had he felt so helpless, not since Myra's death. And this time he was responsible. And yet . . . as he glanced at the nearest console, he saw many green indicators where before there had been yellow and red. The n-space matrix was still distorted, but stabilizing—

There was a sudden spike in the external matrix.

"There they are!"

He snapped his gaze back to the star pit. Directly in its center was Claudi again—looking frightened, but striding forward as though she were going to climb right out of the star pit. At her side was Roti Wexx'xx. Behind them, the storm abruptly faded to dark, leaving a sky full of stars. As the two passed out of view, something new appeared in the center—a large, irregular cloud of dust or gas, with something inside it growing bright . . . *exploding*.

"Secure for impact, all decks—!" Thornekan's voice choked off when he saw something appear in the center of the explosion. It was a Human face, and it looked like—

"Claudi?" Melnik breathed.

Sudden new voices boomed in Thornekan's head, incomprehensibly. It was not Claudi's face, but a face that resembled hers. It seemed to be speaking. He understood clearly just one word: "SORROW." Then the face faded, and in the center of the expanding conflagration he glimpsed black shapes swarming, scattering, fleeing, many of them flaring incandescent white, before shriveling and darkening. The remaining Throg-shapes drew together and somehow seemed to gather energy—and with a strange distortion of light, shot away into the distance and vanished. And the explosion darkened, leaving only the stars; and the stars blurred, and in their place was the familiar view of the starstream.

Thornekan turned to look at the consoles. The n-space distortions were gone. Len Oleson was staring at the readouts in disbelief. He looked up. "We seem to be underway without interference—"

"Captain!" squawked Liza. "Someone else coming through down in the circ-zoo!"

Thornekan's heart leaped. He spun to say to Melnik, "Maybe you had better—"

But John Melnik was already running out the door.

Claudi hugged her mother, crying; and then she grabbed Sheki and hugged him, too. Baako was there with Lopo, and even Baako held still to be hugged for a moment. Joe Farharto was trying to herd the lupekos back to their enclosures, but Claudi cried out imploringly until he agreed to let them stay. Lopo panted in relief, and Baako murmured, "Rrrr-good, good—"

Claudi heard a shout, and her heart pounded. It was her father running across the room. He grabbed her up in a bear hug. *"Claudi, Claudi!"* he murmured in her ear. *"Little bird, we saw you out there! We saw you! We were so afraid for you!"*

For a long time, she just squeezed his neck and wouldn't let go, wouldn't let go for anything in the world. Finally he pried her arms loose and gazed at her with a beaming smile.

"Fath', oh Fath'!" she gasped, snuffling. "It was awful, awful, awful!"

"I know, Claudi, I know! But it's okay now, it's okay!"

"Yes, yes! I'm sure it is!" the Im'kek wheezed behind her.

"Roti!" her father boomed, turning. "You're alive! You really are! We'd given you up for lost!" He seized the Im'kek's hand and pumped it up and down.

"Yes, yes!" said the Im'kek, grinning. "Alive, alive, alive!"

"What about the others?" called another voice, off to one

side. "Did you see any of the others?" Everyone turned. A fuzzy and too-small holo of Mr. Zizmer floated in front of a portable projector, his voice reverberating from a speaker. And when he repeated his question, everyone suddenly became a lot more somber.

"I'm sorry!" Roti whispered. "All the others—all gone. All gone. So sorry . . ."

CHAPTER 33

It was a puzzled group that was gathered in the conference suite. The kids and their parents were there, plus Mr. Zizmer, and the Im'kek, and the captain and his officers. Thornekan had relentlessly reviewed the events just passed, trying to learn exactly what had happened. Roti, who seemed to have the best grasp of the whole affair, had done most of the talking.

". . . and they showed us, at the end, that they understood about us, a little. Understood that we are not what they thought—not just a plague, not just mindless disturbances," he concluded, adding that he thought they were . . . *sorry,* in some enigmatic Throg way, for what they had done . . . and that their sorrow was reflected, not just in their leave-taking, but in their release of Claudi and himself. "I am sure, Captain—sure that your act helped them to realize," Roti wheezed. "It was when you released them that they *knew* . . ."

"Yes, yes," Thornekan murmured, unable to stop thinking, *You had Throgs in your grip and you could have killed them, and you didn't.* They had been over all that—the

Throgs' astonishment that someone had let them go in order to spare Claudi's life.

Roti's fingers twitched. He was clearly still spinning his mental gears trying to understand it all.

The captain was, as well; but his heart was heavy with pain. The Throgs had left them, but only after exacting the lives of eleven of his passengers and crew. "Why?" he murmured, half to himself. "Why did the Throgs kill the others, if they saw the two of you, and knew?"

"They didn't see, didn't know yet!" Roti answered frantically. "They were dissolved, discorporated, before the Throgs knew! The n-space changes—it happened too quickly—"

"But not to you and Claudi?"

"No! Me they felk'd, and Claudi! Especially when New helped, guided!"

"Then what about the animals?" Thornekan gestured toward the entity sitting silent on the shoulder of Sheki Hendu. A moment ago, it had been in the form of a small reptile. Now it was a wispy reddish ball of light. "This one, for instance. Why'd it survive?"

Roti stared, puzzled, for a moment. "Ah, of course," he exploded. "An energy-being, a shape-transformer—not affected by the n-space disruption! It glided right through."

"But it is changed," Thornekan said. "Isn't that what you said, Sheki?"

Sheki's eyes rotated from the Im'kek to the captain. "Y-yes, sir." He reached up as if to stroke his pet, but his hand hesitated, as if feeling a tingle from the being's glow. "He felt some of it h-happen, I think. With the Th-throgs." As the boy spoke, the entity shimmered and became a darkly iridescent bird—or was it a bat?—muttering in his ear. Sheki listened, lips pursed, then said to the captain, "They d-did something to him. It changed him. He can m-make more shapes now. But he, he felt *them* change, too, I think."

Thornekan studied the boy and his pet, wondering *how* the Throgs had changed Watson—wondering if they had somehow left him as a spy in the Human midst. It seemed unlikely, ridiculous in fact. "What do you mean, Sheki?" he asked, as the bird turned back into a glowing wisp.

"I f-feel what he feels," Sheki said, looking over his shoulder. "We're s-safe now, he thinks."

"Watson feels that we're safe," Thornekan repeated.

Sheki nodded silently.

Thornekan pursed his lips. Could he trust the feelings of an "entity"? He certainly had no more authoritative information. "Maybe," he sighed finally, "Watson is right. Maybe they're really gone for good. I suppose we'll find out. But we still don't know what Ruskin, what *New* wanted, do we? Or whether it succeeded, or whether it's done trying. Opinions, anyone?"

That triggered a confusing, and largely speculative, discussion of the possible motives and character of the star-stream-being, which led only to a more general sense of puzzlement. When the captain finally adjourned the meeting, it was on the one hand with a vast sense of relief, and on the other, with a deep and abiding uncertainty.

It was an uncertainty that was to take a very long time to pass away.

They saw New once more before it was all over.

Claudi and her friends were in class, under Mr. Zizmer's watchful eye, talking about all that had happened. Jeremy had been insisting that it would have been a lot better if they'd just blasted the Throgs out of the starstream, especially after what they'd done to Suze and to all those other people. That got the other kids going, until someone pointed out that if they could have blasted the Throgs, they probably would have.

Claudi tried to explain why that might not have been a good idea, in any case. "We would never have shown them what we were," she said, echoing Roti Wexx'xx's words to her when she'd voiced a similar desire. "They wouldn't have known that we were sent-, sent- . . ."

"*S-sentient,*" Sheki murmured.

"Right," Claudi said. "And the war would just keep going on forever."

Jeremy looked bewildered at this. "You mean, the Throgs are supposed to be *okay,* now?"

Claudi hesitated. "I'm not sure, exactly."

"Perhaps," Mr. Zizmer offered from the front of the class, "you mean that we both learned something about each other. And that's better than learning *nothing*, isn't it?"

Claudi stared, thinking. Yes, they must have learned something. But to tell the truth, she wasn't exactly sure—

"You speak," interrupted a voice, "wisely."

Everyone, including Mr. Zizmer, turned in surprise. The whole side of the room seemed to have turned into a great, wide view of the starstream, like a surroundie. But Claudi knew that it was no surroundie. The face that looked back at them shimmered like mercury. One instant it was Ruskin's face; in the next its eyes gleamed of Ali'Maksam, then glowed like a red sun; the face softened to a woman's, then hardened to become a Tandesko assassin's, then became Ruskin's again. "Hello, Claudi," said New. The class murmured in amazement. "And Sheki— and Captain Thornekan. Roti. And—dare we say it? Jeaves."

The amazement of the class grew as more figures became visible against the starstream.

On the bridge, the image in the star pit blurred. Captain Thornekan glanced at Len, who checked the n-space monitors and turned his hands outward. There was no problem in the n-space configuration. Thornekan drew a breath. Was this what he'd feared—another appearance of the Throgs?

The *entire front of the bridge* suddenly filled with a full, clear image of the starstream. In its center was the face of Willard Ruskin. It seemed to swim and change, as though many personality aspects were shifting through it. Thornekan stepped toward the image, then hesitated.

When the being spoke, it was not to him, but to Claudi and Sheki. The two came into focus off to the right. For an instant, Thornekan feared that they had been taken from the ship again; then he saw the entire class, not quite so sharply focused, and the walls of the deck-school.

The starstream-being turned its gaze and greeted the captain by name.

* * *

Roti Wexx'xx was lost in thought in his cabin, perusing book-slivers, when he felk'd the change around him. The wall of his cabin dissolved, and he drew a slow breath. Was it all going to start again? No . . . he felk'd nothing harmful. . . .

Then the starstream-one appeared, and Roti found himself drawn into a most unexpected conversation.

New spoke, its changing face holding Claudi and her classmates in rapt attention. It spoke in strange and sweeping words of what had recently happened. "By no means was the loss of your friends in vain. Something new exists between Human and Throg that never existed before. A knowledge, a partial understanding of *being.*"

The dim shape of the bridge was visible behind the image of the captain as he spoke in answer. "Maybe," he said. "But can you tell us this: Are we safe? Have the attacks ended? Can you tell us, for once, what you know?"

The being's eyes glowed red, with points of diamond white light in the center. "Is your ship safe? We believe so. The Throgs are far from you now, and still moving. Is Humankind safe?" The eyes flickered. "Who can say? There is much we do not know—of Throgs, and of Humanity."

Thornekan replied, "Tell me something else, then—if you will. Did all of this happen according to some plan of yours?"

New gazed directly at Claudi as he contemplated the question. "Not precisely." A sudden smile graced the face in the stars. "We had much to learn, and there was much that took us by surprise. Roti Wexx'xx, had we known of you—" The eyes glittered, conveying an unreadable expression. Amusement, perhaps?

"Sorry!" cried the Im'kek, his image floating somewhat apart from the captain's. "Did you not felk my presence? Did you not know?"

"We are not omniscient. We do not . . . felk. We are just who we are."

"Wait a minute!" the captain's image demanded. "You won't deny that you purposely engineered a meeting between the children and the Throgs?"

The starstream-being nodded slowly. "Yes, indeed, we had a purpose. But not we alone, as it turned out." And now its eyes shifted, as though searching. *"Jeaves, can you hear us?"*

"At your service!" boomed a voice from the direction of the teaching wall.

Claudi turned, and saw Mr. Zizmer's eyebrows go up. It was not Mr. Zizmer's voice, though it seemed to come from the same place. *Jeaves.* Jeaves was the robot Mr. Zizmer had sent to her during the Throg attack! But hadn't it disappeared in the Throg world?

"We have much of your memory, Jeaves," the starstream-being said. "But had we known what you were thinking—had we only known—"

"Ah. But as Humans like to say, 'All's well that ends well,' is it not?" replied the voice from the wall.

"Who is that speaking?" Captain Thornekan demanded, turning around.

"The IS, captain."

"The intelligence system?"

"More accurately, I am a resident in the IS, placed here to perform certain investigations during the course of the voyage. I answer to the name of Jeaves. If there is any way that I may be of assistance—"

The captain's sputtered reply was overwhelmed by waves of laughter. And the laughter came not from the classroom or from the speakers in the wall, but from the great being that floated outside, among the stars.

EPILOGUE

"Knowledge comes, but wisdom lingers."
—Alfred, Lord Tennyson

Interlude

They were aware of much, and yet there remained so much more that they could not know, might never know. But the one who had so tugged at their heart, so awakened them . . . that one lived, and knew them, and laughed. And that was a reward

She sang
  and we sing
    in her dreams

—but—
Of the dark ones, the Throgs—
  —who can tell?—
  —or know?—

They had done the astonishing: destroying many of themselves, fleeing away down the world-strand, radiating waves of consternation. Was it guilt, this self-immolation? Or something else? Had the Throgs acquired understanding, or just a muddle of confusion and doubt among themselves? It was difficult to feel, impossible to know.

—but—
The dark ones—
—recognized error—

And that gave hope.

New tingled still with surprise at the role of the Im'kek, buying time to bring Claudi to the Throgs, and of the captain and his willingness to give up an advantage so desperately won. How could New have predicted? And Jeaves! Was it pure coincidence that his plans and hopes had matched their own? Perhaps. Or perhaps not, for Jeaves' thinking of old was a part of New, a part of what New was.

New had been helpless to prevent the deaths of the other Humans, and so they had done the only thing they could: opened themselves to the memories and thoughts of the victims, as they passed. It was a remembrance—an immortality of a sort—a joining with the rumbling maelstrom of thought and emotion that was New.

But as for the future—

Would reconciliation come? Would Throgs recognize and respect the Greater Humanity, the Habitat? Or could they know it only in this strand, in the revealing presence of n-space?

—Impossible to know, the link is broken—
—Fleeing now, fleeing—

And so they were fleeing, the Throgs—down the world-strand toward . . . even New did not know where, just that they were already far from this Human ship, far from the Human child and the Im'kek who had shown them that they were not alone. Was it fear? or shame? or regret that sent them flying away? Would they return? Who could say?

Come to sing   ?
  Could they not sing   ?

Instead of attack? Why did they always attack?

—How can we know why?—
—Ever know why?—

CHAPTER 34

Though this part of our story is over, I'm sure that questions remain. Did the starship continue on its journey in safety? Did the Throgs go away to stay? Was the galaxy made safe again for Humanity and its friends?

Yes. Maybe. I don't know.

None of us knows.

I must say that it all ended better than I had feared in my worst moments, but perhaps not as well or at least not as *clearly* as I had hoped in my best. A confrontation that might have ended in disaster, didn't—but neither did it end in a straightforward reconciliation. It ended in mystery, and with a host of unanswered questions.

I'm sorry if you thought I was going to clear up all of the questions for you. I can't. I can say, though, that it ended in safety for starship *Charity* (with the exception of those already lost); and I can tell you now, looking back, that this event signaled the beginning of the end of the Karthrogen "war." There was no truce, nor any further known interspecies communication. But the random attacks grew less frequent, and soon stopped altogether. Still, it's been only a few decades since that happened, and there are those who believe that the Throgs may simply have withdrawn to regroup, to rethink their strategy, to return at another time.

Those pessimists could be right. But let us hope not. Or if the Throgs do return, perhaps they will do so in peace. Who can know what the result of this meeting with Humanity will be?

Did we learn anything about them through all of this? Not as much as we would have liked, certainly. We were left still with no inkling of where the Throgs came from or what they were about, or whether they lived wholly in n-space—or what they were like once you got to know them. Most people, I suppose, couldn't be happier. I'm not so sure, myself.

My Querayn employers certainly would have liked to know more about the nature of the Throgs' consciousness before they'd vanished from the known galaxy. I reported to the Querayn, of course, on all that I had learned. But when I suffered my own loss in the final encounter, it cost me much of the direct information that I had hoped to gather. I'm referring to the robot, my sibling-self, that helped lead Claudi to them and then vanished in the n-space fold that carried Claudi to the Throgs. I lost my direct sensing when that robot disappeared. I also lost a part of myself.

Maybe you think that doesn't matter. But I mourned my sibling-self. Perhaps it increased my empathy for those who had lost friends or family to the Throgs.

And yet, still, I would like to have learned more about them—for myself, for my employers, for the sake of whatever they might have taught us all. And even for what we might have taught them. But that's all matter down the black hole now, I suppose. In later conversations with New, I learned that the starstream-consciousness felt much as I did, though undoubtedly they'd gleaned impressions that might have enhanced my own knowledge, if they could have clearly conveyed them to me. They tried, they really did; but New can be a little hard to follow sometimes.

I expect you'll want to know what became of Claudi and Sheki and the others. I can tell you a little. I can tell you that *Charity* emerged from a starstream node in a great blossom of color and light and with a tremendous *jabber jabber* in the head of every sentient being aboard. Flying on through K-space toward a still distant golden-yellow star named Sherrick, they ultimately reached their destination, the third planet in the Sherrick system, intact and nearly on schedule. Once they were planetside, naturally, life changed. The shipboard cameraderie dissolved as the passengers dispersed to various locations. The kids hated to leave their favorite teacher, Mr. Zizmer; but they got over it in time, as kids do, I'm told. (A year later Claudi and Sheki got a surprise visit from Mr. Zizmer; but that was a bit of subterfuge that I indulged in, sneaking a copy of the Mr. Zizmer program ashore with my newest sibling-self.) I might note that Mr. Zizmer was never the same after knowing those children.

I don't know that Captain Thornekan was ever the same, either. He was in for some pretty harsh criticism for letting the Throgs go, never mind that in doing so he saved the children and most likely the ship. But he weathered the criticism, and he and starship *Charity* continued on down the starstream, making several more stops before cutting across through pokey old K-space to the nearest entry node for the outbound loop of the starstream. During the return journey, I introduced myself to him more fully, and we whiled away the time with many thoughtful and provocative discussions. The captain had a great deal to reflect upon, and I like to think that I helped him in making sense of these events. One of the things we talked about was the relative merits of vengeance and forgiveness on a galactic scale. It was then that I learned just how deeply he had wanted to avenge his wife's death. I can't say that we really resolved the question to the satisfaction of either of us, but it is worth noting that the captain's actual decision in the heat of struggle seems to have been vindicated by history. Upon our return to homeport, Captain Thornekan left starship *Charity*, and I lost touch with him after that.

Meanwhile, on Heart of Heaven, Claudi's family and Sheki's settled down not too far apart on the outskirts of New Wooster, the primary city of the still-new world. Claudi and Sheki made their adjustments to their new school, and though placed in different classes, they were still able to see each other. Roti Wexx'xx became a sort of godfather to Claudi, a concept that initially confounded him, but which made more sense to him once he realized that he didn't actually have to rear the child, but would be given the joy of watching her mature while being her older, perhaps wiser, friend.

If this were a fairy tale, I suppose I would report that Claudi and Sheki grew up and married and had a dozen children and lived happily ever after. But no. They did grow up and marry—but not each other, though they remained lifelong friends. As for whether they lived happily ever after, I don't know that I'm one to judge. What does that mean, anyway? Life is not always easy on a new colony world, and their lives were no exception. I suspect that they found more fulfillment than many. Claudi and Lopo remained inseparable companions, which might have been impossible had not certain officers of starship *Charity* joined forces to purchase the lupeko's freedom from the J. J. Larkus Circ-Zoo. (Baako, it might be noted, stayed with Joe Farharto, though not with the zoo. They elected to remain on Sherrick III when the time came for the circ-zoo to move on.)

And what of me?

I said at the beginning that this story wasn't about me. But maybe I was wrong. Never before had I thought so hard about my own being and my role in Human civilization—or for that matter, in the life-and-sentience process of the universe. Yes, I mourned the losses and cheered the victories, silently, within the placeless little worlds that were my home. And I kept on doing my job as best I could, all the while searching for meaning. I suppose most of us do that, don't we?

I asked Claudi once, long after the events of this story, what *she* thought she had learned—and more specifically, what her thoughts were on God and immortality and so on, after her experiences with the starstream-being. She looked a little wistful and said that those kinds of questions had often come to her mind in the years following the experience. One day she hoped to return to the starstream, because she had some questions she wanted to ask of New. She had never forgotten Scer-Randall's final living act, or the sight of Lanker and the S'rath in the chapel praying. Nor had she forgotten the challenge posed to her by New, in the face of the Throgs: Could she forgive them for all they had done? The answer to the last was yes, perhaps—she supposed she *must*, in fact—but not so quickly nor so easily.

As for the first part of the question, she said she still didn't know for sure. She had not in her young adulthood been attracted to any of the then common religious faiths, but she nevertheless felt certain that there was something greater in the universe than even the starstream-being. New had seemed so Godlike to her, and yet wasn't God; she said it just didn't make sense to her that that was the whole story. I wasn't sure I agreed with that, or even that it answered the question. But I liked the way I felt when she said it.

And I guess I still do.

About the Author

JEFFREY A. CARVER is the author of nine science fiction novels, including the recently published *From a Changeling Star*, to which this book is a sequel. His other books include *Star Rigger's Way*, *The Rapture Effect*, the epic novel *The Infinity Link*, and the forthcoming *Dragons in the Stars*.

Originally a native of Huron, Ohio, Carver has lived in New England since graduating from Brown University in 1971 with a degree in English. In 1974 he earned a Master of Marine Affairs degree from the University of Rhode Island. He has been a collegiate wrestler, a scuba diving instructor, a quahog diver, a UPS sorter, and a word-processing consultant, among other things. His interests include science, religion, nature and animals, underwater exploration, and flying.

He lives with his wife Allysen Palmer and their daughter Alexandra in Arlington, Massachusetts, where he is a full-time SF writer. He is currently working on a new novel.

From the *New York Times*

bestselling co-author of

The Deathgate Cycle

◆ ———————— ◆

Margaret Weis

STAR OF THE GUARDIANS

Volume 1: The Lost King

◆ ———————— ◆

For centuries the galaxy has known only peace. Then came the Great Betrayal and a new order under the heel of Derek Sagan and the Imperium. Though the royal family was destroyed, an heir possessing unique abilities has survived in hiding. Now Sagan has discovered the boy and seeks to use him to tighten his dictator's grip on the galaxy.

◆

Peopled with humans, aliens and wise-cracking computers, a tale of love, hate and ambition, **Star of the Guardians:** *The Lost King* begins a grand adventure that bears the trademark of a spectacular imagination.

DON'T MISS IT!

"As complex and spellbinding a bit of science fiction as I've ever come across."—*Minneapolis Tribune*

THE LAST LEGENDS OF EARTH
by
A. A. Attanasio

"A wonderfully realized, richly detailed and cohesive novel."
—*People*

"A grand and glorious visionary epic . . . I loved it."
—*Robert Silverberg*

Seven billion years from now, millennia after Earth has shattered in the heat of our exploding sun, an alien being reincarnates humanity from its DNA. We are to serve as bait in a titanic struggle between the Rimstalker, reanimator of Man, and the zotl, dread creatures who feed on the pain and suffering of intelligent lifeforms.

Set in the planetary system of Chalco-Doror, which is no more and no less than a vast machine, **The Last Legends of Earth** is a love story, a gripping tale of resistance against alien control, and an examination of the machinery of creation and destruction. It is also a world-building effort on the grandest scale—and A.A. Attanasio's most ambitious and accessible novel to date.

A Bantam Spectra Paperback

AN165